Alison Love grew up at the University of theatre for five years to university to do an MA, then more relations. She is now PR and Press Manager for a leading children's charity, the National Children's Bureau. Alison Love has written several prize-winning short stories; *Mallingford* is her first novel.

MALLINGFORD

Alison Love

BLACK SWAN

MALLINGFORD
A BLACK SWAN BOOK : 0 552 99771 4

First publication in Great Britain

PRINTING HISTORY
Black Swan edition published 1997

Set in 11/12pt Linotype Melior by
Kestrel Data, Exeter, Devon.

Black Swan Books are published by Transworld Publishers Ltd,
61–63 Uxbridge Road, London W5 5SA,
in Australia by Transworld Publishers (Australia) Pty Ltd,
15–25 Helles Avenue, Moorebank, NSW 2170
and in New Zealand by Transworld Publishers (NZ) Ltd,
3 William Pickering Drive, Albany, Auckland.

Reproduced, printed and bound in Great Britain by
Cox & Wyman Ltd, Reading, Berks.

For Barry, as always
and in loving memory of Martin

Chapter One

'Where is he now?'

'He's gone into the studio. I just hope he doesn't swipe something. Gerald will be furious if he swipes something.'

'Gerald won't notice. Besides, he's too stupid to know what's worth taking. William, stop wriggling.'

'I can't help it,' said William, who was a stolid boy of eleven, with a coarse halo of red hair. 'There isn't room for both of us.'

'Don't whine,' said Cosima. She raised herself on her knees so that she could see over her brother's head. They were crouched in the tree-house which had been built for her ten years ago, when she was eight. It smelt of damp leaves and of creosote; a smell half unpleasant, half wonderful, which reminded Cosima of her childhood. Through the rough porthole she could see the stable block, which formed an elongated L-shape, its flinty walls buttressed in red brick. A large green Land Rover was parked on some gravel nearby.

'I've got a splinter,' said William, accusingly.

'Shut up,' said Cosima. 'Roddy's coming out.'

The green door of the stable block opened, and a tall man stepped into the courtyard. He was about thirty, dressed in sharp-creased beige trousers and a cashmere golfing jumper. For a moment he paused, and looked around him, surveying the house and its grounds with an air of satisfaction; the air of a man of property, not of a trespasser.

'Look at him,' hissed Cosima. 'Anyone would think he owned the place.'

7

'He does own it,' said William. 'Ouch. This sodding splinter really hurts.'

Cosima held her breath, willing her cousin Roddy to turn away, towards the Land Rover. But he did not. Instead he put his hands in the pockets of his expensive trousers and began to walk meditatively towards the clump of chestnut trees at the edge of the yard. Then, slowly, he raised his head.

'Cosima!' His voice was calm and slightly nasal.

'Damn and blast,' said Cosima.

Roderick was looking directly towards the tree-house, squinting a little because of the sun. It was May, and the light was clear and cold. Cosima tugged fiercely at the tail of brown hair which hung over her shoulder. Her hands were slim and long-fingered and ingrained with dirt.

'You'd better talk to him, Cos,' said William. 'We can't stay up here for ever. What if Gerald comes back and finds him?'

Cosima scowled, and hunched her legs so that she could knot the laces of her plimsolls. Her shoes were very old, the rubber at the toes disintegrating.

'Fat lot of use you are,' she muttered. Then, carefully, she lowered herself over the edge of the wooden platform, her right foot seeking the familiar first step of the rope ladder. When her hold on the greasy brown rope was secure, she let herself swing gently out of the tree-house, and began to climb down the ladder. Roddy blinked at her as she made the last deft leap to the ground.

'Ah,' he said. 'There you are.'

'Yes,' said Cosima. She stared across at him, challenging him to ask why she had been hiding. But Roderick merely smiled, an affable unrelenting smile.

'Isn't William coming down too?' he asked, in a benign voice. 'Well, never mind; it's you I came to see. How are you, little cousin?'

'I'm all right,' said Cosima, in an ungracious voice. 'We weren't expecting you.'

'I realize that.' Roderick turned and glanced in the direction of the house. 'Can we talk?'

'I've got work to do. In the garden.'

Roderick laughed. 'Don't be so mulish, Cosima. You wouldn't be able to work if you were still hiding from me, would you?'

'Yes, but since I'm not I'd better get on with it,' said Cosima, and she began to stride across the courtyard, away from the clump of trees. Her face was hot with annoyance. Roddy always made her feel like this: uncomfortable, and somehow trapped. When she was a child he had often teased her, with a facetiousness that she had failed entirely to comprehend: his jokes had seemed part of the overall strangeness of her mother's family, into which she could never quite fit. Now, although she could not have said that Roddy teased her exactly, she had the same feeling of mistrust, as though there was something happening that she did not understand.

The slabs of the yard were cracked and uneven, with weeds sprouting lustily between them. Roddy stumbled on the flagstones, trying to match his step with Cosima's. A battered-looking hen with rusty brown feathers fluttered out of his way.

'It's quite important, you know,' he said. His voice had a faint upper-class whinny.

'So is the garden,' said Cosima. 'It's how we make our living, remember?'

'All right, little cousin,' said Roderick peaceably. 'Have it your way.'

In silence they walked towards the house, which stood harmoniously in the centre of the little valley, the green slopes of the South Downs rearing up on either side. Mallingford was a tall square building, with a row of gable windows like half-shut eyes. Its walls, like those of the stable block, were made of stone set with rows of flint, encrusted with yellow lichen. Several of the roof tiles were broken or missing, gaping in one place to reveal the dark rafters beneath.

There was, even at this distance, a faint, dispiriting smell of mould.

'I suppose your father's teaching this afternoon, is he?' asked Roderick, as they reached the path which led to the gardens. Cosima gave a wanton kick at some pale yellow toadstools in the shaggy grass.

'Look, Roddy, don't muck about,' she said. 'You know Gerald goes to the art college on Wednesdays. That's why you came this afternoon. All right?'

'All right.' Roderick grinned at her, a sudden wolfish grin. His face was long and pink, with pale hair which had receded to display a high shiny forehead. As far as Cosima could remember he had always looked like this, even when he was a boy of eighteen. 'I'll be honest. I wanted to talk to you without – ah – without fear of reprisals.'

They were passing a clump of willows now, set around a sluggish green pond. Beneath the branches stood a pair of primitive granite blocks, with rudimentary faces carved upon them, like the ancient statue-menhirs of Corsica. One face had a smile on its lips, slight and sly; the other, smaller block had dumb gaping eyes and a solemn circle for a mouth. The effect was comic but disturbing, as though the larger stone, like a troll, had been petrified in the act of persecution, and would come back to sinister life once darkness fell. Cosima glanced at the statues. They were the work of her grandmother, Stella Deighton. At one time they had faced their own reflections, mirrored in the pond's clear surface, but now the water was too thick to cast much light, and they stood alone in the gloom of the willows.

'I don't know why you bother with us,' said Cosima to Roddy. They had reached the walled garden now, which contained the vegetable plot. 'You must have better things to do.'

'I have other things to do. Not necessarily better things.' He pushed open the wrought-iron gate and stepped into the vegetable garden. 'God, this must be the only part of the whole place which isn't going to rack and ruin.'

The garden had been freshly dug, the earth brown and rich. It was divided into distinct patches, separated by narrow mud paths. In one corner a primitive greenhouse had been created with some thick sheets of clear plastic; opposite this makeshift building stood a long wigwam of bamboo, with bean stalks winding up the poles.

'Well,' said Cosima, reaching for a hoe which was lying on the path, 'we've all been working damned hard in here.'

Roderick leaned against the wall. 'Even your father?' he asked, in a suave voice. 'Somehow I can't see him with a spade in his hand.'

Cosima started to jab energetically at a clear patch of soil, refusing to rise to the bait. 'Gerald's doing very well at the art college,' she said, blandly. 'The students adore him.'

Roderick gave a sceptical harrumph, and pushed himself away from the wall. Cosima noticed with satisfaction that the sleeves of his beautiful pink and blue jumper were streaked with dirt.

'Cosima,' said Roddy, 'my father and I have been thinking.'

'Oh, yes?'

'The thing is – we're very worried about the state of the house. To be honest, it's falling apart. Another winter and it could be uninhabitable.'

Cosima thrust the hoe into the earth. 'So, what?' she said, flippantly. 'You're going to throw us out?'

'Don't be stupid. We wouldn't do that.' Roderick paused. 'I don't think we could, anyway. Under the terms of the lease your father has the right to stay here for the rest of his life. But we've got to do something, you know.'

'Such as?' said Cosima, in an unco-operative voice, still hoeing. Roddy was always coming up with schemes to get his cousins out of Mallingford: virtually every time he came to see Cosima he had a new idea. Last autumn he had tried to persuade her that she and William should abandon Gerald and move to Courtney Park, where their mother's family lived, before the cold weather set in. There had been no question of doing it, of course. Even William, who could be stubborn over the most unexpected things, had turned white with horror at the thought.

'Well,' said Roderick now, 'we think we're going to reclaim the outbuildings.'

The hoe froze in Cosima's hands. 'What?' she said. 'But you can't do that.'

'Actually, we can. I was looking at the lease the other day. It doesn't mention the outbuildings; it only refers to the house.'

Cosima stared at her cousin, who was smiling nervily, his hands shoved into his trouser pockets.

'But that was Stella's studio,' she said. 'All her stuff's there.'

'As a matter of fact,' said Roddy, 'it's partly because of Stella we'd like to renovate the place. Look, Cosima, can't we go inside? I want to explain this properly and I can't do it with you behaving like Tess of the d'Urbervilles.'

'Sorry,' said Cosima, 'but we don't all have the privilege of being rich and idle.' She dropped the hoe, and stomped towards the makeshift greenhouse.

'You could be rich and idle too, if you wanted, little cousin,' Roderick said mildly, watching Cosima as she bent to lift a black plastic tray of broccoli seedlings.

'Don't start all that again, please.'

With her free hand Cosima pushed the loose tendrils of hair back from her face. They felt moist and curly with sweat. For some reason which she could not explain, she liked the idea of Roddy seeing her at her worst, grubby and hot, dressed in ancient khaki jodhpurs and an Aertex shirt. The shirt had been dyed apple green to freshen it, but the colour had taken badly, and the fabric was covered in dense lurid streaks.

'Anyway,' she said, 'what can you do with the outbuildings? They're useless without the house.'

'As a matter of fact – well, we're toying with the idea of setting up some kind of – ah – what you might call a Stella Deighton museum.'

'What?'

'You heard me. A sort of museum. To show Stella's studio to the public.' Roddy paused for a moment. 'Don't you think that's a good idea?'

Cosima looked at him, a seraphic smile spreading across her face. 'I think you're barmy,' she said.

'I don't see why,' said Roderick, hurt. 'People pay to go to Charleston House, or whatever that Bloomsbury place is called, and none of their work is a patch on Stella's. I don't imagine they have anything like the dovecote on show, either.'

'Probably not,' said Cosima. 'But at least they've got a proper road, instead of a mudtrack.' She crouched to plant the first seedling. 'And they don't have a tenant taking pot-shots at anyone who comes near the place.'

As soon as she said this Cosima's stomach gave a lurch. Fool, she thought, fool. So busy being smart that she walked straight into the trap Roddy had set. He of all people would remember Gerald wedged into the attic window, threatening to pepper the whole Courtney family with his shotgun. In her mind she could still hear the crack of the warning shot he had fired across the treetops. Her hands shook as she tried to firm the earth around the roots of the broccoli plant.

Without speaking, Roddy stepped forward and squatted beside her, the sharp crease of his trousers flattening across his knees. Cosima stared at his shiny nut-brown shoes, unable to look up.

'You see, little cousin,' he said softly, 'you know as well as I do that things can't go on like this. Admit it.'

13

Cosima did not answer. Her hands, caked with earth, were still trembling.

'You mustn't think you're being disloyal to your father, Cosima,' said Roderick, in the same silken voice. 'We've got to face facts. It might be too late to stop Gerald from falling to pieces, but we can at least save the house.'

He was so close to her now that she could smell his skin, an unexpectedly sweet scent, like talcum powder. If he touches me, she thought, with sudden clarity, I'll hit him.

'And of course,' he went on, 'if it works out, we should all make a few bob from it.'

Cosima took a breath. 'I see,' she said drily. 'So it's a way of buying us off, isn't it?'

Roderick's hand, which had been hovering as if to pat her thigh, withdrew.

'You're such a cynic, little cousin,' he said, straightening up. 'Why don't you trust me? I want to stop the rot before the damage is irreparable. I don't see what's so wicked about it. Mallingford's a very beautiful place. You of all people should know that; you've lived here all your life. Besides, don't you think Stella would have liked a bit more glory? She was a very popular artist in her heyday. We owe it to the public to open up the place.'

'Possibly,' said Cosima, extracting another seedling from the tray. The trapped feeling that Roddy engendered was darker and tighter than ever, making it hard for her to breathe.

'Of course,' Roderick went on, 'it's early days yet. We've got to check the feasibility of the whole project before we sink any cash into it. Or start persuading other people to sink their cash. But this is a good time to start new projects. We're in a boom, after all, thanks to Maggie's government. Money sloshing about everywhere.'

'I wouldn't know,' said Cosima.

'Oh, believe me, there is. And I don't see why you

shouldn't start making your pile, little cousin. You're nearly nineteen, after all. Whatever happens you'll be needing cash.'

Roderick paused. His face had turned even pinker from the effort of kneeling.

'Anyway,' he said, 'what I'd like to do is to bring someone round to have a look at the place. A marketing consultant called Tom Nettleship. He's American. I met his boss at a charity bash in the City last month, and he sounds a bright boy. He should be able to give us a bit of guidance.'

Cosima shook the soil from the filigree roots of the plant in her hand, and carefully pressed it into the raked earth.

'Why ask me?' she said. 'You're the owners.'

'Yes, but I'd like him − ah − I'd like him to meet you. It would lend the whole thing a bit more credibility if he could actually talk to a member of Stella Deighton's family. Don't you agree?'

Slowly Cosima got to her feet, and tucked her frayed shirt into her trousers. Roderick was watching her obliquely, a faint smile on his lips.

'It's up to you,' said Cosima. 'Personally I still think you're barking mad.'

'But you will meet this chap Nettleship?'

'All right. As long as you fix it for a day when Gerald won't be here.'

'Yes, I had thought of that,' said Roddy. 'After all, I don't want blood on my hands.'

'It'll be your blood if it's anyone's, I'm afraid,' said Cosima, eyeing her cousin solemnly. 'You know how Gerald feels.'

Roddy's glance faltered, and skittered away from hers.

'You're probably right,' he murmured. Then, aloud, he said: 'Well, I'll let you know when I've made the arrangements, shall I?'

'Yes,' said Cosima, 'you do that. And now, if you don't mind, I'd better get on.'

'You're not being very hospitable, you know, little cousin,' said Roddy, in a querulous voice.

'Oh, come on, Roddy. I've got work to do, even if you haven't.'

'All right,' said Roddy, 'all right. I'll be in touch.'

He hovered for a moment by the gatepost, like an actor uncertain of his exit-line; then he turned on his heel, and strode off the way he had come.

Once Roddy had gone, Cosima sank to her knees at the edge of the broccoli patch, suddenly faint with the imminence of change. Roddy was right, of course; she knew that. She had known for months that something had to be done, although she had shelved that knowledge in some secret part of her mind. But it was true that the house was gradually succumbing to damp and decay, one room after another becoming uninhabitable; and if the house fell apart, God alone knew what would happen to her father. Cosima pictured, for a moment, her father's face. It was gaunt yet somehow gleeful, as though he had a trick or two up his sleeve which he was not yet prepared to divulge. However much she tried she could not imagine Gerald living anywhere but Mallingford: he seemed to belong to the place as much as it belonged to him. She took a slow deep breath. Her nerves thrilled with fear, mixed with a perverse excitement, the excitement of knowing that something was certain to happen, and that it was quite beyond her control.

Then she looked up and saw that William had come into the garden. In his arms he was carrying a large moth-eaten cat: Salvador, the black and white bruiser who kept down the rats.

'Roderick's gone,' he announced.

'Yes, I know.'

'He left Salvador shut in the stable block,' William went on indignantly. He squeezed the cat, who uttered a surprisingly tolerant squeak. 'I'm going to the kitchen to give him some milk. Then I'm going to see if any of the hens have laid.'

'Well, hurry up. I need you to come and help me with this broccoli.'

William eyed the patch of earth dispassionately. 'Yes,' he said. 'You do, don't you? You've made a pig's ear of it so far.'

Chapter Two

Tom Nettleship gazed across the office to the window where Alastair, his boss, was standing, peering inquisitively through the Venetian blinds. The blinds were pale grey, in keeping with the careful colour scheme of the premises, which looked like a chic expensive hospital tricked out in white and chrome. Restlessly Tom stirred three lumps of sugar into his coffee.

'Jeez, Alastair,' he said, 'why don't you go yourself? You'll handle it much better than I will.'

Alastair tweaked once more at the blinds. For the last five minutes he had been watching a smart young woman in the street below as she paced up and down outside a wine bar. The office occupied the cramped but fashionable third floor of a tall building near Cambridge Circus, on the busy fringes of Soho.

'She's still waiting,' he said. 'Looks to me as if she's been stood up. Do you think I should invite her in for a drink?'

'No, I don't,' said Tom. 'She'd probably give you a smack in the mouth. Anyway, we've got work to do.'

'She might be grateful to me for rescuing her,' said Alastair, thoughtfully; but he twanged the blinds shut and sat down at his desk once more. Alastair was a small, flashy, well-dressed man, who had the bowed legs of a jockey and the dark good looks of a fallen angel. Indeed, Tom sometimes thought of him as Mephistopheles to his own lumbering Faust. Tom himself was massive by comparison: six feet four inches tall, with wiry brown hair and long limbs that seemed to have a will of their own. His nickname as a boy in Minneapolis had been Stumblejohn, because of his uncanny ability to break everything he touched. This capacity to do damage had made him, in adult life, at once awed and belligerent.

'I don't understand why you're so worried, Tom,' Alastair said. 'You're perfectly capable of handling it. I expect you know more about that arty-farty stuff than I do. I'd never even heard of Stella Deighton until I met our young friend Roderick.'

Tom scowled. 'Yeah, well, I'm not exactly an expert myself,' he said. 'And I don't know the first thing about the British aristocracy. I'm sure to stick my big feet straight in it.'

'No, you won't. Roddy Courtney's a businessman. Shit-hot, according to my friends in the City. You won't have to worry about protocol: that's not the name of the game.' Alastair poured himself coffee from the jug. 'He's brought us in because he wants to make the most of his assets. Apparently the place has been standing there for years, wasting away. He wants to get some return on it.'

'Didn't you say he had sitting tenants? They won't be very happy about a queue of tourists in their backyard.'

'Oh, Roddy says they'll play ball. They're family; did I mention that? Stella Deighton's son married Roddy's aunt or something.' Alastair took a mouthful of coffee and picked up his grey telephone. 'Besides, if it comes off there should be money in it for everyone. Don't start looking for problems before you've even seen the place, Tom.'

Tom gave a non-committal grunt, and watched as Alastair punched out the numbers on his phone. They had been working together for a year, since Alastair had wooed Tom away from a much larger company by the simple ploy of doubling his salary. What I need is a tough bastard to do the dirty work, he had said, with a candour Tom found disarming, so I can concentrate on schmoozing the punters: that's what I'm good at. In fact Tom found himself doing Alastair's donkey work rather than his dirty work, handling the day-to-day business of the marketing company while Alastair wined and dined his clients; but none the less he relished the image of himself as a tough bastard. After the past confusions of his life it seemed to him rather an honest, uncomplicated thing to be.

'Anyway, I'd like to get in with our young friend Roddy,' Alastair said, the receiver tucked under his bluish faintly stubbled chin. 'He's got a lot of irons in the fire, and I wouldn't mind having a stake in them.'

'Yeah, but if this one's a turkey—' began Tom.

'Phil?' said Alastair, into the telephone. 'It's Alastair Weston. Still on for lunch? Terrific. See you there at half twelve. *Ciao*.' He blipped the button to disconnect the line. 'Don't be so negative, Tom. It'll be good experience. And I'm too busy at the moment to spend time chasing business. I think we might be about to clinch the deal on this cigarette. Belmont, they're calling it, to appeal to the girls. I tell you, that one could be serious money. Half the marketing firms in the country won't touch fags: we can sting them for all they've got. No, you do the Mallingford trip.'

'Well, all right,' said Tom, 'but don't fire me if I screw up, will you?'

'Ha!' said Alastair, without mirth. Still holding the telephone, he wandered back towards the window and glanced down at the street. 'Oh, she's gone. Pity.' He began to dial another number. 'You might want to do some research before you go, Tom. Find an art dealer or someone to brief you on this Deighton bint: what her stuff sells for, that kind of thing. Keep stumm on the project though, won't you? We don't want anyone else getting their mucky hands on it.'

'Yeah, yeah,' said Tom, rising from the slippery white leather sofa on which he had been sitting. 'I went to business school, remember? I know all that shit.'

He scooped up his coffee and went into the reception area, shutting the paper-thin door of Alastair's office behind him.

'Hi,' he said to the receptionist, who sat behind a semicircular desk adorned with pink and cream carnations. 'Any messages?'

The receptionist was, unexpectedly, a beautiful Asian woman of twenty-five called Shabnam. She was the successor to a string of exquisite blonde girls who had one by one fallen first in bed and then in love with Alastair, and, after a suitable period of taking messages from his newer conquests, had tearfully resigned. Alastair had picked Shabnam on purpose because she was stunning enough to impress visitors to Weston Associates, but far too strong-minded to indulge in sexual frivolity. Tom in particular she treated with a cool dignity, as though she could not be bothered to decide whether or not she liked him. Accustomed as he was to hard-nosed jolly American girls, he found this aloofness disconcerting.

'Giles from *Marketing Week* rang about those advertisements,' said Shabnam, demurely consulting her notebook, 'and Kate Snell asked if you could call her at the office. And the second post came about fifteen minutes ago. Here.'

'Great,' said Tom, with the false enthusiasm that Shabnam so often induced in him. He shifted his coffee cup to his left hand so that he could take the sheaf of letters. As he did so the cup, as if of its own volition, tilted on the saucer and spilt cold brown dregs over Shabnam's tidy notebook.

'Oh, Christ,' said Tom. 'I'm sorry, Shabnam.'

'That's all right. I'll get a cloth,' said Shabnam. At her own speed she stood up and strolled towards the kitchenette in her exotic sapphire trousers. Tom watched her for a moment before deciding it would make matters worse to offer his help. Instead he pushed open the door to his own room. Tom's office was much smaller than Alastair's, little more than a cubicle built of plywood, with a dusty window overlooking the side wall of the next door building. It contained an ivory desk, a very uncomfortable chrome chair, and a huge weeping fig tree which sporadically dropped pointed yellow leaves on the grey carpet. Tom dumped the post on his desk and picked up his telephone to ring Kate Snell.

Kate was the beauty editor of a glossy magazine; she and Tom had been dating, as Tom called it, for the past five or six months. Their relationship was physically passionate, but also, to Tom's relief, casual. He had fled to England from the shipwreck of a youthful marriage, and he was not yet ready to think about the future. He was not even sure how long he intended to stay in London. His parents, kind plain people baffled by his self-imposed exile, constantly asked when he was coming home, and he would hear himself say, across the pellucid transatlantic lines, I'm not through here yet, Mom. I'll come home when I'm through.

Kate answered the phone at once.

'Hiya,' said Tom. 'Shabnam told me you rang.'

'Oh, yes.' Kate had a high voice which sounded shrill on the telephone, although in real life it was softer and sweeter. She was a pretty young woman of twenty-four, with dark hair cut voguishly short and a small trim aerobicized body. 'We've been invited to dinner. Sally, my editor, asked if we'd like to come to dinner next Tuesday. I said I'd check with you, but it's OK, isn't it? We haven't fixed anything for Tuesday. And it's the first time Sally's invited me to her place.'

Tom could hear the note of excitement as she spoke. Kate was an ambitious girl, constantly trying to improve her prospects. In theory he admired this go-getting urge, although in practice it sometimes grated upon him. He had always imagined that English girls would be gentle creatures, less competitive than their American counterparts.

'Yeah, fine,' he said. 'I don't want to be too late,

that's all. I've got to drive down to Sussex on Wednesday.'

'Oh? What for?'

'Alastair's dumped something on me. I've got to go visit the place where Stella Deighton – the artist, you know – used to work, to see if it's worth opening it to the public.'

Tom heard Kate sniff in amusement.

'I'm surprised Alastair has even heard of Stella Deighton,' she said.

'He hadn't,' said Tom. 'Mind you, I don't know that much about her either. The only picture I can remember is the really famous one: that self-portrait, in the straw hat. I'm planning to do a bit of research this afternoon. The Tate Gallery's got some of her paintings, hasn't it?'

'I think so, yes.' There was a moment's silence; then Kate said: 'So. Are we meeting tonight?'

'Sure,' said Tom, 'if you'd like to. I'll be through about seven thirty. We could have dinner.'

'OK. Come round to my place and I'll cook.'

'Oh,' said Tom, surprised. Normally Kate reserved dinners at home for special occasions, birthdays or reunions after business trips, when it was likely that they would spend most of the evening in bed together. He wondered why she was proposing so voluptuous a celebration now, on an ordinary weekday.

'You do like my cooking, don't you?' she said, sounding faintly aggrieved.

'Yeah, sure I do. That'll be lovely, sweetheart. I'll see you later.'

When he had rung off Tom pushed his chair back and clasped both hands at the nape of his neck, allowing his mind to play upon the prospect now before him. Kate in bed was both tender and enthusiastic. She had none of the diffidence he had encountered in other women: his ex-wife Becky, for instance, who always made him feel as if he were somehow hurting her. Tom thrust his long legs under

23

the desk and kicked over his wastepaper basket. An avalanche of apple cores and screwed-up letters tumbled over the carpet. Automatically he rose to gather them from the floor, trying as he did so to shut out Becky's ghost, her pained and pretty face, her cultured Boston voice as she said, Tom, this just isn't working out. It was still too dangerous to think about Becky. He dropped the rubbish with a clang into the silver bin, and took out his A to Z of London, to find the best way to the Tate Gallery.

Chapter Three

Stella Deighton acquired Mallingford, back in 1920, through a combination of good luck and misunderstanding.

She came across the house by chance one afternoon in August, as she was walking across the South Downs, her infant son Gerald in a knapsack on her back. Stella liked walking. She was a strong and fiercely solitary woman, capable of rising at dawn and marching ten miles to fetch the milk and post the letters before she set about the real business of the day. On this particular afternoon, however, she was walking to escape. Stella had been spending the summer in a rented farmhouse not far from Lewes, with a bunch of art school friends from her days at the Slade. It was one of those arrangements hatched in optimism after a good dinner on a fine spring evening, when it seems an insult to all present even to imagine squabbling over the butcher's bill or the chopping of the firewood. But as the weeks passed, small grievances gathered like stormclouds, and at last erupted into a sudden terrible row. Stella could not tolerate rows. Wordlessly she laced her boots, hauled her son from the stone-flagged kitchen where he was playing, and strode out of the little farmhouse into the smooth dark hills. As usual she had no plan in her head; she was propelled by a simple instinct, that it was better to act than to react, better to move than to stand still.

Although she had often walked across the hills surrounding Mallingford, she had never paid much attention to the place, and would not have done so now had she not been thirsty. It was a warm day, and in her haste to leave Stella had not brought with her any water. Seeing the house, she turned off the path and began to scramble down the rough green slope. Somebody there would give them a drink, especially when they saw Gerald. He was a beautiful child, with translucent skin and bright, serious grey eyes: one of Stella's artist friends, commissioned to paint the altarpiece for a local church, had used him as a model for the infant Christ. Stella's son was the product of a short, casual affair with a young psychiatrist, eager to prove his theory that sexual ecstasy enhanced the creative powers. The experiment had not been a successful one: Stella found the psychiatrist's efforts to excite her at best ludicrous and at worst humiliating, and she was disinclined to give him much credit for the several paintings she produced during their affair. They had already agreed, amicably enough, to call off the experiment when Stella discovered that she was with child. She did not in the least want a baby, but she had seen too many friends mangled by back-street abortions to do anything but brazen out her pregnancy.

The first thing which struck Stella about Malling-ford, once she got to the bottom of the slope, was its absolute stillness. Although it was not far from the road or from the neighbouring farms, the hills sur-rounding it were just high enough to give an aura of seclusion. Stella, her nerves strained from the claustrophobia of her shared farmhouse, felt as though she might absorb this new peacefulness through the very pores of her skin. She walked slowly across the grass. Gerald, who had been wailing as she jolted down the hill, had fallen into a spellbound silence. As she passed the orchard Stella could hear the wind rustling among the trees, could smell the sweet, faintly sinister scent of ripe apples. All of a sudden she wanted this place more than she had ever wanted anything, except to paint.

She drew closer to the house, wondering why nobody had yet appeared to speak to her. The gardens

26

did not seem neglected: they were tidy and well kept, and most of the fruit in the orchard had been harvested. If she had had a more whimsical nature, she might have imagined herself in some time-slipped domain, mysteriously abandoned like the *Marie Celeste*. Quietly she strode across the courtyard in her tight-laced leather boots, to the back door, which was painted blue.

'We'll see if there's anyone here, shall we?' she said, twisting her neck so that she could just see her son's face, bobbing cherubically at her shoulder. Then she made a fist and rapped sharply on the panels of the blue door. No answer. She rapped again, listening for the sound of steps in the corridor beyond. When it was clear that no-one would come, Stella hoisted Gerald more securely upon her back and walked round to the front of the house. Here, too, the grounds had been recently tended, with a neat gravel drive and a small oblong of grass. Stella crossed, not to the porch, but to the first of the tall ground-floor windows. She stood on tiptoe and peered into the room. It seemed to be a large room, but it was foreshortened by an ugly wooden screen, and all Stella could see was a row of three bare iron bedsteads, lined up as they might be in a dormitory. She sank back upon her heels, satisfied. The house had clearly been used as some kind of hospital during the War, but as far as she could make out it was no longer occupied. She pressed her hands against the sill, which was warm in the late golden sunlight. Stella so rarely wanted anything that when she did her desire had the force of a moral imperative. She adjusted the straps of her knapsack, and set off along the track to the village.

It did not take her long to establish that the house belonged to the Courtneys: they owned most of the surrounding land, including the best part of two villages. Mallingford had originally been a farm, but the Courtneys had used it as a sort of annexe, pretty enough to tempt superfluous dowagers away from

Courtney Park. In the 1800s an ambitious younger son tried to take it over and refurbish it in the new style; but he lost all his money in a gambling scandal, and proceeded to shoot himself in the upstairs drawing room, with one of his pearl-handled duelling pistols. After this catastrophe the house had fallen from favour, and in 1915 the family willingly handed it over to the authorities, to be used as a convalescent home. Now, as Stella had observed, it was standing empty. She walked briskly back to her gloomy farmhouse, and wrote to Sir George Courtney, asking to lease the house.

Finding Mallingford was Stella's piece of luck; next came the misunderstanding.

Sir George Courtney was a clever, melancholy, rather sentimental man of fifty-five. During the War he had lost two sons from wounds and a wife from influenza, and he was haunted by a terrible sense of the wrongness of things. This sense, which in another man might have turned to outrage, in Sir George had turned to guilt: he felt that he could — should — somehow endeavour to atone for the destruction of the known world. When he got Stella's letter he assumed that she was a war widow, struggling to begin a new life for herself and her son: she had signed herself 'Mrs Deighton', a style she had adopted shortly after Gerald's birth, more from convenience than from any wish to deceive. Sir George wrote back at once inviting her to come and see him. He had been wondering what to do with Mallingford now that it was no longer a convalescent home, and this seemed to him the perfect combination of philanthropy and sense.

The sight of Stella confirmed his belief that she represented that rare and satisfying thing, a good cause. Stella was, all her life, a serious-looking woman. She was not imaginative about clothes, and had no ambition to dress like Dorelia John or the Russian Ballet dancers. When she met Sir George she wore a plain grey gabardine suit, with her hair in a tight golden bun, the embodiment of a respectable young matron. She did not dither or giggle, and she answered his questions in a firm clear voice which he found refreshing: the widows of his sons, now living at Courtney Park, were nervy flighty vapid girls forever weeping or chattering over the breakfast table. Perhaps it was the fear that Stella too might prove weepy which prevented Sir George asking explicitly about her late husband; perhaps it was a gentlemanly reluctance to probe into subjects he suspected would be painful. Afterwards he had no idea how he had spent an hour interviewing her without arriving at the truth of the case, but the fact remained that the words *artist* and *unmarried* were never uttered.

As for Stella, it did not occur to her that she had won her house on false pretences. She packed her belongings with a solid sense of joy, certain that she had found the place where she would spend the rest of her life. The little community of artists greeted her announcement with regret and relief. They were sorry because her departure implied that their social enterprise had somehow failed; but at the same time they secretly agreed that living with Stella had been nobody's idea of Utopia. It was not only that her talent undermined their confidence; it was also her remorseless dedication. While the others would sit drinking black tea and smoking Turkish cigarettes, lamenting the hardships of the artist's life, Stella would be in the studio, working at her easel like a grim energetic Valkyrie. She made the rest of the group feel trivial; a sin which was difficult to forgive.

Nevertheless, they were generous people, and they cheerfully set about helping her to move house. They borrowed a handcart from a local farmer which they loaded up with Stella's things, her bits of furniture, her canvases, her trunk of hardwearing clothes. Then they dressed in their most exotic costumes and accompanied her to Mallingford, in dazzling procession. Stella strode at the front of the cavalcade, while Gerald sat on top of the cart like a young raja, a Chinese parasol held over his head. One of Stella's housemates, a dark young man called Julius Murdoch, had brought his violin, and he played a succession of whirling Irish jigs as they marched over the Downs, to which the women, less burdened than the men, began to dance.

They were halfway there when the skies abruptly clouded over, and it started to rain, the kind of thin, drizzling rain which drenches slowly and thoroughly. Gerald's paper parasol fell apart; the dancing women seemed wild as gypsies, their flying hair dark and wet. But still they marched on, to the skirl of the violin and the occasional hopeful whoop of the dancers, across the ridge and down into the valley. And that was how Stella Deighton arrived at Mallingford; to the utter consternation of Sir George, who had come to welcome his sober tenant to her new home.

Once she had moved in, Stella wasted no time in reorganizing the house. She bought a job lot of second-hand furniture at a sale in Brighton; she chose powdery emulsion in three different colours to paint the drab rose-papered walls; she took on a middle-aged couple from the village, Mr and Mrs Maybrick, to see to the cooking and the gardening. All these under-takings turned out surprisingly well; better, perhaps, than Stella in her haste deserved. The furniture proved to be solid, seaworthy, and free of woodworm; the Maybricks were hardworking and God-fearing.

For the most difficult task, the decoration of the rooms, Stella engaged the help of three of her erstwhile housemates, who were finding life in Sussex more expensive than they had expected, and were running short of funds. While Stella herself spent the mornings in her makeshift studio at the back of the house, these three went staunchly to work, wielding large brushes which left tough dark threads of horsehair stranded upon the walls. Two of them were women, a plump untidy pair called Dora and Molly; the third, Julius Murdoch the fiddle-player, fancied himself in love with Stella, despite the fact that he was never able to maintain more than five minutes' conversation with her.

The arrangement worked well. Although the three painter-helpers sometimes grumbled amongst themselves about having no time for their own work, they were relieved to be living rent-free, and in their different ways they were absorbed in the task before them. Dora and Molly, although they could not bring themselves to admit it, actually found decorating far more satisfying than painting: it inspired in them a boldness and a verve normally stifled by the pressure to create great art.

It was different for Julius, who regarded the transformation of Mallingford as a pure labour of love, the building of a bower for his idol. He had not in any case been able to paint for months, since his passion first took root. Nothing he did could be worthy of Stella; the little he began he destroyed almost at once, nauseated by its crassness. Apart from his work on the house, his main occupation was to indulge in long tortuous discussions with Dora and Molly, to whom he had confessed his lovelorn state. These discussions took place in the morning, while Stella was working, or late at night in the draughty kitchen after she had gone to bed. The girls, who had known her for much longer than Julius, were hugely interested in his feelings, and they never tired of advising what he should do next, analysing each casual word that Stella bestowed upon him. The trouble was that none of the discussions seemed to bear any true relation to Stella herself. More than once Julius made up his mind to speak – was bolstered in his resolve by his friends' encouragement – marched up the stairs to the studio – and then found himself utterly floored by the baffling presence of the real Stella, more distant in the flesh than ever she was in the lengthy intimate debates from which she was absent.

It was Dora who suggested that, to further his

campaign, Julius should take a special interest in Gerald. Since moving to Mallingford the boy had been allowed to run wild, indulging in one mischief after another. He ate wormy fallen apples in the orchard and was sick for two days; he tumbled into the pond and had to be fished out by Molly, who lost a shoe in the khaki slime; he trampled the young tomato plants which Maybrick the gardener had painstakingly nurtured. All these escapades were greeted by Stella with an air of good-humoured resignation. She was never unkind to Gerald, but she had no natural sympathy for the needs of a small boy. Now that he could walk and talk she stopped thinking of him as a baby; instead she treated him rather as she treated the adults in her life, with a sort of remote tolerance, holding him quizzically at arm's length. It did not occur to her that he might be incapable of amusing himself, or that the freedoms thrust upon him might make him miserable and afraid.

Gerald's upbringing – or lack of it – was a frequent topic of conversation among the painter-helpers: they discussed it almost as often as they discussed Julius's adoration of Stella. Although none of them had read Freud, vague concepts from his work had percolated down to them, and they all firmly agreed that what Gerald needed was a father figure. Molly, who could never quite forgive the shoe, maintained that he also needed the odd judicious slap. It was true that Stella had sent him to bed after the episode with the tomatoes, but that was more to mollify the gardener than to chastise Gerald.

Once it had been mooted, the notion of taking on Stella's son intrigued Julius, adding new substance to his passion. As Dora energetically pointed out, the fact that Stella had a child at all meant she could not be untouchable: she had had one lover, there was no reason why she should not have another. Rather to Julius's disappointment, neither Dora nor Molly knew who Gerald's father was. But Dora was right: she was not unattainable. As he laboured over the yellow emulsion in the attic bedrooms, Julius found new daydreams replacing the old stale ones, daydreams in which he hunted for butterflies with Gerald, or rescued him from unspecified dangers, to receive the mature and incomparable barrage of Stella's gratitude.

Unfortunately the real Gerald, like the real Stella, was more intransigent. Julius's first overtures ended in failure. For one thing, it was very hard to speak to Gerald. At mealtimes he was too frantic for his mother's attention to take much notice of anyone else, and during the day he would run off whenever he saw a grown-up coming. (Julius sometimes wondered if this was because Molly had secretly been administering the judicious slaps she had recommended.) Presents, too, were useless. Picture books Gerald would gleefully dunk in the pond, and toys unnerved him. When Julius, on a trip to London, bought him an expensive jack-in-a-box, he screamed with such terror that the entire household – even Stella – came running to see what was wrong.

Nevertheless, little by little, Julius made headway. As the year slowly advanced, he managed to find amusements for Gerald, mushroom-picking in the misty fields, netting sticklebacks in the village stream, playing with paint or crayons. With his luminous grey eyes Gerald bore a haunting resemblance to Stella, and Julius could fancy, at their more harmonious moments, that he was in subtle communion with the woman he claimed to love. He had to admit that Stella herself did not appear to have noticed the friendship he had struck with her son. Occasionally he tried to engage her in discussions about Gerald, so that he could reveal his new knowledge of the boy; but Stella would merely say, oh yes? in an abstracted voice, and continue with whatever she was doing.

In September, when the quinces in the orchard were plump and golden and the decoration of the house was nearly complete, Julius was summoned to Liverpool to see his mother, who was slowly dying of tuberculosis. As always when he was away from Stella's aloof presence his passion seemed a solid and a certain thing. He came back after five days determined that he would this time declare himself. With him he brought an old wind-up gramophone which he had found in his bedroom at home, and a heavy sheaf of records: fragments of opera, Strauss waltzes, the Irish tenor John McCormack singing sentimental ballads. He set up the machine as soon as he got back to Mallingford, opening the window so that the music drifted out across the gardens, like a lure, to draw Stella to him.

But it was Gerald that he drew; Gerald who, unbeknown to Julius, had missed him intensely while he was in Liverpool. Stella, herself oblivious of Julius's absence, had not thought to explain it to her son, and he had spent the past few days in a state of unhappy confusion, unable to understand why his guardian-playmate had so abruptly vanished. When he hurtled into the sea-green drawing room to find Julius quite simply there, he gave a great whoop of joy and threw himself into his arms, or more precisely at his legs, with the force of a small cannon. Julius, in the act of changing the record, promptly dropped 'Roses from the South' on the wooden floorboards, where it broke with a loud crack.

The crack thrilled Gerald. Gleefully he pounced upon the shiny black pieces and began to hurl them against the wall. They shattered noisily, like demon confetti.

'Stop it,' said Julius. But the relief of seeing his friend return had given the boy a fierce new energy. Gusting with laughter, he snatched another record from the pile and smashed it at Julius's feet. Julius reached out to grab him, but he danced away, grinning. In his grey eyes – Stella's eyes – was a tormenting gleam.

'Stop it,' said Julius again, his nerves, already strung up by the long expectant journey, jarring with the noise. Gerald gave a high-pitched silvery giggle. Then he dived once more for the pile of records. Julius dived too, his right arm outstretched to seize the boy. As Gerald sprang backwards, a record in his hand, Julius caught him a sudden accidental thwack across the head. The force of the blow startled Julius as much as it did Gerald: his hand stung with the shock of it. They stared at each other for a moment, stunned; then Gerald took a breath, and began to howl, great gulping howls which echoed in the once quiet room.

Julius turned. Stella was standing in the doorway, just as he had imagined her, in her long blue skirt and her grubby painter's smock, the hair working loose from its knot. He had a horrible feeling that everything had gone wrong.

'Hello, Stella,' he said lamely. 'I'm sorry about Gerald. I didn't mean to hurt him. It was an accident.'

But Stella did not deign to answer. She marched across the room and swept up the squalling Gerald, with his red wet face. As she walked out she gave Julius a single baleful glance.

There was no sign of Gerald for the rest of the day, and after dinner Stella told Julius that she thought it would be better if he left Mallingford. She knew that he was fond of Gerald, but it was obvious to her that their friendship made the boy over-excited and harder to manage. Besides, the work on the house was nearly done, and the girls could easily finish the rest. She said all this quite gently; so gently that Julius wondered if Dora or Molly had welshed upon him, and told Stella his secret. He sat miserably in his upright chair, not bothering to argue. As he was repacking his things he realized that it was the longest conversation he and Stella had ever had, outside the fertile confines of his imagination, in the whole year he had spent at Mallingford.

He left the next morning at dawn; his own poetic idea, to spare Stella the embarrassment of seeing him again, and to avoid goodbyes. When he reached the gate he looked back once, and thought he saw a face at Stella's window, but he was already too far away to tell for certain.

In fact Gerald had woken at sunrise, disturbed by the faint unavoidable sounds Julius had made leaving the house. He had crept into Stella's room, where his mother was deeply asleep: all her life Stella slept like the dead, a heavy conscienceless sleep. Gerald had looked at her for a moment, and then climbed up to the window seat, to watch the sky split in lurid streaks of grey and pink; and he had seen Julius walking slowly along the path, his knapsack on his back. Afterwards Gerald would claim that this was his first memory, the memory which tainted all others: the gangling beloved figure of his first friend, vanishing for ever, like the wayfarer in a German song.

Chapter Four

The night before Tom Nettleship's visit, Cosima sat in the room which had once been her mother's, looking for something to wear. On the dressing table stood a large paraffin lamp, shedding its patchy light across the floor, where great sheaves of material were spread, bronze-coloured velvet, scarlet taffeta, the odd pink wisp of maribou. Cosima, cross-legged in the middle, was gazing at these bits of finery, her eyes glassy with despair.

This room was quite unlike any of the other rooms at Mallingford. Cosima's mother, Annabel Courtney, had been scathing about Stella Deighton's simple, Arts and Crafts notion of interior design, and after she married Gerald she had brought with her, more or less intact, the contents of her bedroom at Courtney Park. There were gilt-edged mirrors, candy-striped curtains, satin cushions trimmed with lace. A row of wardrobes had been built against the wall, smelling of fibreglass, and a deep white carpet had been fitted to cover the polished floorboards. Now, nearly twenty years later, the room looked like a dusty shrine to a forgotten goddess. The fabrics were faded, the mirrors had become rusty and pockmarked; even the clutch of stuffed animals on the chaise longue seemed eerie rather than endearing. Nobody had used the room since Annabel's death, seven years before, in a skiing accident.

'Oh, God,' said Cosima aloud, contemplating the sea of designer dresses around her. She had had a vague idea that it would be easy to find something smart and businesslike amongst her mother's clothes, but as she turned the tiny golden key in the wardrobe door and smelt the great waft of cloves and stale lavender, panic rose in her chest. There was simply so much of it: cashmere jumpers on scented hangers, rows of billowing ball frocks, funny little hats stacked up on the shelves. In most respects a lazy young woman, Annabel had been obsessively tidy when it came to her clothes. Everything was ranged with a tragic neatness, according to season or shade or style.

'Oh, God,' said Cosima again. Hopelessly she fingered the crunchy silk of a dark blue cocktail dress. Many of her mother's things had scarcely been worn; they still had price tags fixed to them, or tissue paper tucked lovingly around their collars. Shopping had been Annabel's *raison d'être*, far more consistent than her erratic passion for Gerald. She had shopped expertly, zealously, plundering Brown's and Harvey Nichols with a blithe disregard for her rustic situation. Cosima could still remember her coming back from London, carrier bags strung like slave bangles on her arms, her eyes bright and dilated as though she had been drinking champagne. Looking back now, she sometimes wondered if Annabel had in fact been drinking champagne, or even conducting feverish love affairs in London hotels, but on the whole she thought not. It was, quite simply, shopping, the spending of her personal allowance on beautiful, unusable things, that had thrilled her to the point of ecstasy.

The flame of the paraffin lamp lurched and flickered in the wind. There had been no electricity at Mallingford since the previous winter, when Gerald refused to pay the bill and tore the grey meter out of the broom cupboard. It's no good, thought Cosima, suddenly, I can't go through with this. She got to her feet, and was about to bundle her mother's clothes back into the wardrobe when there was a knock on the bedroom door.

'Come in,' said Cosima.

The door opened with a creak — all the doors at

Mallingford creaked – and Morag, the housekeeper, came in.

'I've brought you some Bovril,' she said. 'I thought you might want it.'

'Oh,' said Cosima. 'Thank you.'

Normally she was irritated when Morag came to find her, bearing unwanted drinks and biscuits as an excuse for her intrusion. Tonight, though, it was a relief to be interrupted. She took the proffered mug, and sat down on the quilted satin stool by Annabel's kidney-shaped dressing table.

'How are you getting on?' asked Morag. 'Have you found anything yet?'

She sounded brisk and jolly, clearly delighted by this desecration of Annabel's shrine. Cosima waved her hand in the direction of the white wardrobes.

'Well . . . to be honest, it's all a bit much.'

'Your mother's things do fit you, don't they?'

'Some of them do. I'm not as slim as she was.'

'Puppy fat,' said Morag. She perched uncomfortably on the edge of the pink chaise longue, crossing her solid legs.

'Well, whatever. I haven't tried anything on yet.'

Morag picked up the maribou stole between her thumb and forefinger, examined it for a moment, and then let it fall.

'She certainly didn't stint herself, did she? I don't know why we don't sell off some of this stuff. It would fetch a few quid in Brighton. I suppose your father wouldn't hear of it.'

Cosima sipped her Bovril which, for economy's sake, Morag had made much too weak. She decided not to point out that Gerald had preserved Annabel's room from inertia, not devotion. At the time of her death they had been in the middle of an acrimonious separation; the latest – and, as it turned out, the last – of several such estrangements. It was the Courtneys who brought Annabel's body back from Switzerland and made all the arrangements; Gerald had not even attended the funeral. Neither had Cosima, who at eleven was deemed too young for such an ordeal. She had not been sorry to miss the grim polite rituals, but it made it more difficult for her to believe that Annabel, always an absentee mother, had vanished for good. Even now, as she sat here in the neglected candy-pink bedroom, she half expected Annabel to burst in, shrieking at the great joke of having been presumed dead.

'I expect her clothes are all terribly unfashionable now, anyway,' said Cosima to Morag, cradling the hot mug of Bovril in both hands. Although the spring days were warm, the nights fell sudden and chilly as winter, and there was no fire in the room.

'What sort of thing are you looking for?' asked Morag. Cosima gave a shrug.

'I don't know. I should try to look businesslike, so most of the frocks are out. She must have had some suits, or a decent pair of trousers.'

'I'd wear a skirt if I were you,' said Morag, sagely. 'Men prefer it.'

'Do they?' said Cosima, trying to suppress a grin. Men prefer it, indeed; as if Morag would know. The housekeeper was a squat dark woman in her forties, with eager, bulbous eyes and a shadowy moustache on her short upper lip. Cosima often thought – as she was thinking now – of the difference it would have made to Morag's life if she had been better looking. Not beautiful, necessarily; just ordinary, neutral, not-ugly. As it was, Morag seemed doomed to invest her passions in a series of eccentric causes. In her early youth she had been a scout mistress; then she had turned to a virulent form of evangelical Christianity; then to an archaeological project in Umbria which proved to be a hoax. Gerald was the latest of her grand causes. She had encountered him when he gave a guest lecture at the art college, where Morag was a secretary; and from that moment she began, with a single-mindedness as impressive as it was terrifying, to

40

manoeuvre her way into his life. Nine months later she moved to Mallingford, where she had been for the past four years, living rent-free in exchange for her considerable practical gifts. Cosima's attitude to Morag was one of cheerful contempt, but she had to admit that they could not have managed without her. She was the only person who knew when they were short of firewood for the Aga, or how much paraffin they needed for the lamps. It was Morag who had started the vegetable plot and arranged to sell the produce to local farm shops, and it was Morag who had inveigled the art college into letting Gerald teach there for half a day each week.

Cosima put her mug on the dusty glass top of the dressing table, and picked up the bronze opera cloak lying on the floor.

'What about your hair?' said Morag. 'You ought to do something with it, you know.'

'I thought I'd tie it back,' said Cosima, diffidently scooping up its tawny mass in her free hand.

'I could put it up for you, if you like.'

'You won't be here,' Cosima said, quickly. 'You'll have to drive Gerald to college.' The thought of Morag's stubby fingers tugging and twisting at her scalp made her shiver.

'Yes. Pity, really. I'd have liked to see what this chap makes of the place. You will be civil to him, won't you?'

'Of course I'll be civil,' said Cosima, in an irritable voice. 'Not that it'll make any difference. He'll take one look at the place and run a mile.'

'I wouldn't be too sure. If you ask me, it's a brilliant idea, setting up a museum here.'

Cosima swept up the velvet cloak and started shoving it back into the overstocked wardrobe. 'Try telling Gerald that,' she said, drily.

'Oh, we'll persuade Gerald when the time comes,' said Morag. 'Don't do that, Cosima. Hang it up properly or you'll spoil it. No, the real problem is to make sure that we're in control, not your cousin Roderick. I don't see why he should cream off the profits when it's Gerald's inheritance they're trying to flog.'

'Roddy says we should all get something out of it,' said Cosima. She hated the way Morag took charge of everything, particularly where Gerald was concerned, assuming that only she had the power and the judgement to prevent catastrophe. Nevertheless, she stopped trying to cram the bronze cloak into the cupboard, and reached for a clothes hanger.

'Well, yes,' Morag put down her Bovril mug with a clatter. 'That's the sort of thing he would say, isn't it? Come on, then. Let's see what we've got here.'

She stood next to Cosima, staring into Annabel's dark closet. The sick wave of panic rose once again in Cosima's throat.

'The trouble is,' she said, 'I can't remember ever seeing her wear the sort of thing I need. If she wasn't in one of her frocks she was wearing jodhpurs or her dressing gown.'

Morag gave a tut, and then, with malicious energy, plunged her hands into the line of clothes. A moment later she pulled out a yellow chiffon dress, with a huge flounced skirt.

'Tcha,' said Morag. 'I shudder to think how much your mother spent on this sort of rubbish. When Gerald was living on toast and packet soup, I expect. Put this back, will you, Cosima?'

'She did have her own money, you know,' said Cosima. Morag did not answer. Instead she unhooked a tweed skirt and coat, in subdued shades of lavender.

'This might do,' she said.

Cosima pulled a face. 'Too hot,' she said.

'Well,' said Morag, 'I'll put it to one side, just in case.'

She dropped the tweed suit over the scrolled end of the pink chaise longue, where the hanger struck a fluffy white rabbit on the head, toppling it sideways.

Automatically Cosima picked the rabbit up and stroked its dusty nylon fur.

'Too young,' she said, as Morag hauled out a floral cotton dress with a white piqué collar.

'You are young.'

'That's why I don't want to look it.'

'All right,' said Morag, resignedly, and she buried her face once more in the wardrobe. A few moments later she pulled out a dark velvet suit.

'This might be a possibility, I suppose.'

'Let's have a look.' Cosima put the rabbit back with the other animals on the chaise longue. 'Can you move out of the light? I can't see properly.'

The suit was bottle green, with an extravagant quantity of black frogging: it looked like a fashionable parody of an Edwardian riding habit. Thoughtfully Cosima held it up against herself.

'It's a bit – kooky,' said Morag, frowning.

'Kooky?' Cosima laughed. 'I don't know what you mean. I like it.'

Morag flattened her hair with her hands. She had dark rather frizzy hair, cut short and straight. 'You'd better try it on,' she said.

'All right,' said Cosima. She hesitated for a moment, hoping that Morag would leave the room while she undressed; but the housekeeper reached for her abandoned Bovril and settled herself on the chaise longue. Oh, well, thought Cosima, I don't care; and she pulled her jumper over her head. It smelt of earth and paraffin and, comfortingly, of her own sweat.

'Be careful with that blouse,' said Morag. 'Silk stains so easily.'

Cosima slid into the shirt, cool and foreign after the musty warmth of her jumper. The buttons were fiddly, and she turned her back as she did them up, in case Morag should observe her fumbling and offer to help.

'What's it like? Too small?'

'No, it's fine,' said Cosima, wriggling into the green suit. When she had pulled on the jacket she

43

stepped forward to show Morag. 'There,' she said. 'How's that?'

Morag stared at her thoughtfully and nodded. 'Well, it fits, more or less. Have a look.'

Slowly Cosima turned to her reflection in her mother's dusty mirror; and a peculiar thing happened. Like Narcissus, she fell in love. Cosima had never been a vain girl. Her clothes, ancient school uniforms and trophies from the Oxfam shop, had not encouraged her to spend much time looking at herself; besides, she disliked the way her body had swelled and sprouted when she reached adolescence, and she did her best to ignore its ominous ripening. But now the figure in the glass seemed as thrilling and as mysterious as a fictional character: she could hardly take her eyes from the eyes in the mirror. This must be how Annabel felt, she thought suddenly; this must be what intoxicated her. Perhaps I am my mother's daughter, after all.

'What d'you think?' asked Morag, sounding impatient.

'I think it's rather nice,' said Cosima, in a careful voice, because she did not want Morag to see the unholy rapture in her face. There was something wicked about falling in love with yourself; she knew it was something for which the fates punished you.

'It'll do,' Morag said. 'If you ask me, the shirt's a size too small, but I don't suppose there's anything we can do about that. Your mother can't have been very well endowed in the chest department.'

'Mmn,' said Cosima, who was not listening. She was still entranced by her own reflection. The glow of the paraffin lamp, which usually irked her with its dimness, endowed upon her now a special magic, bringing out the streaks of gold in her long hair. A person who looked like that could do anything; a person who looked like that could charm this visiting stranger, could outwit Roddy, could save Gerald's soul. Her own power seemed to crackle in the air, like lightning.

Morag drank the last of her Bovril and stood up. On

44

her face was the satisfied expression of one who has solved yet another problem. She did not seem to have noticed Cosima's rapt absorption in her own image.

'You'd better root about for some decent stockings,' she said, a note of finality in her voice as she reached for Cosima's empty mug. 'And I should take those things off if I were you. You don't want them spoilt before tomorrow, do you?'

'All right,' said Cosima, watching the girl in the mirror speak, essaying grandeur. 'Thank you, Morag. You can go now.'

But Morag had already gone.

Chapter Five

The traffic lights in Lewes High Street turned green. Tom Nettleship whistled through his teeth as he manoeuvred through the town, scanning the ancient houses for a glimpse of the White Hart Hotel. It's a huge place with a flag, Roddy had said, in his drawling and, to Tom, quintessentially English voice; you can't miss it. The spring weather was crisp and unreliable. Tom had driven down from London at breakneck speed, while the humped blue silhouette of the South Downs grew nearer, like a shadowy promise.

The hotel was a large white building on the corner, just before the street plunged downhill towards the river. Tom checked his watch. One o'clock: bang on time. Outside the door stood a painted plywood figure in knee-breeches, with a menu pinned to its chest bearing the legend *Thomas Paine recommends*. Tom grinned, remembering his high-school history lessons. Two centuries ago Thomas Paine had plotted democracy in the upper rooms of this inn, although it was hard to believe that he would have wished to be commemorated like this, lending his name to pan-fried breast of chicken and Sussex ploughman's lunch. Tom made his way into the bar, a smoky timbered room overlooking the High Street, and ordered a pint of local beer. Then he sat on a wooden bench by the fireplace and waited. The church clock struck the half-hour. Roderick was late. Tom's stomach rumbled as the usual doubts – wrong day, wrong time, wrong place – crowded in his head. At last he asked the barmaid to bring him some roast beef sandwiches; and he was unheroically in the middle of them when Roderick appeared, wearing a green waterproof jacket, wellingtons and a flat tweed cap.

'Ah,' he said, 'you must be Tom Nettleship.' The sight of Tom trying to gulp down his crusts amused him, and he gave a whinnying laugh. 'I see you've sorted out some lunch. Sensible man. Let me get myself a pork pie, and I'll join you.'

Wrong-footed, Tom watched as Roderick sauntered towards the bar. He had expected a gracious aristocrat, a character from Evelyn Waugh, perhaps, or P. G. Wodehouse. Instead there was an arrogance about his new client – the cold-fish handshake, the permanent smile – which set his teeth on edge.

'So,' said Roddy, when he came back, 'you found this place all right, did you? I told you you couldn't miss it.' He cut his pork pie neatly into four. 'How long have you been over here? Alastair did tell me, but I've forgotten.'

'A couple of years,' said Tom. 'I came over to do my MBA at Cranfield, and then kind of stayed.'

Most of the Britons he knew were flattered by the notion that he could not bring himself to leave, but Roddy merely looked at him with his opaque blue eyes.

'You've still got an accent,' he said, in a faintly accusing voice.

'Well, yes, I guess I have. My mom would be upset if I lost it.'

'Really?' said Roderick, surprised. For a moment he chomped at his pork pie in silence; then he began: 'Couple of things I should mention. As I've told you, the situation at Mallingford is complicated. The fact is, my family owns the whole of the estate, including the outbuildings, which is the part I want you to see—'

'The outbuildings?'

'Where Stella Deighton had her studio. The house itself is leased rent-free to Stella's son Gerald. For life; at least in theory. It's a long story, which I won't bore

47

you with.' Roderick took a mouthful of beer, which left a pale moustache on his still paler upper lip. The 'I won't bore you' was said crisply, as though he were reproving Tom for inquisitiveness. 'The outbuildings, though, are ours to use.'

'And Gerald doesn't support the project?' Tom asked. Roderick shot him an unfriendly glance.

'That's what I've been trying to explain. Gerald doesn't know about it. Not yet, anyway. Look, I'd rather not go into it in any great depth. There's no point until we've come to some decisions. Gerald can't block anything: it's not in his power. I only mention it because you should know you won't be meeting him.'

'Oh,' said Tom, digesting this. 'Who will I be meeting?'

Roderick ate another wedge of pie. 'My cousin Cosima. Gerald's daughter. Again, I won't bore you with the details of our family peccadilloes.' He paused for a moment, chewing. 'I'd like to involve Cosima as much as possible. She's rather an unfortunate case. Got a perfectly good head on her shoulders but she's not been given much opportunity to use it. I'd like to give her a shot at this.'

Tom's heart sank. He could imagine what Cosima would be like: a half-witted debutante with a voice like Roderick's. He had met dozens of girls like that, at parties in Kensington and charity dinners, ruddy-faced girls who wore hairbands and snorted when they laughed. With any luck, though, Cosima would be too dim to do much damage. Across the table Tom gave Roddy a brisk smile.

'Fine,' he said. 'You're the client.'

'Yes,' said Roddy, drily, 'I am. Let me make one thing clear, though: I want you to be candid with me. We're serious about making money from this, and we've got no intention of wasting our time if it's a no-hoper. So I'm depending on your opinion. Your honest opinion, that is.'

'Sure,' said Tom, lifting his hands as if to show that he carried no weapons. 'I'm an honest guy.'

'Good,' said Roddy. 'I'll remember that.'

When they had finished their lunch they trudged out to the car park behind the White Hart, where Tom had left his sky-blue Porsche. Roderick gazed at it dispassionately.

'I think my Land Rover might be more serviceable,' he remarked. 'The road out to Mallingford's rather bumpy.'

Bumpy's not the word, Tom thought grimly, as the Land Rover jolted past fields of grass and spiky young corn. The track was unmarked and deeply rutted, and it seemed to be leading nowhere. Thick clouds had crept across the sun, dulling the green and gold of the countryside. The hedges were scattered with white May blossom, as though they had been dredged with icing sugar. In a ploughed field nearby a tractor was systematically spewing out brown gobbets of manure.

'Courtney Park's on the right,' said Roddy, in a casual voice, as they skirted a pothole. 'You can just see it through the trees.'

Tom caught a glimpse of a pale Georgian frontage before it was once again obscured. The family seat, no doubt, which Roddy would in due course inherit. Tom's distaste for his client intensified. Then the Land Rover cornered and, abruptly, he saw that they were in a low valley like a bowl, surrounded by dark ridged hills. At the heart of the valley was a cluster of buildings, nestled among a crop of seedy-looking trees.

'Here we are,' said Roderick, as he drew to a halt. Tom opened the door of the Land Rover. There was a smell of fresh earth, and a remarkable quietness about the place. Once the engine was switched off he could hear nothing except his feet on the gravel and the distant singing of unidentified birds. It gave him an odd, dream-like feeling, as though he had been here before.

'We'll go and find Cosima,' said Roddy, slamming shut the car door. 'She'll be expecting us.'

'I guess those are the stables?' said Tom, gesturing towards the block of buildings on his left. On one corner the roof was crowned with a tarnished weather vane, in the shape of a long gilt sow, suckling three ill-formed piglets. Beyond the stables he could see the fissured lantern of an old dovecote.

'That's right,' said Roderick. 'We'll give you the Cook's tour later.'

There was a sudden rustling in the shrubs which bordered the yard, and Tom glanced across just in time to catch sight of a boy's face, solemn and staring. Then the face vanished, and a moment later he saw the boy's bottom, in yellow shorts, retreating into the trees.

'Jeez,' he said. 'You don't have intruders, surely?'

Roderick gave a high-pitched laugh. 'Oh, no. It's my cousin William. Cosima's little brother. He's at that age where he'd rather die than be sociable.'

There was a self-conscious note in Roderick's voice, and it occurred to Tom that he was nervous. His eyes kept darting from side to side, as though he were on the lookout for someone or something, although what it might be Tom had no idea. When they reached the house Roddy lifted the latch of a dilapidated blue door. Inside the corridor smelt of burnt bread and mildew. Tom followed his client into a large kitchen with flagstones on the floor and a dirty iron stove. Standing by the stove was a tall girl, with a large, moon-like face and brown hair, tied loosely back with a ribbon. She was wearing an extraordinary velvet suit, and she stared across with burning desperate eyes, as though she were about to be dragged before a firing squad.

'Hello,' mumbled Cosima. As she spoke her face turned hotly scarlet. Tom put out his hand.

'Hi,' he said. 'Tom Nettleship. I'm from Weston Associates.'

Cosima looked at the hand and stepped forwards, away from the security of the stove. Her own hand was warm and not quite clean, with short nails. She can't be more than eighteen, thought Tom, noting the hectic colour of her cheeks. He felt unexpectedly sorry for her.

'How do you do?' said Cosima. Tom smiled, and then, remembering Roderick, turned to include him in this ceremony of greeting. But Roddy was standing mute by the kitchen table, staring at Cosima as though he had never seen her before. For a dizzy moment Tom wondered if the whole thing might be a hoax, one or both of these unlikely characters playing a part in some unfathomable upper-class plot. Then, at last, Roderick spoke.

'Well, little cousin, I didn't know you could look like that.'

Cosima fixed her eyes upon her feet, in polished lace-up boots, and muttered something Tom could not properly hear, about her mother's wardrobe.

'Well, very nice too,' said Roderick. 'You should dress like that more often.'

She gave an involuntary squirm. So she doesn't like him either, thought Tom, with a flash of glee.

'Would you like something to drink?' Cosima asked. 'Some tea?'

'Not for me, thanks,' said Tom, whose stomach was still swilling with beer and gobbled sandwiches.

'We'll have tea after we've seen the outbuildings,' Roddy said. He paused for a moment. 'Gerald got off all right, did he?'

A wary glance passed between the two cousins. Cosima nodded her head, and the tension seemed at once to lift from Roddy's long pale face.

'Good,' he said. 'Let's go, then, shall we?'

Tom stood aside to let the girl pass through the kitchen door. She lowered her head and seemed to butt her way out of the room, her fists grasping the folds of her skirt. He wondered what she normally looked like, that her appearance now should cause Roddy such consternation. The suit was visibly

51

expensive, but it was also visibly old-fashioned: Kate, for instance, would not be seen dead in it. Now that her blush had faded he had noticed too that there were inexpert dabs of rouge, Coppelia-like, on her cheeks, which made her look like a child who has raided the dressing-up box. Tom tried to imagine what Gerald, her father, was like, that he so obviously put the fear of God into Roderick. The thought of anyone putting the fear of God into so complacent a being as Roddy was rather pleasurable.

'This place is beautiful. Out of this world,' he said to Cosima, as they walked, all three, towards the stable block. 'Have you lived here long?'

'Yes,' said Cosima.

'You were practically born here, weren't you, little cousin?' said Roderick. Cosima did not reply. Above the outbuildings the hillside rose like the tiered wall of an amphitheatre.

'You must understand,' said Roddy, 'the studio is rather – ah – neglected. You need to use your imagination when you're looking at it.' He paused, and glanced at Tom. 'But then, that's what you people are supposed to be good at, isn't it?'

He put his shoulder to the wooden door, which had swollen in the damp weather, and it gave way with a judder. Tom stepped inside. What struck him first, despairingly, was the chaos of the place. Like the house, the studio smelt musty, peppered with another, sharper scent, a solvent of some kind. The old stable partitions had been torn down, leaving lumpy scars in the emulsioned walls, and had been replaced with wooden screens, covered in crudely painted Art Deco patterns. On the table stood an ancient wind-up gramophone and some chipped 78s. The floor was of stone, so dusty that it made Tom sneeze.

'Atmospheric, isn't it?' said Roderick. 'You can really imagine Stella working here. It's as if she's just left the room.'

'Yeah,' said Tom, playing for time. The studio

seemed to him no more than a cultured junkyard. He touched the wooden screens, the paint thickly whorled in great bursts of scarlet and emerald and egg yellow. 'Does anyone use this place still?'

'Gerald does; my father.' Cosima's voice was breathy and reluctant. 'He did those screens. We've got a couple of his canvases, too, in the same style. He's quite a successful painter too, you know.'

'Of sorts,' said Roddy quickly. 'I don't think he can be classed with Stella, exactly.' He glanced at Tom. 'Gerald was responsible for some of those lurid sci-fi posters that were terribly popular in the Seventies. I don't know if you had them in America but here everyone seemed to be buying them. Tolkienesque, I believe they were. There was a whole series of them.'

'Oh,' said Tom, 'I remember. Yeah, they were really hot over in the States. All the kids got them. My brother Scott had one on his bedroom wall. They had wacky titles, didn't they? *Zenox confronts His enemies.* That kind of thing.'

'That's right,' said Roddy. 'As I say, they were terribly popular.'

Tom tried to visualize his brother's poster. He had a recollection that the picture had both excited him and given him nightmares, although he could not now think why. As far as he could recall it showed a tall man with messianic eyes, his arms outstretched, looming above a crowd of terrified people. In the distance some buildings were burning, the ruins stark against the orange horizon. Of all the pictures he ever saw as a boy it was the one which had seemed least to resemble his home life in Minneapolis, its emotions were so extravagant, its primeval landscape so dramatic.

'I must ask Scott what happened to it,' he said aloud. 'I should think it's a collector's item now.' He crossed the floor to examine an old potter's wheel which was beginning to rust about the spindle. 'What about Stella's paintings? Have you got many of those?'

Cosima shook her head. 'Not really. Mostly we've just got unfinished stuff; sketches and so on.'

'The great majority of Stella's work's been sold,' said Roderick. 'I believe Gerald flogged quite a few paintings after she died. Of course, we've got some pictures up at Courtney Park. A lovely one of Mallingford in autumn. My father has it hanging above the fireplace, in his study. And half a dozen others; I forget what.'

Cosima looked at her cousin for a moment, dispassionately. Then she turned to Tom. 'I'll show you what I mean,' she said, in a confiding voice which seemed to exclude Roddy, and she led the way round the corner to the other arm of the L-shaped building. This part of the studio was brighter, with picture windows built into the thick walls. Tom could see motes of dust dancing in the light. Two easels stood on the stone floor, each holding a picture: one a half-finished landscape, the other a charcoal sketch on Ingres paper which bore a clear resemblance to the famous self-portrait Tom had seen in the Tate Gallery. Stella wore the same neat straw hat, hung with fake cherries, and in her eyes was the same watchful expression. She looked a little like Cosima.

'Yes,' said Tom, 'this I recognize. It's the self-portrait, isn't it? The one they've got in the Tate.'

To his surprise Cosima smiled, a wavering smile which lightened her large pale face. It occurred to him that despite her oddness she was a beautiful girl. Beneath the cack-handed blobs of rouge her cheeks bore an elusive bloom, like a new apple.

'I was thinking that perhaps a chronological exhibition might be best,' Roddy said. 'To show the genesis of some of Stella's pictures. From first sketch to finished canvas. That should attract the punters, shouldn't it?'

'Yes,' said Cosima, in a demure voice, 'you could always loan the pictures you've got up at Courtney Park, couldn't you, Roddy? If you can remember which ones they are.'

Roderick flexed his lips. Not for the first time Tom had the feeling that he was a cipher in some private, hostile dialogue between the two cousins. In his mind he rehearsed the conversation he would have with Alastair when he got back to London. Forget it, he would say; if you ask me there's serious trouble brewing. And if we're not careful we'll get caught in the crossfire, believe me.

'That is a possibility,' Roddy said, interrupting this rather satisfying reverie. 'Open to negotiation, anyway.'

'Well,' said Tom, in a bullish voice, 'we'll need a hell of a lot of finished pictures if we're going to attract the general public. I don't think there's any doubt about that; not when they can see Stella's best works in the Tate any day of the week. We've got to have something more to offer.'

Roddy smiled silkily. 'Oh, I'm sure it can be arranged,' he said. 'Although I'm not sure I agree with you entirely, Tom. The other day I had a look at that place in Rodmell that the National Trust has got, Virginia Woolf's old house, and they really don't have much to show there. Just a few books and some old cushions, as far as I could see.'

So much for wanting me to be candid, thought Tom; I should have known better. He took the charcoal sketch from the easel to examine it more closely. Beneath it was a watercolour, of a walled garden with a curlicued iron gate. It was simple and straightforward, the shapes delineated by a few confident lines, leaving the eye to fill in the gaps.

'Hey,' said Tom, 'that's great.'

Roderick stepped up, squinting at the picture. 'Yes, very pretty,' he said. 'I don't think I've ever seen that one before. Where did it come from, Cosima?'

Cosima's face had once more turned crimson. 'It's mine,' she said. 'I didn't realize it was there.'

'It's terrific,' said Tom.

'A talented girl, aren't you, little cousin?' Roddy

said, benignly, as if he had rights of approval over Cosima's talent, although he had clearly never seen the picture before. 'Perhaps we ought to pack you off to art school. Make the most of your gifts.'

Cosima muttered something unintelligible, gazing at her feet. Tom looked at the picture once more. After the *gravitas* of Stella's work its simplicity was charming; the sort of painting that you could live with.

'Will you let me buy this?' he heard himself say.

Cosima stared at him. 'What? For money?'

Roderick began to laugh, his high-pitched whinny of a laugh.

'Good heavens,' he said. 'Well, there you are, little cousin. Your first ever sale. You didn't expect that, did you?'

'I mean,' said Tom, 'I don't know how much you'd want—'

'I've no idea,' said Cosima, her face clouding in distress. Tom wished he had not suggested buying the picture. Stumblejohn, he thought, with a familiar dismay at his own clumsiness.

'If you'd rather not part with it—' he said, gruffly.

'No, it's not that—'

'Twenty-five quid,' Roddy chimed in. 'That sounds like a fair price; wouldn't you say, little cousin?'

Cosima gave a wordless shrug.

'Look,' said Tom, his own face warm with embarrassment, 'don't sell it if you don't want to.'

'No, it's all right,' said Cosima, looking up at him. Her eyes were a deep clear grey, luminous as water. 'I don't mind. Twenty-five pounds is a lot, though.'

'No, it's not,' said Roderick decisively. 'Of course, I shall demand ten per cent, as your agent.'

Cosima shot him a bleak uncomprehending glance.

'Don't worry, little cousin. I'm only joking.' Roddy paused for a moment, rubbing his hands. The mutual confusion of Tom and Cosima seemed to have instilled in him a new energy. 'We'll sort out the filthy lucre later, shall we?' He stepped towards a glass-panelled

56

door at the back of the studio. 'You'll be pleased to hear that we've saved the best till last. We'll show him the dovecote, shall we, Cosima?'

Behind the stables was a patch of overgrown grass, with large smooth cobbles placed here and there, forming a causeway which led to the dovecote. It was beginning to crumble, the bricks decaying in the dubious embrace of a rampant sweet-brier.

'How old is this?' Tom asked.

'I'm not sure,' said Roderick. 'Seventeenth century, I think. Of course, no birds have been kept here for decades.'

In the door was a large old-fashioned key, growing rusty. It gave a satisfying scrape and clunk as Roderick turned it. Going in was like walking into a church: the same smell of damp stone, the same aura of dimness, pierced by discrete shafts of light from the high leaded windows. Then Tom realized that the plastered walls were covered in endless, self-repeating murals, their colours deep and rich, like cave paintings. He took a breath. The paintings were casual but intense: exotic animals with horns and webbed feet and fiery tongues, tall floating figures like the heroes of some uncharted mythology. In one place he saw the same figure portrayed eight times, each distillation growing sharper, like a photograph coming into focus.

'What do you think, eh?' said Roddy at his shoulder, proudly. 'In my view, this is the pièce de résistance of Mallingford. It's badly in need of restoration, of course. But once it's been restored – well, can you imagine?'

Tom put out his hand and touched the cold crumbly plaster of the wall. 'It's amazing,' he said. 'Kind of like a temple. When did she do it?'

'Oh, throughout her life, I think,' said Cosima, who was prowling near the door. 'Nothing's been changed in here since she died. It used to be Stella's private place.'

Tom looked more closely at one of the animals, a

scaly bird-like creature, with fierce pink plumage and a tender woman's face. 'It's extraordinary,' he said, tasting the word as he uttered it. 'It's like seeing someone's subconscious. Especially given that most of Stella's work is so – well, so low-key.'

Cosima nodded at him energetically. 'Yes,' she said. 'I sometimes think that it's sacrilege for anyone at all to come here.'

'Now, now, little cousin,' said Roderick. 'Don't say that. We're hoping to attract Joe Public, remember?' He turned towards Tom, a note of expectancy in his voice. 'So? What do you think? Have we got a project or not?'

'Well . . .' said Tom. He hated it when he was jumped like this into giving public answers. Besides, he found Roddy's blithe confidence infuriating. Then he realized that Cosima was watching him, her face taut with anxiety. Poor kid, he thought, without knowing quite why.

'Oh, I think so,' he said, before he could stop himself. 'Perhaps not a museum, as such; that might be asking a lot. It's a competitive business these days. But let me have a think about it. I dare say I can come up with a plan.'

As he spoke he had a sense that he had made a commitment he would afterwards regret, like the slapdash hero of a fairy tale whose promises come back to haunt him in all their literal solemnity. It's the atmosphere in here, he thought, that's all; it doesn't necessarily mean anything. He looked across at Cosima, who was standing with her hands pressed together, an expression of curious radiance on her face. If we don't do this, thought Tom, I shall never see her again. The idea made him feel, for a moment, dreadfully sorry.

'Good man,' said Roderick. 'That's what I thought you'd say.'

Tom turned, irked by the satisfaction in his voice. 'Of course,' he said, to be annoying, 'we'll have to fix the problem with Gerald Deighton. This won't work with a hostile tenant on the doorstep.'

'Oh,' said Roddy, 'I'm sure you can handle Gerald, can't you, little cousin?'

'I can try,' said Cosima drily.

Roderick glanced at his watch. 'Well, since we're more or less agreed, let's go back to the house for tea,' he said.

Tom took a last slow look at the dovecote walls, at the enticing curves of the female figures, the dazzling unexpected colours of the animals. The sheer energy of it was thrilling: he wished he could engrave it upon his memory. Then he felt the pressure of Cosima's hand on his forearm.

'Don't worry,' she said. 'There'll be plenty of time, you know.'

And with a secret smile she moved away, out into the clear air of the garden.

Chapter Six

From the moment Stella moved into Mallingford the villagers began to gossip. They said that she had set up an artists' colony, where they smoked opium and preached free love and socialism. They said that Julius Murdoch was Gerald's father, and that he had refused to marry Stella because he already had a wife and family in Liverpool. One or two of the more sophisticated scandalmongers went so far as to suggest that the hapless Dora and Molly were lovers, though this particular tale was incomprehensible to most of the rural community.

All these stories were brought to Sir George Courtney's breakfast table with shocked delight by his daughters-in-law. Neither of these upright young women could understand why Sir George had chosen Stella as his tenant, when he might so easily have let Mallingford to what they indignantly termed 'one of our sort'; a family with eligible sons, perhaps, who might have rescued them from the anticlimax of their widowhood. They also, in secret, harboured a certain resentment that the house had not first been offered to them. Alicia, the wife of Sir George's elder son, thought her status as mother of the new Courtney heir should have been recognized by the gift of Mallingford; while Violet, who had only been married for a month when her boy-husband met an obscure but, she was assured, 'clean' death in the Battle of the Somme, hankered for the independence of her own household. The young widows were too much alike not to clash with a frequency which irked Sir George to the point of madness; but they were shrewd enough to recognize that on certain points they would do well to join forces. And so, although Alicia and Violet each privately hoped that she would be the one to benefit from Stella's eclipse, they were united in their ambition to rid Mallingford of its notorious and quite unsuitable tenant.

Sir George had not been to the house since his ill-timed visit of welcome, although he had seen Stella on several occasions in the year of her tenancy: when she came to pay the rent, and, once or twice, as she was walking through the village. He was in no doubt that he had been bamboozled by her, and he felt torn between annoyance at the deception, and a desire not to lose face by admitting his error. This inner conflict was compounded by the chatter of his daughters-in-law, who, it seemed, could not open their mouths without relating some new story of the immorality at Mallingford, like ugly sisters dropping toads and snakes from their lips. Sir George knew that if even a quarter of these revelations were true, he ought to take action; but at the same time the careful malice which Alicia and Violet displayed prompted in him an unexpected sympathy for Stella. It was all very well for his daughters-in-law to titter and gasp in outrage. They had a secure and luxurious roof over their heads, and unless they committed some act of exceptional folly the Courtney estate would provide for them for the rest of their lives. Stella had had to fend for herself, on her own, in less than comfortable circumstances. Although he could not altogether commend the path she had taken, Sir George admired the competence and the dignity with which she had followed that path.

Nevertheless, when the popular account of Julius Murdoch's expulsion reached his ears, he resolved to cut short Stella's tenure of Mallingford. Julius's sad departure had been embroidered by the locals into a fantastic tale of lust and perfidy. One version had it that Stella had found him in bed with both Dora and Molly, while another – whispered, this one – hinted

61

that the young man had endeavoured in some un-
mentionable way to corrupt the child Gerald. It was
this second version which decided Sir George. He
was sentimental about children, especially handsome
children, and he had been struck by the sight of Gerald
in his bedraggled finery, riding on top of the handcart.
His own heir, Alicia's boy, was something of a disappointment to him: not a splendid creature like
Gerald, but a pudgy chinless specimen with a shrill
voice which resembled his mother's. Sir George felt
that, if nothing else, it was his duty to protect Gerald
from harm; and he went upstairs to his study to write
and give Stella notice to quit.

It was then that Stella's famous luck once more came
into play. That morning she had been strolling in the
orchard at Mallingford where Maybrick the gardener
was harvesting apples, and it occurred to her that she
should offer Sir George the first fruits of what was,
after all, his land. With the basket of apples she sent
a note asking if he would care to call upon her the
following day to see the success of her renovations.
This note was conveyed to Sir George just as he was
about to seal the letter curtailing Stella's lease. After
examining the invitation for a moment, he folded his
own letter and put it away in one of the little pigeon-
holes in his beautiful cherrywood desk. He would visit
Stella first, and see what she had to say for herself;
then he would make up his mind. A solid feeling of
satisfaction filled him, as though he had resisted the
temptation to do something small-minded and quite
possibly unfair.

Alicia and Violet were startled when, at breakfast
the next day, Sir George announced that he would be
paying his tenant a call that afternoon, and would not
be home for tea.

'But, Father,' said Alicia (both the young widows
called Sir George 'Father'), 'surely you don't have to
meet her. Won't it do just to write?'

'She has invited me to see what she's done with the

house,' said Sir George, in his mild implacable voice. 'It would be rather discourteous – wouldn't it? – to refuse.'

He arrived at Mallingford promptly at half past three, in the sleek black motor car which he had bought just after the War. Beside him on the passenger seat was a spray of flowers from the garden at Courtney Park, shaggy amber chrysanthemums and Gloire de Dijon roses, like bits of crumpled silk. Stella herself answered the door when he rang. She was, as usual, soberly dressed, in a beige print frock and smooth lisle stockings. Sir George had forgotten her dark grey eyes, which struck him once more with their absolute candour. No wonder he had been hoodwinked, he thought; he would be hoodwinked again tomorrow.

Stella accepted the flowers with a grave bow.

'Do come upstairs and have some tea,' she said, in her unsmiling, rather formal manner. Sir George stepped inside, across his own threshold. He saw at once that Stella had entirely transformed the house. The busy floral wallpaper had been torn off, and the walls washed in chalky emulsion, which he could still smell. The floorboards had been varnished to the colour of treacle toffee – he could smell the varnish, too – and there was a vast red Turkish carpet in the hall, with one or two holes in it where the moths had attacked. In the corner was a hatstand, draped with bright Liberty shawls and a number of straw and felt hats, which had been trimmed with artificial cherries and pink silk camellias and little scraps of ribbon. Stella put Sir George's own hat carefully on a peg in the midst of this milliner's gallery, and she led him up the stairs to the drawing room at the front of the house.

This room, which Sir George remembered from before the War as stuffed with dark mahogany furniture and several tiers of ornaments, was now huge and airy. The windows were hung with white muslin, drifting in the breeze like the sails of a delicate schooner, and set here and there in the room were bamboo screens which Dora and Molly had covered in coarse green and blue cotton. The walls were green, too, a misty green which made Sir George think, quite suddenly, of the lagoon at Venice. It was more than thirty years since he had been to Venice, and at least ten since he had thought about it; but as he stood in Stella's drawing room it all came back to him, the glorious dampness of his hotel bedroom, the murky scent of the canals, the blend of exhilaration and fear with which, after dark, he had strolled alone through strange alleys, never knowing if he might meet a sudden dead end, or, perhaps, his own sudden death: Venice had the flavour of a dangerous city, where cut-throats might lurk in every shadow. In fact, the death Sir George encountered had been of an altogether different and quite metaphorical kind. Too fastidious a young man to be tempted by whores in England, he found their exotic Venetian equivalent another matter; although even then he preserved the formula of romantic love by giving his attentions only to one woman, a neat slender girl of about seventeen named Rosanna, who lived near the Campiello San Zulian and had astonishing bushes of black hair under her arms and between her legs. Sir George had not imagined that such extremes of sensation were possible short of dying, or that physical delight could be so richly and so frantically caught up with the emotions. At the same time, he somehow knew that this was not an experience which could ever be repeated; it was certainly not an experience compatible with marriage. In the dutiful process of begetting sons upon his wincing bride, it never occurred to him to compare Isobel, his wife, with Rosanna, or to be disappointed in the comparison; and over the years the image of Venice and the green canals and the musky shuttered room above the Campiello San Zulian had faded.

'Will you sit down?' said Stella, gesturing towards a

blue armchair. Sir George sat, disconcerted by the flood of his own libidinous memory. Had he been a more self-righteous man, he might have blamed Stella for the calling up of those lost images, as though the atmosphere of moral laxity around her had revived such wanton thoughts. But Sir George was much too fair to ascribe guilt to anyone but himself. Chastened, he perched on the edge of his armchair, his back supported by a heap of tapestry cushions.

A middle-aged woman in an apron came in, carrying a tray of cake and tea things. Sir George recognized her at once; he knew all the local people, by name and by family as well as by sight.

'Good afternoon, Mrs Maybrick,' he said, as she put the tray down on the low table in front of Stella. Mrs Maybrick gave the requisite bob of acknowledgement.

'Sir George,' she said, without surprise, and she made her way from the room, leaving Stella to pour hot water from the brass kettle into the teapot. Sir George leaned back, allowing himself to become a little more comfortable in the armchair. Mrs Maybrick's presence had reassured him. She was a sensible and entirely respectable woman, and she would hardly be working at Mallingford if the house were filled with degenerates. Sir George watched Stella make the tea, not with exaggerated daintiness, as Alicia was wont to do when they had company, but tidily and unself-consciously. She is a very *handsome* woman, he thought, putting out one hand for his cup.

'You seem to have settled in,' he said, rather drily. Stella glanced up, first at Sir George, then at the drawing room.

'I've made it my own,' she said. 'But that was in the terms of the lease, wasn't it?'

'Oh, yes,' said Sir George, taking a hot mouthful of tea. Evidently Stella had read the lease in detail; there would be no room for manoeuvre there. If he wanted her to go, he would have to put it in writing, and give her six months' notice. But he wasn't at all convinced that he did want her to go. In the silence which followed he examined his tea cup, which was of green lustreware, with a strand of gold about the rim.

'Have some cake,' said Stella. 'It's one of Mrs Maybrick's.'

Sir George took a slice of the yellow cake. Then he cleared his throat, and said: 'You know, there have been a great many tales about you, in the village and thereabouts.'

Stella's eyes widened in surprise. 'Tales? What kind of tales?'

Sir George looked abashed. He did not feel in the least like the dutiful landlord reminding his tenant of her obligation to uphold the moral standards of the community. Confronted with Stella's air of rectitude, he felt as though he were the one at fault, forced to defend tittle-tattle.

'Well,' he said, rather feebly, 'you know the sort of things people say. Tongues wag, especially in small places.'

'Oh,' said Stella, in a relieved, dismissive voice. 'Yes, I suppose they do. Although what they find to say about us I can't begin to imagine. We lead a terribly quiet life.'

'And there are – what? Four of you living here?'

'Three, and my son Gerald.' Stella shot another glance across at Sir George. 'That was in the terms of the lease too.'

'Yes. I'm not questioning it—'

'At present I have two women friends staying with me; they've been helping me to redecorate the house. But I don't doubt they will want to go back to London in due course. They've already spent a year down here, and they have their own lives to lead.'

'There was – wasn't there a young man, as well? One of my daughters-in-law saw him; in church, I think.'

'Julius?' For the first time Stella's face lit up with golden amusement. It was obvious she knew what Sir George was hinting at, and obvious too that, for her, the notion of Julius Murdoch as an object of sex and scandal was quite ridiculous. 'Yes, Julius was staying here too. He's gone now.'

'Ah,' said Sir George, not at all sure where that item of knowledge left him. Stella was still faintly smiling, although it was not a smile Sir George felt he could share.

'As I say,' she went on, 'we lead a very quiet life. Do eat your cake.'

Obediently Sir George broke up the slice of cake on his plate and put a piece of it in his mouth.

'What I would like to ask,' Stella continued, 'is if I might use the stable buildings as a studio. They're quite empty, and I don't imagine I shall ever want to keep horses.'

'Well . . .' mumbled Sir George, his mouth full of sweet buttery crumbs.

'The dovecote, too, looks as though it might fall into disrepair if nobody uses it. Of course, in return I would make the place serviceable. Whitewash the walls and so forth.' Stella leaned forward for a moment, across the tea table, as though offering a concession. 'I know that it's not in the terms of the lease.'

'That's not quite the point—' Sir George began, having swallowed his cake. He was interrupted by the sound of the door opening, and the rapid thudding footsteps of a boy entering the room. It was Gerald, dressed in a dirty sailor's suit which was too small for him. His corn-blond hair had been allowed to grow long, and its tangles made him look like Lucifer in childhood. When he saw Sir George he stood quite still in the middle of the floor, his grey eyes fixed upon the visitor.

'I expect he wants cake,' said Stella, in a benign dispassionate voice. 'There's usually cake at this time of day. Gerald! Would you like some cake and some milk?'

Gerald said nothing. He was still looking at Sir George.

'Hello,' said Sir George lamely. Although he sometimes had conversations with Charles, his grandson and heir, he was not accustomed to spending time with children, and he had no idea how to address a boy of Gerald's age. He was not even sure if Gerald was old enough to talk.

'He looks very like you,' he said instead, to Stella.

She bowed her head, rather ironically, and said again: 'Gerald, would you like some cake?'

Still Gerald did not speak, or make a sound of any kind. He seemed wound up like a spring with his own secret mischief. For a moment longer he stared Sir George in the eye, as compelling as a hypnotist; then he gave a sudden leap forward and with one hand snatched the half-eaten slice of cake from Sir George's lustre plate.

'Oh!' said Sir George, more in shock than disapproval. With a small high squeal of delight, Gerald dived into the corner of the room, and hid his booty behind a tall stoneware pot of pampas grass.

'You'd better have another slice,' said Stella to Sir George, in a temperate voice. 'I'm not sure why he wants to snatch yours when he could have a piece of his own, but I suppose that's what children are like.'

Gerald, meanwhile, was peering at Sir George through the great pale fronds of the pampas grass, occasionally giggling as he stuffed cake in his mouth. Sir George was astonished. In his own house no child would have been allowed to flout authority in so blatant a fashion; his grandson Charles was thrashed for much lesser offences. Silently he took another slice of cake, and began to eat it. He felt rather foolish at having his tea stolen by a small boy.

'I'll ring for Mrs Maybrick to fetch some hot water,' said Stella, who was examining the dregs of the teapot. Sir George nodded. He was aware of Gerald, a sailor-suited predator dancing at his elbow. I'm damned if the little blighter's having my cake this time, he thought, tightening his grip on the soft brown crust.

'Lively chap, isn't he?' he remarked to Stella, hoping that she might take notice and make Gerald stop. A sense of persecution rose hotly in his chest, like yeast.

'Oh, yes,' said Stella, in an abstracted voice. 'Full of energy. I've no idea what he does all day.' She paused, and put the lid back on the teapot with a clunk. 'I won't charge you for the whitewash or the labour, obviously.'

'What?' said Sir George, who had forgotten about the stables in his effort to defend his cake. Gerald was still dancing from one foot to another, making little teasing feints in the direction of Sir George's green lustre plate.

'And I'll consult you before I make any structural changes, of course,' Stella went on blithely.

'Of course,' said Sir George, automatically, clapping his hand down protectively. Gerald subsided for a moment, with a chuckle, and his eye caught Sir George's. The boy's face was alert, and smiling with glee. Of course, thought Sir George, he's *playing*. The boiling sense of persecution began to evaporate. He felt that he was not Gerald's victim but his accomplice. And the child had spirit, he would say that for him; not like his own querulous grandson, who seemed forever anxious about getting his feet wet or spilling butter on his shirt cuffs, and would never have dreamed of attempting to play with his grandfather.

Mrs Maybrick came in, bearing another kettle of hot water. 'Sit down properly, Gerald, and have your tea,' she said, in a matter-of-fact voice. Gerald glimmered once at Sir George, and then, surprisingly, he did as he was told, retiring to sit beside Stella on the scrolled sofa.

'I hope he hasn't been bothering you, sir,' said Mrs Maybrick, as she poured milk into a cup for the child. 'He gets excited when we have visitors.'

'Oh, no,' said Sir George amiably. 'Boys will be boys.'

Stella, meanwhile, was lighting a slim brown cigar, as though this conversation had nothing to do with her. Sir George was accustomed to society ladies who smoked, but none of them did it as easily and as naturally as Stella. He felt as if he had stumbled on some other world; not as comfortable a world as his own, to be sure, but more colourful, more exciting, a world of promise; the kind of world he had half divined during those distant weeks in Italy, and had then abandoned. He stretched out his legs, and accepted another cup of tea. How ill at ease Violet and Alicia would be in this room, he thought, with quiet enjoyment. He gazed at the plain green walls, and thought once again of Rosanna, and how the afternoon sun used to chink through the shutters of her small sweltering bedroom.

'Yes,' he said, picking up the threads of his discussion with Stella, 'I don't see why you shouldn't use the stables as a studio. You're right: they'll only stand empty otherwise. Make something of them; why not?'

Stella lifted her head and smiled at him. It was the same smile that Gerald had given him, conspiratorial and bewitching; and Sir George had the sudden obscure feeling that he was lost, doomed to be Stella's champion and to ride into battle on her behalf for the rest of his natural life.

'Oh, yes,' said Stella, 'I think I could make of them something quite interesting.'

And she flicked the ash from her cigar nonchalantly into her lustrous tea plate.

After this, Sir George became a regular, if diffident, visitor to Mallingford. His daughters-in-law disapproved, of course, but they were too conscious of their dependent position to express that disapproval except through the medium of injured little sniffs. As for Sir George, he found Stella's companionable silence as easeful as a beech wood on a blistering day. At first he took to appearing at teatime once or twice a week, to sit in the sea-green drawing room and relish the perfume of Stella's cigars. Then, as plans for overhauling the stable block took shape, he came more often, to observe and to advise. He offered Stella his own workmen to help with the enterprise, making good the brickwork and putting in the new windows; to his own astonishment, he even lent a hand white-washing the building, gently chaffed by Dora and Molly. The girls, emboldened by their success in renovating Stella's house, were attracting commissions from friends and wealthy acquaintances to decorate their homes. Shuttling between London and Malling-ford, they took advantage of the refurbished stables to set up their drawing boards and their workbenches and their metal dye baths. The dovecote, however, remained exclusively Stella's. As soon as the inner walls had been covered with terracotta plaster, she took possession of the great iron key, and in her tacit indomitable way made it clear that this was to be her territory, an inviolable place where she was not to be disturbed.

On his visits now Sir George would often dally for half an hour with Dora and Molly, watching them sketch outrageous fabric designs or varnish tea trays or boil up vile-smelling buckets of size on a small gas ring. Occasionally the impish idea crossed his mind that he should invite them to come and 'do up' Courtney Park, and he took a sly delight in imagin-ing the horror of his daughters-in-law as Dora and Molly wrought havoc with the family heirlooms. Once, when Alicia had been particularly bossy about com-mandeering a suite of rooms for Charles, he went so far as to ask the two women to look over the house; but at the last minute he relented and cancelled the visit, not so much from respect for the two young widows as from a feeling that it was unfair to submit Dora and Molly in their delightful ragbag clothes to Alicia's chilly scrutiny.

He did, however, over the next few years, buy half a dozen of Stella's paintings, most of which he hung in his study. Sir George had mixed motives for his purchases. It was true that he liked Stella's work, which charmed him far more than the ornate still lifes and the sporting prints which filled Courtney Park. He also had a canny sense that the pictures might one day be extremely valuable. Stella was by no means a household name, but she had had paintings accepted by the Royal Academy as well as the New English Art Club, and her work was a reasonable if not a sure-fire investment. Certainly Sir George did not feel that he was buying the paintings out of charity; although there was an element of charity in the timing of his purchases. In his first interview with Stella she had told him that she had a small private income, derived from a childless uncle who had owned a successful ironmongery. At the time Sir George presumed that this income would be adequate to pay for the lease of Mallingford. But as he grew to know Stella and to observe the frugal running of her household, he had a gnawing fear that her funds might run short and that, too proud to admit it, she would hand in her notice, taking Gerald with her. And so, a couple of times a year, two or three weeks before the quarter's rent was due, Sir George would spend half an hour poking around Stella's north-lit studio, and then, in a reticent voice, would propose a figure for the canvas of his choice. If Stella knew what he was about, she did not say so, and she never accepted anything other than a fair price for the pictures. For his part Sir George did not insult her by offering to waive the rent in lieu of payment: he always took the trouble to write her a cheque, in guineas, with his black emphatic signature upon it.

In this way he tactfully supported not only Stella, but also her child. With the passage of time Sir George became more and more attached to Gerald. His own grandson, Charles, had been absorbed without rebellion into the conventional snobberies of public school, and even when he was at home Sir George found little joy in his company. He was a rather self-satisfied boy, who took for granted the privileges of his position, the splendours of the house, the dutiful posse of servants, the endless opportunities to ride and fish and hunt. With his grandfather he adopted a tone of careful reverence, addressing him as 'sir', in a manner which Sir George found both artificial and faintly patronizing. Gerald, on the other hand, was fun. He seemed to live entirely out of doors, bounding through the countryside, turning somersaults, swarming up trees, like a fair-haired Robin Goodfellow. Sir George took delight in teaching him to identify flowers and the songs of birds and, at night, to recognize the stars. He showed him the mysterious cloud-ponds scattered across the Downs, which seemed never to dry up in the hottest of weather, and explained to him how the ancient Britons had used the flints embedded in the chalky hills. He taught him to shoot rabbits, too, digging out an ancient shotgun of his own so that the boy could practise in the Mallingford gardens. To the dismay of Alicia, he brought him to Courtney Park and let him ride Charles's pony, which Gerald did with much greater verve than Charles himself, pelting towards fences with a lack of fear which Sir George found startling. The boy enticed Sir George into escapades which, five years before, he would not have dreamed of attempting. They tramped across the Downs on hot summer afternoons, and clambered across the rocks to bathe in the grey ice-cold sea at Hope Cove. Once or twice they spent the night under canvas, inexpertly cooking sausages over a camp fire. On those nights Sir George, who woke at dawn now that he was growing older, would watch Gerald as he slept, snuffling gently against the blankets. He would breathe in the scent of woodsmoke and damp grass, tinged with a sharp smell that he vaguely characterized as boy, his senses flooded by a feeling of absolute calm.

'You ought to be more careful, Father,' said Alicia, one afternoon when Sir George had come home with his legs scratched by brambles and his breeches torn beyond repair. 'We worry about you, Violet and I; don't we, Violet?'

'Yes,' said Violet, 'you're not young any more, you know, Father.'

Sir George gave a peaceable smile, but did not bother to answer. Of course he was no longer young; he could not think why Violet spared the breath to tell him so. And yet the discovery of this other family and this other self had given him an appetite for life which he had not felt since his own far-off boyhood, and which, through the sombre intervening years, he had never imagined he would feel again.

Chapter Seven

'Alastair not back yet?' Tom asked, as he walked into reception. Under his arm he was carrying a flat oblong parcel, wrapped in white paper.

'No, not yet,' said Shabnam. 'I'm expecting him any time.'

'Any time is right,' said Tom. Shabnam gave him a functional smile.

'I'll ring through when he arrives,' she said, politely dismissing him. Tom nodded, and opened the door to his office. He was feeling restless. All day Alastair had been out at obscure business meetings, which meant that he had not yet been able to talk to him about Mallingford. A great deal of what Alastair did with his time was obscure to Tom. At first he had resented this, feeling like a novice excluded from the true mysteries of a black art; later he wondered if it was simpler than that, and Alastair was merely slacking, veiling his long boozy lunches with the illusion of hard graft. Now, however, Tom was reconciled to the way Alastair worked, his social contacts, his endless wheeling and dealing. He was a fixer, and if some of his deals seemed shady, that was part of his witchcraft.

Tom put the parcel down on his desk and began carefully to loosen the white tissue. Inside was Cosima's painting, which he had just collected from an art shop in the Charing Cross Road. Framed, the picture had an air of authority, just as a printed page has authority over a hand-written one. The edges of the paper had been cropped, giving a further density to the delicate image at the centre. Tom looked at it thoughtfully. He was planning to give it to Kate; a decision he had reluctantly made because he could find nowhere in his own home where it might go. His rented flat near the Portobello Road was very much a man's flat, stridently decorated in black and white and red: wherever he tried to put it, the fine lines of Cosima's painting were blasted by his stark walls. Nevertheless, as he looked at it now he felt an ache of regret to be parting with it, and he was beginni g to waver when the telephone rang.

'Hello?' said Tom.

'Hello, my son. Shabby says you wanted to see me.' Alastair always called the receptionist Shabby, with cheerful disregard for her elegance and her feelings. 'Why don't you come on through?'

'OK,' said Tom. He hung up, flicked the tissue paper back across the painting, and reached for his brown cardboard file.

'Have a seat,' said Alastair, who was standing at the chrome drinks cabinet. 'What do you fancy? G and T? Fizz?'

'Not fizz,' said Tom. 'I'm meeting Kate at six thirty. It's not worth cracking a bottle.'

'It's always worth cracking a bottle,' said Alastair, hoiking some champagne from the miniature fridge. 'Do the honours, will you? I must have a shave.'

Tom took the chilled green bottle and began to tear the foil from its neck. 'What have you been up to?' he asked.

'Oh, a few irons in a few fires. Nothing to report as yet.' Alastair took an electric razor from the top drawer of his desk. 'Where are you meeting Kate?'

The champagne fizzed over Tom's left hand as he popped the cork. To Alastair's despair he had never mastered the knack of opening the bottle properly, so that it smoked but did not spill.

'Over in Kettners,' he said, shaking his wet fingers. 'Come and say hi, if you want.'

'Yes, I might do that. I'd like to see Kate.' Alastair pulled his chin taut as he began to shave. 'I can't stay long, though. I've got to have dinner with a girl I met the other night at Stringfellows.'

'Tough,' said Tom, pouring champagne. With his free hand Alastair accepted a glass.

'How was your trip to – what's its name? Mallingbridge?' he asked.

'Mallingford. It was OK.'

Alastair's razor buzzed nimbly along the curve of his throat. 'Yes? So tell me.'

Tom took a mouthful of his champagne, which was dry and exquisitely creamy. One of Alastair's greatest talents was for buying champagne.

'Well,' he said, 'it's miles from anywhere. And the house itself isn't part of the deal. It's on a more or less permanent lease to Gerald Deighton, and they can't get him out.'

'Terrific,' said Alastair. 'What's the good news?'

'I guess the studio might be worth seeing, if we could borrow some decent pictures to put on show. And there's an amazing dovecote in the grounds of the house. Covered in Stella Deighton originals. It's wild. The real problem is that the place is a mess. And there seems to be a family feud going on between the Deightons and your friend Roddy. Half the time I was there I felt like the referee at a really mean ballgame. I tell you, it wasn't fun.'

Alastair put his razor back in the desk drawer, and took out a pocket mirror and a red Swiss Army knife. 'What did you think of Roddy?' he asked, flicking open the blade of the knife with his thumbnail.

'I couldn't stick him,' said Tom. Alastair grinned.

'I thought you might feel like that. He's a bit of a turd. But a rich turd.'

'Oh, sure. I'll suppress my animosity for the sake of a nice fat fee,' said Tom, lightly. He drank some more champagne. 'The Deighton girl's OK.'

'Who?'

'Gerald's daughter. I met her while I was there.'

Alastair looked up sternly from his desk. 'I hope

you're not planning to break company rule number one,' he said. 'Thou shalt not sleep with the client.'

'Jeez, no. She's only eighteen. Anyway, some of us are in relationships. We don't need to sleep with clients; or pick up girls in Stringfellows.'

'All right, all right.' Alastair gestured towards his pocket mirror, on which there was now a thin line of white powder. 'Do you want some of this, Tom?'

Tom shook his head. 'No, thanks.' He watched as Alastair took a fat multi-coloured plastic straw and flared his nostrils. 'I don't know why you bother.'

'Yeah. Cocaine is just your body telling you you earn too much.' Quickly and carefully Alastair ran the tip of the straw along the line, snorting up the white powder. 'I don't care, I like it. Puts me in a good mood.'

He sniffed once or twice, to clear his nose. Then he put away the knife and the mirror, and said: 'Where does the Deighton girl come into it? Is she putting up some of the cash?'

'No. It's Roderick's way of getting the Deightons on side. He wants Cosima to persuade Gerald to co-operate.' Tom paused for a moment. 'Plus there's the fact that he fancies her rotten.'

As he spoke Tom realized that this was true, and that it explained Roderick's unease with his cousin. He wondered why the idea had not struck him before. Alastair groaned.

'Oh, Christ,' he said. 'Are you telling me this whole thing's a set-up so that Courtney can wangle some girlie into bed? Jesus. The lengths people go to just to get laid.'

'Well, that's only part of it,' said Tom. The notion of Roddy taking Cosima to bed was peculiarly repugnant to him. 'He's a devious guy. One thing's for sure: he wants to make money from the place.'

Alastair reached languidly for the champagne bottle. 'You think it's a can of worms, don't you?'

Tom held out his own glass to be refilled. 'I don't know. We're not looking at a goldmine, that's for sure, although I guess we could make something of it. But my gut reaction is that we should steer clear.' He remembered standing in the dovecote, with Cosima squeezing his arm and saying, there'll be plenty of time; and he felt a twinge of disloyalty, as though he were betraying an oath. You're being soft, Nettleship, he said to himself, you'll never get on if you're soft; and, hardening his heart, he went on: 'I'll write a report if you think it's worth the time, but I don't think we should get involved. It smells like trouble to me.'

Alastair was silent, swilling champagne thoughtfully around his mouth. Then, as if he had not heard Tom, he said: 'Let's go with it; at least for the time being. I want to stay in with Roddy Courtney. He could put a fuck of a lot of business our way.'

'Oh,' said Tom.

Alastair opened his eyes wide. They were a deep blue, and very bright. 'Look, Tom, I'm not saying I don't trust your judgement. You know I do. But you don't make your first million by playing safe. We can always pull out if it looks as though we might get burnt. And in the meantime, I tell you, Roddy Courtney's a valuable asset. I want us to have a good crack at seeing what we can get out of him.' Alastair finished the last of his champagne. 'Tell him you'll set up a sponsorship deal. He'll like that. I get the impression he doesn't want to bankroll the whole show.'

'And what if he calls our bluff, and asks to meet this sponsor?'

'Then we find him someone. Jesus, Tom. Don't be dense. It shouldn't be that difficult, not at the moment. I'm sure old Brian Edwards would be more than willing to put a few quid in something respectable.' Alastair waved the champagne bottle enticingly. 'Shall we kill it?'

Tom glanced at his watch. It was twenty to seven. 'I can't,' he said. 'I'm late already.'

'She'll wait,' said Alastair, still holding the bottle in front of Tom's nose. 'That's what girls are for.'

'I know she'll wait, but she'll be mad when I get there.' Tom got to his feet, slapping his pockets to check for his wallet and his keys. 'Are you coming?'

Alastair stretched out his hand for a teaspoon which he dropped into the open neck of the champagne bottle. 'OK,' he said. 'I'm coming.'

Outside the sky was tinged with huge flamingo-pink clouds. They crossed Cambridge Circus, and turned the corner into Romilly Street, where Kettners' neon sign glowed green.

'What's that?' asked Alastair, nodding towards the white parcel. It was just the wrong size for Tom to hold comfortably under his arm, and he kept shifting his fingers to stop them from going numb.

'Present for Kate,' he said.

'Jesus. She's got you where she wants you, hasn't she? Christ, Tom. She'll be hauling you up the aisle before you know it.'

'No, she won't,' said Tom. 'It's not like that. She's not like that.'

They were in Kettners now, edging their way through the crowds towards the bar.

'Tom,' said Alastair, 'they're all like that, believe me. Ah, look. There she is.'

Kate was sitting in a wicker chair, dressed in a Chinese silk waistcoat and a pair of tight black trousers, with a black bow tie at her throat. She was drinking a glass of Buck's Fizz. As usual, she smelt rather strongly of a gaudy perfume which Tom did not recognize. Kate was always checking out new products for the magazine she worked for, and she never wore the same scent twice. Tom was much too reasonable to object to this, but sometimes, when he took her in his arms, he missed that moment of blissful recognition, where sight, touch, and smell all cohere and say, this is the loved one.

'Sweetheart,' he said now. 'Sorry I'm late.'

'I'm used to it,' said Kate, smiling up from her winged chair. 'Hello, Alastair.'

'Katie, darling.' Alastair kissed her on both cheeks. 'Is this what the best dressed snooker player is wearing this year? You look lovely.'

'Thank you,' said Kate, in a serene voice. She always treated Alastair as one might treat a recalcitrant schoolboy, firmly and sweetly.

'Have you been waiting long?' said Tom. 'I'm really sorry.'

'That's all right. Look, there's a stool over there. Why don't you grab it? God, this place is like Paddington Station.'

'But that's why we love it,' said Alastair. 'In with the in-crowd. What are you drinking, Katie? You're not diluting perfectly good champagne with orange juice, are you? You'll OD on vitamin C. Tom? More of the same? Okey-cokey.'

'Cokey being the operative word,' said Kate perceptively, when Alastair had plunged into the wedge of bodies lining the bar. 'I shudder to think how much money's gone straight up that man's nose.'

'Yeah, I know,' said Tom, sitting on the stool beside Kate's shiny black knees. 'But you try stopping him. I like the gear, Kate. It's cool.'

'What's in the parcel?' asked Kate, prodding the white tissue with a crimson fingernail.

'Show you later. How's tricks?'

'Fine. Sally wants me to do a piece on bubble baths for the next issue so I've got a load to test drive.' Kate gestured to a large green Harrods bag beside her chair. 'What did Mr Hyperactive say about Mallingford?'

'He wants me to press on with it. Thinks we might end up best buddies with Roderick Courtney.'

'The creepy rich chap?'

'Yeah. Personally I think he's crazy, but he's the boss. Listen, do you want to eat here? Because I ought to put our name down for a table if you do.'

Kate sniffed. 'Are we lumbered with Alastair for the evening?'

'No, he's got some floozie lined up. Sorry, sweetheart, but I expect she is a floozie. He met her in Stringfellows.'

'I wish he'd give it a rest,' said Kate. 'I thought the Eighties thing was fidelity.'

Tom tucked his feet more comfortably beneath his stool. 'If you ask me old Alastair just hasn't found the right woman.'

'The right harem, you mean,' said Kate. 'I don't think one woman would have the energy to cope with him.'

Alastair came back with three crystal flutes of champagne precariously balanced between his fingers. 'Here we are,' he said with satisfaction. 'I bought you the real thing, Katie. I'm not having anyone say I didn't do my bit for a pretty woman. Haven't you given Kate her present, Tom?'

'Oh,' said Kate, pleased, 'is that a present for me? You didn't say.'

'Oh, he's so gauche and inexperienced. I don't know why you hang out with him. Go on, then, Tom.'

Inwardly Tom sighed. He had been hoping to give Kate the picture later, when they were alone together, and he could savour her response. But now her neat pointed face was alight with anticipation. He reached for the white parcel.

'There,' he said. 'Small token of my esteem. Or something.'

'It looks like a fairly large token to me,' said Kate. She glanced across at him, questioningly. 'You never give me things, Tom. What is this?'

'Well, I saw it, and I kind of thought – oh, go on. Just open it.'

Kate tore impatiently at the parcel. 'It feels like a picture. Is it a picture? God, I love having presents.'

Tom watched her face as she scrunched up the tissue paper, and the painting was at last revealed. She stared for a moment; then she raised her eyebrows.

'Oh,' she said. 'It's rather nice.'

'It's an original,' Tom said, proudly. 'By Stella Deighton's granddaughter, no less. That's the gate of the walled garden at Mallingford.'

'Is it?' Kate examined the picture more closely. 'I don't think I've ever had an original painting of my own. Thanks, Tom.'

She leaned forward and kissed him on the cheek. Her perfume this evening was a floral one, spiked with the heavy scent of gardenias.

'I expect that could be worth a bob or two in a few years' time,' said Alastair. 'I should look after it, Katie.'

'Yes,' said Kate. 'I will.'

She rewrapped the picture and slid it down to the floor, next to her plastic Harrods bag.

'You like it, don't you?' said Tom, stung by her lukewarm reaction.

'Oh, yes,' said Kate, picking up her glass. 'It's sweet. And awfully nice of you to think of it.' She drank some champagne, her large gilt earrings rattling; then she turned to Alastair and said, teasingly, 'I hear you've made yet another conquest. Who is she?'

Alastair gave a little moan. 'She works for a telly company. Why do I do it, Katie? I must be mentally retarded.'

'I think you probably are,' said Kate. 'Where are you meeting her?'

'That Malaysian place in Frith Street. Her idea, not mine.' Alastair screwed his face up wistfully. 'Maybe I won't bother. I'd much rather stay with you. We could have dinner and go to a club. That would be fab. Don't you think that would be fab?'

'No,' said Kate, briskly. 'We're a very boring couple on the quiet, you know. You go and meet your ladyfriend. Go on, Alastair. Push off.'

Alastair sighed, and got to his feet. 'You're so masterful, Katie. I don't think Tom deserves you.' He bent and kissed her lightly on the mouth. 'OK, you two. Off I go. See you in the morning, Tom.'

Kate watched him go, her lips folded, her cheeks flushed. Then she turned and smiled at Tom. 'Hello, darling,' she said. 'Let's start the evening properly now, shall we?'

But Tom was looking at Cosima's picture, still half swathed in tissue paper. Kate had put it face-down against her chair, which somehow made matters worse. He struggled for a moment with himself; then, accusingly, he said: 'You don't like it, do you?'

'What? Oh, the painting. Yes, I do. I mean, I'm sure it'll grow on me.'

'Great,' said Tom. He took a gulp of champagne, as if it were medicine. The bubbles shimmered aggressively in his nose.

'Oh, Tom, don't be like that. It's just that it's not something I'd have chosen myself. It's a bit sort of – well, abstract for me. A bit modern.'

'I thought you'd really like it,' said Tom, in an injured voice.

'I do like it. It'll look lovely in the bathroom.'

'Oh, terrific, Kate. I give you an original painting and you stick it in the bathroom. Terrific.' He picked up his empty glass. 'I'm having another drink. What about you?'

Kate did not answer, but sat implacably upright in her wicker chair, thin brown hands fisted. Then she said: 'Look, Tom, when you give someone a present it's theirs, OK? And they can do what they want with it. If you're so bothered about what happens to the picture, you should have kept it.' She paused for a moment, gave a sniff and added: 'Or saved it for Becky. I'm sure she'd have adored it.' She had a way of saying Becky's name as though the word were in quotation marks, making it sound at once pretentious and absurd. This always surprised Tom, who did not understand why Kate should be jealous of his ex-wife.

'Oh, come on,' he said. 'I bought it on impulse. I wasn't thinking about Becky.'

'But you weren't thinking of me either, were you?' said Kate, at once.

Tom slumped upon his stool. He had forgotten how fiercely Kate fought back whenever they argued; quite unlike Becky, who had been inclined to weep and sulk. And she was right, of course: he had not been thinking of her. If he had been thinking of anyone, it was Cosima, that odd time-warped girl with her bunched bronze hair and her velvet suit.

Sensing her advantage, Kate went on: 'I mean, every once in a while it would be nice to know that you do think about me when I'm not there.'

'Of course I think about you,' said Tom, rather weakly. 'Don't be silly.' As he spoke he wondered whether it were true. He had a sneaking feeling that he only really remembered Kate when he was prompted to do so, by her phone calls, or the need to make plans for the weekend, or by glimpses of girls who resembled her. It was not a thought of which he was particularly proud.

'Well, good,' said Kate, stretching out her hand, 'because I think about you rather a lot. In case you hadn't noticed.' She ran her fingers through the stiff curls of his hair; then she slid her hand to his ear and gave the lobe an expert pinch, sharp, but not quite painful. 'Listen, I'm really not very hungry. Why don't we just go back to my flat?'

Tom looked across at her. The expression on her face was at once playful and determined: he could hardly admit to her that he was starving. From the restaurant across the hall came the smell of pizzas baking. Regretfully he pictured the tiny galley kitchen in Kate's flat, where there was never anything but white wine, cornflakes and instant coffee.

'Sure,' he said, 'if that's what you want.'

'It's what *you* want, isn't it?' said Kate, with a little knowing smile. She gave his ear another tweak. There's a hidden agenda here, thought Tom, but Christ knows what it is. He seized Kate's hand and pulled it towards his mouth. Her palm smelt of cosmetics, that sweet expensive scent like nothing which ever occurs in nature. Tom was not certain that he liked the smell, but something about it was intoxicating.

'OK,' he said, releasing her hand, 'we'll get a cab to your place.'

Chapter Eight

Roddy helped himself to watery scrambled eggs from the silver chafing dish, and sat down at the long table, opposite his father. Weekend breakfast at Courtney Park was an old-fashioned affair, eaten in the dining room, with a row of hot dishes lined up on the sideboard and an electric tea urn permanently on the boil. A couple of years ago Sir Nicholas, Roddy's father, had suggested abandoning this formality – it was hard work for the cook, and a great deal of the food went to waste – but his children had been clamorous with indignation. Home would not be home without proper breakfast.

'So,' said Sir Nicholas, amiably, as he buttered lukewarm toast, 'it's all systems go, is it?'

Roderick sprinkled pepper over his eggs. He hated the note of amusement in his father's voice, as though any project he conceived must by definition be somehow comic.

'I don't know yet,' he said. 'The report this Nettleship chap sent me was interesting. He doesn't think it would be viable to turn the place into a full-scale museum, but he's had some other ideas. A study centre, perhaps, or something like that.'

'Ah,' said Sir Nicholas.

'And,' Roddy went on, bullishly, 'he said he was looking at the possibility of corporate sponsorship. Sounded rather hopeful, actually.'

Sir Nicholas bit a half-moon from his slice of toast. 'Oh, well,' he said, in a philosophical voice. 'At least that means we won't have to foot the bill on our own.'

Roderick eyed his father with dislike. Sir Nicholas was a tall, bland, good-looking man in his late fifties. He had the same colourless brown hair as Roderick, but his features were much sharper, a finer nose, a more prominent chin: indeed, he looked like the mould from which Roderick had, inexpertly, been cast. He had decided to hand over to Roddy the bulk of the family's business some years before, while he himself pursued a well-intentioned public career: he was active on several charity committees, and held a couple of directorships. At one time he had considered becoming an MP, but he despised the new values of the Conservatives, and could not contemplate belonging to any other political party.

'I don't know why you're so sceptical, Father,' said Roddy. 'I'm not exactly a novice when it comes to setting up deals.'

'No, no,' said Sir Nicholas swiftly, because he was not an unkind or an unfair man. 'I'd like to minimize our risk, that's all.'

'Anyway,' Roddy went on, aggressively shovelling eggs into his mouth, 'nobody else has come up with any ideas about what to do with the place.'

Sir Nicholas stretched out his ivory hand to take another piece of toast from the rack. 'It's a shame you couldn't persuade those youngsters to decamp,' he observed. 'Then we could have gone in with all guns blazing, and shifted the bounder. I dare say that if we'd called the police after that incident with the rifle we could have had him out months ago.'

'Well, yes, I agree. That would have been the ideal solution. But since it can't be done, we have to make the best of it. And personally I think it's about time we reaped some benefit from the Deighton connection, instead of the other way round.'

Sir Nicholas dolloped pale orange marmalade onto his plate. All his movements were slow and deliberate. 'That's a fair point,' he said, 'as long as we do reap some benefit, you know.'

'Father,' said Roderick, 'that's exactly what I'm trying to ascertain.'

Sir Nicholas smiled. 'All right, all right. Message received and understood. I'll leave you in full control.' He took a mouthful of tea, which was strong and slightly stewed. 'Mind you, I'd like to have a meeting with this marketing chap of yours at some stage. Before we jump in feet first.'

Roderick pushed his eggs around his plate. 'Yes, of course,' he said, in the clipped voice of one who is just managing to suppress exasperation. 'As I keep telling you, it's early days yet.'

'And what about young Cosima? Does she think it's a plan worth pursuing?'

'I haven't shown her Nettleship's letter yet. She seemed surprisingly co-operative the day he was at Mallingford. Came out with all sorts of things about Stella that I certainly didn't know.'

Sir Nicholas lifted his white linen napkin and gave a fastidious dab to his lips. 'Don't be too manipulative, Roddy, eh?' he said. 'I know it doesn't suit our purposes that Cosima should be so attached to her father. But the fact remains that she is attached to him; quite deeply attached, from what I can gather. And she's not had a particularly easy life. I don't think it would be fair to play games with her loyalties.'

'Oh, for heaven's sake, Father,' said Roderick, irritably. 'I'm not playing games. Besides, you underestimate Cosima. You haven't seen her since Aunt Annabel died. She's not a little girl any more; she's a very pragmatic young woman. She's perfectly aware that something has to be done about the house. And about Gerald, too. She hasn't said it in so many words, but I think she realizes that he needs professional help.'

'Needs horsewhipping, if you ask me,' said Sir Nicholas pleasantly, tossing his napkin aside. 'Though I suppose it's a little late for that. He's not violent with the children, is he, do you think?'

Roderick shook his head. 'Oh, no. Not at all. The only people he seems to attack are outsiders.' He paused for a moment, ruefully. 'Me, for instance.'

'Tcha,' said Sir Nicholas. 'Damn that lease. The Lord alone knows what possessed the old man to give him rights to the place for life.'

'Philanthropy, perhaps?' suggested Roderick, in his silkiest voice.

'Hardly,' his father said, annoyed, as Roddy had known he would be. Sir Nicholas regarded philanthropy as his own special province: he had gone so far as to call himself 'philanthropist' in his entry in *Who's Who*. 'More like perversity, in my view. I've always thought that the First War left him with a screw loose.'

'Well,' said Roddy, 'unfortunately we have to live with the consequences. And I think my solution is the best we can find, for the time being.'

Sir Nicholas stood up, his chair scraping the bright parquet floor. 'At least it should provoke action of some sort,' he conceded. 'Even if all it does is to give us an excuse for arresting our friend Gerald for threatening behaviour. I'll be in my study, Roddy, if anyone wants me.'

Roderick watched his father go. Sir Nicholas's study was one of the most comfortable rooms in the house, and he spent a great deal of time there, looking out at the clipped lawn and the fountain. Nominally he used it for work, although Roddy suspected that it was as much as a refuge as an office. Privacy was difficult to achieve at Courtney Park. The house buzzed with a particular kind of trivial activity, supervised by Lady Courtney, who was forever organizing trips to church, or brisk walks, or rubbers of bridge. No doubt she would breeze into the dining room any moment now, to chivvy Roderick into finishing his breakfast and coming with her to morning service. Decisively he put down his fork and got up. The thought of his mother's robust prodding manner set his teeth on edge. He

would go out into the garden; ... would think to
look for him there.
...he Courtney Park grounds we... ...mal and ex-
...in the French style, with de... ...ng hedges
of sto... beds scissored into the ...rass. Oc-
ing upon ...s were placed here an... ...d... beneath
fountain, towa... ...al replicas, not the ...lumps
he acquiesced in h...th, ...et lawn. Often on Su...the
the day partnering h...r in th...e demands, and sp...
activities which his ...ther dis...ed; otherwise he ensconced himself in th...estate office, which was in the
gate-house, to get on with some work. But today he
wanted to be on his own, to think things through.

He turned to look a the benign golden frontage of
the house, across the dip of the ha-ha. Through a
first-floor window he could just see the figure of Sir
Nicholas, evidently reaching for a book from the shelf.
What an old fraud, thought Roddy, with a shudder of
contempt. He liked to think that he despised his father.
After a lifetime of empire-building, Sir Nicholas had
bluntly withdrawn from politics at precisely the time
when, in Roddy's view, his influence and contacts
might have borne fruit. The Thatcher government was
not afraid to engage the talents of the unelected; Sir
Nicholas — and possibly Roddy — might have had a
dazzling new career, and made a fortune into the
bargain. But instead Sir Nicholas had opted for his
charities and ballet companies, leaving Roddy to do
his best with the family business. To make matters
worse, he seemed to be holding even this at arm's
length. However great Roddy's success on the stock
market, however brilliant his running of the estate,
he never seemed to elicit from Sir Nicholas more
than a quiet, half-smiling response. Every so often
Roddy caught himself having grandiose multicoloured
fantasies, of his father and himself on an election

91

platform, ... press conference, Sir Ni...
thumping ...oulder ecstatically, all mo...
detach... seen his father's face. As far... the
he had... imagining it. ...eous shout
Could... lately he turned on his ...pointing pair
Disom th... distant lawns... younger sister.
ho... of the ...rocks; ...
of... at the d... of ... he said to himself,
b... I am right ab... Mal...
...cking up stones, no... wha his opi... may be.
As Roddy thought of ...lling for the image of Cosima
focused suddenly and sharply i his mind: so sharply
that it seemed an almost physial pain, like a kick in
the stomach. He gave a small voluntary groan, and
at once looked around to mak sure that nobody had
heard him.

Roddy had been brought up - chiefly by his mother
- to believe that love and marriage occurred with a
smooth inevitability which quite precluded suffering.
You could be silly about it, of course, like his aunt
Annabel, and get into scrapes; but for most people,
people like him, the transition from one sort of family
life to the next was calm and comfortable. Roderick
had always assumed that at some stage a nice, well-fed
girl of his own class would materialize and would
simply cheerfully take him on: accompany him to
hunt balls and charity premieres, organize dinners at
Courtney Park, eventually produce a clutch of sleek
strapping children to bear his name. It was only when
he reached his thirtieth birthday that he realized
nothing of the sort had happened. There had been
girls, of course: the right kind as well as the wrong
kind, glossy Carolines and Emmas who adored spending the weekend with his family, and dropped massive
hints about their suitability as future Lady Courtneys.
But something about this very eagerness curdled
Roddy's enthusiasm. He preferred the less suitable
girls, the drama students, the Australian waitresses.

would go out into the garden; nobody would think to look for him there.

The Courtney Park grounds were formal and exquisite in the French style, with dense oblong hedges and flower beds scissored into the turfy grass. Occasional statues were placed here and there beneath the trees: classical replicas, not the crude vital lumps of stone which adorned Mallingford. His feet crunching upon the gravel path, Roderick strolled past the fountain, towards the croquet lawn. Often on Sundays he acquiesced in his mother's demands, and spent the day partnering her in those country-lady social activities which his father disliked; otherwise he ensconced himself in the estate office, which was in the gate-house, to get on with some work. But today he wanted to be on his own, to think things through.

He turned to look at the benign golden frontage of the house, across the dip of the ha-ha. Through a first-floor window he could just see the figure of Sir Nicholas, evidently reaching for a book from the shelf. What an old fraud, thought Roddy, with a shudder of contempt. He liked to think that he despised his father. After a lifetime of empire-building, Sir Nicholas had bluntly withdrawn from politics at precisely the time when, in Roddy's view, his influence and contacts might have borne fruit. The Thatcher government was not afraid to engage the talents of the unelected; Sir Nicholas – and possibly Roddy – might have had a dazzling new career, and made a fortune into the bargain. But instead Sir Nicholas had opted for his charities and ballet companies, leaving Roddy to do his best with the family business. To make matters worse, he seemed to be holding even this at arm's length. However great Roddy's success on the stock market, however brilliant his running of the estate, he never seemed to elicit from Sir Nicholas more than a quiet, half-smiling response. Every so often Roddy caught himself having grandiose multicoloured fantasies, of his father and himself on an election platform, or at a press conference, Sir Nicholas thumping his shoulder ecstatically, all mockery and detachment purged from his face. As far as he knew he had never seen his father's face ecstatic, but he could not help imagining it.

Disconsolately he turned on his heel, away from the house. From the distant lawns came the raucous shout of one of the peacocks; a mangy, disappointing pair bought at the demand of Henrietta, his younger sister. But I am right about Mallingford, he said to himself, kicking up stones, no matter what *his* opinion may be. As Roddy thought of Mallingford the image of Cosima focused suddenly and sharply in his mind; so sharply that it seemed an almost physical pain, like a kick in the stomach. He gave a small involuntary groan, and at once looked around to make sure that nobody had heard him.

Roddy had been brought up – chiefly by his mother – to believe that love and marriage occurred with a smooth inevitability which quite precluded suffering. You could be silly about it, of course, like his aunt Annabel, and get into scrapes; but for most people, people like him, the transition from one sort of family life to the next was calm and comfortable. Roderick had always assumed that at some stage a nice, well-fed girl of his own class would materialize and would simply cheerfully take him on: accompany him to hunt balls and charity premieres, organize dinners at Courtney Park, eventually produce a clutch of sleek strapping children to bear his name. It was only when he reached his thirtieth birthday that he realized nothing of the sort had happened. There had been girls, of course: the right kind as well as the wrong kind, glossy Carolines and Emmas who adored spending the weekend with his family, and dropped massive hints about their suitability as future Lady Courtneys. But something about this very eagerness curdled Roddy's enthusiasm. He preferred the less suitable girls, the drama students, the Australian waitresses.

For nine months he had been obsessed by a young woman who worked in the wine bar near his City office, a brash independent large-breasted girl from Sydney, who had never given him more than a damp kiss at closing time; then he had a short unsatisfactory affair with a red-haired Scottish girl, a temporary secretary who disappeared without notice back to Airdrie.

The very impossibility of these girls intoxicated Roddy. He sometimes thought that the world would crash if he ever brought one of them home to Courtney Park, to meet his mother. Not that the girls would have come. They shrugged off Roddy's wealth and connections with a disregard all the more seductive because he knew it was not feigned. When he boasted of those other women, the friends of his sisters and the sisters of his friends, who would have fainted with pleasure at such an invitation, these girls stared him out with disbelief, and an indifference he found ravishing.

The peacock cried again. Roderick had reached the little pavilion where the croquet things were kept, a pretty square building covered in wisteria. Beside the door was a long white bench, facing the lawns. He sat down, feeling the damp wood cold against his thighs. Cosima, of course, was not impossible; at least, not impossible in the way the Sydney barmaid and the Scottish girl had been. He let his mind prowl carefully around the idea of her, as one might prowl around a fire, or a jungle creature. It was true that she did not encourage him, exactly, but then she was still very young; too young not to be farouche and clumsy. And there was the whole business of her devotion to Gerald. Father's right, Roddy thought, grudgingly; I'll have to be careful, I don't want to alienate her. He was conscious of a sense of terrible difficulty, as though he were trying to shape a substance both precious and quite unmalleable. It made his stomach knot up.

A drop of rain fell upon the sandy earth beside the

pavilion. Roddy looked up into the solid pale sky. He wished he could remember what Cosima had been like as a child. He knew that, when Annabel was alive, the little girl had often been dumped at Courtney Park, but he had no proper recollection of her. The only memories he had were false ones, based on details his mother had told him: what a scrawny silent creature Cosima was, who barely tasted her food; how she refused to unpack her suitcase, insisting on keeping it ready for the unspecified day when she would be collected and taken home to Mallingford. All these things Roddy could visualize, from his mother's faintly outraged descriptions, but it was not the same as remembering them.

The drizzle intensified, shrouding his view of the house in a thin grey mist. Pensively Roddy stretched out his legs. If only she would confide in me, he thought, I would make it right for her; I would. The idea was so abruptly poignant that his mind shied away from it. He stood up, and tried the door of the pavilion, although he knew that it would be locked. Through the dusty window he could see a sheaf of croquet mallets and some fold-up canvas chairs, neatly stacked. The clumps of wisteria blossom hung like fragile mauve grapes. Perhaps she needs to find her feet, learn some confidence, he thought, staring at the heap of chairs. Perhaps then she might – ah – then she might *appreciate* me. He wondered if he should allow her to talk with Tom Nettleship on her own. At least then she might feel that the Mallingford project in some way belonged to her; she might even become enthusiastic about it. Anything, thought Roddy, to wean her away from Gerald. He turned away, back towards the rainy lawns. Cosima had liked Tom, as far as Roddy could judge. It might be that he could win her over where he himself, so manifestly Gerald's enemy, could not.

In the distance Lady Courtney, sheltered by a Prussian blue umbrella, emerged from the front door.

Time for morning service. Roddy watched her for a moment, marching in the direction of the garage with small determined steps. Perhaps I should go with her after all, he thought; and, stepping from the narrow veranda, he began to run lightly towards the house, his feet squeaking on the wet grass.

Chapter Nine

'You've got to help us,' said Cosima, in a soft, urgent voice.

'What?' said Tom, taken aback. They were sitting under the beech trees at the top of Chanctonbury Ring. Before them the South Downs spread out towards the sea like a series of upturned bowls, lusciously green. In the distance a cuckoo was calling, its voice resonant and, to Tom's ears, strangely artificial.

It was his second visit to Sussex. Roddy had asked him, over a sparse expensive lunch in the City, if he would go and meet Cosima and explain to her in person his proposal to turn Mallingford into a study centre. I want her to feel she has a say in things, Roddy had remarked with what was, for him, an unusual diffidence. And so, three days later, Tom found himself driving down to Brighton, where he met Cosima in a brown and cream café not far from the seafront. To his surprise – and rather to his shame – her face lit up at the sight of him with a sudden trusting rapture.

'Tom!' she said at once, putting down her white china cup. She was wearing a blue pleated skirt, like a school uniform, with a shabby waxed jacket slung over the back of her chair.

'Hiya,' said Tom, as he eased himself into the seat next to hers, his knees jamming against the wrought-iron struts of the table. 'How're you doing? Can I get you another drink or something?'

Cosima shook her head. 'It's such a beautiful day,' she said. 'Let's get out of here and go for a walk. You've got a car, haven't you? We could go up to Chanctonbury Ring.'

Tom hesitated. He would much rather have stayed in the chic comfort of the café having tea and cakes. The previous night he had spent with Kate and, as always when he was very tired, he had developed an insatiable appetite for sweet stodgy food. Besides, he had deliberately put on smart clothes to impress Cosima, a cream-coloured linen suit and shiny new Italian shoes, not what he would have chosen to wear for a country walk. But she looked so eager at the prospect of getting out of Brighton that he did not have the heart to object.

'OK,' he said. 'You're the boss.'

Cosima directed him out of town along a series of country lanes sprinkled with cow parsley, the small lacy flowers clustering above the ragged grass. They parked in a field and negotiated their way along a steep path through some ash trees which creaked in the wind, until at last the woods gave way to open country. In the distance Tom could see a hill on which a coronet of beeches had been planted.

'That's it; that's Chanctonbury,' said Cosima, pointing. A white track lay across the ridge of the Downs like a pilgrim's path, leading to the hilltop.

'What is it? A Roman fort?'

'No, it's Iron Age. An Iron Age temple. The earthworks have been there since something or other BC, but the trees were planted in the eighteenth century.' A fly buzzed in Cosima's face, and she whisked her tail of hair as a pony might. 'I love it here. I'd come all the time if we could afford the petrol. Don't you think it's beautiful?'

'Yeah,' said Tom. He stepped over a cattle grid which lay across the path. 'I guess I'm more of a city person at heart, that's all. My girlfriend calls me Urban Man.'

'Oh,' said Cosima. She said nothing for a moment. Then she asked: 'What's your girlfriend called?'

'Kate,' said Tom. 'She works for a magazine; she's the beauty editor. Writes about lipsticks and face creams and things.' As he spoke he thought how trivial this made Kate sound and he added, firmly: 'She's really clever.'

Cosima gave a nod, as though this was to be expected, and hugged her blue waterproof arms around her chest. Then, in a matter-of-fact voice, she said: 'Roddy says you want to turn the outbuildings into a study centre or something, rather than a museum.'

'Yeah,' said Tom. 'That's right. Of course, we could open it to the public too for part of the time, but I reckon it's more likely to make money if we have some organized events. Weekends for painters, art history courses, interior design, that kind of thing.'

'I see,' said Cosima. She trudged along the chalk path, which was studded with blue flints. 'What does Roddy think?'

'Well, I guess he likes the idea. He agrees with me that it's more likely to be profitable.'

'I bet he does,' said Cosima. They had reached the earthworks at the top of the hill now. 'It's really windy up here. Let's find some shelter and sit down.'

Tom lowered himself gingerly to the ground, wishing again that he had worn something more hardy than his best linen suit. The turfy grass was scattered with the husks of last year's beech nuts. For a moment they sat in silence, listening to the ripe double shout of the cuckoo; and that was when Cosima turned abruptly to him and said, in her deep compelling voice: 'You've got to help us.'

Tom gazed at her. With her hair tied back from her wide pale face, she looked like a Byzantine madonna.

'I don't understand,' he said.

'I'm talking about Gerald,' said Cosima. 'We've got to rescue him.'

There was something needy in her expression; so needy that Tom felt strangely excited. No-one had ever asked him for help before. They always assumed that he would be too obtuse or too clumsy to benefit anybody.

'The thing is,' Cosima went on, 'I agreed to play along with Roddy first of all because I didn't think anything would come of it. I mean, I couldn't imagine anyone paying just to see Mallingford. The place is such a mess, and the Courtneys won't repair it and we can't afford to. Then when you came along and said you thought it might work out, I thought, well, maybe we'll make some money from it.'

'Well, yeah, you might,' said Tom. 'Not for a few years, but—'

'Exactly,' said Cosima. 'Not for a few years. And by then it might be too late.'

Tom shifted his weight on the damp earth. Partway down the slope he could see some ragged-looking sheep, ready for shearing, grazing on the coarse grass.

'I'm sorry,' he said. 'I guess I'm being dense. But I really don't know what you're driving at.'

Cosima stared at her own feet in shabby boxer's boots. 'The Courtneys would do anything to get Gerald out of Mallingford,' she said, in a simple, rather tired voice. 'That's why they're so keen on this scheme. It isn't only that they think they'll make a profit from it. They think Gerald won't be able to stick it, having people milling around the place. That's what they want: to drive him out. And then the place will be theirs to do whatever they like. They can exploit Stella's name as much as they want.'

Tom did not answer immediately. It occurred to him that, little as he cared for Roddy, the fact remained that Mallingford did belong to the Courtneys, and it could not be easy for them to stand by and see the place so wantonly falling apart. But he knew better than to say this to Cosima. Instead he asked: 'Do you think Gerald will be able to stick it?'

Cosima plucked a blade of grass and began to shred it with her fingernails. 'I don't know. I think he'd put up with it if he thought it would make us rich. We need money. And he hates the Courtneys every bit as much as they hate him. They were vile to him when he married my mother; they did everything they could to stop it. At least if he knew that we were making some money of our own he might see it as one in the eye for Roddy and the rest of them.'

'Surely he'll get some satisfaction from the fact that we're promoting Stella's work? I mean, won't he think that's worthwhile?'

'No, I don't think so. Gerald's got mixed feelings about Stella. The thing is, he could have been a great artist if he'd been allowed to do what he was really good at. Not as great as Stella, maybe, but great all the same. He was a brilliant potter, only he gave it up and tried to paint instead. That's why he's always been in Stella's shadow, even after she died. Especially after she died.' Cosima paused for a moment and drew breath. 'No, Stella's greater glory wouldn't be enough to protect – well, to protect his sanity.'

'His *sanity*?' said Tom, startled. Cosima looked at him, her eyes grey and candid.

'Yes. That's what I'm talking about, really. His sanity.'

'Oh,' said Tom. For a moment he was lost for words. He had grown up in a society which failed entirely to comprehend the nature of mental illness, and the idea that Cosima's father might actually be *insane* sent a terrible chill through him. Then he realized that Cosima beside him was quaking where she sat, huddled in her waterproof jacket.

'Cosima?' he said, in an experimental voice, as if to test the water. Cosima gave a shiver.

'Tom,' she said, 'I'm frightened.'

'Frightened? Why?'

'I should never have started all this. I should never have let Roddy bring you to Mallingford. It's going to end in disaster, I know it is, and it will all be my fault.'

'Of course it's not going to end in disaster. Come on.'

'I just think—' Cosima began; and then her voice

failed her, with a small choking sound. She put her hands to her temples in a shielding movement.

'Hey,' said Tom, and he slipped his arm around her blue shoulders. At close quarters she exuded a strange rich scent, like vanilla. 'What is it you're so scared of? Do you think the Courtneys will run off with the profit and leave you guys with nothing?' Cosima made a constricted noise which Tom took to mean yes. 'Sure, I know that's a risk. But it's just a question of getting the deal right. I'll make sure they don't screw you, I promise. Deals are something I'm good at.'

'Oh, Tom,' said Cosima. He could feel the sudden trustful pressure of her face against his chest. After a moment she went on: 'What I couldn't stand is if we persuaded Gerald to say yes to opening the place, and then the Courtneys drove him out and nabbed all the money. I couldn't bear that. Apart from the fact that it would send Gerald right over the edge.' Her voice began to wobble. 'I just don't think he could survive outside Mallingford.'

'It won't be like that. Of course it won't. Look, Cosima, it'll be OK. I promise. And let's face it, we don't even know for sure if this thing will take off. You might be getting scared over nothing.'

'Yes, I know. But I can't help it, Tom. The Courtneys won't give up now they think there's a chance of getting Gerald out. And Roddy's much cleverer than I am. Well, more devious, anyway. I don't want him to wipe the floor with me.'

'Look, he won't,' said Tom. 'Honestly, Cosima. I'll help you.'

As he said this Tom once again had the giddy sense that he was making a promise he could not possibly fulfil. It was Roddy, after all, who was paying him to protect the Courtneys' interests; indeed, it was Roddy who was paying for him to be here on Chanctonbury Ring in the first place. Tom could almost hear the clunk of an imaginary taxi meter as it clocked up the minutes. Guiltily he loosened his grasp on

Cosima's shoulders. 'Besides,' he said, rather lamely, 'for any deal to work it has to be fair to all parties. Roddy knows that.'

Cosima sat upright, delicately shifting from Tom's embrace as though she had suddenly become conscious of her situation. In a calmer tone she said: 'I'm sorry to sound hysterical. But I get so scared. And there isn't anyone I can talk to. Morag pretends to understand, but she doesn't really. And William's much too young to get involved.'

'It's OK,' said Tom. 'I understand.' Now that he no longer had Cosima's warmth leaning against him the wind seemed cold and penetrating. It was growing late, the shadows deepening on the green curve of the hill. We ought to go, thought Tom, but he did not move.

Cosima brushed her hands against each other, to get rid of the fragments of grass she had plucked. Then she said, in a different sort of voice: 'Do you miss America? I mean, don't you feel sort of uprooted, being away from your home? I would, if it were me.'

The question took Tom by surprise. He was so accustomed to people supposing that it must be bliss to be in England.

'Well,' he said, 'sometimes. I miss my folks, I guess. Although they drive me wild when I'm actually with them.' He paused for a moment. 'They're real down-to-earth Americans. I always remember telling my dad I wanted to study sociology at college, and he said, what are you going to do? Open a sociology shop?'

Cosima smiled. 'And did you study sociology?'

'No. I switched to business studies instead. Just as well, I guess: it's what I'm cut out for, business.'

'So why did you come to England?' asked Cosima.

Tom shrugged, about to explain, as he always did in answer to this question, about coming to Cranfield and taking his master's degree. Then he heard himself say: 'Because my wife left me.'

The words seemed to have catapulted from him into the air, without his consent. He had never told anyone

102

about Becky in precisely these words: pride always made him elaborate on the bare fact of her departure. Even Kate had not heard the real story of his failed marriage. The angle of Cosima's head sharpened.

'Oh,' she said. 'I'm sorry.'

'One of those things,' said Tom. He gave a small nervous laugh. 'It's not even as if she left me for someone else. I might have found it easier if she'd – you know – met some other guy. But she just walked out on me. And so I came over here.'

'To escape?'

'I guess. All I know is I couldn't stand it at home.' There was a silence. Cosima looked out over the hills, growing hazy in the lateness of the afternoon. We really ought to go, thought Tom again.

'But now you've got your girlfriend in London?' Cosima said.

'That's right,' said Tom. 'I've got Kate.' It seemed somehow an unsatisfactory answer, but he could not begin to explain why, even to himself. 'Look, do you want to go back to the car? It's getting chilly.'

'All right,' said Cosima.

She got to her feet, slowly, her face cloudy. I shouldn't have told her all that, thought Tom, with sudden regret; she'll think I'm a real loser. Briskly he said: 'Well, I guess the next step is to get the sponsorship deal confirmed. Until that's signed and sealed there isn't much point even broaching the project with your father.'

'It depends how long it's going to take, though,' said Cosima. They were descending the slope now, walking together towards the chalk path. 'I'm worried that he might get wind of it before we've actually talked to him. He's quite a cunning sort of person. And I've already told Morag about it, and she's a dreadful blabbermouth.'

The sun was low in the sky, and the breeze had sharpened. Tom pulled his linen jacket more closely around him, feeling the gooseflesh rise on his arms.

103

'Well, I guess it might alienate him if he thought it was all going on behind his back,' he said. 'It's a question of timing—'

'Careful,' said Cosima. 'The cattle grid.'

'What?' said Tom, stepping blindly forward. The sole of his shoe slid on the smooth metal cylinder. For one heart-stopping moment he thought he would regain his balance; then his right ankle turned, with a subtle crack, and he fell heavily to the ground. Cosima let out a little startled cry.

'Are you all right?'

Tom rolled onto his back, gripping his ankle with both hands. He felt as though his face had turned green with pain.

'Tom!' Cosima was kneeling beside him now, touching his arm.

'My foot,' he managed to say.

'Let's see,' Cosima said, in a businesslike voice, and she began to unlace his shoe. Tom felt her fingers inch deftly against his sock.

'Ouch,' he said.

'Sorry. I don't think it's broken, but I'm not absolutely sure.' Cosima sat back on her heels, contemplating him, a knot of a frown between her dark eyebrows.

'It bloody hurts,' said Tom, who was still feeling sick. He would have liked to cry, out of pain and annoyance, but he could not do so in front of Cosima.

'We'd better get you back to the car,' she said. 'Do you think you can stand?'

'I don't know.' He put the sole of his foot to the ground, experimentally, levering his knee upwards to test the weight.

'I'll help you,' Cosima said. She got up, brushing chalk dust from her blue skirt. Then she held out both hands to haul him up. Even in that difficult moment he was aware of the unexpected strength of her grip.

'Ouch,' he said again, lurching upright. Cosima laced her arm across his shoulders.

'There,' she said, with satisfaction, supporting him. Tom, accustomed to Kate's inconstant exotic perfumes, thought how reassuring the smell of skin could be. He could feel the warmth of her breasts, squashed against his back.

'This is so dumb,' he said, with a half-suppressed wail of frustration.

'It doesn't matter,' said Cosima. 'Let's get moving.'

Like a linked four-legged creature they hobbled along the chalk path. Tom was conscious that Cosima was bearing most of his weight, but he felt too weak to do anything about it. His head ached with shock, and the effort of walking.

'This is the difficult bit,' said Cosima, as they reached the steep incline which led through the ash trees to the car park. 'If I go ahead, can you lean on me?'

'Yeah, sure,' said Tom, 'but will you be all right?'

'Oh, yes. I'm really quite strong, you know. All that gardening. Here: take my hands.'

She turned to face Tom, stretching out her palms as though she were making some kind of offering. Despite the effort of the last ten minutes, her face was serene. Tom reached out and laid his hands across hers, gripping the wrists. Then, carefully, he tilted his weight towards her. Cosima gave a little gasp.

'Are you all right?'

'Yes,' said Cosima. 'I'm fine.' She began to shunt her way backwards down the slope, her head half turned over her shoulder so that she could see where she was putting her feet. Step by step she guided him down the hill, through the shade of the trees. Tom shuffled after her, trying not to use his injured foot.

'Steady. You're going too fast.'

'Sorry,' said Cosima, in a little breathless voice. 'We're nearly there.'

The blue Porsche in the car park looked as cool and

as blissful as an oasis. Cosima took the keys from Tom's pocket, and unlocked the door.

'Ah,' said Tom, in an ecstasy of relief, sinking down upon the passenger seat. Cosima pushed the hair from her face, which was damp and flushed. She seemed rather pleased with herself.

'I think you ought to go to the hospital for an X-ray, in case it's broken,' she said. 'I'll drive, if you want.'

'Oh, God,' said Tom, who had forgotten about driving. He flexed his right foot, testing it, and gave a yelp of pain. '*Can* you drive?'

'Of course,' said Cosima, in a nonchalant voice; adding, more rashly: 'So can William. My little brother.'

'Oh, Lord,' groaned Tom.

'No, honestly. Morag taught us both. She thought it would be useful in an emergency.' Cosima glanced at Tom, diffidently. 'This is an emergency, isn't it?'

'Well, all right. But you'd better take me to Mallingford. I don't want you driving round town looking for a hospital. This car's conspicuous enough as it is; we'll both end up in trouble.'

For a moment Cosima looked mutinous; then she said: 'I suppose Morag can look at your ankle. She used to be a scout mistress; she knows about first aid and things.'

She adjusted the ribbon which tied her mane of hair, and climbed into the driving seat. Her mouth was tense with concentration as her hands and feet explored the controls of the car.

'OK,' she said, at last, in a breathy voice, and she switched on the ignition. Tom fastened his seat belt. His ankle was throbbing, and the pain gave him a dreamy sense of unreality, as though he could not possibly be held responsible for what was happening. Cosima let out the clutch and promptly stalled, the Porsche bucking like a temperamental horse.

'Christ,' said Tom.

'No, honestly, it'll be all right, I promise, it'll be

all right, just let me get used to it.' Cosima rubbed her hand over her hot forehead, took a deep breath, and turned the key again. This time she started the car smoothly, and gently backed it towards the gate-posts.

'Right hand down a bit,' said Tom, as the car snaked out into the lane. 'That's it. Good girl.'

They drove to Mallingford at a stately twenty-five miles an hour, like a royal progress, mostly in second gear. Cosima was bowed over the wheel, her face red, her eyes wide, only swerving twice when impatient drivers thundered past her. At last she manoeuvred the car along the mudtrack which led to the house, easing it around the potholes.

'Thank the Lord,' said Tom, as Cosima pulled up on the gravel, alongside a rusty green van.

'I wasn't that bad, was I?'

'No, no. You were fine. Honestly.' Tom released his safety belt. He felt a fierce desire to sleep, as com-pelling as if he had been drugged.

'Does your foot still hurt?' Cosima asked, as she got out of the car.

'It's all right unless I put my weight on it. Probably just needs strapping up.'

'Morag will sort you out,' said Cosima, offering him her arm once more. She helped him across the over-grown courtyard, towards the back door. The air smelt hauntingly of woodsmoke.

In the kitchen – the kitchen where he had first seen Cosima – a squat dark woman was standing, next to a red-haired boy. They were both wearing striped butcher's aprons, and were companionably stamping out pieces of yellow polenta, using crinkly silver pastry cutters. A vast black and white cat was sitting, sphinx-like, on top of the stove.

'You're early,' Morag said to Cosima, looking up. Then she stopped and stared at Tom.

'This is Tom Nettleship,' said Cosima. 'He's hurt his ankle. Up on Chanctonbury.'

A silent current of knowledge seemed to pass like electricity between the two women. Morag wiped her hands on her apron and bustled forwards.

'Is it broken?'

'I don't think so,' said Tom, allowing Morag to propel him towards one of the yellow kitchen chairs. With more expert but less gentle hands than Cosima's, she took off his shoe and sock, and began to probe his ankle. The flesh looked pallid and swollen.

'Sprain,' she said, after a moment, in a decisive voice. 'Nothing serious. You'll have to rest it, though.'

'Perhaps you'd better leave the car and get the train back to London,' said Cosima. 'Morag will drive you to the station; won't you?'

As she spoke there was the sound of footsteps on the staircase. Again a strange warning current flashed between the women.

'Yeah, I think I should get the train,' said Tom. 'I can pick up a cab home from Victoria.'

But no-one was listening to him. They stood frozen, all three, in the untidy kitchen, while the footsteps grew louder. Then Tom heard a deep, teasing voice: 'Fee fi fo fum, I smell the blood of a British man.'

Cosima gave a shiver. Tom twisted in his chair towards the kitchen door, and before he could say, actually, I'm an American, he came face to face with Gerald Deighton.

Chapter Ten

Stella first saw Cloris Bohun in 1931, at a private view in the Three Shields Gallery in Holland Street. She was standing in front of a red and green tapestry, listening with a ravishing air of concentration to Dorothy Hutton, the calligrapher who ran the gallery, her round soft face tipped to one side like a bird's. Stella – cool Stella who had permitted her body to be used in a psychiatrist's callow experiment, distant Stella whose only passions to date had been for the inanimate, her house, her painting – fell terribly, instantly, irrevocably in love.

'Who's that?' she said to Duncan Grant, the artist, who was hovering at her elbow as he scanned the party for familiar faces. It was Duncan who had persuaded her to come to the Three Shields in the first place. Stella was shy of such occasions, and although on her rare trips to London she liked to take stock of the latest exhibitions, she preferred to do so anonymously. But when she ran into Duncan at Agnew's, the art dealers who handled both his paintings and hers, he had been quietly insistent that she should go with him to Holland Street. Stella and Duncan liked one another, and admired each other's work, but for some reason this very admiration made them tongue-tied when they met, eager to show their mutual goodwill but quite unable to fall into proper conversation. Instead they would make fruitless gestures, issuing vague invitations that the other would accept, to lunches or long weekends, both sensing that these imagined events would never come to pass. Even now, as Duncan said, oh, do come to the Three Shields, it will be such fun, everyone will be so pleased to see you, Stella guessed that once inside the gallery he would abandon her for the first congenial acquaintance he spotted.

'Who?' he said, in answer to her question, hitching up his trousers and blinking three times at the round-faced woman. 'Oh, that's Cloris Bohun. She's a potter. Did a short stint with Roger at the Omega Workshops, I think, just before they closed.'

'Oh, yes,' said Stella. Her heart was beating very fast, and it seemed somehow important not to show her agitation.

'She had an exhibition here a couple of years ago,' Duncan went on. 'Rather good, as I recall. Stella, will you excuse me? I must go and find Mrs Bell.'

'Of course,' said Stella. She gazed at Cloris in her grey and silver dress, and tried to gather up the crumbs of everything she had been told about this woman. Gifted, they had said, witty when she chose to be, good company. She thought she had also heard muttered the word 'parasite' but, then as now, she had no real idea of what was meant by it. A phrase hammered in her head, something from Shakespeare, she thought: my fate cries out. She held her breath and surged forward, like a ship, through the loose throng of people.

'Ah, Stella,' said Dorothy Hutton. 'How nice of you to come. I didn't realize you were interested in textiles.'

'Yes,' said Stella, without listening.

There was a silence, during which Stella could feel Cloris Bohun looking at her, a friendly inquisitive expression on her face. Then Dorothy said: 'Do you know Cloris Bohun? Cloris, Stella Deighton.'

'How do you do?' said Cloris, giving Stella her hand, which was small and warm, with no rings upon it. Dorothy murmured politely about needing to circulate, and she moved off. Stella cleared her throat.

'Would you like to go somewhere and have dinner?' she heard herself say. The mild interest in Cloris's eyes sharpened, not to alarm as Stella had feared, but to amusement. Clearly this was a woman unafraid of adventures.

'Well,' said Cloris, in her rich, rather deep voice, dwelling on the word as though it had at least five syllables, 'I don't see why not. I should warn you, though, that I've only got about sixpence in my purse.'

'That doesn't matter,' said Stella. 'I'll pay.'

'All right,' said Cloris. 'I'll fetch my things, then.'

Cloris Bohun, in 1931, was at a loose end. She had the week before run away from Cornwall, where she had been living in the clear brittle light of St Ives with a burly painter called Matthew Gardiner. Unlike Stella, Cloris did not have a private income, and she was obliged to be more pushy and more pragmatic. She had paid her way through art school by serving as a *massière*, organizing the nude models, finding and arranging the objects for still life classes. Sometimes she worked as a model herself: she was interesting to draw, with her voluptuous figure, which over the years – she was now thirty-six – had become less of an hourglass and more of a luscious cottage loaf. Above all, though, Cloris survived through her love affairs. She had had several liaisons, mostly with men although once or twice with women, usually people richer or more influential than herself. This was not as calculating a manoeuvre as it might have been for a less sexually passionate woman. Cloris dived, not drifted, from one amour to another, each as heady and as sincere as the last. Only when the affairs were over did she look at herself more soberly and think, half in disgust, half in admiration, I'm really a bit of a tart.

The partnership with Matthew Gardiner had lasted for two years. He was a socialist, an atheist and an alcoholic, who was inclined to smack Cloris around on Saturday nights in an aimless kind of way, as though it were a job that someone had to do. The next morning he would have forgotten all about it, and would whistle as he set off to the harbour with his

111

painting things. He always painted on Sundays, even if he did nothing for the rest of the week, because it annoyed the Cornish Methodists. Gardiner was the sort of man who was compelled, almost against his will, to annoy other people. He waged a constant war with the Methodists, who tried to creep up behind him and tip his easel into the sea. Gardiner treated all this as a marvellous comic drama in which he was bound to come off best, until the Sunday when one of the Methodists, a middle-aged man as stocky and as zealous as Gardiner himself, succeeded in pitching the easel and an almost-finished canvas into the choppy water. Gardiner's sense of humour sank as abruptly as the picture. He gave the Methodist a resounding thump round the head, and was arrested by the local constable. At the trial the Methodist flaunted his swollen jaw with a sombre, self-righteous glee. Gardiner was found guilty of causing actual bodily harm, and was sent down for six months.

From the moment he was sentenced Cloris knew that she would not be waiting when he came out. Gardiner's raw enthusiasms, which had originally excited her, now seemed both boorish and boring; besides, she was getting tired of being knocked about. There was also the question of their cottage in St Ives. The rent was overdue, and even if Cloris had been able to clear the debt she did not see how she could afford to keep up the payments alone. And so, on Gardiner's fourth night in prison, Cloris packed a valise – a small one, to allay suspicion – and set her alarm clock for half past six. In the morning, she put on her hat, locked the door of the little house carefully behind her, and walked to the station, where she caught the first train for London. Once there, she drew all the money she had from the bank and cadged a temporary bed from a sculptor friend. Then she set about finding work of some kind: a modelling job, perhaps, or a commission for some ceramics, preferably with a hefty advance payment. It was in this quest that she had gone to the

Three Shields, nicely turned out because nobody ever gave you anything when you looked shabby and desperate, hoping that her luck would turn.

'Where do you want to go?' said Stella, when they had left the gallery. Over her grey and silver crêpe dress Cloris had put on a cloak of charcoal-coloured velvet, with a turned-up collar which emphasized the curves of her face. Her eyes were brown and deep-set and glittering.

'Well . . .' she said, dallying a moment on the pavement. Since her flight from Cornwall she had been living on currant buns and cups of tea and the occasional bottle of Guinness to cheer herself up, and the prospect of a square meal, paid for by someone else, was almost more than she could bear. Nevertheless, she did not want to propose too expensive a place in case Stella thought her a scrounger.

'I'm not really familiar with this area,' Stella said. She peered anxiously around the street, fearful that at any moment Cloris might say, oh, well, never mind, I'll be on my way. But Cloris, sensing Stella's panic although she did not yet realize its true cause, took pity upon her.

'Let's walk for a while, and see what we can find,' she suggested, defying the pangs of her stomach, and they fell into step, strolling towards Kensington Church Street. It was a dull evening in late April, with a sharp wind which snatched incessantly at Cloris's dark grey cloak. Occasional drops of rain spattered the pavement.

'And where do you live?' asked Stella, in a careful, constricted voice. She had registered the ringlessness of Cloris's fingers, but she knew that this alone did not make her a free agent. Cloris gave her umbrella a twirl.

'Oh,' she said, airily, 'at the moment, on a studio floor in Grafton Street. I'm only just back from Cornwall, you know. Delightful, but terribly quiet. Don't you miss London, buried down in Sussex like that? I'm sure I should.' Cloris paused at the window of a small smoky restaurant. 'What about this? It looks all right, don't you think?'

The restaurant had rickety tables covered in red gingham, and lugubrious waiters with long grubby aprons. They sat in the corner, Cloris's grey umbrella propped against the wall.

'So will you find rooms in London?' asked Stella, once they were settled. Cloris studied the menu. Now that she was so close to eating she could think of nothing else, caught up in a rapture of anticipation. Her stomach stirred and rumbled.

'Oh, yes, I expect so,' she said, willing the grumpy waiter to come and take their order, if possible bringing the bread basket with him.

'I suppose,' said Stella, 'you wouldn't contemplate living in the country again? Now you've left Cornwall.'

The waiter ambled towards them, a pencil in his hand. Come *on*, thought Cloris, gripping the sides of her wooden chair.

'Well,' she said, 'I'd like to see a bit of life first, I think. I wouldn't rule out anything, though.' She bestowed a magnificent smile upon the waiter as he stood poised beside their table. 'I'll have the oxtail soup and the lamb cutlets, please. And could we have some bread and butter?'

Stella ordered at random, unable to contemplate anything as gross as eating. As an afterthought she asked for a bottle of red wine.

'I imagine you'd need to find quite a large place, if you're going to work there,' she said. Cloris's eyes skittered to the table beside theirs, where a couple were tucking into Irish stew and mashed potatoes.

'Ideally, yes, but one can always make do,' she said, in a distracted voice, failing to meet Stella's gaze. Stella, who had never in her life cared about social skills, thought miserably, I must be boring her. Then Cloris looked across with another of her wide confiding smiles.

'I'm sorry,' she said. 'I'm just dreadfully hungry.'

114

'Ah,' breathed Stella; and so the story came out, of Matthew Gardiner and the escape from St Ives, of the cheap buns and the cups of tea, of Cloris's hunt for a job to tide her over. She was accustomed to singing for her supper, and she told the story wonderfully, with a droll inventiveness, never once implying that she had been frightened or distressed. Stella watched her with a delight so intense it verged on pain, dazzled by the animation of Cloris's face. All the while she talked she ate: her own dinner and most of Stella's as well as the contents of the bread basket, neatly and rapidly slipping the food into her mouth.

'Where are you staying?' Cloris asked Stella at last, as they were drinking their coffee. It was dark now, and the night seemed to press against the glimmering windows of the restaurant.

'In a hotel near Victoria,' said Stella. 'I usually stay there when I come up to London.'

Neither spoke for a moment. Stella tried to lift her coffee cup, but her hand was trembling too much. The notion that Cloris would simply vanish was so unbearable it made her throat dry.

'Well,' said Cloris, 'that was a wonderful meal. And very timely. Thank you.'

She reached out for her furled umbrella, her chair creaking as she did so.

'Come back with me,' said Stella, all at once. Cloris let her hand fall. There was a sudden new spark in her eye.

'What?' she said, in an amused, faintly challenging voice. 'To Victoria or to Sussex?'

'Both,' said Stella.

And that was how they spent their first night together, in a dowdy yellow room with chintz curtains which did not meet in the middle. Although it was Stella who had instigated the liaison, once she was alone with her beloved she was overcome with awe, and with an exalted desire which could not readily be translated into lips and flesh and fingers. It

115

was left to Cloris to effect the consummation of the affair; something which she did with compassion, recognizing the nature of Stella's confusion, and also with competence. She had always taken a quiet pride in her ability to give pleasure, as though it were a practical accomplishment quite divorced from any emotion she might feel.

By morning Stella was enslaved. She went with Cloris to fetch her valise from Grafton Street and then she paid for her train ticket to Sussex. They bowled along past Redhill and Haywards Heath, Stella gazing incessantly at her lover, committing to memory every detail of her face. As for Cloris, now that she had been rescued she let herself succumb to the exhaustion of pure relief. She ate an enormous lunch at Overton's before they caught the train and fell deeply asleep in the carriage, her cheek crushed against the rattling window.

They reached Mallingford at sunset, trudging up the lane from the village. Cloris's hair was wispily askew under her little grey hat, and, footsore, she had allowed Stella to carry her valise.

'We're almost there,' said Stella, encouragingly, striding ahead in her stout flat shoes. Then, as they passed beneath the horse chestnuts which sheltered the house, there was a sudden thrilling whoop, and in the half-light a dark goblin figure leaped down from the trees, blocking their path. Cloris let out a scream. The goblin steadied itself, with a grimace; and Cloris saw that it was a boy, wearing shorts and a ragged blue jersey, his face deliberately smeared with mud.

'Oh, Gerald,' said Stella, in a weary tolerant voice, 'I do wish you wouldn't do that kind of thing.' She looked solicitously over her shoulder at Cloris. 'This is my son, Gerald.'

'Your son?' said Cloris.

'Yes. Did I not tell you I had a son? Gerald, this is Cloris Bohun. She's come to stay.'

Gerald said nothing, but continued to stand in their

116

way, glowering at his mother. He had grown into a slender sinewy boy, the brightness of his hair faded to a shaggy golden brown. For most of the afternoon he had been roosting sulkily in the tree, waiting to see his mother's silhouette appear on the path. He was always angry when Stella went away, but this time his resentment was sharpened by the fact that Sir George, too, had apparently abandoned him. The friendship between the old man and the boy continued to flourish, although now Sir George was nearly seventy their outings together were no longer so boisterous. They were more inclined to sit watching the sea than to swim in it, and to trot sedately through the grounds of Courtney Park than to pelt their horses at fences and ditches. At the moment, however, Charles Courtney was home from school for the Easter holidays, and Sir George felt obliged to devote to his grandson the time he would normally have spent with Gerald. At thirteen, Gerald was old enough to understand that both his mother's absence and his friend's were temporary, but they still induced in him a sullen ferocious mood, which seemed to hang in the air, black and tangible.

'Hello, Gerald,' said Cloris, trying to sound friendly, in spite of feeling that this was altogether too much for her to cope with in one day. The fact that Stella had blithely omitted to mention the existence of a son stirred up sudden shadowy doubts in Cloris's mind about the character of her new lover. Most of all, though, she wanted a bath, another meal – she was ravenously hungry again – and a clean warm bed, preferably to herself.

Gerald stared at Cloris in her high-collared cloak and her pretty squashed hat. Since the days of Dora and Molly there had been regular visitors coming and going at Mallingford, and he was not sure why this one seemed so different. He was conscious that his mother, instead of facing him on the path, was standing to one side, as if in deference, watching Cloris. Furiously, without knowing why he did it, he pursed his mouth and spat, a single efficient jet of saliva. Cloris flinched, although she was much too far away for the spit to touch her.

'Gerald!' cried Stella. But Gerald had gone, gambolling off into the trees like the goblin he had at first appeared to be.

'Well,' said Cloris, drily. 'What a welcome.'

Stella put her hand on Cloris's arm. The act of touching her beloved, even so slight and so chaste a touch as this, made her tremble.

'Oh, darling,' she said. 'He's a difficult child, that's all. It means nothing, believe me.' She picked up the valise, which she had let fall in the shock of seeing Gerald. 'Come on, darling. We're nearly home.'

Taking Cloris by the hand, she led her slowly and tenderly towards the house.

Chapter Eleven

'Of course,' said Gerald Deighton, 'my mother should never have had a child. Certainly not a man-child. She always preferred the company of women. And then, she was jealous of me, naturally.'

Tom wrapped his stiff grey blanket more closely around his shoulders. He was lying on a green sofa, in the upstairs drawing room at Mallingford. On the table stood a candelabra, which smelt of hot wax.

'That is what made it so difficult to pursue my own career,' Gerald was saying, with little wise nods of his head. His long yellow fingers were busily rolling a cigarette.

'Yeah,' said Tom. 'Stella must have been a hard act to follow.'

The rhythmic swaying of Gerald's head did not falter. 'Very difficult,' he said. 'Impossible, in fact.'

Tom blinked across at him, hoping that he would not disgrace himself by falling asleep. It was nearly midnight. Morag the housekeeper had strapped up his ankle in fierce swaddling bands, and it was throbbing hotly. He had the impression that his foot was enormous, like a helium balloon, but much heavier.

'You were quite successful, though, weren't you?' he said. His eyes were prickly with exhaustion and with dust. 'Some of your paintings sold.'

'Ha! Trivial stuff,' said Gerald. 'No-one wants to be remembered for trivial stuff.' He looked across at Tom. 'Are you tired?'

'No,' lied Tom, stung by the challenge in Gerald's voice. He looked much older than Tom had expected, and much frailer: a pale gaunt man with high

119

cheekbones and limpid grey eyes, like Cosima's. His hair was long and shaggy, redeemed from squalor by its cleanliness. He was wearing black trousers and a loose open-necked shirt.

'They think I don't know,' Gerald said, in a conversational voice. As he spoke he got to his feet and crossed to the table. Then he licked his thumb and forefinger, and carefully trimmed the wick of one of the candles. He did it so nimbly his hands might have been fireproof.

'Don't know what?' asked Tom. It was like sitting next to loonies on the subway in New York; you were always on your guard in case they turned nasty. Not that Tom ever talked to loonies on the subway, or anywhere else for that matter.

Gerald smiled at him now, a sweet mature knowing smile. 'And I suppose you're in it up to your neck?' he said pleasantly. 'I suppose that's why you're here.'

'I don't know what you mean,' said Tom. His scalp was prickling now, as well as his eyes. Again he had the reeling quagmire sense of one negotiating madness.

'I hope you won't deceive my daughter, that's all,' Gerald said, leaning forward to light his roll-up at the candle flame. He made a little sucking noise as he did so.

Tom shifted the hem of his blanket so that it did not scratch his neck. 'I don't intend to deceive anyone,' he said. The thing about mentally sick people – and Gerald must be mentally sick; even Cosima thought so – was their cunning. He had read that somewhere. You thought of them as purely vulnerable, when really you should be taking account of their artfulness.

'I'm aware,' said Gerald, 'of the reason why no-one has spoken to me. You all think I'll disapprove, don't you? I expect that little shit Roddy thinks I'll start a massacre.'

'Well,' said Tom, 'even Cosima thought you wouldn't like the idea. Of the study centre, I mean.'

'Ah. So that is what he's planning.' Gerald shot a

triumphant look in Tom's direction. Shit, thought Tom, he's wiping the floor with me. He wished that Cosima had stayed to give him moral support. She had spirited herself off to bed hours ago, after dinner; an unexpectedly flavoursome dinner of slow-cooked lamb with herbs and roast polenta. They had eaten it, all five of them, at the kitchen table, Gerald delivering what seemed to be a gaudy parody of himself, to the visible discomfort of his children. Cosima had retreated into an aloof silence, and Tom had yet to hear the boy William utter a word. There appeared to be no question now of Tom's attempting to get back to London that night. After the meal Morag had driven him in her rusty van to the village pub so that he could ring Kate and tell her what had happened, and by the time they got back to Mallingford both Cosima and William had vanished.

'So. Do you disapprove?' asked Tom, trying to outstare Gerald.

'Why should I?' Flightily Gerald turned his back on his guest, and crossed to the dilapidated window seat. 'I don't give a damn what the Courtneys do to this place, as long as they don't trespass on my rights. Have I shown you this, by the way? A tidy little bloodstain on the wall. Come and see. Where Frederick Courtney shot himself back in eighteen hundred and two. Unfortunately none of his relatives have seen fit to follow his example.'

Tom declined to haul his bound leg from the sofa and hobble across to look. Instead, bullishly, he said: 'So as far as you're concerned we can press on?'

'As far as I'm concerned you can do what you like.' Gerald squinted over his shoulder. 'Don't oblige me to meet the little shit, though, if you've got any sense. He has an unfortunate effect on my metabolism.'

Tom suppressed a grin. He wanted to ask Gerald how, if he so despised the Courtneys, he had come to marry one of them, but he suspected that Gerald would regard the question as impertinent. It *was* impertinent, though Tom would still have liked to know the answer.

'Yeah, I think we can manage that,' he said. 'Of course, it might be a wild goose chase. We haven't done a business plan yet.'

None of this seemed to interest Gerald Deighton. He stood at the window, with his back to Tom, extravagantly smoking his meagre cigarette.

'I would have thought,' he said at last, 'that there was quite enough of Stella in the Tate to satisfy anyone. She's eclipsed Gwen John. Poor old Gwen's stuff is consigned to the bunker. Stella's got rooms and rooms devoted to her.'

Tom adjusted his leg on the frayed cotton of the sofa. It was not a very comfortable sofa: the horsehair padding was lumpy and uneven, and he could feel the pressure of the ancient springs.

'Of course,' Gerald went on, 'she had talent. Not like that silly tart Carrington. Or the fat one – what's her name? – the sister of that novelist who topped herself. Lived round here.'

It was on the tip of Tom's tongue to say, enthusiastically, 'Vanessa Bell' when he realized that this was a performance: Gerald strutting his stuff for the stupid Yankee, spouting all the things he was sure Tom would want to hear.

'I thought Stella didn't go much for the Bloomsbury crowd,' he said coldly. Gerald turned to him and smiled again, as if acknowledging the point scored.

'No,' he said. 'Apart from old Duncan she couldn't stand them. Arrogant and spiteful; especially the Woolves. She could hardly bring herself to write to Leonard when Virginia did herself in.' Companionably Gerald stubbed out his cigarette and came to sit on the arm of the sofa. 'Horrible death, mind you. So slow. At least if you're swept off to sea the waves knock you senseless first.'

'I guess so,' said Tom. He watched as Gerald took the tobacco pouch from his pocket and began serenely to roll another cigarette.

'I like you, you know,' said Gerald, glancing up from the flimsy white paper in his fingers. 'So does Cosima. You've got backbone. I don't know why you're doing business with a little shit like Roderick.'

'Well—' began Tom, caught off guard. He was flattered, not only by the notion that Cosima liked him, but that Gerald should have observed Cosima liking him. Gerald, however, was not listening. He slid from the arm of the sofa onto the seat, next to Tom's bandaged leg.

'My wife had a horrible death too,' he said, in an amiable voice.

'Oh?' said Tom. 'A skiing accident, wasn't it?'

'In a sense. Have you ever been skiing?'

'Yeah,' said Tom, warily.

'My wife was addicted to it. She went all the time, practically every winter. She should have known better, of course, being so experienced.'

He's going to tell me something grisly, thought Tom, with a sense of dread sharpened by his desperate tiredness. He would have liked to leave the room, or at the very least cover his ears, but it seemed impossible to do anything except listen to Gerald's pleasant, confiding voice.

'Yes,' he was saying, 'she'd had a long lunch, with all her affluent friends, and afterwards she decided to go for a ski. Hopped on the ski lift, got halfway up the mountain, and they switched it off for the night.'

'What?'

'The ski lift. I thought you said you'd been skiing? They switch off the ski lift when it starts to get dark.' Gerald examined his roll-up before licking the edge of the paper to seal it. 'So there was my wife, suspended on her little chair, hanging on to the cable, way above the Alps. Couldn't jump down, of course; much too high.'

'What happened?'

'Oh, they found her the next day. When they started up the motor, and her chair came swinging round.

123

Must have been quite a shock for them, first thing in the morning. Mind you, they say it often happens.'

'Christ,' said Tom, picturing the killing bleakness of the mountainside. Gerald was right: it was a horrible death, death by ice, the sort of death which haunted you.

'I hope it doesn't give you bad dreams,' said Gerald, in a bland voice, standing up to light his cigarette. 'Morag's put you in the attic, hasn't she? Next to Cosima? No ghosts there. Well, not many.' He sucked in the candle flame. 'Have I shown you some of my work?'

'No,' said Tom, in despair. He had hoped that Gerald's mention of bedrooms meant that he would shortly be released, and at this lurch to another subject he felt a surge of panic. He tried to console himself by thinking how he would describe this scene to Alastair: the drawing room, the candles with their long leaping shadows and their sinister winding-sheets, the loopy old man. Alastair would lap it up, accuse him of exaggerating, sit there greedy for more.

'Here,' said Gerald, lifting the candelabra to light a patch of wall that had until now been in darkness. Tom caught a glint of varnished frame, but could see nothing else. He slid his leg from the sofa. At least if he were on his feet he might be able to leave the room afterwards, slip out without offending Gerald.

'My best-known work,' said Gerald. 'It sold thousands.'

Tom detected a note of irony, but it was difficult to judge what was real and what fake in Gerald's act. Slowly he made his way to where the old man was standing, the candles held high. Molten wax had dripped onto his wrist, but he took no notice.

'Jeez,' said Tom. There before him, in its lurid original glory, was *Zenox confronts His enemies*. The contours of the oil paint, thickly applied to the canvas, were thrown into weird relief by the raised candles.

'I see you recognize it,' said Gerald drily. Tom gazed

at the picture. It seemed so absurd, so wholeheartedly belonging to the fashion of another era, that he found it touching.

'Well, it was really popular in the States,' he said, sounding apologetic. 'My brother Scott had it on his bedroom wall.'

Gerald gave a brief shout of laughter.

'I had a family to support, you know,' he said. 'And even Stella did a poster or two, back in the Thirties.'

'Yeah, sure,' Tom shifted his weight so that he could stand more comfortably, 'You should have it reprinted. That sort of sci-fi stuff goes down a storm.'

'Does it?' said Gerald, unimpressed.

'Could make you some cash,' Tom said, remembering his conversation with Cosima on Chanctonbury; how she had said, with fierce simplicity, we need money. It seemed an infinitely long time ago.

Gerald gave a shrug, which shook the trembling candle flames. 'Too late now for cash,' he said. The cigarette, forgotten in his hand, gave off a pungent scent, sharp as marijuana.

'Well,' said Tom, after a moment, 'I think I might go up to bed.'

Gerald said nothing. He stared at the painting, as though he had not heard. Tom glanced around the drawing room. It had just occurred to him that he would need a light of some kind to guide him to the attic, and that the only candles were firmly in Gerald's grasp. Exasperation rose in his throat. The black corridors beyond the drawing room seemed to imprison him with their solidity, quite impenetrable.

'It's not unusual, to ruin your own life,' Gerald said, in a conversational voice, as though answering a question Tom had just put to him. 'Hundreds of people do it. Although most of them are spared the knowledge that they've done it.'

Tom put out his arm and leaned on the cold plaster

wall, in an agony of tiredness. He felt like crumpling to the floor and wailing aloud.

'I, of course, have the privilege of knowing,' the old man went on, sweeping away from the painting and placing the candelabra back on the table. Tom stared at it longingly. Only good manners prevented him seizing it and rushing off, in search of the narrow staircase which led to his bedroom in the attic.

'The real rogue is time,' said Gerald. He dropped his cigarette and ground it into the floorboards with a carpet-slippered heel. 'You should remember that. I thought I had ruined my life when I was twenty or so. I assumed that I had ruined my life, and that nothing thereafter would matter.'

'Yeah,' said Tom, still leaning against the wall. Gerald's words sank into his dazed consciousness like cool round pebbles.

'It goes to your head,' Gerald was saying. 'That kind of fatalism. You get drunk with it. You get drunk with the idea that you're damned. It's only afterwards you see that you weren't damned, then. But you are damned now.'

'Look—' Tom began, heaving himself away from the wall. This was ridiculous: he was falling asleep where he stood. Then he saw that Gerald's mouth had turned downwards like a rubber quoit, and that he was beginning to cry, quite soundlessly. Tom could not remember when he had last seen a man cry.

'Look,' he said again, mortally embarrassed, 'shall I fetch someone? Cosima, or . . .' The name of the squat housekeeper evaded him. Gerald did not speak. His narrow shoulders quivered, fragile as the shell of a long-dead sea creature, ornate and hopelessly brittle. One of the candles guttered and died.

'Here. Sit down.'

Tom moved forwards, his ankle twingeing beneath the weight as he guided Gerald towards the window seat. The old man's long fingers grasped at his forearm. He still shook with the force of his inner storm.

'Let me fetch Cosima.'

Gerald, on the shredded cushions of the window seat, made a small inarticulate noise which Tom thought might have been 'Yes'.

'I'll have to take the candles,' said Tom, grasping the stem of the candelabra. It was thick and slippery with wax. When Gerald made no move, he raised the candles high, and limped off, into the wide black corridor. All the floorboards creaked, and the house smelt horrible, like a stale cake tin. He jarred his injured foot on the stair, shock waves of pain running up his leg.

The door to his room had been left open so that he would recognize it, a nightlight glimmering beside his bed in a saucer of water. It seemed as innocent and as welcoming as a water lily. For a moment Tom was tempted to abandon Gerald and simply go to bed. Instead he rapped smartly on the door next to his. From within he heard Cosima inside give a low, bedraggled moan; then she said: 'Who is it?'

'It's me: Tom.'

'Come in,' said Cosima. She sounded so unsurprised that for one startled moment Tom wondered if she had expected him to come knocking at her door. Then he realized that she was still more or less asleep. She sat up in her narrow iron bed, pushing aside the tousled mass of her hair.

'Cosima,' said Tom, 'it's your father. I don't know what's wrong, but he's really upset.'

'Oh,' said Cosima, struggling to the surface. 'I'll come down. Where is he?'

'In the drawing room. We were talking – well, he was talking, and then he suddenly started to cry.'

Cosima nodded her head, as though she had heard all this before, and she pushed back her nest of blankets. She was wearing a large white shirt, its long tails covering her thighs. The buttons were open at the front, and Tom could see the glistening curves of her breasts, like pretty apples.

127

'My dressing gown. On the peg by the door,' she said, rubbing her cheeks. Tom unhooked a shadowy garment, slippery and faintly sticky, like a fish, and handed it to her.

'Thanks. Light my candle, would you? There are some matches on the dressing table.'

Tom's hands groped across the surface of the dressing table until he found the box.

'I'm afraid I had to leave him in the dark,' he said, as he struck the match. He was starting to feel guilty about Gerald. Should he have left the old man in the black drawing room? Should he have allowed him to talk so much in the first place, wearing himself out?

'Yes, all right,' Cosima said, without listening. She took the candle Tom had lit, and led the way to the stairs.

'Does this happen often?' asked Tom, hobbling after her.

'Not often. Sometimes.'

They had reached the drawing room now. As Tom brought in the candelabra he saw that Gerald was sitting where he had left him on the window seat, like a hunched grasshopper, quaking. Cosima, her dressing gown flying like a bird's dark wings, crossed the room and took him in her arms, without speaking. Tom heard her utter little soothing noises in the back of her throat, obscure maternal noises. He thought of Prospero and Miranda – no, of Lear and Cordelia, mad father and tender daughter, caught up in a black prison of their own making. He put the candelabra on the table, and for a moment longer he watched them, the oval of Cosima's face blankly tilted above the leathery weeping face of her father. Then, quietly, he picked up Cosima's lighted candle, and made his way to the attic stairs.

Chapter Twelve

The sun shone blearily through the chestnut trees, casting dappled shadows on Cosima's drawing block. She was sitting in a canvas chair, sketching the house with some stubby pastels she had found in Stella's studio. Like Stella herself, she had sketched the house dozens of times, from all angles and in all lights, and she was drawing it now, not from inspiration, but from a desire for peace. It was reassuring to hone her skills on familiar territory; each meticulous stroke of crayon on paper soothed her with the tranquil solidity of a caress.

Two days had passed since Gerald's tearstorm in the candlelit drawing room. During that time her father had stayed upstairs, demanding soup and soft-boiled eggs which he ate in bed, strewing gritty fragments of shell over the counterpane. His face was whey-coloured, as though he had been bled by a host of invisible leeches. Nervous exhaustion, said Morag, in her most knowledgeable – and, to Cosima, most exasperating – voice. Whenever Gerald was ill Morag guarded him like a solicitous dragon. She prepared tantalizing dishes for him, to the detriment of the household's other meals; she refused to leave the house in case he should ring the bell at his bedside; she even tried to roll his cigarettes, although she made such a mess of it that Gerald irritably snatched the tobacco pouch from her damp red fingers. Cosima herself had scarcely seen her father, and he had not, to her knowledge, asked for her. This normally happened in the aftermath of Gerald's emotional crises. It was as though he resented Cosima for having witnessed his terrible weakness, and needed to withdraw, to put some space between himself and his daughter, until he had regained his equilibrium. Intuitively Cosima understood the reasons for his withdrawal, but she could not help finding it painful, especially with Morag lording it so confidently over the sickroom.

Tom's car, meanwhile, was still parked on the gravel, close to where Cosima was sitting. He was coming to collect it at the weekend, on his way to the opera at Glyndebourne. Cosima angled her crayon to etch the random pattern of flints in the wall of the house. Her day with Tom had acquired the quality of an hallucination, at once dazzling and improbable: she could not now believe that she had ever sat there, under the beech trees at Chanctonbury, asking him for his help. As she changed her black crayon for a brown one she wondered whether he had by now forgotten their conversation. After all, he had sounded so casual talking about his ex-wife, about his girlfriend in London. The words echoed in her mind: she's called Kate, she's very clever. For a moment Cosima felt like a shadowy Cinderella, a minor character in someone else's story. Then she thought, with sudden obscure confidence, no, it's not like that; it means more than that. I'm sure it means more than that.

The bonnet of Tom's car was standing upright while her brother William peered at its glossy innards. William had a passion for machines. He had already dismantled and re-assembled the car radio, as well as a personal stereo which he had found in the glove compartment amongst a heap of maps and sweet papers. Cosima had the older-sisterly feeling that she ought to stop him doing anything to the car, but she felt too lazy to move. They had spent the morning in the vegetable garden, planting out tomatoes, and her back was aching. Besides, she liked knowing that William was there, fiddling about with the car. He seemed to be linked to her by a harmonious silence.

A house martin swooped out from the gutter of the house. Cosima picked out an indigo crayon to mark it in her drawing. The gutters at Mallingford always clogged with birds' nests in the spring, and nobody had the heart – or, more to the point, the ladders – to dislodge them. Then behind her she heard the motor of the Porsche purr into life.

'Hey,' she said, turning over her shoulder, 'I don't think you ought to do that.'

William leaned out of the driver's seat. His coarse red hair was tufted with earth and with oil.

'Why not?' he said. 'He let you drive it, didn't he?'

'That's different. It was an emergency.' Cosima put her drawing block on the grass and stood up. Her tired feet winced in her plimsolls.

'It's all right,' said William, sliding from the car. 'I know what I'm doing.'

He stuck his head into the open bonnet once more, his lower lip caught between his teeth with the solemnity of a grown-up. Cosima noticed that his cotton shirt had split under the arms.

'Don't start taking it apart, that's all,' she said.

'If I do, I'll put it back again. I managed with those other things, didn't I?'

'Yes, but a car's different,' said Cosima; adding, less confidently: 'Isn't it?'

William gave a mature shrug. He pulled out the dipstick and examined it.

'Bet it guzzles oil and petrol,' he said. Then, losing interest, he reached up and closed the blue bonnet with a click. 'I suppose we'll have to give him back that cassette player when he comes?' he said, in a hopeful voice.

'Of course we will. We can't just nick it.'

'It's not nicking, exactly. He's probably forgotten about it,' William said, persuasively. 'Finders keepers.'

'Don't be such a scavenger. Even if he has forgotten, he'll still want it back. He's not made of money.'

131

Cosima picked up her sketchbook and sat down once more in the saggy canvas chair. At her shoulder William hovered like a doubtful cherub.

'Cos,' he said, after a moment, 'do you think Dad's going off his rocker?'

'No, I don't. He's been like this before; remember?'

'I don't like it when he cries,' said William.

'Oh, Will,' said Cosima. She would have hugged her brother, but she knew that if she tried he would wriggle strenuously out of her arms and run away. William hated physical contact of any kind. The only creature for whom he ever showed affection was Salvador, the cat.

'It is going to be all right, isn't it?' he said, in a testing sort of voice.

'Of course it's going to be all right. The good thing is that Gerald's told Tom he'll agree to opening up the stables. Which means we should have some money to sort the house out. We might even have electricity again. You'd like electricity, wouldn't you, Will?'

'Yes,' said William, persistently, 'but what about Dad? Is he just going to get worse and worse?'

'No, of course not. He got over-excited when Tom turned up, that's all.'

'But what if he gets over-excited when people start coming to see the stables? He might be really ill.'

There was a terrible quaver in William's voice. Cosima risked putting her hand on his arm, gently. She was touched by his anxiety for Gerald, who had never shown much real interest in his son. Cosima, born in the first tumultuous flush of his passion for Annabel, had always been Gerald's favourite child; William, product of a botched reconciliation, he seemed merely to tolerate, as one might tolerate a foundling or an evacuee.

'That's different,' said Cosima, in a soothing voice. 'He'll have time to get used to the idea. It won't take him by surprise, the way it did when he found Tom in the kitchen. Honestly, Will. It'll be all right.'

William gave a soundless nod, and moved out of Cosima's reach. Then he said: 'Whose side is Tom on, anyway? He's not on Roddy's side, is he?'

'No,' said Cosima. 'Actually, I think he's on my side.' As she said this she remembered the expression on Tom's face, watching her as they sat side by side on Chanctonbury Ring. The memory gave her an inner glow, as though she had some kind of secret information. 'He doesn't like Roddy very much.'

'Good,' said William, with satisfaction. He began to stomp back towards the Porsche. Then he stopped, and pointed along the path, towards the gate at the end of the valley. 'Look,' he said.

Cosima stood up. In the middle distance three dark figures were approaching, in Indian file, up the pot-holed drive.

'Who are they?' said William.

'Don't ask me,' said Cosima. 'I've no idea.'

The leader of the group swung an agile leg over the wooden gate. He had long black hair, like a Goth's, and boots which reached to his knee. When he had climbed over the gate he put out his hand to help the first of his companions, a girl in a ragged purple frock.

'I expect they're lost,' said Cosima.

Nevertheless she moved closer to where William was standing, just in case. It was difficult to get lost near Mallingford: the public footpaths were meticulously signposted with brash yellow waymarks. The three figures drew nearer. At close quarters Cosima could see that they were young, not much older than herself, with pasty faces and gangling limbs.

'Hello!' she called out.

The black-haired young man stopped, about six yards away from her. 'Is this where Gerald lives?' he asked. His voice was unexpectedly refined.

'Yes, it is,' said Cosima, guardedly. 'Why do you want to know?'

Slowly the three shuffled towards her. Cosima noticed that the girl's hair was tinted aubergine, to

match her dress. She looked like Nefertiti, her eyes
laden with kohl. Behind her stood a narrow-
shouldered boy in a shapeless mohair jumper.

'We're his students,' said the Goth. 'At the art
college, you know. We came to see if he was OK.'

'Oh,' said Cosima. 'Yes, he's OK.'

'Right,' said the young man. 'The college had a call,
see. To say that he couldn't teach today because he
was ill. So we thought we'd skive off and check him
out.'

'He's in bed,' said Cosima, in an uncompromising
voice. She could sense that William was squirming
behind her, ready to make his escape from these
unwanted visitors.

'But it's not – like – *serious*, is it?' the girl said. She
was half standing, half leaning against the Goth, like
a flower in need of water.

'No,' said Cosima.

'Any chance we could see him?' The boy in the
mohair jumper gave a nervy ingratiating smile. 'We've
come all the way from Brighton.'

'He's probably asleep,' said Cosima. 'He's been
sleeping a lot.'

'Can't you go and see?' wheedled the mohair boy.
Cosima realized that they were all three staring at her
with hungry eyes. There was no doubt about it, Gerald
had ignited a hot flame of adoration in his students.
She was about to refuse when it occurred to her that
these rivals for Gerald's attention would put Morag's
nose seriously out of joint. Cosima smiled.

'Will,' she said, 'go and find out how Dad is, will
you? Ask him if he'd like to see . . .'

'Stefan and Marcus,' said the Goth.

'And Kirsty,' said the aubergine girl, looking
aggrieved.

William said nothing, but he wriggled one last time,
and ran off in the direction of the house.

'It doesn't really matter if he can't see us,' said
Stefan, the Goth, in a conciliatory voice. 'The main

134

thing was to check that he was OK. That nothing had happened to him. We had to find out, you know.'

'How did you get here?' asked Cosima.

'Oh, we hitched part of the way. Then we walked. Not easy to find, is it?'

'I suppose not,' said Cosima, who was wondering whether it would be polite or rude to ask them to sit down when there were no chairs except her own. Just as she was thinking this, the girl Kirsty crumpled gracefully onto the grass, her purple dress billowing around her.

'She's whacked,' said Stefan. 'We shouldn't have let her come, Marcus.'

'Oh, she's all right. You're all right, aren't you, Kirst?' Marcus gave the girl a comradely prod with his foot. Then he said: 'Are you Gerald's granddaughter? I didn't know he had any family.'

'Daughter,' said Cosima.

'He's brilliant,' said Stefan. 'He's the best teacher in that whole dump. I'd jack it in tomorrow if it wasn't for Gerald.' He reached into his fringed leather jacket and brought out a squashed pack of cigarettes. 'D'you want one?'

'No, thanks,' said Cosima, who had been put off smoking by the stench of Gerald's endless roll-ups. She watched as Stefan lit his cigarette. The scent of the match lingered in the air, acrid and sulphurous.

'It's amazing, this place,' said Marcus, looking around him. 'I don't suppose we could have a look round, while we're waiting for Gerald?'

'Well . . .' Cosima hesitated for a moment. Then she thought, why not? After all, hordes of people would soon be tramping through Mallingford, most of them much less sympathetic than these three. 'All right,' she said. 'I'll show you Stella's studio, if you want.'

Kirsty made a little moaning noise. She was lying flat on her back now, her hair spread Medusa-like on the grass. Cosima noticed that she had an amethyst stud in her left nostril, like a single immaculate eye.

'Come on, Kirst,' said Stefan. 'Shake a leg.'

Cosima waited until Kirsty had got to her feet, and then she led the way towards the stable block. The art students made her feel uneasy. She hardly ever mixed with people of her own age, and she was not sure what she would find to say to them. She also felt curiously hurt by the fact that Gerald had not mentioned her existence, or William's, to his pupils.

'It's amazing, isn't it?' said Stefan, staring around him. 'Amazing atmosphere. It must be great living here.'

'The place doesn't belong to Gerald, though, does it?' said Marcus. 'I remember him saying he thought he was going to be kicked out. Said he'd got landlord trouble.'

'Who hasn't?' said Stefan, in a lugubrious voice. He blew a smoke ring, carefully, his red lips pursed.

'Well, it's all a bit complicated,' said Cosima. 'He won't be kicked out, though.'

'I should hope not. Bloody criminal idea,' said Marcus. Despite the warmth of the afternoon he showed no inclination to take off his straggly black jumper; nor did he show any signs of overheating. His face remained sallow and impervious, with a few spots around the mouth.

'He's quite old, isn't he?' said Stefan. 'I mean, you don't notice it, because he's a shit-hot teacher. But he must be knocking on a bit. You can't throw people on the street when they're knocking on. It's not right.'

'How many of you are there in Gerald's class?' asked Cosima.

Stefan grinned. He had large, rather yellow teeth, stained with nicotine. 'Well, originally there were twenty-five, weren't there, Marcus? But now it's down to a hard core of about six. Those of us who appreciate him.'

'Yeah,' said Marcus. 'I don't know why there's all that fuss about old Stella when it's Gerald who's the

136

real bloody genius. He's the one who should have his stuff in the Tate.'

Cosima, who admired her grandmother's work, said nothing. She wondered just what Gerald had done with his class of students to kindle such adulation. Although she had always been pleased by her father's success at the art school, she had never really thought about it: it was merely what Gerald did on Wednesday afternoons, to supplement their income. Now she felt jealous of the tracts of time he shared with his pupils. Cosima had never been able to discuss her own painting with her father. Once or twice, when she was much younger, he had asked to see what she was doing, and had remarked on her use of colour or the perspective she had chosen; remarks she had valued all the more because they were serious and critical rather than admiring, the remarks one working artist might make to another. But that was a long time ago. Cosima could not remember when Gerald had last expressed any interest in her pictures, and she was much too fastidious a girl to show them to him unasked. Thoughtfully she put out her hand to lift the latch of the stable door.

'Oh,' cried Kirsty, suddenly. 'Here he is!'

Cosima looked up. Gerald, in his white nightshirt and his blue silk dressing gown, was striding out across the yard. With his long white hair he looked like a zealous Old Testament prophet. Behind him came Morag, nagging him about the wisdom of leaving his room.

'Far out,' hissed Marcus. All three students had turned in Gerald's direction, like acolytes at a shrine. The devotion in their eyes was as bright as patent leather.

'Ah,' said Gerald, stretching out his arms, 'hello.'

Morag at his back was still muttering ominously.

'We wanted to check that you were – you know – all right,' said Stefan, in a bashful voice. 'The college got a call to say you were ill.'

137

'He *is* ill,' said Morag. 'He should be in bed.'

Gerald flapped his hand at her impatiently, as though she were a gnat he wanted to swat.

'Nothing serious,' he said, 'as you can see. Morag, fetch some refreshments, will you? These people have come a long way.'

'They wanted to see the studio,' said Cosima, who still had her hand on the latch.

But Gerald was not listening. Instead he was gazing at the art students, as though he might soak up the very essence of their adoration. For a long moment nobody spoke. Then, belligerently, Morag said: 'Squash.'

'What?' said Gerald.

'That's all there is to drink. Orange squash.'

'All right, all right,' said Gerald pettishly. 'Just get it, will you?'

Cosima realized that Morag was trying to catch her eye, in the hope that she would help to fetch the drinks, but steadfastly she ignored her. She did not want to be excluded from whatever was about to happen between Gerald and his pupils. After two or three attempts Morag stopped coughing and winking, gave an irritable sigh, and stomped off towards the back door.

'Don't bother with the studio, Cosima,' said Gerald to his daughter, in an imperious voice. 'There's nothing very interesting in it. Let's have a look at the dovecote. I've talked to you about the dovecote, haven't I? My mother's subconscious, there for all to see.'

'Oh, yeah,' said Stefan. 'I remember. You said once it was the best thing she ever did.'

Gerald's white nightshirt trailed in the grass as he led the way round the back of the stable block. The arrival of the art students had filled him with a new vitality, his eyes burning.

'Oh, yes,' said Gerald. 'Of course, I was never allowed in here when she was alive. She was as careful about this place as she was about her private parts.

138

More careful, perhaps, if my existence is anything to go by.'

The boys gave a snicker. Cosima felt shocked. She had often heard her father rant about Stella, but never like this, in public, and never so lewdly. In silence she watched as Gerald turned the rusty key in the lock.

'*Voilà*,' he said, with a flourish, throwing open the door of the dovecote. The art students tiptoed forwards, their faces sharp with curiosity. After the warmth of the afternoon the air was moist and cold.

'Hey,' said Marcus, 'this is amazing.'

Gerald stood smiling on the earthen floor, relishing the students' astonishment.

'Wow,' said Stefan, staring around him. 'Wow. What was she on? Acid, or what?'

'Oh, nothing, Stefan, nothing, I assure you. Stella didn't need drugs. I told you: it's her subconscious breaking out.'

'It's incredible.' Marcus reached out with his long waxy fingers and touched the cold walls. 'Much more interesting than all that representational shit.'

'Well, I doubt if Stella would have agreed with you,' said Gerald. 'This was what you might call her *cahier*. First sketches, you know. Work in progress. She painted it, and then she hid it from sight.' He crossed towards the section of the wall which was covered in mythical beasts. 'This, it might interest you to know, is a portrait – quite a good portrait, as it happens – of Cloris Bohun, the potter. Painted from memory, of course.'

Gerald pointed towards the pink bird of prey, with long curved talons and the face of a woman: a round, gentle face, with large brown eyes. Cosima glanced across in surprise. That particular creature had always intrigued her – the face was so sympathetic and the claws so terrible, sharp and bloodied like a huntsman's spurs – but nobody had ever suggested before that it was a portrait of Cloris. She wondered if Gerald was making it up, in his desire to impress the art students.

Her father could never resist the temptation of playing to the gallery.

'Cloris, of course, was the only person Stella really cared for,' Gerald was saying now, in a nonchalant voice. Kirsty stood opposite the bird/woman, examining it.

'She's got a nice face,' she said at last, ingenuously. Both the boys laughed.

'I think these are more interesting,' said Marcus, gesturing towards an evolving series of geometric shapes on the opposite wall. 'It's a shame she didn't do more stuff like this.'

'Yeah,' said Stefan. 'It's the kind of thing you used to do, isn't it, Gerald? I really like it.'

'Yes, it's a little like the paintings from my abstract period,' said Gerald, in a lofty, rather precious voice. 'Of course, Stella did everything first. I was a mere imitator.'

'Bollocks,' said Stefan, robustly. Gerald smiled.

'Did you really not come in here until Stella died?' asked Kirsty, who was trailing her fingers negligently along the powdery walls.

'No. Well, not properly,' said Gerald. 'I told you: it was Stella's private place.' He threw a bright glance at Cosima, for the first time acknowledging her presence. 'Ironic to think of it being thrown open to the great unwashed, isn't it, Cosima?'

'Not exactly the great unwashed,' said Cosima. She hoped that Gerald was not going to choose this moment to argue about her plans for Mallingford. It would be so like him, to agree in private, and then to deny it all as soon as he had a receptive audience.

'What do you mean?' said Marcus. 'You're letting the public into this place?'

'We have plans to do that, yes,' said Cosima, firmly, before Gerald could speak. All three of the art students looked at her.

'Well, I think it's a good idea,' said Stefan, after a moment, in a faintly defensive voice, as though he

140

expected the others to disagree. 'Art's not for the elite. Let the people see it, too.'

'Stefan,' said Gerald, 'you're so *egalitarian*.'

He made it sound a quality both earnest and un-glamorous. Stefan, beneath his stubble, flushed.

'I just meant—'

'Personally,' said Gerald, smoothly, 'I'm doing it for the money. We should make a fortune. Isn't that right, Cosima? It's all Cosima's idea, you know.'

Oh, God, thought Cosima, I should have known. He's punishing me for talking to Roddy. Gerald was smiling at his daughter, but there was a glint of malice in his eyes which Cosima recognized. Her heart sank. In this mood her father was quite capable of baiting her until she had to fight back the tears: he could, when he chose, be a relentless and gifted tormentor. She noticed too that the expression on the art students' faces had changed. Their gaze was charged now with suspicion, as though Cosima might prove to be one of the enemy, not on Gerald's side at all. I'm going to nip this in the bud, she thought, and she took a breath.

'Look,' she said to Gerald, in as blunt a voice as she could manage, 'if you don't want to open the place up, we won't. You only have to say so.'

Gerald's eyes widened for a moment, surprised by her temerity in calling his bluff. Then, still smiling, he feigned innocence.

'Oh, but I didn't say that, did I?' He looked at the art students, appealing for their support. 'I agree with Stefan; I think it's a wonderful idea.'

'Well,' said Stefan, encouraged, 'I just feel too much art is kept behind bars. If you ask me, people ought to be banned from having private collections.'

'Yeah, but it's not as simple as that,' said Marcus, at once. Clearly this was an old quarrel between the two boys. 'It isn't the fact that art's kept behind bars which stops us seeing it, it's the fact that we're not taught properly. I mean, we're not taught to *see*. We're taught to appreciate conventional art forms, but

141

we're not taught to look outside. That's why people still buy shit reproductions of Van Gogh and bloody Raoul Dufy when they could have something that really is original. Something challenging.'

Gerald looked at Marcus with sudden interest, distracted from the business of persecuting Cosima.

'Well, maybe,' he said. 'I think you're forgetting two things, though, Marcus. One is the power of the art mafia, which, let's face it, controls what's available. The other is the woeful timidity of public taste.'

This last phrase he enunciated with scornful precision, and both the boys laughed. Kirsty, who was leaning with one purple shoulder against the abstract designs Marcus had admired, said, in a whining voice: 'Can't we go outside and sit on the grass? It's creepy in here.'

'Oh, Kirst,' said Marcus. 'You're such a wimp.'

'No,' said Gerald, with unexpected tenderness, 'she's tired, I expect, aren't you, Kirsty? She's come a long way. Let's go and sit down.' He held out his blue silk arm, with old-fashioned grace, for the girl to take. 'Do you know, Kirsty, there's a copper beech in the garden here which is exactly the colour of your hair? I'll show it to you later, when you've had a rest.'

As they passed Cosima, standing silent at the door, Gerald half tilted his head in his daughter's direction and, without meeting her eyes, said: 'Make yourself useful, will you, Cosima, and go and see what's happened to Morag?'

Sometimes Gerald let fall commands like this affectionately, as a way of restoring contact after a quarrel; but in his voice now there was no hint of imminent forgiveness. Cosima, knowing herself dismissed, nodded, and began to make her way gloomily across the courtyard.

Chapter Thirteen

The three years which followed her meeting with Cloris were the happiest of Stella's life. Under the benign influence of her lover, she learned, quite gradually, the difficult art of having fun. Instead of burying herself in her studio from early morning to midnight, she began to dally over breakfast and supper, reading the newspapers aloud, laughing at private jokes, listening to scratched 78s on the gramophone which the long-forgotten Julius Murdoch had left behind. Cloris taught her to ride a bicycle, which she did very slowly, with meticulous dignity, along the Sussex lanes; she persuaded her to go to concerts in Lewes, and to visit her illustrious neighbours in Charleston and Rodmell. They went to London more often too, on long weekend jaunts filled with theatre visits and dinner parties and private views, which satisfied Cloris's yearning for crowds and for noise.

Perhaps more surprisingly, during those three years Stella was also at her most productive. In the past she had worked laboriously, making endless preliminary sketches, agonizing over every angle, every shadow, staring for hours at her canvases before she would at last admit them to be complete. Now, although she spent less time in her studio, when she was there she painted with a speed and a fluency she would not have believed possible. Pictures which once would have taken her two months or more were accomplished in ten days. Wit, for the first and only time, came to her work. She accepted a commission from Jack Beddington of Shell-Mex for a poster, and she polished off a series of jewel-bright canvases depicting Biblical heroines in modern dress: Judith fearsomely elegant in black and silver, Naomi and Ruth with pastel feathered hats, Bathsheba sweet and seductive in a long amber tea gown. Bathsheba had a plump face and deep-set brown eyes. She was closely modelled on Cloris; one of the many portraits which Stella produced of her beloved.

Cloris herself, despite the distractions of sitting for Stella, found it much easier to work in Mallingford than ever she had done in London or St Ives. There she had never had enough room for storage or for glazing, and she had constantly been obliged to wheedle other potters into giving her space in their kilns. Now she took over the area in the stables which Dora and Molly had once used for their furniture and their painted screens. She set up her kick-wheel and her workbench, lining the walls with slatted wooden shelves where her pots stood in rows. She and Stella bought bricks from a supplier recommended by Sir George Courtney, and during the summer of 1931 they built a wood-fired kiln behind the stables, mixing the mortar themselves, their heads wrapped in chequered scarves like a pair of gypsies.

The house, too, blossomed in Cloris's care. Her nomadic life had given her a knack for turning temporary lodgings into something resembling home, draping shawls over nasty rented armchairs, arranging candles or bunches of flowers on drab mantelpieces. With the acres of Mallingford at her disposal, she played house with joy. Each morning she would spend half an hour discussing menus and household chores with Mrs Maybrick, who had grown stout and weary and varicose, and was grateful to have a more down-to-earth mistress to serve. It was Cloris who had the hot water geyser put in the bathroom and Cloris who arranged for electricity to be installed in the house and the stable block. She would have included the dovecote in her plans, but Stella was adamant that she did not want electric light there, and certainly did not want workmen toiling in and out of her secret domain. This vigilance over the dovecote occasionally troubled Cloris, although she was too mature a woman to take her exclusion from the place personally. She knew from experience that even in the most intense partnerships some kind of privacy is essential, a hidden reservoir nourishing the qualities on which love depends.

More troubling, in the beginning, than Stella's obsession with the dovecote was the question of Gerald. For the first three months of her stay at Mallingford Cloris did not see the boy except fleetingly, as he slipped behind the trees in the orchard or dived out of the kitchen door. He ignored mealtimes, raiding the larder instead whenever he was hungry, and for every night he spent in his attic bedroom he spent at least two sleeping rough.

Stella seemed unperturbed by his behaviour. 'Oh,' she said blithely, when Cloris questioned her, 'he has phases like this. I don't believe in restraining him. He'll settle in time if we let him be.'

Cloris, however, was not reassured. She had a guilty fear that she had driven the boy away, and that he might in his obstinacy starve, or die of exposure. Although she would never have been so disloyal as to discuss Stella with Mrs Maybrick, she and the housekeeper reached a tacit agreement, that Mrs Maybrick would prepare the foods Gerald particularly liked, seed cakes and potted beef and hard-boiled eggs, and would leave them in the larder for when he came foraging. Sometimes Cloris hid behind the pantry door, watching the boy as he snaffled his provisions. She had herself been compelled to scrape and scrounge, though never in so literal a fashion, and she felt a curious one-sided sympathy for Gerald. Besides, he was, even in the gangling throes of adolescence, a beautiful boy; exactly the sort of child Cloris would have liked if her erratic life had allowed her such a luxury.

It was Sir George's influence which brought Gerald back from the wilderness. Like his young friend, Sir George realized at once that Cloris was quite different from the others whom Stella had invited to Malling-ford, although he could never have said why. He knew only that Stella was now in some way *taken*, as she had hitherto been free; a piece of knowledge that touched him with a tremor, like a distant pealing of bells, which he did not recognize as regret. Nevertheless he and Cloris got on extremely well. She was sensitive enough to realize that here too her presence might be seen as an intrusion, and she made a point of giving Sir George a warm welcome on those after-noons when he unceremoniously dropped by. He came less often now that his health was faltering, perhaps once a fortnight. Then he would sit ensconced in the sea-green drawing room for an hour or so, quite silent, as though storing up its stillness for some future need.

It was on just such an afternoon, when Stella had locked herself away in the dovecote, that Cloris plucked up courage to tell Sir George her anxieties about Gerald. She knew about the old man's special relationship with the boy from Mrs Maybrick. Even Stella, normally oblivious of what her son was doing, had once or twice said, oh, he must be off with Sir George.

The old man listened to Cloris attentively, leaning back in the winged armchair which he appropriated on his visits.

'Of course,' he said, 'Gerald has always been an unruly boy. He takes things from the kitchen at Courtney Park too, you know. Once he made off with a roast guinea hen.' He smiled quietly at the memory. 'My daughter-in-law was furious.'

'Well, I'm glad,' said Cloris, in a robust voice. 'I mean, I'm glad he does get enough to eat. But I can't help feeling that he shouldn't be running wild like this.'

Thoughtfully Sir George stretched out his legs, wincing a little at the rheumaticky pain in his hips.

'What Gerald needs is an occupation,' he said. 'The village school bores him, and has done ever since he could read, so there's no sense making him go there, and he's too young for college. But he ought to be engaged in learning of some kind. Idle hands, and so on. Is there any tea left in the pot, Cloris, my dear?'

Cloris put her hand to the cheek of the pot and refilled Sir George's cup with orangey Indian tea. Then she said: 'I'd gladly make time for him if it weren't for the fact that he won't come near me. I thought at first he might get used to my being here, but it's been weeks now. Months.' She stirred her own tea. 'Does he speak with you at all, about how he feels?'

Sir George looked mildly shocked at this idea. 'No. I can't say that we talk, exactly, in that kind of way.' He took the sugar tongs and dropped two lumps into his cup. 'What does his mother think?'

The words 'his mother' Sir George spoke with a certain oblique tenderness, as though he could not bring himself to mention Stella's name. Cloris gave a shrug.

'Stella says he'll settle down if we let him be. But I'm not convinced that she's right.'

Sir George said nothing. For a moment Cloris was afraid that she had lost his sympathy by daring to suggest that Stella might be wrong. She watched him consider his teacup: the same green lustreware he had used on his very first visit. Then he gave a sigh.

'Well,' he said, 'I'll try and talk to Gerald. Do my best to persuade him to – ah – to play more of a part in the household.' He leaned forward to put the green cup on the low lacquer table. 'And if you can think of things he might be enticed into doing, well, I dare say that would help.'

Cloris did not know when Sir George spoke to Gerald, or what he said; but after this conversation she

147

would sometimes glance up from her kick-wheel or from dipping biscuit-fired pots into saucepans of glaze, and find Gerald watching her through the stable windows. At first he vanished as soon as he knew that she had seen him; until one morning, as she was thumping a new batch of clay on her workbench to get the air bubbles out, when she saw the boy peering at her through the dusty glass, his fingers gripping the window sill. This time she managed to look him in the eyes, and to hold his gaze. It was an extraordinary sensation. Afterwards, in her mind, Cloris compared it to Jacob wrestling with the angel, although she was not sure which was the angel, she or Gerald. They stared for a full minute or more, like a pair of cats jockeying for precedence, neither prepared to admit defeat. Then, at precisely the same moment, they looked away. Cloris gave her clay another whack, slid her eyes skywards, and realized that the boy had disappeared.

This strange soundless interchange marked the beginning of their friendship. By the time winter came, Gerald had once more been absorbed into the daily life of Mallingford, and, more particularly, into the routine of the studio, under the guidance of Cloris. He had always been fascinated by the studio. In the past he had often wandered in to watch his mother at work, and she had generally ended up giving him paint and paper of his own to stop him clamouring for her attention. From the outset Stella had tacitly assumed that her son would have artistic talent of some kind. She had not been at all surprised when his pictures turned out to be promising, with a strong if crude grasp of colour and of form. Several times she had given the pictures a professional once-over, explaining their faults and virtues to Gerald with a level of comradely interest quite unfamiliar to him. But, as with his emotional development, she expected his skills to bloom spontaneously; she had certainly not spent the time to map out what he might do next, or encourage him to learn new techniques or new ways of seeing.

It was Cloris who now took on herself the business of teaching Gerald. She had spent half her life hanging around art schools hoping for modelling jobs, and the experience made her a gifted tutor. Her original plan was to help Gerald learn to draw, but, as light relief, she let him loose in her pottery from time to time, to play, and to practise making shapes which he could then gleefully squash into nothing. That was how she discovered his gift for ceramics. The boy seemed to discover a life in the clay, a secret elasticity from which he moulded glorious unexpected forms. Cloris taught him to throw pots on the kick-wheel, and from the first moment he seemed to know what to do, drawing the clay to the centre of the wheel, plucking it and smoothing it as if it were a living creature.

'You know, he's extraordinarily good,' said Cloris to Stella, as they were going to bed. They slept on the first floor, beneath a patchwork quilt over which the redoubtable Dora and Molly had toiled for months. Cloris would have preferred a room of her own, but when she had proposed it Stella had grown stiff and silent, and she had not had the heart to press the point. 'I think he could easily make a living from ceramics. Well, more than a living: a name. He's certainly as good as I was at his age.'

Stella was taking down her hair. It was half gold, half grey now, but still very thick. She drew it into three strands to plait it; otherwise it fell into Cloris's mouth as they made love.

'He wants to paint, though, doesn't he?' she said, in an abstracted voice. 'I'd always imagined he would paint.'

'Possibly. What I'm saying is that the skill he has is quite remarkable.'

'Mmn,' said Stella, weaving her strands of hair. The act of plaiting made her think of the act of love, which, a year after meeting Cloris, still caused her fingers to quiver. Cloris, meanwhile, did not speak. She often suspected that Stella did not take her work seriously, that she regarded it as somehow inferior to her own: a craft, not an art, incapable of real profundity. As a rule she absorbed this prejudice without rancour. She was, after all, earning almost as much as Stella, even if she lacked the awestruck reviews which Stella attracted in newspapers and art magazines. But the idea that her life's work might be too trivial a calling for Stella's son irked her horribly. She slipped out of her scarlet kimono and climbed into the bed.

'Of course,' she said, 'I love teaching Gerald. I think there'll come a stage, though, when he ought to learn from someone else. In a year or two perhaps. I wouldn't want to impose my particular style on his. Maybe he should work with Bernard Leach in St Ives. Or go to Japan.'

Absorbedly Stella fastened her plait. She could see Cloris in the mirror, sitting upright against the pillows in her prim white nightie. Desire like a mouth gaped inside her.

'Yes,' she said.

'What?' said Cloris. Stella stroked the wisps of hair back from her wide forehead.

'Darling, let's not talk about Gerald,' she said, in a coaxing voice. 'There'll be plenty of time to decide what he ought to do.' She put down her comb and threw off the Paisley cashmere shawl she was wearing round her shoulders. 'Besides, I'm sure he wants to paint. He's always said so.'

'Really?' said Cloris drily. 'I hadn't noticed you asking him lately. In fact, I hadn't noticed you paying him much attention at all.'

A cloud passed over Stella's face. 'Please, darling,' she said, 'don't let's discuss it now. It's bedtime.'

Cloris punched at one of the pillows behind her back. Her cheeks were flushed like apples with annoyance.

'I don't see how you can simply assume you know

what he wants to do,' she said. 'Besides, if he does have a gift for ceramics, you should encourage him to make the most of it, shouldn't you?' She glanced sharply across at Stella, who was hovering doubtfully beside the bed in her unbleached calico smock. 'Unless you think making pots is beneath him.'

'Oh, darling.' Stella sat down on Cloris's side of the mattress, and took her lover's hand. Her face had cleared now she thought she had fathomed the reason for Cloris's irritation. 'I do value your work, you know. Really I do. You mustn't ever think I don't.'

'That isn't quite the point,' said Cloris; but she said it more gently, mollified by the candour in Stella's eyes. She allowed Stella to draw back the quilt, and to start undoing the tiny shell buttons of her night-dress. Then she said: 'We ought to make some plans for Gerald. He's a very gifted boy.'

'Oh, yes,' said Stella, slowly loosening the pale buttons. 'He's quite young, though, remember. And I couldn't afford to send him to art school anyway.' She pushed back the shoulders of Cloris's nightdress to expose her breasts, spilling out against the fine white cotton. They were very large and very soft, the sallow skin stretched in a way that Stella found both touching and erotic. 'Don't let's talk about Gerald now,' she said again.

'You never do talk about him,' said Cloris, with a faint protesting laugh. But Stella was kissing her breasts, and Cloris could never resist the terrible urge to give pleasure. She let the moment slip just as she let Stella slide her warm calico weight into their shared bed.

She did not, however, forget her plans for Gerald. Remembering what Stella had said – that she could not afford to send her son to art school – Cloris set about teaching the boy in a more systematic fashion, binding him to her as though he were her apprentice. When the village church, at Sir George's behest, com-missioned some hand-thrown candlesticks for the

151

altar, Gerald accompanied Cloris to discuss the specifi-
cation, and although it was she who designed the
candlesticks, it was Gerald who made them. He
learned to slice pots from the wheel with a wire like
a cheese-cutter, and to trim their bases when they were
leather-hard; he learned the alchemy of mixing glazes,
using the jars of powder which Cloris like a sorceress
had lined up on her studio shelf; he learned to stack
the wood-fired kiln and to stoke it so that it reached
the right fierce temperature. Accustomed as she was
to working in isolation, Cloris revelled in the boy's
companionship as well as in his burgeoning skills. She
did not again raise the subject of Gerald's education
with Stella, while for her part Stella seemed not to
notice the amount of time which her lover devoted
to her son. Once or twice, to be sure, she mentioned
Gerald's ambition to paint, but only casually, as if it
were an event far into the future which need not be
considered yet.

It was a year later, on a mild afternoon in October,
that the demon struck. Cloris and Gerald had been
firing a batch of pots, taking turns to watch the kiln
overnight so that the temperature in the brick oven did
not fall. It was a particularly important firing because
they were experimenting with a new glaze, based on
some wood-ash they had gathered from the autumn
bonfires, which Cloris hoped would fire to a rich
crimson red. All day they had been waiting for the kiln
to cool, unable to settle to any other sort of work; and
at last, at about five o'clock, they put on protective
gloves and opened up the bricks of the oven. That was
how Stella found them when she came out of her
studio. Their heads were bowed together, Cloris's tied
up in a red bandanna, Gerald's bleached gold by the
sun.

'Look!' said Cloris, in triumph, turning to show
Stella the first piece she had salvaged. It was a bowl
the size of a soup plate, with a magnificent sunburst
at its centre: exactly the crimson Cloris had wanted,

flecked with blue and with gold. The expression on her face and on Gerald's was identical. In that moment jealousy swept through Stella like a forest fire, unforeseen and all-consuming. She felt as if the joy in Cloris's eyes – a joy she had not inspired, a joy she could not share – had touched her with a branding iron, and she knew with a certainty as absolute as it was sudden that she would have to make Gerald leave Mallingford.

Chapter Fourteen

'It's Dickensian,' said Kate, tossing her sleek head. 'Terribly creepy. Like Miss Havisham's house in *Great Expectations*. It makes you think of dead cats.'

Alastair gave a delighted chuckle. 'Don't tell Brian Edwards that,' he said.

'No, but honestly. I don't know how you could bear to stay overnight, Tom. And *eat* there. I couldn't have swallowed a thing. I bet it all tasted like armpits.'

'It was OK,' said Tom. He arranged his strapped ankle more comfortably upon the tartan rug. They were sitting on the lawn at Glyndebourne, waiting for Brian to arrive. Beside them stood a large wicker hamper, propped open to reveal the picnic which Alastair had brought, of caviar and pâté and cold roast duck: expensive conventional delicacies, none of which Tom really liked. The weather was hot and claustrophobic.

'We were met by the ugliest woman I've ever seen in my life,' Kate went on, in that same high-pitched artificial voice, revelling in Alastair's attention. 'God knows I've seen some ugly women, especially when the mag's doing those before and after pieces. But this one – oh, dear. I thought I was in a Hammer horror film. The Bride of Frankenstein. She was hideous.'

She gave each syllable of the word 'hideous' the same histrionic emphasis. Tom resisted a puerile urge to smack her.

'What about the daughter? The luscious Cosima Deighton?' asked Alastair, with a gleam of malice in Tom's direction. Kate ran her small quick fingers through her hair, which was glistening with gel. She

154

wore a tight green dress made of raw silk, fashionable and incongruous beneath a black leather jacket.

'Oh, *sweet*,' she said. 'Just a bit dopey. Of course, she adores Tom. You can see it a mile off.'

'Really?' said Alastair. 'House rules, remember, Tom. No screwing clients.'

'For God's sake,' said Tom. He took a mouthful of champagne, and leaned back on his elbows.

'What about the loony old man?' asked Alastair. 'Did you see him, too?'

'No. I expect they'd locked him in the attic,' Kate said, with a giggle. 'Honestly, Tom, I hope you know what you're letting yourself in for.'

'Oh, don't worry, he's got it all under control; haven't you, Tom? The old man really liked you. You mark my words, Katie, Tom's going to pull this one off.'

Tom did not answer. He was not looking forward to the afternoon ahead. Like many of Alastair's contacts, Brian Edwards sounded at best improbable, and at worst criminal. He was a builder who had made good in Docklands, and now wanted to acquire, in his own phrase, a better class of customer. It was obvious that Alastair had lured him with the prestige of the Courtney name; as far as Tom could tell, the man had never heard of Stella Deighton. This would have mattered less if Tom had felt that he could rely on Kate to support him through the social niceties of the day, but in this salty mood she would be no help at all. Ever since the accident at Chanctonbury Kate's manner towards him had subtly changed. It was not that he had expected her to be sympathetic about his ankle. Kate was never sympathetic over minor ailments like bad colds or upset stomachs: she always behaved as if they were somehow your own fault. What surprised him was that she had become offhand and, for much of the time, unavailable. I'm really busy at work, she had said, when Tom questioned this; you don't mind, do you? When he asked her if she would drive him down to Sussex early in order to collect his abandoned car, she made a point of consulting her diary as though Tom should be aware that she might have better things to do.

It had been a mistake to take her to Mallingford; Tom realized that now. His growing passion for the place had blinded him to the fact that any outsider, and Kate in particular, would see the house as he had first seen it, a ramshackle heap miles from civilization. The visit had been a disaster. At each pothole in the road he felt the jolt through Kate's body rather than his own; the shabby trees, the broken gateposts, he saw with her eyes. Even the miraculous stillness of the valley seemed sinister rather than soothing, now that he heard it through Kate's resolutely urban ears. He could sense her beside him in the driving seat, fizzing with irritation and dislike.

Morag had greeted them enthusiastically, and invited them into the kitchen, which was awash with cold tea and toast crumbs. She offered them drinks, an offer which Kate, accepting, took to mean gin and tonic, but in fact meant watery orange squash. Then one of the hens wandered into the room, and Kate, who was frightened of birds, gave a squeal, and was at once annoyed with herself for squealing, and annoyed with Tom for putting her in a situation where she had been prompted to squeal. Cosima's arrival did not improve matters. She was wearing her work clothes, her hair clumsily bunched behind her, and she looked both gauche and gloomy, quite unlike the radiant companion who had walked with him on Chanctonbury. At the sight of her Kate shot Tom a sly sidelong glance, prickly with irony. He gulped at his orange squash so that they could take their leave as quickly as possible.

Cosima came to see them off, slouching behind as they walked towards the Porsche. Tom dallied for a moment until she drew level.

'Are you OK?' he murmured.

'Mmn,' said Cosima. She was gazing at Kate as she sashayed gracefully across the courtyard in her Glyndebourne finery. Kate had pushed her sunglasses onto the top of her head, and she looked like an exotic Mediterranean insect, with glittering vast eyes and an iridescent thorax. The simile disconcerted Tom even as it occurred to him: he was sure it could not be right to compare your girlfriend to an insect.

'I'll see you there, then,' Kate said, rattling her bunch of silver keys. Her little red Metro was parked next to Tom's car on the gravel.

'Sure,' said Tom. 'Will you be able to find your way?'

'Oh, I'll follow you. You're not going to hang about, are you?' said Kate. She reached into the back of the Metro and pulled out Tom's dinner jacket, dangling it from the tip of one finger. 'Here. You'd better have this.'

'Thanks.' Tom stepped forward to take the jacket, stumbling as he did so. Kate's elegance made him feel more of a buffoon than usual.

'See you, then,' said Kate. She waved her arm in a vague gesture, casually intended to include Cosima, and climbed into her car.

'Won't you be hot in those clothes?' Cosima said.

'I guess so,' said Tom, 'but it's obligatory.'

He poked his finger into the breast pocket of his jacket, and pulled out the bow tie he had stowed there, like a sombre gleaming butterfly. Both he and Cosima looked at it. Tom had the feeling that Cosima had been dismayed by Kate's presence, and he would have liked to reassure her, without of course denying the nature of his relationship with Kate.

'How's Gerald?' he asked, instead.

'Oh, he's all right. Well, actually, no, he's not all right. He's being horrible to me, to get back at me for doing a deal with Roddy.' Automatically Cosima brushed a speck of dust from the shoulder of Tom's shirt. Then she looked up at him. 'Don't worry. He's still keen on the idea of turning the place into a study

157

centre. He's even asked the students from his class at the art school if they'll come and help with the renovations.'

'That's great,' said Tom. 'We're seeing the sponsor today: he and his wife are coming to the opera with us. That means we should get a commitment in the next week or so, and it'll be all systems go.'

Kate, who had turned her car towards the road, tooted her horn. Tom unlocked the Porsche.

'Are you safe to drive?' asked Cosima, frowning at his strapped foot.

'Yeah, I'm fine,' said Tom, as he slid into the seat. He could see Cosima's earth-stained fingers gripping the metal door frame, her large anxious face bent towards him. Kate's little horn tooted once more.

'You'd better go,' said Cosima. 'She's waiting.'

Tom started the engine. 'I'll see you. Take care.'

Cosima gave a little nod, and she pushed shut the car door. Then she turned and walked to the house, not staying to watch him drive off.

Kate's red car bobbed on his tail all the way to Glyndebourne, at once tantalizing and reproachful. I should talk to her, thought Tom, wearily, as he negotiated the narrow lanes; I should find out what's bugging her. But he did not, and once they reached the house it was too late: Alastair, as usual, imposed his mood upon theirs, wafting them towards the wonderful picnic site he had staked out near the yew trees. After that any sort of privacy became impossible.

'Do you think Brian is going to like it here?' Kate asked now, greedily holding out her glass for more champagne. Alastair swung the heavy bottle by its neck.

'I'm not sure if he'll *like* it. He'll be bloody impressed, that's the main thing. It was a bugger getting hold of these tickets. Tom? More fizz?'

'No, thanks,' said Tom.

'I think it's marvellous,' Kate said. She stretched out

158

her limbs upon the car rug, luxuriating. 'Lovely food, lovely drink, lovely clothes—'

'Not to mention a bit of singing,' said Tom.

'Don't be such a snob. It's the whole occasion that makes it so special. You've got to admit that. The opera's only part of it.'

'Yes. Shame you've got to have the opera, really,' said Alastair, thoughtfully refilling his own glass. 'I hope Brian sits through it. It's some modern thing, isn't it?'

'*Rusalka*, by Dvořák,' Kate declaimed, reading from the fat elaborate programme.

'Never heard of it.'

'Pleb,' said Kate, with satisfaction, although she did not herself offer any further information. Tom cleared his throat. He had been taken to see *Rusalka* in New York by Becky's parents, just after they were married, and he had a vague memory of hordes of girls in green chiffon.

'There's a famous aria in it,' he said. '"Song to the Moon". You're bound to recognise it.'

'If you say so. Ah, look. There's Brian.'

Brian was a burly crop-haired man in his forties, wearing a glossy dinner jacket and a large velvet bow tie. In his wake trotted a sleek woman in yellow satin, not quite young enough to be his daughter.

'Second wife, eh?' murmured Kate, as they all three stood up.

'Bitch,' whispered Alastair, with admiration. Then, aloud, he said, in a hearty voice: 'Brian! Welcome.'

'Ah, so you've got the shampoo flowing already, Alastair. That's what I like to see,' said Brian. He had a strong South London accent, and a bone-crushing handshake. 'You must be Tom. Looks like you've been in the wars.'

'Slipped on a cattle grid, didn't you, Tom?' said Kate, with a grin.

Brian gave a shout of laughter; then, turning towards Kate, he asked: 'And whose better half are you?'

'I'm Kate,' said Kate. Normally phrases like 'better half' made Kate obstreperous, but now, to Tom's surprise, she angled her head flirtatiously in Brian's direction. Brian took her small hand in his enormous one, and kissed it.

'Kate's my girlfriend,' Tom said, belatedly.

'I'm also the beauty editor of a very influential magazine,' said Kate, 'in case you were wondering.'

'You should talk to Wendy. She spends her life reading magazines, don't you, Wen? *Ideal Home* and all that crap.' Brian glanced over his shoulder at his wife, who was accepting a glass of champagne. 'Don't give her too much. She's driving back to London so I can get ratarsed. That's the point of this, isn't it, eh? To get paralytic.'

'Absolutely,' said Alastair, easing the cork from another bottle. 'Tom, give me a glass for Brian, will you?'

Tom limped towards the hamper and took out one of the crystal flutes.

'Are you interested in music, Mrs Edwards?' he said politely to Brian's wife, who was sipping at the champagne Alastair had given her. She had expensively streaked fair hair, and an unusually deep tan for so early in the summer.

'Oh, don't ask her. She knows bugger all about it,' said Brian. 'Barry Manilow's about your limit, isn't it, Wen?'

'I like ballet,' said Wendy, in a very small, very girlish voice. Brian guffawed.

'I know what it is you like about ballet,' he said. 'You're wasting your time, though, love. They're all poofters. Yes, that's right, Alastair, fill it up. Cheers.'

'Alastair tells me you've done brilliantly down in Docklands,' said Kate, as they sat down once more. Brian seemed to take up a vast amount of space, squeezing the others to the edges of the rug. At close quarters he smelt strongly of cigar smoke and of gin. It occurred to Tom that he was already rather drunk.

'Yes, I've made the odd million,' said Brian, in an offhand voice. 'Right man in the right place at the right time. And there's more to be made, if you've got the contacts. Eh, Alastair?'

'Yes,' said Alastair. He refilled Brian's glass, which was already empty. 'That's why I think this project is exactly what you need, Brian. It'll bring your name in front of a whole new clientele. Tom thinks this idea to set up a study centre could be really hot, don't you, Tom?'

'Well, we're picking up on a trend,' said Tom, recognizing his cue. 'If you read magazines like *Harper's* they're full of ads for interior design courses, that kind of thing. Arts and Crafts for wealthy housewives. I guess we can tap that market, as well as getting trade from tourists who want to see where Stella Deighton lived.'

Brian shifted his weight on the rug and began to examine the contents of the hamper.

'Sounds good,' he said. 'I hope this pâté's foie gras, Alastair?'

'Of course it is. From Fortnum's. What else would I give you, Brian?' said Alastair. He paused for a moment, while Brian dug a stick of celery into the jar of pâté. Then he went on: 'The Courtneys were delighted when we told them you might come on board, weren't they, Tom?'

'Oh, yeah,' said Tom. He remembered the sharp gleam in Roderick's eye at the prospect of someone else's cash to use. Then he thought of Stella's dovecote, with its other-worldly atmosphere. He tried to picture Brian there, lumbering round the damp plaster walls, guffawing at the raspberry nipples of the bird-woman.

'Let's face it,' Alastair was saying, in his most blandly persuasive voice, 'the Courtney connection on its own could be worth a fortune, never mind our plans for Mallingford.'

'It's all right, Alastair,' said Brian. He ate the last of his celery and stretched out his legs, crumpling

Wendy's yellow dress as he did so. 'You don't have to keep up the sales pitch. I've more or less made up my mind, as long as we can get the sums right. Let's forget about business and get pissed, shall we?'

'A decisive man,' said Kate, sweetly. 'Just the kind I like. Alastair, darling, top me up, will you?'

Glass in hand, she stretched across the rug, revealing a great deal of neck and bosom for Brian's benefit. Jeez, thought Tom irritably, what's she playing at? He had seen Kate charm powerful men before, but she was usually subtle about it, listening to their achievements, laughing at their witticisms, not thrusting her cleavage in their faces. Tom shot a glance at Wendy to see if she had noticed, but Wendy seemed spellbound by the growing throng of people in their dinner suits and magnificent ball frocks. She had her eyes fixed on a glamorous middle-aged woman dressed in crimson taffeta.

'So what's the form?' asked Brian, digging another celery stick into the velvety mound of pâté. 'When do we start the nosh?'

'Not till after the first act, I'm afraid,' said Kate. 'Then there's a long interval, an hour and a half or something. That's when you eat.'

Brian chomped at the celery. 'You obviously know the ropes,' he said. Tom noticed that he was looking straight at Kate's breasts.

'Oh,' said Kate, in a blasé voice, 'I've been here once or twice. I'm not an opera buff, mind you; not like Tom.'

'I'm hardly a buff,' said Tom gruffly. He was aware that this had not been intended as a compliment. 'I think you'll like *Rusalka*. It's very romantic. All about a water nymph who gives up everything for love.'

'Nymphs, eh?' said Brian. 'Could be fun. Do you get girls showing their tits in operas?'

'I bloody well hope so,' said Alastair. 'The tickets cost enough. Brian, your glass is empty. We can't have that.'

In the distance a bell began rhythmically to chime.

'I guess we should make a move,' Tom said, putting his hand on the edge of the hamper to lever himself upright.

'What, already?' said Alastair. 'I was going to open another bottle.'

'Too late,' Kate said cheerfully. 'Come on, Alastair. Stir your stumps.'

They walked across the grass in the direction of the house. From this angle the building seemed to be composed of a series of different-sized blocks, made of terracotta brick delicately inlaid with white. On top of one of the taller blocks a red flag fluttered half-heartedly from a white flagpole. Behind the house the Downs reared up, vividly green and unexpected.

'I hope it doesn't last bloody ages,' said Brian. 'I'm starving. I must say, some of these picnics look good.'

He sauntered across towards an unattended hamper, and peered at its contents. Then, before Tom could stop him, he reached out and grabbed a leg of cold chicken.

'Oh, Brian,' said Wendy, with a giggle. 'Trust you.'

'Well, sod 'em,' said Brian, biting into his chicken. 'Dickheads shouldn't leave it lying around, should they? Asking for it to be nicked.' He hoisted a bottle of champagne from the silver ice bucket on the table beside the hamper he had just raided. 'Hey, Alastair, is their shampoo better than ours?'

'Nobody's champagne is better than ours,' said Alastair, modestly. 'If it were I'd have to kill my supplier. Tom, have you got the tickets there?'

Tom led the way across the light brown parquet floor to the auditorium entrance. The usher, an elderly man with a gilt medallion hung on a ribbon about his neck, smiled and tore the stubs from their tickets.

'Hold this for me, would you?' said Brian. 'I must take a leak.'

He handed the usher the chewed bone of his chicken

163

leg, and, with a chortle, slipped off nimbly in the direction of the lavatories.

'Oh, Brian, honestly,' said Wendy, in a breathy indulgent voice, as she followed him. The usher meanwhile was staring bemusedly at the chicken bone.

'I'll bin that for you,' said Tom, coolly. He dropped the bone into the metal wastebasket, and with his clean hand reached into his pocket for a handkerchief to wipe the grease from his fingers.

'Quite a character, eh?' said Alastair, gazing in the direction Brian had gone.

'If you like that kind of thing,' said Tom. 'You realize he's half-cut, don't you?'

'Of course he's half-cut. So am I. So's Katie, aren't you, darling? I must say, you've made a conquest there, Katie. Old Brian's dying to get into your knickers.'

'Alastair, don't be vulgar,' said Kate, hunching her bare shoulders. 'I'm trying to do my bit for you two, that's all. Keeping him sweet.'

'Well, that's very noble of you, darling. Don't you think it's noble of her, Tom?'

'Yeah,' said Tom. 'Heroic.'

'Mind you,' said Alastair, 'I expect he's bloody terrible in bed. That type usually is; I've got it on good authority. All mouth and trousers.'

'All mouth and no trousers, I should think,' said Kate, with a giggle.

'Jesus Christ,' said Tom, in an irritable voice. 'If you ask me the guy's a complete prick.'

'Ssh,' said Alastair. 'Here they come. Brian, I think we'd better find our seats.'

In the auditorium Alastair deftly manoeuvred Kate between himself and Brian. Tom took his place at the end of the row, next to Wendy, who was arranging the slippery folds of her yellow dress.

'It's quite small, isn't it?' she said, looking around the auditorium with an air of disappointment. 'I

164

thought it would be more like Covent Garden, you know. More glamorous.'

From two seats away Tom heard the familiar ring of Kate's laughter, although she was too distant for him to discern the joke. Dutifully he smiled at Wendy.

'Well, it's a different set-up, you know. Glyndebourne's a private residence, which just happens to have an opera house in the front room. No gold and glitz like Covent Garden. I guess that's part of its charm.'

'Oh,' said Wendy. She clicked open her Kelly bag, took out a packet of chewing gum and unwrapped the foil from one of the sticks. As an afterthought, she offered the pack to Tom.

'No, thanks,' he said. He watched as Wendy rolled up the pale strip of gum and popped it into her mouth. Along the row Kate laughed at another unheard joke. Tom glanced in her direction. She was flushed and smiling, clutching the programme to her breast. Then the house lights began to dim, and the curtain rose on what seemed to be an Edwardian nursery, equipped with iron beds and a brightly painted rocking horse. There was a vast curtained window, through which a fake full moon glimmered, and at the front of the stage hung a wooden swing.

'Are those the nymphs?' Wendy murmured, as a bevy of girls in white nightdresses scurried across the stage, whooping. One of them was pushing a wicker bath chair in which sat an old man, with pointed ears and a grey beard. Tom glanced at Wendy and nodded, hoping to shut her up. The nymphs launched into a high-spirited chorus, like a bacchanal.

'Which one's Rusalka?' said Wendy, in Tom's ear.

'I don't know,' said Tom curtly. He was conscious of a stirring and a tutting from the man in front of him. On stage another young woman had entered, with a mass of reddish hair falling down her back. She reminded Tom of the girl in a Whistler painting he had seen in the National Gallery in Washington DC, an

165

adolescent girl in a white dress, gawky and passionate. Then, as the young woman turned the broad plane of her face towards the audience, he realized, with a shock, that she resembled Cosima.

'Where are all these tits, then?' whispered Brian.

'Ssh!' said Kate, with a half-suppressed giggle. The man in front of Tom turned and fixed Brian with an icy cultured stare. Meanwhile the girl in white had crossed the stage and was sitting in the wooden swing, her face lifted so that it caught the artificial moonlight. The expression on the face was achingly pure. Oh, Cosima, thought Tom suddenly, Cosima.

'That must be her,' said Wendy, in a complacent tone, as though no-one would otherwise have guessed the fact. The cultured man in the next row gave a loud exasperated sigh. Swaying gently on the ropes which held her swing, Rusalka began to sing the 'Song to the Moon', in a sweet high yearning voice.

'She's a bit fat, isn't she?' murmured Wendy to Tom.

Tom did not take his eyes from the gleaming water nymph on her swing. The adoration in her face seemed so clear, so candid, untouched by doubt or confusion. I want *that*, thought Tom, with a terrible impossible pang of desire; I want that.

'Tell him, oh, tell him how I long for him,' sang Rusalka, gazing at the flimsy silver moon. Then Tom became aware of a different sound, closer to home, a deep rhythmic scraping sound. It took him a moment or two to recognize it as a snore.

'Oh, for Christ's *sake*,' hissed the cultured man. Tom turned. Brian had slumped in his seat, his great bulk heaving in time to his ferocious snorts. Both Kate and Alastair were staring at him, aghast. Tom leaned across.

'Let's get him out of here,' he whispered.

'Right,' said Alastair. He reached past Kate and gave Brian's vast arm a nudge; then, when nothing happened, a sharp prod. Brian grunted, and his head jerked upright.

'Come on, Brian,' said Tom, in a firm undertone. 'We're going.'

Brian blinked. In the dim light of the auditorium his skin seemed unnaturally pallid.

'What? Oh. All right,' he said, with surprising docility, and he lumbered to his feet. Tom took one last look at the rapt face of the water nymph, who, oblivious of this disturbance, was still singing. Then he led the way to the foyer.

'Let's go and finish our picnic, and fuck off home,' said Alastair, under his breath. Tom nodded.

'I guess that would be diplomatic,' he said.

'Actually,' said Kate, 'I don't think Brian's very well.'

Brian was standing by the door, his head bowed, while Wendy clutched solicitously at his arm. Beneath his tan his face was clammy and green.

'Oh, Christ,' said Alastair.

'I think he needs to go to the bathroom,' Wendy said, in a delicate voice. She was still chewing her stick of gum.

'All right,' said Alastair. With an air of pained resignation he slid his arm across Brian's enormous shoulders, and angled him in the direction of the lavatories. 'Come on, Brian.'

'Champagne on an empty stomach,' said Wendy, a note of faint accusation in her voice, as though her husband's condition must be somebody's fault.

When Alastair came back, a few minutes later, he was on his own, his face pinched and rather weary.

'Brian's OK now,' he said, 'but he needs some fresh air. I've taken him to your car, Wendy. I think it might be a good idea if you drove him home.'

'Oh,' said Wendy. 'All right, then.'

'I'll walk you to the car park,' Alastair said. 'I'm sorry your first visit's been such an anticlimax.'

'Well, what a disaster,' murmured Tom. Kate pushed at her stiff slicked hair.

'Yeah,' she said. Through the auditorium doors Tom

heard a muffled flurry of applause. He thought once more of Rusalka's dazzling silvery face, so like Cosima's.

'Look,' he said, 'I'm going to see if I can slip back in and catch what's left of the first act. Why don't you wait here for Alastair? You don't really want to see the opera anyway, do you?'

'Tom,' said Kate, in a small voice.

'What?' said Tom. The orchestra was striking up again: he knew he should slide through the doors now, before the singing began. Then he realized that Kate was crying, fat crystal tears tinged with mascara.

'Katie?' he said, in amazement. He had never seen Kate cry before.

'Oh, Tom,' she said, her face puckering like a four-year-old's, and she groped inside her leather jacket for a tissue.

'Here,' said Tom, pulling out his handkerchief. Kate took it and buried her wet face in it.

'Can we go outside?' she managed to say. 'I don't want Alastair to see me like this.'

'OK,' said Tom. He put his arm around her shoulders and led her into the empty sunlit garden. The yew trees were beginning to cast squat shadows on the lawn.

'It's just—' Kate began. 'I just feel – I can't go on like this.'

'What?' said Tom again.

'Not knowing where I stand. I mean, we've been together for six months now. I have to know if you're serious about this or not.'

'Oh, God,' said Tom. He propelled Kate towards a wooden bench overlooking the gardens. In the pit of his stomach there was a sick tight feeling.

'Well, come on,' said Kate, lifting her tear-stained face. '*Are* you serious?'

Tom did not reply. He wanted to say, pleadingly, can't we just carry on the way we were? It was fine, the way we were. But he knew that of all the answers he could give now that was the most unthinkable.

'Tom, I know that what's her name – Becky – really screwed you up. But you've had months to get over it. Years.' Kate mopped at her eyes with Tom's handkerchief. Then, in a different voice, she said: 'This smells of chicken.'

'Yeah, I used it to wipe my fingers. After your friend Brian played his little joke on the usher.'

'He's not my friend,' Kate said, sounding peevish. 'I wanted to show you that other men find me attractive, that's all.'

'Kate,' said Tom wryly, 'I find you very attractive. You know I find you attractive.'

'Oh, yeah. With my clothes off.' She blew her nose, and in a gentler tone, she said: 'Tom, I don't like being like this. Playing games and stuff. But I need to know.'

Tom gazed across the lawn, which was littered with carefully laid picnics, awaiting their owners' return. He thought of Gerald Deighton in the dark drawing room at Mallingford, of that mellifluous voice saying, it's not unusual to ruin your own life. Hundreds of people do it. Who am I kidding? thought Tom, with a flash of bitterness so powerful it seemed like thirst or hunger, an appetite which must be satisfied. I'm never going to have more than this, I'd better make the most of it. Aggressively he turned towards Kate on the wooden bench. Her eyes were still sparkling with the tears she had shed.

'Do you love me?' he demanded. She seemed taken aback by the question.

'Well, yes, of course I do. I mean, we're good together, aren't we? We want the same things.' Sensing a shift in his mood, Kate slipped her arm through Tom's, drawing her face towards his glossy black shoulder. She smelt of sandalwood and of hair gel and of champagne. 'All I'm asking for is some kind of commitment. What's so terrible about that?'

Tom said nothing. He stared once more at the yew

169

trees, at the tartan rugs spread on the lawn, at the wine glasses sparkling where they caught the sunlight. In the deepening sky he could see a chalky fingernail of moon. He gripped Kate by the shoulders and began to kiss her, roughly, feeling the cavern of her mouth open under his in astonishment. He dimly knew, as he kissed her, that she thought he was answering her question, when in fact he wanted only to blot out that pale unattainable face which so resembled Cosima's.

Chapter Fifteen

'Don't look so scared, little cousin. They won't bite.'

'Yes,' said Cosima crossly. 'I know that.'

She was sitting aloft in Roderick's Land Rover as they jolted along the lane out of Mallingford. Cosima would much rather have travelled to Courtney Park with Tom, but she had not been given the choice. Her cousin had simply informed her that there was to be a meeting with her uncle Nicholas and the sponsor from London, and that he would collect her at half past ten.

'You're looking very nice, anyway,' Roddy said, sliding his eyes from the wheel towards Cosima's knees. 'Is that dress one of your mother's? It's pretty.'

Cosima did not speak, but gave a fruitless tug at her long cream-coloured skirt. By daylight the dress, which was of crêpe with satin panels on the shoulders, seemed too garish for a business meeting, and she wished she had chosen something less flamboyant. Exposure to other girls had eroded Cosima's self-confidence. Kirsty she had not minded: her clothes were as peculiar as Cosima's own, although she found the tiny glowing amethyst in the art student's nostril intriguing. Kate, however, was another matter. This time when Cosima had raided Annabel's wardrobes, half hoping that she would again fall beneath the spell of her own reflection, she had instead been haunted by the image of dapper little Kate, dancing towards her car in green silk and black leather. The following day Cosima had wheedled from Morag some of the money they got for the vegetables, and had cadged a lift into Brighton. She bought three women's magazines from W. H. Smith's, and sat on the windy promenade poring over them for nearly an hour, as the waves crashed on the pebbly slopes of the beach. Then she went to Boots and purchased some hairpins, a palette of eyeshadows and a smooth amber-coloured lipstick quite unlike the squidgy ancient pinks and purples in her mother's collection. With these she set to work in front of the pocked mirror in Annabel's room, practising the art of coiling up her hair and smudging powder on her eyelids, until she looked what she had begun to think of as 'normal'. Even so, she was troubled that she had not got the knack of make-up at all. Her face felt as stiff as a sheet dipped in starch: she was afraid it might splinter if she smiled too much.

'My pa's looking forward to seeing you again, you know,' said Roddy, shifting the gears of the Land Rover. 'He says he hasn't set eyes on you since you were about twelve.'

'No, I suppose not,' said Cosima. Her throat was becoming dry as they drew closer to the house. Gerald knew, of course, that she was going to Courtney Park to discuss the future of Mallingford, but he had not in so many words sanctioned her visit. When she had last night explained that she would have to speak on his behalf, he had merely nodded as though it was not worth discussing, and had fixed his attention on the cigarette he was rolling. This morning at breakfast there had been no sign of him, and although Cosima was relieved that he had not encountered Roddy, she felt uneasy at leaving without his blessing, however oblique.

'There,' said Roderick, with satisfaction, as the handsome frontage of Courtney Park came into view. 'Isn't it beautiful?'

He drew up alongside the front door. Cosima climbed out of the Land Rover, trying not to catch her heels in the hem of her dress. She noticed Tom's blue car parked beside the house, next to a huge silver

Mercedes. In the distance a peacock gave a shrill soulless cry.

'You used to come and stay here quite often, little cousin,' Roddy said, as he wiped his feet on the coir mat in the porch. 'Do you remember?'

'Oh, yes,' said Cosima, breathing in the forgotten scent of Courtney Park. The house smelt subtly, as it had always done, of beeswax, shot through with a faint whiff of dog. She had never been happy here, although she had been given a very pretty room with chintz curtains, overlooking the gardens, and her uncle in particular had done his best to help her feel at home. But the luxuriousness of the place made her miserable. She was so sure of breaking or spoiling something, and she hated the unrecognizable foods which the servants piled upon her plate. It had always been a vast relief when she was brought back, as inexplicably as she had been sent, to the ramshackle security of Mallingford.

'We're having the meeting in Father's study,' Roderick said, putting out his arm to guide Cosima towards the staircase. She gave her skirt a twitch and scurried forward, out of his reach. The house seemed unchanged, the same huge Chinese vases with dried flowers in them, the same dark glossy furniture. On the stairs, which were slippery and treacle-coloured, there were antique Turkish carpets of different patterns, the ends tacked together with large stitches. Cosima remembered the stair carpets from her child-hood. She had been puzzled as to why her uncle, so palpably rich, had not bought matching carpets; then she had sat on the staircase trying to decide which of the patterns she liked best, and had been in the act of unravelling the stitches which attached her favourite to its neighbour when her aunt, Lady Courtney, found her and tersely sent her out into the garden to play.

They were on the first floor now. Through the door of her uncle's study Cosima could hear men's voices, followed by a sudden deep guffaw of laughter. Stand-ing in the dim corridor she froze.

'Don't worry, little cousin,' said Roddy, in her ear. 'I'll look after you.'

She felt his hand touch her hip in her tight crêpe dress.

'I'll be all right,' she said, fiercely, and she jerked open the door. The three men in the room turned at once towards her, their suits dark and shadowy, their faces a blur. She was beginning to panic when Tom stepped forward, looming and familiar.

'Cosima,' he said, and bending down he kissed her on the cheek. His aftershave smelt warm and leathery. For a moment, as they looked at each other, it seemed they were the only people there in Sir Nicholas's study. Then a tall, elderly man crossed the floor, his hand extended.

'Hello, my dear. I'm your uncle Nicholas. I don't suppose you remember me, after all these years.'

He shook her hand warmly and firmly. Cosima, nervous that Tom's kiss might have made her uncle believe that he too had licence to kiss her, felt a surge of gratitude for his tact.

'I do remember you,' she said, 'I think.'

Sir Nicholas laughed, a sympathetic easy laugh, not at all like Roderick's self-conscious neighing.

'Well, no matter,' he said. 'It's nice to see you, Cosima. Roddy, get your cousin some coffee, will you? And let me introduce you to Brian Edwards.'

The huge sandy-coloured man in the corner of the room raised his hand, but made no move towards her.

'Hi,' he said, in a relaxed voice, eyeing her with a thoroughness she did not think entirely polite. He was wearing a blue suit, with a bright yellow silk tie loosened at the neck. Cosima took the china cup and saucer which Roderick offered her, filled with milky coffee from a gilt cafetière on the sideboard, and sat down. The chairs were ornate and uncomfortable, with shiny seats. As a child she had occasionally been allowed into her uncle's study to choose a book or to play with the green and brown globe which stood near the window seat, and she had always liked the room. It seemed more peaceful than the rest of the house, and the pictures – most of them Stella's paintings – reminded her of home, although only one of them was actually of Mallingford: a smudgy autumnal view of the house, with the little green pond in the foreground. She noticed that it was still hanging in its old place, above Sir Nicholas's wide mahogany desk.

'Cosima's here on her father's behalf,' Tom said, drawing up a chair next to hers. His proximity was reassuring, as if they were on the same side of the battle lines, although he did not actually look at her. 'As we explained to you, Brian, Gerald Deighton's not in the best of health, which is why he can't be with us today.'

'Yes, poor bugger,' said Brian cheerfully, swallowing his coffee. 'Can we start, then, now we're all present and correct? I've got to be back at Canary Wharf by lunchtime.'

'Certainly,' said Sir Nicholas, sitting behind his desk. 'I think you're probably best placed to summarize the situation, Tom, aren't you?'

'Sure thing,' said Tom. From his briefcase he took a sheaf of glossy reports, spiral-bound in grey plastic, and began to pass them around the room. 'As you'll see from the business plan, I've gone into a couple of options. I gather that in theory public money might be available, but I don't think we want to go that route. For one thing, it would limit the potential for recouping our investment, and we'd lose time waiting for decisions to be made. I'm not familiar with how these bodies work, but if it's anything like the States they aren't exactly quick off the mark.'

Cosima looked at the amber lip-print on the rim of her coffee cup. She had a strange feeling of dissociation, as though she were watching herself sitting in this opulent room with these slickly dressed men. Tom's deep confident voice was to her as indecipherable as music. She noticed that his wiry brown hair was beginning to curl over his shirt collar, as though it needed cutting. Not for the first time she wondered what it would be like to touch his hair, to feel it spring up against her hand like the coarse grass of the Mallingford lawns.

'I propose two things,' he was saying. 'We set up a charitable trust, the Stella Deighton Foundation, the Mallingford Trust, whatever you want to call it, to deal with the restoration of the property. Then we set up a limited company which would handle the profit-making side: painting classes, courses in interior design, and so forth. That should give us maximum tax benefits without restricting our options. As you'll see from the plan, Brian has agreed to make a sizeable donation in order to get things up and running. He'd also like the option to buy thirty per cent of the shares in the limited company when we set it up.'

There was a moment of silence, during which Sir Nicholas looked across the room, first at his son, perched in the window seat, and then at Brian Edwards. Brian was drinking his coffee, a faint smile on his lips.

'Well,' said Sir Nicholas, 'that doesn't sound unreasonable. What do you think, Roddy?'

Cosima thumbed through her glossy grey report as her cousin was doing, composing her face as best she could into a knowledgeable expression. The figures on the last page danced in their columns like the stately partners in an old-fashioned quadrille.

'No, it's not unreasonable,' said Roddy, in a crisp voice, 'although I think we need further discussion on exactly how we plan to set up the company. In a rather less – ah – a less public environment.' He turned towards Brian, who was sitting beside the window, his huge legs stuck out before him on the red and blue rug, looking unexpectedly amiable. 'Family matters, you know.'

'Oh, yes,' said Brian, easily, 'I've already gathered

that there's a problem with the old man. You don't actually have rights to the house, do you?'

'Well, technically we *own* the house,' said Roddy at once. 'So in that sense, yes, we do have rights to it. Unfortunately my great-great-grandfather in his wisdom saw fit to give Gerald the lease of the place for his lifetime.'

Cosima was aware of her uncle glancing sharply at Roderick, as if in warning. Then, in a smooth voice, he said: 'Sir George – my great-grandfather – was a patron of sorts to Stella Deighton. That's how we come to own several of her best paintings.'

Sir Nicholas gestured to the picture of Mallingford above his desk. Cosima looked up at it once more. She suddenly remembered how, when she was a child, she had stared at the picture for minutes on end, half believing that if she concentrated her energies powerfully enough she could transport herself into the limits of its frame, and be back home again. When she was small she had never quite been able to understand why, if you wanted something badly enough, you could not make it happen by an act of will.

'Oh, no,' she heard Roddy saying, in a jovial voice, 'we have Cosima's word on that; don't we, little cousin?'

'What?' said Cosima, surfacing.

'Brian was asking whether Gerald would disrupt proceedings. But he's well disposed to the whole venture, isn't he?'

'Yes,' said Cosima, who could feel her face turn hot and red.

'Of course,' Tom put in swiftly, 'this is a risk, at all levels. It's going to involve a hell of a lot of expenditure, as you'll see from our budgets. Not just to get Stella's studio into a fit state for visitors, but to make sure we can feed and water them to the kind of standard they'll expect. Later on, sure, we may be able to use the house, but of course that would mean further investment. And although I think we're all reasonably confident that we've tapped a market here, we're none of us psychic. I mean, who knows? we might suddenly go into recession.'

Both Roddy and Brian barked with laughter at this idea.

'Fat chance, my son,' said Brian. 'Fat chance. I for one will be up shit creek if we do.'

'Tom has a point,' Sir Nicholas said, soberly. 'Personally I can't see how the boom in property can be sustained for any length of time, and Lord knows what will happen then. I think, though, we're all agreed that this is a risk worth taking.'

'Oh, yeah,' Brian said, in a nonchalant voice.

'Well,' said Tom, 'what we're suggesting is an exercise to test the water. We've worked out how much it would cost to give the studio a facelift: nothing structural, just a lick of paint to make the place presentable. Shouldn't take more than a couple of months to do. Then we'll have an open day to launch the trust, early in September, for the local community and a hand-picked bunch from the art world. That should give us an opportunity to see how the land lies. We'd probably get press interest, too. Brian's offered to pay half the event costs as an act of goodwill. So we just need to know today if you'll match his funding, Sir Nicholas?'

Through his half-moon spectacles Sir Nicholas was examining the figures which had so resolutely defied Cosima's understanding. He said nothing for a moment, staring down his long fox-like nose at Tom's report.

'Well, fair's fair,' he said, at last. 'It makes sense for us to share the burden. And I agree it's better to start with a small-scale exercise before we jump in feet first.' He looked at Tom over the top of his gilt glasses. 'You would oversee the project, Tom, would you?'

'Oh, sure,' said Tom. 'I mean, obviously I have other clients to service. But this is top of my agenda.'

'As long as you keep a tight rein on the budget, that's the main thing,' said Roddy. 'Isn't it, Brian?'

Brian took no notice of this remark. He put down his coffee cup and stuck out his jaw. Cosima noticed that it was beginning to run to fat, like a bulldog's.

'Mind you,' he said, 'I'd better make it clear here and now that if the open day doesn't pan out I'll want to review my position. I haven't got money to burn; although you try telling that to my wife.' He gave a brief shout of laughter. The other men smiled politely.

'Oh, if the open day doesn't pan out we'll all be thinking again, never fear,' said Roderick. 'Well, Brian, I think that's probably all we need to discuss for now. The rest, as I say, is family business. I take it we're not planning to sign any papers at this stage?'

'Nah,' said Brian. 'Gentlemen's agreement, don't you think? We'll shake on it. That's how the best deals are done.' He put out his vast paw and pumped briefly but energetically at Roddy's hand.

'Thank you for your time, Mr Edwards,' said Sir Nicholas. He rose to his feet although he did not actually move from behind his desk. 'I look forward to seeing you in due course. Roderick will see you to your car; won't you, Roddy?'

Roddy nodded at his father, and he escorted Brian from the room. For a moment Sir Nicholas, Tom and Cosima all looked at the door which had closed behind them.

'Well,' said Sir Nicholas languidly, 'I suppose we can't afford to be squeamish if we want new money to invest. Cosima, my dear, would you like some more coffee?'

'Thank you,' said Cosima. She noticed that Tom was grinning as he took her cup to be refilled, but she was not sure why. 'I'm sorry if I seemed stupid just now.'

'Not at all,' said Sir Nicholas. 'I'm quite aware that this isn't an easy position for you.' He took off his half-moon spectacles and folded them up. 'How is your father, by the way? And William? How is William?'

'They're all right,' said Cosima, in a grudging voice.

'Roddy tells me that your brother's rather a shy boy. Doesn't have much to say for himself,' said Sir Nicholas. Cosima shrugged.

'I suppose so. He's very interested in machines. That's his big thing at the moment.'

'Oh?' said Sir Nicholas, curious. 'I wonder who he gets that from. He's still having lessons from the housekeeper, isn't he?'

'From Morag, yes,' said Cosima. She was silent for a moment; then, abruptly, she said: 'I don't want them to be left out of this, you know. William and my father. I want them to benefit.'

'Of course,' said Sir Nicholas. 'They will benefit. But at this stage I think it's much better for them to benefit through you, don't you?'

Tom brought Cosima her coffee and put one hand reassuringly upon her shoulder. She could feel the warmth of it through the gleaming inappropriate satin of her dress.

'Sir Nicholas and I had a talk while we were waiting for Brian Edwards to arrive,' he said. 'We've come up with a couple of ideas I think you should hear.'

As Tom was speaking the door opened, and Roddy walked briskly into the room, clapping his hands together.

'Congratulations,' he said. 'Brian's quite a find. I do like to see a businessman who's prepared to stick his neck out.'

'Personally,' Sir Nicholas said, in a fastidious voice, 'I think he's a monster. But a wealthy monster, which suits the present purpose. Roderick, we were explaining to Cosima her financial position.'

'Ah,' said Roddy, pouring himself more coffee. 'Have you told her about the job yet?'

'What job?' said Cosima.

'I was coming to that,' said Tom. He leaned towards

Cosima, his hands on his thighs, as though he could by the sheer size of his frame shut the two Courtneys from her view. His eyes, close to, were brown, with flecks of green in the iris. 'We think that the Mallingford Trust, or whatever it's called, should employ you on a formal basis. I've made provision in the figures for a paid administrator, and I don't see why it shouldn't be you. That way you'd have a salary of your own, even if it wasn't much. And you wouldn't have to slog away in the vegetable garden all the hours of the day.'

'Oh,' said Cosima, startled. There was a silence.

'You don't seem enthusiastic, my dear,' said Sir Nicholas, in a gentle voice.

Cosima swallowed, so painfully that she felt the whole room could hear it. She tried to imagine what Gerald would say when he knew she was on the Courtney payroll.

'It's just—' she began, 'well, I can't see how I could *use* a salary. Except for myself, which isn't the point.'

Carefully Sir Nicholas rearranged three of the objects on his large mahogany desk: a fountain pen, a crystal paperweight and a silver-framed photograph of Lady Courtney as a young woman. Then he said: 'Let me be candid with you. It's obvious that we can't wait much longer if we're going to save Mallingford from becoming completely derelict. But we as a family cannot countenance the notion that your father should gain directly from any investment that we make. We'd rather see the place burn down.' There was a faint note of apology in his voice as he said this. 'That's why it's so important for you to take an active part in our plans. In a certain sense you speak for Stella.'

'You mean,' Cosima heard herself say, 'if I play ball you'll turn a blind eye to the fact that Gerald might possibly profit from what we're doing?'

'Oh, come on, little cousin,' said Roddy. 'Don't be so prickly. We're trying to do you a good turn. If you're earning some money at least you can make sure that whatever happens Gerald doesn't end up dossing on the streets.'

'Roddy, shut up,' said Sir Nicholas, in an infinitely weary voice. 'That is the most unhelpful thing you could possibly have said.' He pushed back his chair and stood up. Cosima watched as he came to sit on the corner of his enormous desk and leaned towards her. 'I can see, Cosima, that we're forcing you into the real world perhaps before you're ready. In the real world, I'm afraid, you have to make decisions based on what is expedient, not necessarily what you believe is right. Do you understand what I mean?'

'I think so,' said Cosima. She felt herself mesmerized by her uncle's pale blue eyes, so like and so unlike her mother's, trained upon her like a pair of search-lights.

'What makes it very hard for you, Cosima,' Sir Nicholas went on, still looking at his niece, 'is that nobody else in this situation wants exactly what you want. That's why you have to make the decision yourself. I realize you feel compromised by the idea of taking our money. But I believe that this is the best way of salvaging what's left of Mallingford, and it does at least give you the opportunity of helping your father at the same time. You have to trust me on that.'

Cosima said nothing, but threw a sudden desperate glance in Tom's direction. Noticing this, Sir Nicholas drew himself upright.

'Why don't you go away and give the matter some thought?' he said, in a more casual voice. 'We don't want to press you into a commitment that you'll regret, Cosima; really we don't. Tom will drive you home, and you can have a think about it.'

'Hey,' objected Roderick, 'I was going to take Cosima back to Mallingford.'

'Oh, I'm sure Tom doesn't mind. It's more or less on your way, Tom, isn't it?'

'More or less,' said Tom.

'No, it isn't,' said Roddy; but Sir Nicholas took no notice.

'Let me know what you've decided in a day or two, eh, Cosima?' he said. 'You can always telephone me. Or Tom, if you'd rather.'

Slowly Cosima got to her feet. 'Yes, all right,' she said. 'I don't mean to be awkward, it's just—'

'You need time to think. Of course,' Sir Nicholas smiled at her. 'It's been delightful to see you anyway, my dear, after so long.'

'Thank you,' said Cosima, allowing herself to be ushered out of her uncle's study towards the staircase. One of the dogs, a ragged black spaniel, was trotting across the hallway towards the dining room.

'Roddy,' said Sir Nicholas, 'go and get rid of that bloody animal, will you? You know your mother hates having lunch in a room that stinks of hound.'

'All right,' said Roddy, grudgingly. 'I'll come and see you soon, little cousin.'

In the porch Sir Nicholas shook hands first with Tom, then with Cosima. 'Well,' he said, 'we'll speak soon, yes?'

They walked in silence towards the car. Tom unlocked the passenger door, and held it open.

'Where do you want to go?' he asked, as he climbed into the driver's seat.

'I don't care,' said Cosima. 'Let's just get out of here.'

'OK,' said Tom, pulling on his safety belt. He swung the car round with blissful ease, and sped along the drive away from Courtney Park.

'Handsome place,' he said, as the gold façade of the house dwindled in his driving mirror.

'Yes,' said Cosima, in a forbidding voice. She put both hands up to her face, and rubbed her eyes. Tom glanced across at her.

'You've smudged your eyeshadow,' he said.

'I don't care,' said Cosima. She stared through the windscreen at the fields unfolding around them, the silken ears of green-gold barley, the dazzling yellow flowers of rapeseed. In the distance she could see the tower of the village church near Mallingford. 'There's a bridge just round the corner here,' she said. 'Can we stop for a minute?'

'Sure,' said Tom. 'Whatever you want.'

He drew up on the grass verge just before they reached the bridge, which was humped and narrow. Cosima opened the car door and climbed out, carefully, to avoid the clumps of wilting nettles.

'Ouf,' she said, with a great sigh, as though she had been deprived of oxygen for the last hour.

'Are you OK?' asked Tom. He followed her as she marched towards the bridge. It crossed a small, fast-flowing stream which meandered between the fields towards the river Ouse. Cosima, in her lavish cream dress, flung her arms across the stone walls and leaned forward.

'Are you OK?' said Tom, again. He laid both hands on the parapet, which was rough with lichen. Cosima stared into the stream, the shallow waters eddying around the pebbles. One or two shadows, which might have been fish, darted from side to side.

'It was your idea, wasn't it?' she said, at last.

'The job? Yes. I suggested it to Sir Nick, and he really liked the idea.' Tom paused for a moment. 'He's fond of you, you know.'

'Of course he's fond of me,' said Cosima. 'He thinks I'm a Courtney.'

'Well, and he's quite clear that you should get your share when we set up the company. You and William.'

There was a defensive note in Tom's voice, as if she had accused him of reneging on a promise. Cosima gazed for a moment at the gliding shadows in the water. Then she said: 'The point is, I can't simply do nothing, can I? You think that by doing nothing you're not making a decision, but it isn't true. Even if I said no to my uncle, it doesn't mean things will stay as they are.'

'No,' said Tom, carefully, 'it doesn't mean things

will stay as they are. Something will change, whatever you do. The house might crumble. Your father might get sick. Or something quite different might happen. But you're right: things won't stay as they are.'

'So I might as well do it, mightn't I?' said Cosima. A beech leaf had caught in the pebbles now, and formed a wake in the stream's flow. 'I might as well accept the Courtneys' money, and hope for the best.'

Tom did not speak. Cosima, who had expected him to say at once, yes, you should, twisted her head so that she could look at him. He too was staring into the stream, frowning. At last he said: 'Don't you trust Sir Nicholas?'

'Tom,' said Cosima, gravely, 'he told me in so many words not to trust him.'

'I guess so,' said Tom. 'He seems a decent fellow to me, that's all. He's got your interests at heart.'

'My interests, yes, possibly. But not Gerald's.' She gave a slight crooked smile. 'That's why, you see, I have to think about it. Because in the end I'm responsible.'

'Well, maybe, except that your father's a grown man—'

'Come on. You know that's not the point.' Cosima gripped the stone parapet with both hands and leaned back. 'I am going to say yes, you know. I am going to take the money. And the consequences. I need a breather first, that's all.'

They both watched as the current dislodged the beech leaf, and towed it through the water until it was out of sight.

'Cosima,' said Tom, at last, 'there was one thing your uncle said, about nobody else in this situation wanting exactly what you want.'

'Yes?' said Cosima. Tom reached out and took her hand, still lying on the parapet. He turned it palm upwards and, to her astonishment, kissed it. She could feel his mouth soft and slow against her skin.

'Well,' he said, 'I think I do want exactly what you want.'

Cosima stood transfixed for a moment, her hand still clasped in his. The memory of the kiss seemed like fire in her bloodstream. Then she thought of Kate, in her glorious green dress, frolicking across the courtyard at Mallingford. Gently she pulled her hand away.

'No, Tom,' she said, quietly, 'I don't think so. Come on. We'd better get moving. You've got to drive back to London this afternoon, haven't you?'

Chapter Sixteen

Stella went to see Sir George on a stormy wet morning at the beginning of November, to ask him for the money to send Gerald to London. Despite the blustery weather she came from Mallingford on her bicycle, and by the time she arrived her clothes were hopelessly rumpled beneath her waterproof cycling cape. In this state of disarray she rang the doorbell at Courtney Park and waited for the maid to admit her.

Courtney Park was now emphatically the domain of Alicia. Violet, once her rival and companion, had seven years before married a wealthy timber merchant from Lewes, and become the mother of three boisterous sons. The marriage was, in Alicia's view, a social disaster, rendered more deplorable by the fact that Violet seemed very happy. She did not appear to mind the fact that she had married beneath her, and she exuded the unmistakable aura of sexual contentment. Alicia herself had grown portly and indomitable in the service of the Courtney dynasty. Her ambitions were focused entirely upon her son, who was at Cambridge, dabbling in Classics and learning to row. She continued to mistrust the tenant of Mallingford, though on the whole her antagonism towards Stella had softened; not least because it was evident by now that Sir George would not take it into his head to propose marriage to the woman, and in any case she was rather too old to produce offspring who might challenge the patrimony of Alicia's adored Charles. Her only regret – at least, her only acknowledged regret – was that Sir George did not appear to feel particularly warmly towards his grandson. She knew, however, that this lack of affection would not prevent Charles inheriting the Courtney estate and so she did not trouble herself over her father-in-law's eccentricities.

Nevertheless Alicia felt a stab of anxiety when she caught sight of Stella, shaking out her wet cape in the hall of Courtney Park. From the top of the stairs she watched as the maid showed the visitor into the downstairs cloakroom where she could tidy herself before seeing Sir George. She noted coolly that Stella had aged since she had last glimpsed her in the village, the lines scored more deeply from nose to mouth, the cross-hatching more pronounced around her eyes. There was in her face an unhappy determination which Alicia – herself unhappy, herself determined – found disturbing. She would have liked to intercept Stella on the staircase and ask what she had come for, but of course that was impossible. Alicia had never done more than tilt her head courteously in Stella's direction if ever their paths crossed, and she had no intention of condescending so far as to speak to her now. The moment she heard the cloakroom door open she whisked away into her own upstairs drawing room, not for the first time wishing that the walls of Courtney Park were thin enough for her to eavesdrop upon Sir George's business.

Stella, meanwhile, unaware of Alicia's presence, was steeling herself for her interview with her landlord, just as she had done nearly fifteen years before when she came to negotiate for the lease of Mallingford. For all the warmth and ease of their friendship she felt nervous at visiting Sir George on his own territory. As the maid showed her into his study she was conscious of her hands tightly clenched in the pockets of her coat.

Sir George was standing at the window, next to the green and brown leather globe, looking out across the storm-buffeted garden.

'Stella, my dear,' he said, 'how nice to see you. You don't visit me often enough, you know.'

Stella smiled. Although as a rule she had little imaginative awareness of other people's feelings, she had all the same registered the *tendresse* which Sir George had nurtured for her. She watched him cross the room, leaning rather heavily on his stick.

'How is Cloris? And my young friend Gerald? I've been – ah – laid up for the last few days: I haven't seen much of him. All right, is he?'

'Yes, he's all right,' said Stella. 'Although – it's actually because of Gerald that I've come. I hope you don't mind.'

Sir George raised his eyebrows at her, cradling his stick between both hands as he sat down. Stella for the first time noticed how ancient those hands were, the veins raised and gnarled like tree roots, the skin mottled with liver spots.

'Of course not,' said Sir George. 'I have a great affection for my young friend Gerald; you know that.'

Stella pulled her chair round so that she was facing the old man. 'I'm concerned for his future,' she said. 'It's no life for a boy, out in the country with two middle-aged women. Of course, both Cloris and I have done our best to give him an occupation of some kind, but he needs more than that now.'

A glimmer of a smile appeared on Sir George's face. 'And so you want him – apprenticed in some way?'

'I want him to go to art school in London. He has always had a gift for painting, ever since he was a small boy: I recognized it at once. And there is only so much that I can teach him.'

'Ah,' said Sir George. He shifted his weight in the chair. Stella felt a pang of fear.

'Do you not agree that it would be best for him to go?' she said.

Sir George paused for a moment; then: 'Yes,' he said, 'yes. I'm sure that you're right. Especially since, as you say, he has a gift. Although Cloris tells me she thinks his talent is for ceramics.'

189

Stella gave Sir George a careful confiding smile. 'Cloris is a little biased in that respect,' she said.

'Ah,' said Sir George again. 'And you think London, do you?'

'Of course. London or Paris: there's nowhere else for a first-rate artist to study.'

'And Paris you can't afford?' said Sir George.

Stella gazed across at her benefactor. 'I can't afford London,' she said, simply. 'That's why I've come to you.'

Sir George leaned forward and raised himself upon his stick. Laboriously he made his way back towards the window.

'I hope,' said Stella, 'that you're not offended?'

Sir George fluttered his hand in a brief movement of deprecation. He gazed out for a moment at the neat lawns, the windswept trees, the fountain turned off for fear of frost. At last he said: 'What do you wish me to do? Would you like me to give you a certain sum for safe keeping, on the boy's behalf? Or would you prefer it if I made provision for him in another way? An allowance, something of that kind?'

Stella held her breath in the sheer wonder of getting what she wanted. It was a moment or two before she could speak at all; then, essaying thoughtfulness, she said: 'Perhaps an allowance. That would encourage him to learn independence.' As she spoke she felt, for the first and only time, a twinge of guilt that she was so blithely playing God with her son's life; but the guilt was at once transformed by the peculiar alchemy of Stella's nature into self-righteousness. She was, after all, doing Gerald a service, buying for him a future at the risk of her own dignity. He should be grateful, she thought, firmly, when she had left Courtney Park and was careering along the windswept lane back to Mallingford; he really should be grateful.

Gerald *was* grateful; indeed, he was ecstatic. He ran about the house in a frenzy of excitement, throwing into Stella's old trunk all his clothes and a vast assortment of objects he wanted to take with him to London, despite the fact that he would not leave the house until after Christmas. Stella's plan was to enrol him at the Slade, where she herself had studied, and to find him rooms nearby where he might get his breakfast and his dinner. To her own surprise she felt as excited by the plan as Gerald himself; although in her case it was because his departure was now a decided thing, and its imminence seemed to alter the whole atmosphere of Mallingford. She had not felt so alive since she had first brought her lover home to Sussex.

Only Cloris did not share the general enthusiasm.

'It's terribly good of Sir George,' she said, carefully, to Stella, as they were drinking thick black coffee one night after dinner in the sea-green drawing room. 'But don't you think he's rather young? He's only just seventeen.'

'Oh, nonsense,' said Stella, lighting a cigar. 'You and I were independent at seventeen, weren't we, darling? And it did us no harm.'

Gerald, too, gave Cloris no satisfaction. He seemed to have lost all interest in the pottery, and on the few occasions when Cloris wheedled him into helping with what had been joint commissions he was quite unable to concentrate on the work in hand. He ruined a set of candlesticks by trimming too much clay from their bases, and when Cloris asked him to take his turn stoking the kiln he wandered into the studio and let the fire go out.

'But I thought this was what you wanted to do,' she said, almost in tears, not so much at the disaster to the firing as at Gerald's capriciousness. He looked at her, widening his grey eyes with sudden candour.

'Oh, no. I've always wanted to paint. Of course I've wanted to paint,' he said, in a nonchalant voice, as though this were something too obvious to need discussion. Cloris turned her face away because she was so afraid that she would cry. The phrase, thankless child, echoed in her mind.

'Well,' she said, in a stiff, schoolmarmish tone which she used to control the trembling of her voice, 'I hope you've been over to Courtney Park to thank Sir George for his generosity.'

'Oh, yes.' said Gerald casually. 'I have. He's very pleased for me. Is that all, Cloris? Can I go now?'

Both Cloris and Sir George were at Lewes station to see Gerald off. It was a very cold, very bright winter's day, and the station master had lit the stove in the waiting room; but Gerald, looking absurdly young in a tweed overcoat, insisted on staying outside so that he could see the first plume of smoke as the train appeared. Cloris lent her arm to Sir George, who seemed frailer than ever, bony and shrivelled as an elderly cicada. The whiff of coal made her feel nostalgic for her old vagabond life. She was accustomed to being the traveller, not the staid figure left behind on the platform, waving an ineffectual handkerchief. In the distance she heard the judder of the train and the long plangent note of its whistle.

'Here it comes!' whooped Gerald, with a glee he was much too ingenuous to hide. Cloris gave Sir George's arm a squeeze. She had of course been invited to go to London, but to Stella's surprise, since Cloris was normally avid for such escapades, she had refused. I've got too much work to do now I don't have Gerald to help me, she had said, the note of reproof barely suppressed in her voice. Both women knew that there was more to it than that, but neither, for the present, sought to delve deeper. If Stella had been asked, she would have said, confidently, it'll be all right once we have the house to ourselves.

The station master helped Gerald to heave his trunk into the guard's van; then the boy came pelting along the platform to rejoin his mother. They stood shoulder to shoulder, two golden-haired grey-eyed seraphs, both their faces alight with anticipation. Gerald's cheeks were flushed with effort, Stella's with the cold.

'Well,' said Gerald, 'goodbye.'

Cloris watched as Sir George manfully shook hands with his protégé. Then, conscious of the need for propriety in so exposed a place, she put up her cheek primly to be kissed, first by Stella, then by Gerald. Unused to such manoeuvres, Gerald bent clumsily forward, and she felt the coolness of his boy's mouth as it touched her neck, just below the ear. She gave a start.

'Sorry,' said Gerald, at once.

'Darling,' said Stella, 'I'll see you the day after tomorrow. Goodbye, Sir George.'

'Goodbye,' said Sir George. 'Good luck.'

There was a flurry of steam and of whistles. Gerald leapt into the carriage and put out his hand impatiently to his mother.

'Come *on*,' he said, tugging her towards the open door.

Arm in arm, Cloris and Sir George stood on the platform until the train had disappeared. Neither of them spoke. As the old man renewed his grip on her wrist Cloris was conscious of a dreadful sense of loss, communicated to her by some unearthly method, like telepathy or osmosis, all the more powerful for being silent. In fact Sir George was thinking of his dead sons. They too had left from this platform, bright-faced, impatient, looking far too young for the life ahead of them; and he had never seen them again. The notion that he had seen Gerald for the last time loomed in the distance with a dark, almost tangible certainty, like the figure of death itself.

As for Cloris, she could still feel on her neck the shock of the boy's inept kiss. It had awakened in her skin nerves which she had thought entirely becalmed by her years of domesticity. In the morass of emotion which Gerald's departure had engendered she was aware of a terrible new excitement.

Chapter Seventeen

'So you think we'll be ready for Thursday?' said Tom to Morag, the housekeeper, as she was showing him to his room. He had been put in the attic once more, next to Cosima. The room had gable windows, thrown open in the August heat, and there was a wooden bed with honeycomb blankets and an old patchwork quilt.

'I don't see why not,' said Morag, who had insisted on carrying his brown calfskin bag upstairs. 'I admit I thought those students would be a waste of space, but they've really put their backs into it.'

'Great,' said Tom. 'I'm looking forward to seeing the place. How's Gerald?'

Morag shrugged. 'Up and down. He seems very excited about the open day, though. I always said to Cosima that he'd come round to it in the end.'

Tom took his bag from Morag and slung it onto the bed. Then he opened the heavy gilt clasp. 'I've brought you these,' he said.

From amongst his clean clothes he unearthed two bottles of champagne, which in London had seemed the most appropriate house gift he could bring. Now he wished that he had loaded the car with something plainer and more serviceable, fruit or cake or fresh pasta from Old Compton Street, to relieve Morag of the task of catering for a houseful of hungry workers. The three art students from Gerald's class had moved into Mallingford to help refurbish the outbuildings. They slept, dormitory style, in the old stables, and ate – voraciously, according to Morag – three times a day in the kitchen.

'Oh,' said Morag, accepting the bottles, 'thank you. I'll take them downstairs. You know where the bathroom is, don't you?'

'Sure,' said Tom. From his bag he pulled a sheaf of cotton polo shirts. 'Where's Cosima?'

'In the studio with the others, I expect. She's trying to do her bit. Especially as she's the only one who's actually getting paid for this.' Morag gave a sniff, swinging the champagne bottles like clubs as she did so. When Tom did not answer, she said: 'Well, I'll leave you to unpack. Lunch is at one o'clock.'

'Terrific,' said Tom. He watched as Morag's squat figure retreated through the door. Then he turned to examine his room, in what seemed to him now the great luxury of solitude. After their conversation at Glyndebourne Kate had begun tacitly to assume that they would spend every night together, in his flat or hers, and he could not remember when he had last slept alone. She had even cleared a space in her stuffed wardrobe where Tom could leave clean shirts and weekend clothes. What's more, she had started bringing home estate agents' details of pretty maisonettes in Fulham, which she would leave on the coffee table where Tom could not fail to spot them. He knew that he ought to be panicking at these blatant signals of intent, but to his own surprise he felt nothing: only a dreamy passivity, as though all this were happening to somebody else. When, occasionally, he did experience a tremor of alarm at the joint future Kate envisaged, he thought only, I won't do anything yet, I'll wait till I go to Mallingford, I'll have time to think about it then.

He gazed for a moment through the attic windows at the overgrown courtyard and the dark green trees; then he started to unpack, pulling open the drawers of the little wooden chest beside the door. Both the chest and the headboard of his bed had been painted in swirling pastels, depicting a powdery blue skyscape of birds and clouds. On the bedside table stood a glass tumbler of flowers, an apricot-coloured rose with a few sprigs of honeysuckle, which someone – Cosima, perhaps – had brought to make the room more welcoming. With his forefinger Tom stroked the velvety petals of the rose. He wondered if it were indeed Cosima who had put the flowers there. Carefully he slid his soft pile of shirts into the top drawer, which had been lined with scented paper.

When he had unpacked he made his way outside into the courtyard. The brilliance of the sun struck him like a steely shield of light. As he crossed towards the stable block he noticed that the door of his Porsche, parked on the gravel next to Morag's rusty green van, was half open. In the driving seat there was a small shadowy figure, intently leaning over some unseen object.

'Hey,' said Tom. 'What are you doing?'

The figure stiffened, as though about to take flight, but then clearly thought better of it. Instead a shaggy tentative head appeared above the roof of the car. It was Cosima's brother, William.

'You don't mind, do you?' he said. 'I didn't think you'd mind.'

'Mind what?' said Tom, opening the passenger door. He saw that on the boy's knees, its face towards him, was a large black and white cat. Around the animal's neck were draped the headphones from his personal stereo.

'Salvador really likes listening to music,' said William. 'See.'

He pressed the start button on the stereo, and held the padded headphones up to the cat's triangular ears, holding them in place with both hands. Salvador flinched, and tried to toss his head; but when he found he could not free himself he settled once more upon William's knees, closing his eyes in an expression of absolute resignation.

'See?' said William again, this time with a note of triumph in his voice.

'I guess you're right,' said Tom. He slid into the passenger seat, next to the boy and the cat. 'I'm not sure he's crazy about my taste in music, though. What's he listening to?'

'I can't pronounce it,' said William, holding up the plastic cassette box. The tape contained highlights from Puccini's operas. It had been a birthday present from Becky, offered rather snidely since she herself thought Puccini vulgar. Tom laughed.

'Maybe we should try him with something else. Jazz or something.'

'His favourite's *Clair de Lune*. He always comes into the studio if we put that on the gramophone. Only the record's cracked now and it keeps playing the same bit over and over. Most of our records are cracked, actually.' William stopped squeezing the earphones, and at once the cat shook them off, gently, so that the chrome semicircle slid down his neck. Then he twisted his head and began fastidiously to lick his front paws.

'Yeah,' said Tom. 'Looks to me like Puccini gets the thumbs down.'

'Oh, well,' said William. He unthreaded the wires which had become entangled in the cat's limbs. 'You know, I wanted to keep your cassette player last time. When you left your car here before. Only Cosima told me not to.'

'Did she?' said Tom. 'Well, I guess you can borrow it while I'm staying here, if you want.'

'Can I?' William eyed the cassette player with new respect. 'Honestly?'

'Sure. I won't really need it. You're interested in machines and things, aren't you? Cosima said you were.'

'Well, yes, I am, except that we haven't got many machines here. It's really boring. I've taken the kitchen clock to pieces about a million times.' William paused for a moment; then he reached under the car seat and brought out Tom's mobile phone. 'I don't know what

197

this is, but it's been bleeping a lot. Every couple of minutes it's been bleeping.'

'Oh, God.' Tom put his hand out for the phone. 'You didn't try taking this to pieces, did you?'

'No,' said William, indignantly. 'Anyway, it's a sealed unit. What is it? A telephone?'

'Yeah,' said Tom. 'That's right. A mobile phone. I guess I'd better check for messages.' He flipped open the mouthpiece and pressed the redial button to call his office in London. After three rings he heard Shabnam's voice. It sounded cool, bored and infinitely far away, as though she belonged to a different planet.

'I've been trying to reach you,' she said, rather testily. 'Alastair wanted a word before his meeting, but he's left the office now.'

'I'm sorry. I forgot to take the phone into the house with me. What did Alastair want?'

'He needs to know if you're still on course for the open day next Thursday. We've had a call from a freelance journalist who wants to come along and cover it for the *Sunday Times*.'

'Hey, that's terrific,' said Tom. 'Yeah, tell him we're still on course. I haven't finished inspecting the place yet, but everything seems fine. I'll call you pronto if there's a problem; OK?'

'OK,' said Shabnam, and crisply she hung up. Tom clicked the phone unit shut, conscious of William's enormous eyes fixed upon him in fascination.

'You can have a go with it if you like,' he said. 'The call rate's really expensive, that's the only thing.'

William shook his head. 'There's no point,' he said. 'I don't know anyone with a telephone. Do you want me to take you through to the studio? They're all in there. Gerald's in there too, although he isn't doing any work. He just sits and talks.'

'Yeah, sure. I guess I'd better go and have a look.' Tom slipped the telephone into the pocket of his chinos. 'Have you been helping them out, William?'

William lifted Salvador from his knees and lowered

the cat to the ground, where it at once scampered off towards the house.

'A bit,' he said, 'when I've got time. Someone has to keep the garden going, in case this doesn't lead to anything.'

Tom followed William towards the stables, chastened by the boy's matter-of-fact assumption that the endeavour might after all fail. The sun felt liquid on the back of his neck. He wondered what state Gerald was in, whether his excitement about the open day was a good sign or an ominous one. No doubt the old man would relish the prospect of meeting a *Sunday Times* journalist. Tom grinned to himself, picturing Gerald as he trotted out his grandiose tales of Stella and the Bloomsbury group, of Frederick Courtney's suicide in the upstairs drawing room.

'I take care of the hens, too,' William was saying. 'You know, collect the eggs and make sure they're not getting broody. You really have to understand hens to do it properly. Cosima's useless. She looks in all the wrong places.'

They had reached the door of the stables now. The wood had been daubed a glossy bright green, and a piece of corrugated paper was propped against the wall, on which the words 'wet paint' had been thickly scrawled in the same colour.

'Well,' said William, 'there you are.'

He hesitated for a moment and then, before Tom could say anything to stop him, he made a small skipping movement and ran off, at high speed, towards the clump of chestnuts. Tom's last glimpse of the boy was as he swarmed up the trunk of one of the trees, towards some invisible haven in the lower branches.

Tom took a breath, and gingerly put his hand to the latch to push open the shining door. 'Hello?' he called out experimentally.

'Tom! Ah, there you are. Morag said that you'd arrived.' It was Gerald, enthroned in a canvas chair like a film director's. Despite the heat he was wrapped

199

in a blue woollen blanket, and he wore on his head an extravagantly wide-brimmed hat. Wafting between his fingers was, not the usual hand-rolled cigarette, but a small cigar. Its sweet pungent smell seemed to enhance the other, stronger smell of paint which filled the room. 'Quite a transformation, don't you think?'

'Sure,' said Tom, looking about him. The objects which had been littered around the stables were now heaped in the middle of the room, shrouded in a vast dust sheet, and the walls, once stained and pallid, were a dazzling white. Two lanky young men stood on ladders slapping emulsion on the ceiling, while at their feet a girl in a paint-spattered blue smock was stirring the contents of a large tin with a bamboo stick. There was, as yet, no sign of Cosima.

'Stefan, Marcus,' said Gerald, waving his cigar in the direction of the ladders, 'this is Tom Nettleship. Our marketing consultant. He's come to see how we're getting on.'

The phrase 'marketing consultant' was weighted with irony, as though it were an absurd title for anyone to have. The young men looked up from their work and stared at Tom, faintly hostile.

'Actually,' said Tom, returning the stare, 'I've come to lend a hand.'

'Yeah?' said one of the boys – the one with long dark hair – sardonically, eyeing Tom's neat expensive clothes. Both Stefan and Marcus wore torn jeans and baggy shirts, smeared with white paint.

'Yeah,' said Tom. 'As a matter of fact, I'm quite accomplished with a paintbrush.'

'I'm sure you are, dear boy,' said Gerald, grinding his cigar stub on the dusty stone floor. 'Don't let Stefan wind you up. The nymph sitting on the floor, by the by, is Kirsty. Kirsty, say hello to Tom.'

'Hello,' said the girl in the blue smock, glancing up from her tin of emulsion. Tom noticed that her face was extravagantly made up, her eyes lined in dark blue, her mouth a deep unnatural purple which he

200

found morbid against the pallor of her complexion, like a vampire's.

'Now, Tom, make yourself useful and put another record on the gramophone,' Gerald said, in an imperious voice. 'Then you can come and help me decide which of these photographs we want to put up. I've got a whole box of them here.'

'OK,' said Tom, crossing to the table where the old wind-up gramophone stood. On the turntable was an ancient 78 of Dinu Lipatti playing Chopin waltzes. 'Any requests?'

'Let's have that Irish singer doing "Danny Boy",' Kirsty said. 'I like that one.'

'Oh, Kirst. You're so wet,' said Stefan, vigorously smacking his paintbrush across the ceiling. A gobbet of emulsion landed on Kirsty's blue shoulder.

'Hey,' she said, but without heat, as though she were used to this kind of thing. 'Careful.'

'OK,' said Tom. '"Danny Boy" it is.' He slid the Chopin into its thin paper sleeve and began to sort through the records on the table. As William had said, most of them were cracked or chipped, and they were all unexpectedly heavy. At last Tom found John McCormack singing the 'Londonderry Air'. Carefully he lowered the great silver needle onto the disc. A hiccuping noise at once emerged from the gramophone, followed by the scratchy swell of an orchestra.

'Now,' said Gerald, 'pull up a chair and look at these. Cosima found them in one of the cupboards when we were clearing up. I thought we could do something with them.'

Tom sat at Gerald's elbow. On his knees the old man had a marbled box file, open to reveal a heap of old photographs and some press cuttings. The photograph on top of the pile showed a woman at once recognizable as Stella, standing by the pond at Mallingford. She was smiling, but the smile seemed at odds with the wariness of her eyes, as though it had been pasted onto an otherwise sombre face.

'My illustrious mother,' said Gerald. 'You recognize her, of course? This was taken when she was in her early forties. Just after I went to art school.'

Tom picked up the photograph. 'Who took it?' he asked.

'Oh, Cloris, I should think. Cloris Bohun, you know; the potter. Stella gave her a box Brownie to keep her amused. She needed things to amuse her, did Cloris.' Gerald riffled through the contents of the box file. 'Do you want to see what she looked like? There's a snap of her somewhere which Stella must have taken. Ah, here she is. This is Cloris.'

He handed Tom a dog-eared picture of a small plump sweet-faced woman, who had one hand raised to push the hair back from her forehead. She was wearing a flowered summer dress with buttons down the front, its tight waist emphasizing the curves of her figure.

'She's pretty,' said Tom. 'Is she the one Stella loved?'

'Yes, that's right. She's the one Stella loved. The only one she really loved.' Gerald took the picture back and picked up a folded piece of newspaper. It was yellow and leathery with age. 'My mother's obituary in *The Times*. You'll see they gave her plenty of column inches. You and I won't get obituaries like that, eh, Tom?'

'I guess not,' said Tom, who had never thought about it. He was unfolding the press cutting when, with a rattle, the studio door slowly opened and Cosima came in backwards, carrying a tray of mugs in both hands.

'Tea break,' she called, to the room at large.

'Brilliant,' said Stefan, putting down his brush. He and Marcus began at once to descend from their ladders. Tom stood up.

'Hi, Cosima,' he said. Cosima looked across at him and blinked.

'Hello,' she said. Like the art students she was wearing shabby stained clothes, but there was something different about her, something smarter, which

Tom could not at first identify. Then he realized that she had had her hair cut. The ragged tail of hair which he remembered had become a smooth tawny bob, ending just above her shoulders. Tom was simultaneously aware of how well it suited her, and of how much he missed her old tangled mane. He had a sudden image of the bright locks of her hair tumbling as the scissors sheared through them.

Cosima put the tray on the floor and, picking up one of the mugs, brought it across to her father.

'There you are,' she said. Gerald rose to his feet, throwing off his blanket as he did so. The photograph of Cloris Bohun fluttered to the ground.

'Cosima, I wish you wouldn't treat me like an incontinent old fool,' he said. 'Leave it on the tray, will you? I'm quite capable of fetching it myself when I'm ready. I don't need you to wait on me hand and foot.'

'I'll have it, Cos,' said Marcus, in an undertone, taking the mug from Cosima's hand. Tom noticed that the boy was more or less the same height as Cosima, and that they were both wearing white collarless shirts which hung loose outside their trousers. He felt an abrupt stab of jealousy.

'It's looking terrific in here, Cosima,' he said, in a loud voice, to draw attention to himself. 'You must have been working really hard. All of you.'

'Oh, well . . .' Cosima gave a shrug, and drank from her mug of tea. 'The boys have done most of it. And Kirsty, of course. A couple more days and we'll be ready to start putting up pictures. Have you seen the photographs we've found?'

'Yeah,' said Tom. 'They're great. We can really do something with those.' The last note of the 'Londonderry Air' died away, and the gramophone began once more to hiccup. Tom lifted the needle off the record and slotted it back into place. Then he said: 'The good news is we might have a journalist from the *Sunday Times* at the open day. I got a call through this morning. Of course, it isn't definite; nothing's ever definite with the press. But it seems to me like there's a good chance of it.'

'The national press, eh?' Gerald, who had been poking around among the paint tins, looked up at once, a sharp gleam of pleasure in his eyes. Tom wondered why there was always something frightening about Gerald's face when it expressed pleasure, as though his joy by definition meant misery for someone else. 'That's excellent. I knew we'd get the local rags, but the *Sunday Times* is excellent.'

Cosima looked at her father, doubtfully. 'I hope we're ready, that's all,' she said.

'Oh, we'll be ready. Of course we'll be ready,' said Gerald. 'Ready and waiting.' He drew his blanket around him with his long fingers and sat down once more, gracefully. 'Cosima has managed to persuade her uncle to lend us some pictures. You haven't told Tom that, have you? Now she's on the Courtney payroll she can do what she wants.'

'It's not like that,' said Cosima, in a weary patient voice, as though she had had this argument before. Gerald took no notice.

'I'm not saying there aren't some advantages to having a daughter in the pay of the enemy,' he went on suavely, opening his small square tin of cigars. 'These, for instance. I haven't had one of these for ten years. The food's better, too. I was getting very tired of Morag trying to be clever with minced beef and cabbage.' He struck a match and lit his cigar. 'No, at least Cosima's putting it about, I'll say that for her.'

Kirsty, who was eating a chocolate biscuit, gave a nervous giggle and promptly choked.

'For God's sake, Kirst,' said Marcus, thumping her on the back.

'Tell her to drink some tea,' said Stefan. 'Kirst, have some tea.'

While Kirsty was still coughing, her blue mascara liquefying around her eyes, Cosima turned to Tom. 'Come and see the rest of the studio,' she said. 'We've finished the decorating there; it's just a question of what we do next.'

Tom followed her past the geometric screens to the other, brighter section of the stable block. The walls were white here too, dazzling in the sunshine. On the floor there were two sleeping bags, each with a cushion at one end.

'We haven't put any of our pictures up yet because we're waiting for the ones from Courtney Park,' said Cosima. 'Roddy won't let us have them until Wednesday. He's worried about security.'

'Well, I guess he has a point,' said Tom, still looking at the sleeping bags. Why were there only two? Surely even if Kirsty were sexually involved with one of the boys they would hardly share a narrow sleeping bag every night. So which of the three students slept elsewhere? And if so, where exactly did they sleep? Aloud he said: 'Do you know which paintings they're planning to lend? That way we could do a plan of where we'd like to hang everything, to save time when they arrive.'

'Yes, I know most of them,' said Cosima. She too looked down for a moment at the pair of sleeping bags. Then she said: 'Kirsty's been spending the night in the house. On the sofa in the upstairs drawing room. The floor in here's too hard for her.'

'Oh, right,' said Tom. He felt at once ashamed and relieved at having his thoughts so expertly read. Cosima was standing close enough for him to smell the vanilla scent of her skin. It reminded him of their descent from Chanctonbury, of her breasts pressed against him as she supported his weight, of her flushed grave face as they made their way down the steep path.

'The boys don't seem to mind it, though,' she said, and she walked slowly towards the door which led to the dovecote. 'Do you think this is all OK?'

'I think it's great. Much better than I'd hoped. The photographs are a real find, too: they'll go down a storm with the sort of people we're inviting, I bet you.

Maybe we should hire some exhibition stands so we can display them properly.'

'Yes, all right,' said Cosima. She was standing by the door now, her hand outstretched to open it. 'Do you want to have a look at the dovecote? We haven't done much in there; I think we really need a professional art restorer to look at it. We've just cleaned up a bit.'

Tom's eyes met Cosima's. In that moment he knew that if he followed her into the dovecote he would not be able to stop himself kissing her. Already it seemed that he could feel the sleekness of her newly cut hair, taste the sweetness of her mouth. His heart was beating very fast.

'Yes,' he said, casually. 'Why not?'

Cosima pushed open the glass door. Then, just as Tom stepped towards her, the phone in his pocket gave a sudden discordant shriek.

'Shit,' he said.

'What's *that*?' said Cosima, startled.

'An infernal bloody gadget my boss made me buy,' said Tom, pulling out the phone. 'It's a mobile phone. Hello?'

'Tom? Is that you?'

'Hi, Alastair,' said Tom, in a resigned voice. He might have known it would be Alastair.

'Did Shabby tell you the good news? About the *Sunday Times* man?'

'Yes, she did. Is that why you're calling?'

'Don't sound so disapproving, Tom. I thought you'd be pleased to hear a voice from the civilized world. Unless you were doing something you shouldn't?'

'Of course not. I'm here to work, remember?'

'Of course you are. Listen, Tom, I think I might come down for this open day myself. As long as we're not too busy.'

'I don't think it's strictly necessary—' Tom began.

'No, I know, but it might be fun. All right, Tom. I'll let you get back to work. *Ciao*.'

Tom clicked shut the phone and looked up at Cosima, who was still standing beside the door.

'Who was that?' she asked. Her steady grey eyes were quite without guile, as though she had no idea what he had been thinking. Perhaps she really did have no idea what he had been thinking. Inwardly Tom groaned.

'Alastair. The guy I work for. He says he wants to come down for the open day.'

'Well, that's not a problem, is it?'

'No,' said Tom doubtfully. What if the day's a failure, though? he thought; I'll look such a fool in front of Alastair. But he could not admit to Cosima, of all people, that the open day might not succeed: she had staked far too much upon it. A shadow of claustrophobia fell across his heart.

'What's wrong?' asked Cosima. Tom breathed out.

'Nothing,' he said, in a resolute voice. 'Come on: let's go and have a look at those photos your father's got. See which ones we can use and get the whole show organized. If Alastair's coming down I want this to be perfect.'

Chapter Eighteen

Once Gerald had left Mallingford Cloris descended abruptly into a mire of boredom. She finished the commissions she had taken on while she and Gerald were working together, but she could not be bothered to go out and seek new ones. With each day that passed she got up later and later, and spent longer and longer mooching around the house in her Chinese silk dressing gown. Nothing that had charmed the old Cloris seemed to charm her now. She let her bicycle rust in the February storms, and when Stella received invitations to dinners and operas and weekend house parties (she was now at the height of her fame and popularity) Cloris would shrug, and say, you go; I'll stay here, thanks all the same. The only person she saw with any pleasure was Sir George Courtney, who, despite his obvious frailty, kept up his visits to the house, avid for news of Gerald.

Stella was appalled by the recalcitrance of her lover's spirit. She had imagined that she could by sheer willpower recreate the first honeymoon period of their affair, and it had never once occurred to her that her plan to expel her son from Mallingford would backfire so irrevocably.

'But what is it you miss?' she would demand, as Cloris sat listlessly in the drawing room, smoking one Turkish cigarette after another. 'Half the time Gerald was horrible to you. And you have me, darling. Isn't that enough?'

Cloris gave a sigh. She was, in her state of malaise, eating too many sweets, and her figure had blown up like a curvaceous Rubenesque balloon.

'I miss having someone to work with,' she said. 'No, it's more than that. I miss having Gerald to work with. You never would believe how gifted he was. How exciting it was to see him learn, and start having ideas of his own. Well, that's what I miss.'

'But I could work with you, if that's what you want,' said Stella, earnestly. 'There are things we could do together. Things we could teach each other. Surely?'

Cloris stubbed out her cigarette and half-heartedly lit another. 'All right, darling,' she said, without enthusiasm. 'Whatever you like.'

For the next few months Stella cast about for things she might share with Cloris. There was no question of Stella herself learning pottery: she knew that she had no flair for it, and even in her painful desire to appease her lover she was not prepared to compromise her talent and make a fool of herself. But she bought books on sculpture and carving, and ordered a set of chisels so that she and Cloris could practise together; if, that is, Cloris ever took off her dressing gown and came into the studio. She bought a camera, too, as a present for Cloris on the fifth anniversary of their meeting. The camera amused Cloris for a few weeks, and she took lots of pictures of the gardens and of Stella, but then she put it to one side and went back to smoking endless cigarettes in the green drawing room. She had lost all interest in the running of the house, and since Mrs Maybrick was now too infirm to come more than once or twice a week, it seemed to Stella that they lived on a permanent diet of cold mutton, tea, stale cake and caramel toffees.

At the back of Stella's mind was the terrible recurrent fear that she was failing to satisfy Cloris. Since their first night together she had rather taken her lover's sexual prowess for granted, assuming that the raptures Cloris provoked in her must somehow be mutual. In her naïveté Stella had never quite lost the notion that technique was unnecessary in the presence of love, and that you could translate emotional passion into physical pleasure simply by your sincerity in wishing to do so. Even now, she could not countenance the idea that Cloris, whom she loved so much, was bored by her in bed: the thought was inadmissible. She allowed herself to fret instead that her beloved, who had after all had a number of heterosexual affairs, might be hankering after men. This fear lodged in her brain like a poison, all the more potent because she never had the courage to challenge Cloris on the point. But she grew increasingly to rely on the lassitude which kept Cloris at home, a well-kept secret, unexposed to the thrills and threats of their wider social circle. She gained great private solace from the fact that the only men Cloris was likely to see were Sir George, who was too old to be a danger, and Gerald, who was far too young.

Gerald himself, meanwhile, had settled happily enough in London. He wrote from time to time, comic high-spirited letters which covered six or seven pages in his huge scrawl. His spelling was execrable. Cloris would read the letters to Sir George as they sat over the tea table, and it was often only when she heard these readings that Stella understood Gerald's endless stream of jokes. Now that her son had gone he seemed more like a stranger than ever. She was relieved that he showed no inclination to come home to Mallingford during his vacations: his social life in London was so much more exciting. He had fallen into a hard-drinking, hard-talking group of left-wing activists, rather older than himself, who were constantly plotting expeditions to Spain or the Soviet Union. None of these plots ever came to anything, but Gerald at eighteen found the prospect of them as intoxicating as the endless bottles of thin gassy beer which his new comrades drank. He was intoxicated too by the women in the group, clever brassy girls who wore tight jerseys and berets and pillar-box-red lipstick. They all treated him as a delicious sort of pet, stroking his coarse golden hair and exclaiming at his beauty; although to

Gerald's disappointment these fondlings never led to anything more.

It was on a May morning, nearly eighteen months after Gerald had first left Mallingford, that Stella went up to town for a meeting at Agnew's, the art dealers, and for an evening party in Fitzroy Square. As usual she had asked Cloris to go with her, and as usual Cloris had said no, on this occasion pleading the excuse of a headache. Cloris had reached that phase of depression where it was much easier to be alone than to endure her lover's hopeful attempts to jolly her along. Indeed, as soon as Stella had gone she climbed out of bed and dressed herself properly for the first time in days. The weather was warm and sunny, and her solitude stretched before her like a glorious beach on which she could sprawl and frolic, undisturbed by the weight of Stella's attention. She made herself a bowl of milky coffee at the kitchen range and then she crossed the courtyard to the studio.

Cloris had not set foot in the studio for several weeks, and all around her she saw the marks of her neglect: uncovered clay which had dried out beyond use, flecks of rust on her potter's wheel where she had failed to clean it properly. The room was dominated by two huge lumps of granite which Stella had had delivered a few days before. Her idea was that they should each carve the image of the other, not for sale, but for display in the Mallingford gardens, a semi-mythological testament to their love. Cloris stroked the grainy surface of the stone thoughtfully, almost pityingly. It's no good, she thought, with sudden clarity; this isn't working. For a moment she stood quite still, trying to see into the future. I could be here for the rest of my life, she thought, and she glimpsed a tunnel before her, airless and narrow, as though Stella's great love had trapped her under glass. On the furthest boundaries of her mind, barely acknowledged, hovered the thought that she would like a child, and that unless she moved on soon it would be impossible.

211

It might be impossible in any case; she was already forty-one. Darkness clutched at her, a sense of terrible waste at the time she had lost cocooned here at Mallingford. Then she heard a voice she had not heard for so long she barely recognized it: her own voice, which had guided her through the erratic penny-pinching years before Stella rescued her. Go, said the voice, just as it had done that night in St Ives when she left Matthew Gardiner, go. You've got money in the bank, which is more than you've ever had before. Don't stay to argue or explain. Go.

It took Cloris all afternoon to pack, not because she had much to take, but because she was so scrupulous about what she should leave behind. The camera, for instance, which had been Stella's anniversary present: was that strictly speaking hers, or had she gained it under false pretences, and should she let Stella keep it? There were books, too, and endless scarves and shawls and jewellery and trimmings for her hats, all of which Stella had given her. Cloris, who had by force of habit continued to think of herself as a light traveller, was dismayed by the sheer quantity of objects she had acquired, too cumbersome to carry in her flight, too precious to abandon without regret. In the end, as the drawing room clock struck six, she decided that she would have to stay one more night and leave in the morning. Stella would not be back until lunchtime tomorrow; she had plenty of time to make her escape. In the luxury of this postponement Cloris went down to the kitchen and cut herself some bread and cold mutton. Then, on impulse, she opened one of the bottles of wine they kept for special occasions, a smoky white Burgundy which she particularly liked. The alcohol made her sentimental. I ought to walk around the estate, she thought, as she poured herself a second glass, have one last look at the gardens before I leave.

It was a beautiful evening, the Downs richly green, the stone of the stable block warm in the sunlight.

Cloris leaned her back against the wall, her wineglass in her hand. She had put a record on the gramophone and left the door open, so that the music filtered through into the open air, as mellow as her mood. Like so much else the record was a gift from Stella, who did not herself care for music but who was happy to pander to her lover's taste for popular songs. Dreamily Cloris began to dance to the music, humming under her breath.

'*Who stole my heart away . . .*' she sang, swaying and swooning around the empty courtyard, her face tilting towards her imagined partner's. And then she turned her head towards the house and found herself looking straight at Gerald. Their eyes locked, just as they had done all those years ago, when they had stared at one another through the studio window like a pair of wrestlers.

'Gerald!' said Cloris. 'What are you doing here?' She felt rather foolish at being caught in the middle of her solitary dance. Gerald said nothing. He let fall the knapsack he was holding, crossed the courtyard, lifted Cloris bodily against the wall and kissed her. It was a kiss so violent that for a moment Cloris was not sure she would survive it. Then all the old hungers at once revived, and she could not imagine how in their ferocity she had ever suppressed them. They made love for the first time like that, against the wall; then they went upstairs and made love three times in the brass bed Cloris had for so many nights shared with Stella. Gerald seemed not to notice the half-filled suitcases littered across the floor. He noticed nothing except Cloris's body and his own desire.

'Demon lover,' said Cloris, touching his mouth as they lay on Stella's defiled sheets. Gerald gave his great glittering laugh.

'I know,' he said. 'It's sacrilegious, isn't it? That's what makes it exciting. Kneel for me, Cloris. I've got to have you again.'

Only gradually did Cloris learn why it was that

Gerald had appeared so unexpectedly at Mallingford, that evening of all evenings. He had been thrown out of art school for punching one of his fellow students, 'a bloody fascist' according to Gerald himself, who had maintained that the government should support Hitler as the best insurance against invasion by the Russians. He told the tale with such glee that Cloris suspected he had punched the other boy more from aggressive high spirits than from political conviction, but she did not say so. It was dark now; they had gone downstairs to the kitchen to find something for Gerald to eat, and to finish the white Burgundy.

'They'll take you back, I'm sure,' Cloris said. She was wearing her Chinese dressing gown, her bare feet rubbing against Gerald's beneath the table. The boy gave an elaborate shrug.

'Maybe they will, maybe they won't. It doesn't bother me either way; I haven't been learning much.' He stood up and from the shelf brought down a hurricane lamp. Cloris watched him as he took a taper to light it.

'What are you doing?'

'You'll see. Come on, Cloris.'

Seizing her hand he led her out of the house across the yard towards the dark mass of the stable block. A breeze had blown up, which whipped the hem of Cloris's dressing gown about her bare legs. They were nearly at the door of the dovecote before she realized what Gerald was about.

'We can't,' she said, shrinking away from him.

'Why not? She'll never know. She won't be back until tomorrow; you said so yourself.'

Gerald turned the huge iron key in the lock. It occurred to Cloris how like Stella it was to leave the key there, as though her very prohibition, like a sorcerer's spell, were enough to stop anyone invading the dovecote. Perhaps there was a spell on the place; or a curse. Cloris in the cool May evening shuddered.

'Gerald,' she said, 'don't.'

'Too late for don't,' said Gerald, with a laugh. 'Much too late for don't.'

He opened the door and stepped inside, the lamp held high. Timidly Cloris followed him. The air in the dovecote was chilly and dank; like the sour air she had imagined herself breathing, trapped in the cocoon of Stella's passion. It was a moment or two before she had the courage to look around her. The first thing she saw was her own face, painted on the wall. The trustful expression in the brown eyes stabbed at her so that she nearly cried out in shame at her treachery. Then she saw that instead of a human body Stella had given her the plumage of a bird, with great snatching talons like knives. The talons were tipped darkly with red. Cloris caught her breath as though she had been injured.

'Now,' said Gerald. 'Here.'

He had seized her arm and was pulling her towards the damp earthen floor. Cloris tried to resist.

'I can't,' she said. 'It isn't possible, Gerald. I can't.'

'You have to,' said Gerald, loosening her sash and pulling open her silk dressing gown. The sight of her own nakedness, so easy to expose, reminded Cloris that she was too far gone in her betrayal of Stella for there to be any point stopping now. Besides, she was hungry for Gerald once more. She let fall the dressing gown and subsided to the ground, taking the boy with her.

He had just begun to thrust into her when Cloris heard a voice, calling her name. It was Stella, come home early from London. She froze, impaled where she lay on the dovecote floor.

'She won't know we're here,' hissed Gerald. He made no move to withdraw from her. 'Just keep quiet. She won't look for you here.'

Stella's voice grew louder, with a terrible throat-note of despair, like an Irishwoman's keening. She must have seen my suitcases, thought Cloris, she must know I'm planning to flit. Her heart was thumping so hard and so fast that it hurt. She listened for Stella's footsteps which seemed to be coming nearer and nearer; and then at last she heard the fruitless scraping of the iron key in the lock, and the creak of the door as Stella pushed it open.

Chapter Nineteen

'Careful,' said Cosima. 'These are hired. We have to pay if we break them, you know.'

It was Wednesday evening; the night before the open day. Cosima and William were unpacking wineglasses from a cardboard box, ready for the glamorous terrifying unimaginable hordes who would descend upon them in the morning. The studio, which still smelt powerfully of new paint, was dim in the summer twilight. Around the room stood the exhibition stands Tom had acquired, shadowy against the white walls, on which Cosima had laboriously stuck up photographs and press cuttings and bits of text which she had copied out in black italic script. Here and there were jam jars with ribbons around their necks, containing rather wormy roses from the garden, pink and cream and scarlet.

'So what will the caterers bring to eat?' asked William. He was lining up the glasses on a trestle table which Tom had also hired for the occasion.

'Finger food,' said Cosima, knowledgeably, although she was not at all sure what the phrase meant. Tom had consulted her before making any decisions about the open day, but she was still unclear of the precise arrangements. She knew that the day was meant to start at half past eleven, and that they had thirty-five people and four journalists coming, and that Morag had agreed not to stir from Gerald's side until the last visitor had gone, but apart from this she had only a vague notion of what would be happening. I reckon Sir Nicholas should be the only person to say anything, Tom had declared, in an authoritative voice, that would be less inflammatory than having your cousin Roddy or your father speak; and Cosima had a bizarre vision of a room full of people passing plates and glasses and nodding in absolute silence, while her uncle Nicholas's voice boomed above them.

She had spent the afternoon hanging the pictures from Courtney Park, assisted by Stefan and Marcus; Kirsty, who was feeling sick, had gone to lie down on the sofa. There were eight paintings in all, including the picture of Mallingford from her uncle's study, another of Stella's self-portraits, and a painting of Cloris Bohun in a diaphanous yellow-ochre gown. Sir Nicholas had suggested putting some of Cloris's pots on display, too, and he had persuaded a collector friend to lend a bowl and a pair of candlesticks for the day. Tom had just driven into Lewes to fetch them.

'Will there be any left over?' William asked, surveying the regimental columns of glasses on the white damask cloth. 'Food, I mean.'

'I don't know, Will. I've never done anything like this before,' Cosima said. 'You won't do a bunk tomorrow, will you? After all, I bought you those clothes specially so you'd look all right in front of people.'

'Hmmno,' muttered William, indecipherably. Then he said: 'You quite like having money, don't you, Cos?'

Cosima stiffened, as though she had been accused of something. 'It makes a change, that's all,' she said. 'What's so terrible about that? It's not as if I grabbed it for myself. I spent most of it on you and Gerald.'

'Yes, I know,' said William, patiently. 'That's what I mean. That's what you like about it.'

'You're being annoying,' said Cosima.

'No, I'm not. I'm just telling you. It won't wash with Dad, though. You know that, don't you?'

'Yes,' said Cosima, in a gloomy voice, 'I know that.' She lifted the hem of the damask cloth and slid the empty box under the trestle table, out of sight. 'I just hope he enjoys the open day so much that he decides to forgive me. He'll like talking to journalists, even if he has to put up with having Roddy and Uncle Nicholas here. Where is he, Will? Has he gone up to bed?'

'No, he's in the dovecote, with Stefan and Marcus. He said he wanted to talk to them.'

'Oh? What about?'

'Tomorrow, I think. I don't know.' William adjusted one of the wineglasses and eyed the rows carefully. 'I've finished this, Cos. Is there anything else to do before it gets dark?'

'No, I don't think so,' said Cosima, tucking her crimson shirt into her trousers. The shirt was made of cotton but it had been washed so often that it felt as smooth and as fragile as silk. 'Let's go and see if Tom's come back.'

Outside the air was crisper, with the first fresh hint of autumn. In the half-light the hills seemed dark and enormous, looming like Titans above the valley in which Mallingford stood. The trees rustled in the wind. Then, in the middle distance, Cosima saw a tall figure walking towards them from the house. It was Tom.

'Hiya,' he said, relaxedly. His face had changed in the few days since he had come to Mallingford. It was browner and smoother, as though the lines around his eyes and mouth had somehow dissolved. Cosima, who was still brooding about her father, felt a great rush of affection for him.

'Did you get the pots?' she asked.

'Yes,' said Tom. 'They're in the car. I thought it would be safest to leave them there overnight. It's too dark to see where to put them now, anyhow.'

'Tom,' said William, 'what's finger food?'

'Stuff you can eat with your fingers. Canapés, you know,' said Tom. 'Actually, I came to ask if you wanted some champagne. Morag's taken a bottle into the dovecote for Gerald and the boys, but there's more in the kitchen. What do you say?'

'Yes, all right,' said Cosima. She was grateful that Tom had not suggested they join the party in the dovecote, although at the same time the idea made her feel sad.

'What about you, Will?' Tom said. 'Do you want your first taste of fizz?'

'No, thanks. I think alcohol's pretty disgusting, really. Champagne is alcohol, isn't it? No, I'm going to make sure the hens are all right.'

'OK,' said Tom. 'See you later.'

There was nobody in the kitchen, but Morag had left a champagne bottle, three-quarters full, in a pail of cold water on the floor. She had also lit the oil lamp which hung over the table, creating a wide golden pool of light. Cosima took some glasses down from the cupboard and wiped them with a red chequered cloth.

'Here we are,' said Tom cheerfully, pouring champagne. It frothed violently in the glasses and then subsided. 'Here's to success tomorrow.'

'Cheers,' said Cosima, chinking her glass against his. Their eyes met for a moment and then sheered away. Cosima suddenly remembered how Tom had kissed her hand as they were standing beside the bridge on their way back from Courtney Park. I want exactly what you want, he had said. The words stirred inside her, a sensation at once familiar and incomprehensible. She took a mouthful of champagne, feeling it sizzle against her tongue.

'Let's go outside and drink this,' said Tom, picking up the bottle. 'It's a really lovely evening.'

The moon had risen now, full and silver. In silence they walked across the courtyard towards the little pond. Together Tom and William had cleared the mud and the weed, and the pond now had a good two feet of water in it, reflecting both the moon and the menhir-statues which stood under the willow trees. In the dusk the two statues looked more solid and more sinister than ever.

220

'These are so weird,' said Tom. He put down the champagne bottle at the foot of the larger menhir. 'When did Stella do them?'

'Just before the Second World War. She was on her own here then, I think; it was after Cloris moved on. I'm really not sure what they're meant to be. I always thought they must have something to do with the war, but Gerald says Stella was never very aware politically, so it can't be that.'

There was another silence. Cosima drank some more champagne, and stared at the lopsided face of the moon in the water. Then Tom said: 'Are you OK about tomorrow?'

'Nervous,' said Cosima.

'Yeah, sure. I'll be there, though, remember. I'll make sure it all goes just fine.'

Cosima nodded. 'I've found something of my mother's to wear tomorrow. Silk, I think. Do you want to have a look? To see if it's all right?'

'Sure,' said Tom, 'in a minute. It's so beautiful out here. Look at the moon on the dovecote walls. I'm really in love with this place, you know. I can understand why your father would do anything to keep it.'

Cosima said nothing. The champagne was beginning to go to her head, a delicious, faintly shivery feeling. She put the palm of her hand on the cold granite of the smaller menhir. In her nostrils was the damp but pleasing smell of the pond.

'You've finished your drink,' said Tom. 'Let me give you some more.'

'All right,' said Cosima, holding out her glass. As if in a trance, she watched as Tom leaned to pick up the dark green bottle. The wind drew faint ripples on the pond, shirring the surface of the water.

'You know, I'd really like to stay out here all night,' said Tom. 'Preferably with you.'

Cosima heard herself laugh, a nervous shimmer of a laugh which seemed to come from someone else.

'I don't think we'd be much use tomorrow if we did that,' she said. Tom gave a small grimace, and swallowed the last of his champagne.

'Come on, then,' he said. 'Let's go and look at this dress of yours.'

The kitchen was still empty, the oil lamp burning above the table. Cosima took a candle from the shelf and struck a match to light it.

'You haven't seen my mother's old room, have you?' she said. They were climbing the stairs, and it seemed suddenly terribly important that she should keep talking, that she should not for a moment allow silence to fall. 'It's more or less the way she left it. None of us could face sorting it out, after she died. And I've always felt a bit strange about it because I sometimes used to play in here when I was a little girl, and she got really angry with me for messing up her clothes and things.' She opened the door to Annabel's room. 'I remember once finding her make-up in the drawer and putting loads of it on, and I spilt face powder all over the carpet, and she came back from London while I was in the middle of it and walked into the room, and—'

'Cosima,' said Tom. He was standing in the middle of the floor, looking at her. The candle fluttered in her hand, making the shadows leap. Tom leaned forward, took the candlestick from her, and put it on the dressing table, without ever moving his eyes from her face. Cosima felt as though she were fixed to the spot, like the statue-menhirs, quite incapable of movement. Even the hand which had been holding the candle remained frozen where it was, in mid-air. She tried to say, don't you want to see my dress? but the words would not come out.

'Cosima,' said Tom again, and he kissed her, so suddenly that it took her breath away. For a moment she was afraid she might suffocate; then he let her go and pulled her more gently into the compass of his arms, her face nestled against his huge chest.

222

'I've wanted to do that for the longest time,' he said. She could feel the rumble of his voice against her cheek. The warmth of his body was immediately and infinitely comforting. 'What about you?'

'I don't know,' said Cosima, in a small voice, her face still hidden. Tom's polo shirt smelt of soap powder and warm skin. She felt his hand stroking her hair. Still gently, he tipped her chin upwards and kissed her on the mouth, softly this time, with an intensity she found bewildering. His lips tasted sweet, his breath touched with the fragrance of champagne.

'Hey,' said Tom, his face still close to hers, 'you're a great kisser. Did you know that?'

Cosima said nothing. She would have liked to go away and contemplate alone the experience of having been kissed for the first time, but she dimly knew that this was not possible. To reassure herself she clutched at Tom, pressing her face urgently against his shoulder.

'Oh, sweetheart,' he said at once. 'Come on. Let's sit down.'

He propelled her towards the dusty pink chaise longue, clearing a space among the stuffed animals with his free hand. Then he kissed her again, winding his arms around her. The bristles of his chin grated against her face, a sensation at once rough and yet somehow promising, like the subtle unfamiliar taste of a food you knew you would grow to like. A sharp feeling of triumph shot through her: triumph that she had actually made something happen, triumph that a new part of her life had begun.

'Have you really?' she mumbled, between kisses. Tom pulled his head back to look at her.

'Have I really what?'

'Wanted to do this for a long time.'

'Oh, sweetheart. Since forever,' said Tom, sliding his hands to her waist. In their embrace the crimson cotton shirt had escaped from her trousers and his

223

fingers unexpectedly touched her skin. She gave a sudden shiver.

'What's wrong? You're not cold, are you?'

'No,' said Cosima.

'Because I'm certainly not,' said Tom, with a smile, as he drew her face towards him once more. Something about the smile disturbed Cosima. It had in it a spark of complacency, almost of greed, quite unlike Tom's usual diffidence. For the first time, even as their lips touched, Cosima wondered what these kisses really meant.

'Tom—' she tried to say; but it was no good because he was holding her hard by the nape of her neck, his mouth damp and hungry against hers. She could feel his other hand on her naked back, beneath her shirt. What about your girlfriend? she wanted to ask; what about Kate?

'You're so beautiful,' muttered Tom, in a voice that was almost angry. The hand which had been grasping her neck slid to the opening of her blouse. Instinctively Cosima put up her own hand to cover and restrain it, stiffening in his arms. She was beginning to feel like a city overrun, without defenders.

'You're beautiful,' said Tom again, and dipping his head he bit her on the neck, just above her shoulder. Cosima flinched.

'Ow,' she said, in a sharp childish voice, before she could stop herself. Tom seemed to freeze for a moment; then, slowly, carefully, he let her go, withdrawing his hands. Now that they were no longer touching the room felt cool.

'What's wrong?' said Cosima, a knot of panic in her throat as she sat there among those ageing fluffy toys which had been her mother's delight.

'Nothing,' said Tom, in a small shut voice, 'nothing. Don't you worry about it.' He pushed the hair from his flushed face and stood up. 'I'm sorry if I frightened you. I guess this wasn't such a good idea after all.'

'You didn't frighten me. It's just—'

'Look, Cosima, it's OK. I get the picture.' He pulled a resigned, rather sardonic face, without looking at her. 'I'll leave you in peace. Don't worry: I can find my own way upstairs. See you in the morning.'

When he had gone, and she had heard the door click shut, Cosima sat down at Annabel's dressing table. In the freckled mirror her mouth looked red, as though she had put on lipstick and then smudged it. On her neck there was a bright strawberry-coloured bruise. My face and not my face, she thought; and then, I don't understand anything about this. And she sat staring at that stranger's face, without moving, until the candle guttered and died.

Chapter Twenty

'Good morning, Tom,' said Gerald, cheerfully, as he presided over the breakfast table. 'Ready for the big day, are we?'

Both Stefan and Marcus grinned over their plates of charred toast. Tom smiled back, although he knew the boys' grins were malicious rather than welcoming. During his stay at Mallingford he had managed to make friends with Kirsty, but Stefan and Marcus remained resolutely hostile towards him. Once or twice he had overheard them muttering about 'the breadhead', and although he pretended to be amused by the naïveté of the term, he could not help feeling hurt by their determination to dislike him.

'Oh, yeah,' he said, putting his mobile phone on the table as he sat down. The kitchen chair creaked beneath his weight. He was feeling terrible.

'You don't sound entirely convinced, Tom. Why is that? Getting cold feet at the last minute? Haven't we done enough work getting the studios spick and span for the delectation of your media friends?'

'It's not that,' said Tom. He reached for a piece of toast from the rack, although he did not really want it. 'I slept badly, that's all. Nerves, I guess.'

'Oh, dear,' said Gerald. 'Nerves. Pour me some tea, would you, Stefan, there's a good fellow? I don't know why you're feeling nervous, Tom. I'm sure everything will run to plan.'

'Oh, yeah,' said Stefan, pouring tea from the huge brown pot. 'It'll run like clockwork.'

Whenever he was with Gerald and the art students Tom felt like an outsider. It was as though the others spoke, not a different language exactly, but a dialect he could not quite follow, which constantly made him feel that he had missed the point. It had been like that when he first came to England, he remembered, before he got the hang of the British sense of humour. Wearily he prodded an empty cup in Stefan's direction. Maybe I should just go home to the States, he thought; cut my losses and go. The idea seemed savagely consoling, like an act of self-mortification.

'Is Kirsty feeling better?' he asked, pouring milk from a blue-and-white-striped jug. The milk, un-refrigerated, formed little white flecks on the brown surface of his tea.

'No,' said Marcus, 'she's still got migraine. She thinks it's the smell of paint.'

'That's a bit unlucky, isn't it, if she wants to be an artist?'

'You don't have to use paint to be an artist,' said Stefan, in a patronizing voice, as though this were a fact so obvious that only someone as crass as Tom would question it. 'A lot of Kirsty's best stuff has been collage. And fabric sculptures, that kind of thing. Hasn't it, Gerald?'

'Oh, yes,' said Gerald, who had taken a tin of small cigars from his dressing gown pocket and was lighting one of them, 'she's not without talent, our Kirsty. Has she had any breakfast?'

'Yes,' said Marcus, 'Cosima took her some, about half an hour ago. She's lent Kirsty her room, so she can rest without being disturbed.'

Tom spread butter on his toast. Cosima must have slept badly, too, to be up so early. He tried to imagine how he would greet her after last night's fiasco. His stomach lurched at the memory of his own clumsiness. Without realizing it he had presumed that if he actually kissed Cosima, crossed that daunting threshold between touching and not touching, every-thing would somehow take care of itself. It had never occurred to him that Cosima might remind him,

227

horribly, of his ex-wife Becky: the way she tensed in his arms, the way she yelped, just as Becky used to do, when he did anything even slightly rough. I don't think I can deal with this, thought Tom, reaching for the home-made jam.

'And when can we expect the pleasure of my nephew's company?' asked Gerald, drawing elegantly upon his cigar. Tom shrugged.

'I'm not sure. Not till eleven thirty, I guess, when everyone else arrives.' He and Cosima had agreed that it would be best to play down Roddy's presence at the open day, so as not to provoke Gerald. 'He might not be able to make it at all: he said he might have business in the City.'

'Oh, he'll make it. I know Roddy. He wouldn't miss this for the world,' said Gerald. He rose to his feet, gathering the slippery folds of his dressing gown about him. 'Well, I'd better make ready for the adoring throngs. What time did you say, Tom? Eleven thirty?'

'Yeah,' said Tom, 'that's right.'

'Good. In that case I shall go and avail myself of the last of the hot water,' said Gerald, and, cigar in hand, he swept from the room. Tom watched him go. It crossed his mind that the old man's behaviour was too good to be true, but it was too late to worry about that now. All I've got to do, he thought, is get through today. If I can get through today everything will be just fine. He forced himself to swallow a mouthful of toast, conscious of the inimical silence which had fallen on the two art students.

'Well,' he said, at last, 'I'd better call base camp and check that everything's OK.'

Stefan, who was refilling his mug with tea, glanced across the table.

'Do you get paid a lot for doing this sort of thing?' he asked. It was so obvious he intended the question to be insulting that Tom smiled.

'I guess so. That's how I can afford the flashy car and the mobile phone, you know. It's a tough job, but

228

someone has to do it. Excuse me, will you? I'll get better reception if I go outside.'

After the fine weather of the past week the sky had solidified to a dull milky grey. Tom stood in the yard, punching out the number of Alastair's car phone. He wondered where Cosima was. Maybe I should go and find her, he thought, get the first meeting over and done with. At least then I'll be able to concentrate. He remembered how she had thrust her head against his shoulder, and felt a sudden sharp pang of regret. Christ, Nettleship, he thought, you're such a fool.

Alastair answered the phone almost at once, sounding breathless.

'Alastair? It's me, Tom. Where are you?'

'On the M23. Where do you think? We've just passed all the plebs peeling off for Gatwick. Oh, shit.' Tom heard the blast of a car horn, long and indignant. 'Jesus. The bastard.'

'What is it?'

'Some arsehole in a white BMW cut me up. Listen, Tom, I'll put you on to Kate. Hang on.'

'Kate?' said Tom, surprised.

'Hi, darling,' said Kate, in a sweet excitable voice. 'Sally said I could come down for your little open day. She thinks it might make an interesting feature for the magazine. You know, successful woman artist and all that. The weather's not very nice, is it? Is it sunny where you are? I haven't brought an umbrella with me.'

'No, it isn't sunny,' said Tom. He wondered whether Kate's sudden desire to descend upon Mallingford had been her own idea or whether Alastair, the mischief-maker, had put her up to it. Tom could almost hear Alastair's wheedling Mephisthophelean voice. Go on, Katie, go and see what he's up to. I bet he's up to something.

'Tom, are you still there?' asked Kate.

'Yeah, sure. Listen, will you ask Alastair if the chap from the *Sunday Times* is still coming?'

'Yes, he is. He told me so this morning. Fab, isn't it? Darling, I'd better go. The line's breaking up. We'll see you in about an hour.'

Tom stood for a moment in the middle of the yard. He tried to imagine how Kate and Alastair would view the exhibition in the studio, whether they would sneer at the homely display of photographs, the stark rows of paintings, but his mind went blank. There's nothing I can do about it now, he thought gloomily, walking towards his car. As he did so he caught sight of a figure in red, moving through the trees. His heart pounded. Could it be Cosima? Treading softly he made his way across the grass towards the clump of ragged chestnuts. The leaves were just beginning to shrivel and turn with the coming of autumn. Tom watched as Cosima stopped at the foot of one of the trees and peered into the branches, evidently looking for something.

'Will?' she said. 'Will? Are you there?'

There was no reply; not even a rustling of leaves or the creaking of a branch. Cosima stood there for a moment, her face tilted patiently upwards. She was wearing a red dress covered in small white spots, with kick-pleats in the skirt, which made her look tall and graceful. Tom hesitated. He did not want to alarm her by calling out, but at the same time he was afraid that if she suddenly saw him she might feel he had been spying upon her in some lascivious fashion.

'Hi, Cosima,' he said, at last. 'Has Will done one of his vanishing acts?'

Cosima turned towards him. He noticed that her eyes were faintly puffy beneath her make-up, which for once had been skilfully applied. But she did not seem now to be angry or upset. In answer to Tom's question she nodded ruefully.

'Yes. I did think he was in the tree-house, but you can usually see the rope swinging for a while after someone's climbed it, so I expect he's somewhere else. Will's got lots of hidey-holes.' She paused for a moment, and moved away from the tree in Tom's direction. 'The really annoying thing is that I'd persuaded him to put on his new clothes: the ones I bought specially for today. And if I know Will he'll ruin them.'

'Oh, well,' said Tom. 'If he doesn't want to play ball there's no sense forcing him.' There was a silence. Cosima clasped her arms across her front, each hand holding the opposite elbow. Her silk dress was cut low and Tom could see the pale curve of her breasts. For Christ's sake, he thought, she's only eighteen; she's bound to be nervy. It's up to you to make the first move. He cleared his throat rather noisily.

'Look, Cosima . . .' he began.

'Yes?'

'I'm really sorry about last night. I was way off the beam.'

Cosima stared at her feet, in old-fashioned patent leather shoes with straps. 'It's all right,' she said, in a voice so gruff Tom could hardly hear it.

'Well, no, it's not. I should have realized that – I mean, the fact is, I'm a bit mixed up at the moment.'

Cosima looked up then, her eyes grey and luminous. 'About Kate, do you mean?'

'Well, yes, about Kate. About lots of things, I guess. I really don't know what I want at the moment. And I shouldn't be starting anything until I've got my life sorted out. It's not fair to you. I'm sorry. I'm a real stumblejohn.'

'It's all right,' said Cosima again, very softly, although Tom had a feeling that it wasn't in the least all right. She had let her head fall and was examining her gleaming shoes with unnatural concentration.

'I mean,' Tom blundered on, 'it isn't that I don't – oh, Christ, Cosima. I'm just making this worse. What I mean is, I'm really attracted to you—'

'Tom,' said Cosima, 'will you kiss me again?'

'What?'

'It's only that nobody's ever kissed me before, and

last night I was too confused to notice what it was like. And I think it's something I ought to know.'

Cosima lifted her face and gazed at him. There were two hectic streaks of scarlet upon her powdered cheeks. She looked at once embarrassed and terribly proud. In that moment it seemed to Tom that he had never wanted anyone so much in all his life.

'Oh, Cosima,' he said, and he stepped forward. Beneath his fingers the silk of her dress felt crisp and smooth. He kissed her carefully and very slowly, as though this were the paradigm of kisses, the prototype on which every other kiss they gave or received would forever be modelled. He felt her mouth open under his with a startled tenderness.

'Cosima,' he said, into her hair. The curves of her body seemed to fit with his own as if they were two halves of a whole. 'I'd give anything in the world right now to run away with you. To get into my car and just take off together away from it all.'

'We can't,' said Cosima. She raised her head and began to pull away from him. 'We ought to get back to the studio.'

Regretfully Tom let her go. 'I know we can't,' he said. Then he put out his hand and held her face for a moment, as though it were a ripe exquisite fruit. 'You're right. We'd better get going.'

As they came out from the trees Tom saw that the caterers had arrived, a pair of breezy young women in neat black skirts and frilly white blouses. They were unloading plastic pallets, covered in silver foil, from the back of a yellow estate car.

'Where to?' said one of the women, holding two of the pallets on capable outstretched arms.

'Over in the stable block,' said Cosima. 'I'll show you.'

Tom crossed to his Porsche, leaning dizzily for a moment on the blue metal. I'm in love, he thought, with sudden astonishment; and then, almost at once: God, that's all I need, today of all days. Hardly aware of what he was doing he opened the car boot and took out the cardboard box in which Cloris's pots were stored. I'll have to talk to her, he thought; tonight, when all this is over, I won't go back to London, I'll stay behind and talk to her. The idea seemed to glow in the distance, like a silvery beacon. He slipped his hands beneath the box and carried it towards the stable block.

By daylight the interior of the studio was everything Tom had wished it to be, neat and clean and fashionably simple. The caterers were laying out platters of food, still draped in clingfilm, on the trestle table. Tom carried his box through to the other half of the studio, where Stella's paintings were hanging. Cosima had done the job carefully and well, making the most of the light from the large windows, grouping the canvases so that each picture offset its neighbour. The charcoal drawing of Stella which Tom had seen on his first visit to Mallingford had been placed beside the self-portrait from Courtney Park, which in turn hung beside a reproduction of the more famous painting in the Tate Gallery. From all three it seemed to Tom that Stella's eyes, so like Cosima's, looked out, watching him as he crossed the room. A small bamboo table stood beneath the portrait of Cloris, with a cardboard sign on which Cosima in her neatest writing had put, *Ceramics by Cloris Bohun, who lived at Mallingford from 1931 to 1937*. Tom unwrapped the newspaper from the bowl. It was wide and flat, the inside a glorious crimson flecked with blue and gold. Carefully he positioned it on the bamboo table. Above him Cloris languished in her gauzy amber dress. Tom could not help thinking that she was not Stella's type: too plump, too obviously sensual for the grave ascetic woman in the self-portrait. I bet she played the field, he thought, observing the moist pink mouth and the provocative angle of her chin. Then he remembered Gerald saying, in what for him was a serious voice, yes, she's the only one Stella really loved. He wondered what had

233

happened to Cloris after she left Mallingford. I must ask Gerald, he thought, bending to unpack the pair of candlesticks; Gerald will know. It crossed his mind fleetingly that if he became Cosima's lover he could have endless such conversations with Gerald.

'Tom? Where are you, Tom?'

It was a man's voice: Alastair's.

'I'm through here,' Tom called. A moment later Alastair appeared, jauntily dressed in navy with a white piqué shirt. Even so early in the day his chin looked faintly blue, as if he needed a shave.

'Well, congratulations,' he said. 'It's not nearly as bad as I thought it would be. Rather Mediterranean, actually. I've had holiday villas in Greece that looked a lot worse than this.'

'Thanks,' said Tom drily. 'I didn't think you'd bother coming down, to be honest. Not when we've got so many fish to fry; or so you keep reminding me.'

'Now, now, Tom. Don't be tetchy; it doesn't suit you. No, I thought I deserved a jaunt. And I wanted to make sure that everyone was very nice indeed to Brian. I know you think he's an arsehole but he's worth a fuck of a lot of money, and I've got something else I want him to bankroll. It came to me in Kettners the other night: a real brainwave. Why don't we import our own champagne? Of course, we'd have to go over to Reims to pick a vineyard, but I think I could live with that, couldn't you? So this is the work of the famous Stella Deighton. It's not bad, is it? I thought it would be all squirls and whirls and blobs. No, I can't say I mind this. I don't mind this at all. Have you got anything to drink?'

'The caterers'll be bringing the wine in a minute, I guess,' said Tom. 'Is Kate here too?'

'Oh, yes. She wanted to use the lav. A rather tasty young woman in a red dress took her into the house.'

'Oh,' said Tom, disconcerted. He did not like to think of Cosima and Kate being alone together.

'All I can say is if that's Cosima Deighton I'm not

surprised you've been so keen on this Mallingford lark. Just as well I've brought Katie down to keep an eye on you. By the way, Derek Connor's due at about eleven. Our man from the *Sunday Times*, you know. I told him to come early so you could fill him in on the background. Tom, do find me a drink, will you? I'm bloody gasping. I did nearly a hundred most of the way down the M23. I think I've earned a drink.'

'OK,' said Tom. He put Cloris's candlesticks next to the crimson bowl and strolled through to where the caterers were still laying out the food. There was a large black dustbin filled with ice, from which he could see the green necks of some wine bottles protruding.

'Oh, fabulous,' said Alastair. 'I don't suppose you have such a thing as a corkscrew, ladies, do you? Fantastic.'

Kate appeared just as Tom was pouring white wine. Like Cosima, she was dressed in red: a little scarlet suit which was very wide at the shoulders and very tight at the waist. Her short skirt showed a long expanse of tanned thigh, and she had on a great deal of chunky golden jewellery.

'Hello, darling,' she said, and she kissed Tom lingeringly on the mouth. 'Alastair drove like a maniac all the way here because I said I was so desperate to see you. Wasn't that nice of him?'

'Well, I guess I can think of safer forms of gallantry,' said Tom. 'Do you want a glass of wine, Kate? Alastair's having one.'

'Oh, yes, fine, why not? Start as you mean to go on. It's obviously going to be that sort of day. Don't you think I look nice, darling? I bought this suit specially.'

'Yeah,' said Tom. 'It's terrific.' He tried to dab discreetly at his mouth, nervous in case Kate's bright lipstick had left a mark. Her kiss had eclipsed the taste of Cosima's, just as her perfume had blasted the subtle remembered scent of Cosima's skin. And yet, now that Kate was actually here, Tom was astonished to realize

235

how attractive she was, with her neat well-exercised figure and her enthusiasm and her gamine smiling face. A sense of impossible confusion churned in his stomach.

'I like the photographs,' Kate announced, sashaying past the exhibition stands. 'Stella looks a bit dour, though, doesn't she? Reminds me of the headmistress at my old school. Who's the pretty blond boy?'

'Gerald,' said Tom. 'Cosima's father. You'll meet him later.'

'Oh, I've met him already,' said Kate, airily, accepting the glass Tom offered her. 'He kissed my hand on the stairs when I was coming back from the loo. I thought he was charming.'

'Is this the nutter?' said Alastair. 'The one who wants to blow our young friend Roddy Courtney to kingdom come?'

'Oh, rubbish,' said Kate. 'He's not a nutter at all. I told you: he's a poppet.'

'Well, that's a relief. I want Brian Edwards to feel confident that we can run the show properly. No catastrophes. He needs to know that he's in safe hands. Don't snicker, Kate. This is serious: we're talking big money here. Who've you got coming, Tom? Is there a list? Terrific. Let me have a look and see who I should talk to. It's a shame all these wealthy bastards insist on spending their money on art. I can think of much more interesting things for them to invest in.'

While Alastair was examining the guest list Kate slipped her scarlet arm into Tom's. 'Come and show me Stella's pictures,' she said, making her voice deliberately husky.

'Don't be too long, though, eh, Tom?' said Alastair, glancing up from his list. 'You're on duty, remember.'

'Spoilsport,' said Kate, still clutching Tom's arm as he led her past the Art Deco screens to where the paintings were hanging.

'There,' said Tom, with pride. 'Looks good, don't you think?'

But Kate was not looking at the pictures. She was grasping Tom's elbows, her face lifted enticingly towards him.

'Darling, I've missed you so much,' she whispered. 'Give me a proper kiss.'

'Well . . .' said Tom, straining half-consciously backwards, out of her embrace.

'Come on, Tom. No-one will see us.'

'All right,' said Tom, because it was easier, and he bent to kiss Kate's glossy red mouth. As he felt the expert darting of her tongue he was conscious that this was an act of betrayal, but just who or what it was he was betraying he could not have begun to explain.

Chapter Twenty-One

The discovery of her son and her lover *in flagrante* bereft Stella of words. She could not imagine how she would ever speak to them again: what vocabulary she might use, what tone she might take. She had no language at her disposal for such double treachery. In the darkness she marched back to the house, and she sat in the bedroom she had shared with Cloris, among the suitcases spilling cashmere shawls and white lace underwear. She did not think at all about how the catastrophe had occurred, whether Cloris had started to pack before Gerald arrived, whether they had been planning to escape together, a flight fatally delayed by the impatience of their lust. She saw only the image of their two perfidious bodies, half naked on the dovecote floor.

It was nearly an hour before Cloris came upstairs to find her. She had been weeping, and her face was wet and red. Stella did not speak. She sat on the edge of the brass bed, her hands clasped in her lap, her eyes like granite.

'Gerald's gone,' Cloris said. 'At least, I think he's gone. He ran off into the trees and I can't find him.'

She looked at Stella, waiting for her to answer. When she did not Cloris began haphazardly to flip bits of clothing into her open valise, a green sleeve here, a white petticoat there. The tears ran down her face without her bothering to wipe it. Stella watched her. Gradually Cloris set about packing with greater and greater energy, as though what had begun as an embarrassed quest for something to occupy her hands had become a true purpose. Then she slipped out of her dressing gown and stood for a moment deciding what to wear. Stella looked with a curious dread at the body which had inspired in her such rapture. Cloris pulled on her clothes quickly, nimbly, the tears still flooding her cheeks. When she was dressed she stood upright and gazed at Stella. The expression on her face was at once baffled and bitter.

'Why did you paint me with claws?' she asked.

Later Stella thought of any number of answers to this question. Because you had such a hold on my heart. Because when you made love to me the pleasure was so intense it seemed to be tearing at me. Because you were to me so entirely lovable that I was afraid, and I gave you claws to disfigure you and to remind myself that you could not be perfect. For the next thirty years or more these answers and many others echoed in Stella's mind. But at the time she could think of none of them. She sat on the bed and she said nothing. Cloris looked at her for a moment, waiting for her lover to speak; then she gave a slight miserable shrug and bent to pick up her two suitcases. Stella heard her laboured footsteps as she struggled down the stairs, but she did not hear the house door open and shut.

The night passed. It was morning before Stella came to herself, hunched upon the edge of the mattress, her hat still on her head. Slowly she pulled out the jewelled turquoise hatpin and smoothed back her hair in its tight tidy bun. Her face in the mirror seemed unchanged, as though it were impossible for mere flesh to register the enormity of what had happened. She took off the light coat she was wearing and wrapped a knitted shawl around her shoulders because she felt suddenly cold. Then she went downstairs to the kitchen to brew herself some tea. It seemed to her that the whole place had about it a stunned atmosphere of disbelief, like a would-be suicide who wakes to find herself still alive. She was sure the house was empty.

Gerald meanwhile had spent the night on the studio floor. Like his mother he was quite unable to cope in any rational way with what had happened. When Cloris, trying in vain to pull her dressing gown about her, had said, what shall we do? he had crouched on his haunches thinking how slack her breasts looked now that he was no longer aroused by them. He saw in her eyes a particular gleam, not of enjoyment exactly, but of excitement, as though this were a melodrama in which they each had a lavish part to play. The idea repelled him. With one hand he scooped up the clothes which lay scattered across the dovecote floor and he ran like a freed thing into the shelter of the trees. Once there he dressed himself, and climbed up into the lower boughs of one of the large chestnuts. It was from here that he watched Cloris leave Mallingford, dabbing at her face from time to time as she hauled her two suitcases along the path towards the village. It did not occur to Gerald to stop her any more than it had occurred to Stella. There seemed to him an inevitability about her leaving: it left him alone with his true partner and antagonist, his mother.

As soon as he was sure Cloris had gone he came out from his hiding place and found his way to the studio door. He listened for a moment to the wonderful silence. Then he rolled himself up into a corner of the room where he slept sweetly and deeply for nine hours.

When he woke up the sun was high. It took him a moment to remember what had happened the evening before, and as soon as he did he had the exhilarating sense that his life's business had really begun. He laced up his shoes and he marched, whistling, into the house. Stella was sitting at the kitchen table, pouring tea from the heavy brown earthenware pot. She stared at him as though he had risen from the dead.

'Hello, Ma,' said Gerald, who had never in his life called Stella anything but Stella. He crossed cheerfully to the wooden crockery rack above the sink.

'Gerald,' said Stella, in a voice which seemed

240

cracked from lack of use, 'Gerald. I think you should leave.'

'No fear,' said Gerald, unhooking one of the green lustreware cups. 'This is my home, remember? Anyway, I've been chucked out of art school. So there's not much point going back to London, is there? I might as well stay here.'

'You can't stay here.'

'Why not? Bags of room. Besides, I've told you. It's my home. You've tried to get rid of me once. You're not pulling that stunt again.'

'I'll give you money,' said Stella, in that same hoarse voice, as if she were possessed by a devil who spoke through her lips. Gerald laughed, and reached across her for the brown teapot.

'I don't want money. I want to stay here.' He took a mouthful of the tea he had poured and at once spluttered it out. 'This is disgusting. How long ago did you make it? You'll poison yourself; not that I imagine anyone would care.' He took the pot and tipped its murky contents into the deep porcelain sink, whistling 'Who stole your heart away?' Then he filled the kettle with water from the tap.

'No,' he said, 'I'm going to stay here, you know. I'm going to sleep in your house and work in your studio. I'm going to haunt you. For the rest of your life, probably.'

Stella made a faint noise of protest and lumbered to her feet. The pained blindness of her movements made Gerald think of a hunted animal, a stag or a boar, fatally injured but still capable of damage. The sense of danger thrilled him.

'We'll kill each other,' said Stella. There was a note of appeal in her voice. Gerald smiled.

'Maybe,' he said. 'We'll see, shall we?'

The weeks which followed were the worst of Stella's life. Gerald was as good as his word: he haunted her like an incubus, sleeping in his old bedroom in the attic, rising for breakfast when she did, leaving off work when she left off. He set up his easel next to hers in the studio, and he painted whatever she was painting, stroke by stroke. When she arranged the objects for a still life, a bunch of flowers, a bowl of fruit, Gerald sat beside her and copied her. When she propped up her mirror and began a self-portrait, he sketched her face from life with exactly the same expression in her eyes. It was like being in a torture chamber, deprived of the space and light her spirit needed to thrive. Even when she was alone in bed she was conscious of Gerald breathing above her in the attic, using up the air. Once or twice she broke her usual discipline and failed to go to the studio, but that only made matters worse. If she sat in the kitchen Gerald sat there too, brewing tea and rolling cigarettes with her tobacco; if she stayed in her room he hammered on the door until she let him in, and sat cross-legged on her bed talking incomprehensibly about politics and Spain and the threat of war in Europe. The only place he seemed to avoid was the dovecote; but then, Stella could not bear to go to the dovecote either. The very scraping of the key made her sicken to the stomach.

In the meantime, because Mrs Maybrick still came to the house once or twice a week, Stella was forced to keep up the pretence that all was well. She told the housekeeper that Cloris was away for a few weeks visiting relatives, and that Gerald was on holiday. This was the story Mrs Maybrick relayed to Sir George Courtney, who was recovering from bronchitis in his vast old-fashioned bed at Courtney Park. He managed to write a gracious note to Stella, expressing his pleasure at Gerald's return, but he was not yet well enough to make the much-promised visit to Mallingford. Once or twice Stella in desperation thought she would go to him, explain to him that Gerald was tormenting her, beg for his help. But she knew that it was no use. In the first place she could not have seen Sir George without Gerald knowing and insisting on accompanying her. More important still, he would have failed entirely to understand what she meant. She knew that, wise as he was, this kind of psychological torture was beyond his comprehension, and besides, she had a feeling that Gerald had successfully supplanted her in the old man's affections. Not that she could blame Sir George: it had suited her to play on his attachment to her son, and she could hardly complain now that the tables had been turned.

It was during these claustrophobic weeks that Stella carved the statue-menhirs which stood beside the Mallingford pond. She made them from the two stone blocks once intended for herself and Cloris, as an emblem of their love. She began in part because she could no longer bear to have the blocks littering the studio, and in part because Gerald's watchfulness was inhibiting her in what she regarded as her real work, her painting. She got up particularly early to start, and managed almost an hour of solitude before Gerald, bleary and unshaven, opened the stable door.

'What are you doing, Ma?' he said, gazing at Stella, who had wrapped her head in a blue handkerchief and was sweating from the effort of chiselling away at the stone.

'Nothing,' said Stella. Gerald laughed.

'Of course,' he said, as he pulled up a wooden stool and sat down beside the block on which Stella was working. 'Nothing, of course. Shall I model for you? Would that inspire you?'

'No,' said Stella, but she said it without heat and without hope. She knew that nothing would make Gerald move; and indeed, he sat there all day, his hands idle, watching as she chipped laboriously at the granite. It was slow and difficult work. Stella had intended to carve, from memory, the stylized images of herself and Cloris, but before the morning was out she realized that in this medium she lacked the skill to represent her lover in any way that would satisfy her. Besides, something strange was happening.

Gerald's presence, normally so troubling to her, seemed now to spur her on. Little by little she saw that the crude face she was carving belonged, not to Cloris, but to her son, with his sly taunting smile. From that moment the making of the statues was to Stella a form of exorcism. Once I've done this, she thought, as she tapped at her chisel, once I've done this he will leave. He will leave and I shall have time to mourn Cloris.

'What are you going to do with them?' Gerald asked, when it was obvious that the statues were nearly finished. 'Do you think you'll be able to sell them?'

Stella shook her head. 'No. I'm going to put them in the gardens. Under the willows, I think, by the pond.'

Gerald looked at the two statues, the large with its faint cruel smile, the small with its dumb circle of a mouth. 'I'll help you, if you want,' he said, unexpectedly. 'They'll be too heavy for you to move on your own.'

They shifted the statues on a hot June morning, in absolute silence. It took them over an hour, inching first the small block and then the large across the courtyard and over the shaggy grass which grew around the pond, spattered with yellow dandelions. Stella noticed dark patches of sweat spreading on Gerald's white shirt. He kept lifting his hand to flick his heavy golden fringe from his face, which was solemn and entirely absorbed by the task in hand. For a moment, as though through a crack in the fabric of time, she glimpsed a future in which it might be possible for her to love her son, to enjoy his gifts, to work alongside him as a partner and helpmeet. Then the memory of the two bodies in the dovecote resounded in her head, like the beat of a drum which spells death. No, thought Stella, no. I need him out.

'There,' said Gerald, stepping back with satisfaction once the statues were in place. 'That's perfect.'

Stella nodded. The jeering expression had quite gone from her son's face, as if he had forgotten these weeks in which he had existed only to torment her.

He put his hands on his hips, smiling where he stood at the pond's edge.

'Look,' said Stella. 'You can see their reflections. That's why I wanted to put them here.'

'Can you?' said Gerald, and he turned, stooping over the water in his white shirt. It seemed to Stella that his image was seared upon her mind in ferocious colours, while the rest of the world went black. That was when she pushed him headlong into the pond. Taken unawares he toppled at once, splattering muddy water over Stella's smock. Quite what she had expected to happen she did not know; she had half hoped that Gerald would simply disappear, swept away in some non-existent maelstrom. But the pond was barely two feet deep. Gerald landed on his knees with a smacking noise, his bottom sticking upwards like an ostrich's.

'For God's sake,' he said, as he tried to stand up. At the sight of her tormentor off balance Stella jumped into the water, her stout shoes squelching in the mud. With both strong hands she grabbed at Gerald's head, pulling it downwards. Against her fingers his coarse thick hair felt exactly like her own. For a moment she thought she might succeed in felling him; then he regained his balance and gripped both her wrists, disarming her.

'Oh, no, you don't,' he said; and, putting one palm against the nape of her neck, he forced her face slowly downwards to the murky surface of the pond. 'Let's see how you like it, then.'

Stella gasped as he dunked her head, and got a mouthful of bilgewater. The horribleness of it gave her a burst of new strength. She struggled upwards, ramming her head against Gerald's stomach, so that he fell back into the pond, taking her with him. They were still tussling in the mud when they heard a voice, sharp with bewilderment, calling Stella's name.

'Mrs Deighton!'

Both Stella and Gerald looked up, their hands and

clown-like faces smeared with khaki slime. A small bowed figure, hands clasped, was standing on the stone path. It was Mrs Maybrick, the housekeeper, come to tell them that Sir George Courtney had died in the night.

Chapter Twenty-Two

Cosima picked up a silver platter of cocktail snacks and offered it to Derek Connor, the *Sunday Times* journalist, who was standing beside the display of photographs. He was not nearly as frightening as she had expected: a neat-faced man of about thirty-five, dressed in a very hairy charcoal jacket.

'I hope you're not going to tell me you think these look too pretty to eat,' he said, as he took a tiny chicken vol-au-vent from the parsley-strewn plate. Cosima smiled and shook her head.

'No. Actually I think they're annoying. They're so small that by the time you've decided you like them there's nothing left. And they don't stop you being hungry, do they?'

'Oh,' said Derek Connor, 'I believe they're intended to whet the appetite, not to satisfy it. So is it true that you've lived in Mallingford all your life?'

'Yes,' said Cosima, 'I have.' As she spoke she scanned the room to make sure that Roddy had not drifted into the other half of the studio, where Gerald was holding court. A dozen people had gathered around to hear him, while Morag hovered dutifully at his side. But it was all right: her cousin was still lounging in the corner, talking to Brian and to the little dark man who was Tom's boss. He glanced up for a moment and gave her a faint wink. Cosima looked away.

'But you don't remember Stella?'

'Oh, no. She died before I was born. And anyway, Gerald – my father, you know – wasn't on speaking terms with her for years. Have you met Gerald?

He's next door, talking about the pictures.'

'Yes, I've met him,' said Derek Connor, rather drily. 'Why hasn't this place been opened up before? It's astonishing; especially the dovecote. You don't often find a major new work by a major artist just like that. Do you know if there'll be funds available to restore it properly?'

'Well, I think we're looking into it,' said Cosima. She noticed Kate, Tom's girlfriend, in her chic red suit, working her way across the room, a bright flirtatious smile on her face. I could never be like that, thought Cosima, and the idea made her feel at once proud and sad. She watched as Kate joined the men in the corner, lifting her lips to be kissed by Brian Edwards.

'Of course, it's fascinating to see the self-portraits in context. She did so many, didn't she?' Derek Connor was saying. 'Rather like Van Gogh's sunflowers. To be honest, I'm beginning to prefer the picture you've got here to the one in the Tate. It's from a private collection, isn't it? I suppose an artist as popular as Stella Deighton must have sold most of her work during her lifetime.'

'Most of it, yes. I think my father found a few things after she died. He sort of inherited the place, you know. It was bequeathed first to Stella and then to Gerald by Sir George Courtney. My great-great-grandfather.'

Derek Connor took a fastidious mouthful of wine. 'I suppose everyone tells you that you look like Stella?' he remarked. 'Your hair's a different colour, of course. But otherwise the likeness is remarkable.'

Cosima felt her cheeks redden. 'Well, actually, no. I don't think anyone's ever said that. But then I have led a sheltered sort of life.'

To her surprise Derek laughed so much at this that he nearly dropped his vol-au-vent. When he laughed he looked rather boyish.

'Oh, my dear,' he said, in a mock tragic voice.

'I mean,' Cosima ploughed on, embarrassed, 'I

248

haven't spent much time outside my family. And they all – well, my mother's relatives never really approved of Stella. And my father—'

'Someone ought to write a proper biography of Stella,' said Derek, thoughtfully. 'There's hardly anything serious on her apart from art criticism and footnotes to those endless books about Bloomsbury. I wouldn't mind doing it myself if I could get a publisher interested in commissioning it. I suppose it should be started while your father's still alive, although I suspect that he – well, shall we say he embroiders the truth a little? Presumably he's right though in saying that she had a lesbian affair with Cloris Bohun.'

'I think so, yes,' said Cosima. She looked at the photograph of Cloris in her flowered dress, one small strong hand shading her face. 'Gerald always says she was the only person Stella really loved.'

Derek Connor stood beside her, gazing at the photograph. 'You know she died in childbirth, don't you? Cloris, I mean. It's mentioned in somebody's diary, I'm not sure whose. Or maybe I read it in Nina Hamnett's autobiography.'

'No, I didn't know that,' said Cosima. 'Gerald said that he had no idea what happened to her after she left Mallingford. She and Stella had a row or something and she upped and went. But I suppose it was wartime, and people did lose track of each other.'

'Just before the war, if I remember rightly. Cosima, I think you're wanted.'

'Oh?' said Cosima. She turned to find Tom looming at her elbow. There was a film of sweat on his tanned forehead.

'Sorry to bust in, but I guess we'd better get the speeches over and done with,' he said, in a low voice. 'Do you want to go and find your uncle Nicholas?'

'OK,' said Cosima. 'Excuse me, will you, Derek?'

She slid off through the knots of people to where Sir Nicholas was standing, his head courteously inclined towards a plump middle-aged woman in a virulent

249

green dress. His face brightened at once when he saw his niece.

'Cosima, my dear,' he said. 'Do you need me?'

'It's just Tom thinks we should do the speeches,' said Cosima, when Sir Nicholas had detached himself from the green woman. 'While Gerald's still – well, while he seems to be occupied in the other room.'

'Good thinking,' said Sir Nicholas. He put his hand on the small of Cosima's silken back and gently propelled her forwards to where Tom was standing. 'Let's get on with it, then.'

'Sure thing,' said Tom. He picked up two of the empty wine bottles and struck them against each other so that they rang with a muted hollow note. Sir Nicholas took out his reading glasses. Gradually the hum of the room began to fade. Only Gerald's voice was audible from beyond the screens, declaiming to his captive audience: 'And naturally Stella regarded the work Cloris did as somehow secondary to her own: not art for art's sake, you understand.'

Sir Nicholas took a breath and drew himself up to his full distinguished height. Then he began to speak.

'Well,' he said, in a tone at once relaxed and resonant, 'if you'll excuse me for interrupting the festivities, I'd like to welcome you all to Mallingford, which as you know was Stella Deighton's home for almost fifty years—'

Cosima clasped her hands tightly, trying to focus her mind on what her uncle was saying. She noticed that Kate had inched her way back across the room and was now standing next to Tom, on the far side of the exhibition stands. She seemed to be murmuring something in his ear. Cosima watched as he raised his eyebrows, and then gave a faint lop-sided smile. At that smile, prompted by another woman, she felt her heart leap, though whether it was with affection or with jealousy she could not judge.

'Since my great-grandfather, Sir George Courtney,

might be described as Stella's patron, we do of course have a splendid collection of her work, much of which you can see here today . . .' said Sir Nicholas, glancing down his long nose at the slip of paper in his hand. Cosima was dimly aware that her father, in the next room, had fallen silent. Then through the open door of the stable she saw her brother William. The smart clothes she had bought for him – a brown check shirt and some toffee-coloured chinos – were rumpled and grubby, and there was on his face an expression of dismay. Their eyes met across the studio.

'Oh, God,' whispered Cosima. Derek Connor, who was standing beside her, looked up in curiosity.

'What is it?' he said. He followed Cosima's gaze as she watched William wriggle his way towards her around the edges of the room. 'What a marvellous looking boy. Who is he?'

'My brother,' said Cosima. She stepped sideways, behind a group of local art lovers who were avidly listening to Sir Nicholas's speech. 'Will,' she hissed, 'what's wrong?'

'It's Gerald. He got away from Morag and he's in the courtyard with Stefan and Marcus. They've got some placards or something. And the shotgun. I've been up in the tree-house watching them.'

'Oh, dear God,' whispered Cosima. 'Come on, Will. Let's see if we can head them off before there's trouble.'

'I think it's too late,' said William; but he followed her anyway, weaving his way through the crowds.

'I'd like in particular to thank Brian Edwards for his generosity in sponsoring this venture,' Sir Nicholas was saying. 'I'm sure we're all very happy to see that the business community is prepared to take the long view in supporting the arts . . .'

Cosima stepped out into the courtyard. Her father, in his wide-brimmed hat, carried in one hand his old shotgun and in the other a metal loud hailer. Alongside him were Stefan and Marcus, still wearing their paintdraggled clothes. Marcus was wielding a placard which said, in dark green letters, *Fascists out!*

'Gerald,' said Cosima, in a desperate voice, 'what are you doing?' Her father looked at her, his face bright with a glee which seemed to her superhuman, but he did not answer. Instead Marcus came forward, and put his free hand on her shoulder.

'Look, we're not getting at you, Cosima,' he said. 'Honestly. We realize it's not your fault. It's just we can't let this carry on, you know?'

'All right, lads,' said Gerald, in a hearty voice. He passed the shotgun to Stefan, who proudly slipped his hand around the trigger.

'What are you doing?' said Cosima again, watching the shotgun flail against the sky in Stefan's untrained grasp.

'You'll see,' said Gerald, and he raised the loud hailer to his lips. But it was not Gerald who interrupted Sir Nicholas's speech: it was Cosima, who to her own surprise let out a deafening scream. The scream echoed around the little valley. In astonishment Gerald lowered his megaphone. The rifle which Stefan was holding lurched sideways for an instant; then there was the abrupt crack of gunfire.

After that it all seemed to happen very suddenly. One moment Cosima heard the shot, and the next she found herself being hurled to the ground by Tom, who had apparently come from nowhere. As she fell she was conscious of a circle of faces, their mouths ajar, watching her. One of them, she was sure, belonged to Tom's girlfriend Kate. Then she was lying flat on the courtyard stones, crushed beneath Tom's weight. He felt hot and extremely heavy. She could smell the sharp whiff of gunpowder in the air.

'Cosima! Are you all right?' It was her uncle Nicholas, his gold half-moon spectacles still perched on his nose. Cosima struggled to sit up. Tom, slumped on top of her, was gasping for breath like a landed trout. Meanwhile Roddy had seized the gun from

Stefan and had wrenched his arm behind his back.

'All right, you little shit,' he said. 'We're calling the police.'

'Hey,' protested Stefan, weakly. 'I wasn't doing anything.'

Tom shifted his weight, releasing Cosima. Sir Nicholas helped her to her feet. There was a livid graze along her left arm, and her red spotted dress had torn at the waist. As she stood up, dazed, she met Stefan's startled pleading eyes.

'I wasn't aiming the gun at you,' he said. 'Tell them I wasn't aiming the gun at you.'

'Of course he wasn't aiming the bloody gun at her,' said Gerald. 'For God's sake. Just let him go, will you?'

'If I were you, Gerald, I'd stay out of it,' said Roddy, tightening his grip. Stefan gave a little moan.

'Roddy,' said Cosima, 'please let him go. He's right: it was an accident.'

'I still think we should call the police,' said Roddy, in a grudging voice, but he loosened his hold on Stefan's arm. 'Father, don't you think we should call the police?'

'Hang on, Roddy,' said Sir Nicholas. He turned to the crowd of visitors who were standing outside the stables, their faces blank with disbelief. 'Ladies and gentlemen, I'm sorry for this disturbance. A minor hiccup, I'm afraid. If you'd like to make your way back into the studio, there's still plenty of food and drink . . .'

There was a low uncertain murmur from the watching crowd. Some of the visitors began slowly to amble back into the stables; others huddled in indecisive groups. Cosima reached dizzily out and took Tom's arm to steady herself. He was still breathing very hard and very fast.

'Let's just carry on, shall we?' Sir Nicholas said, in a soft voice. 'Roddy, I can't see much point in calling the police at this stage. No harm's been done, after all. Cosima, my dear, you're not hurt, are you? I think, though, Gerald, we should hang on to the shotgun and hand it in at the police station. You don't want another accident, do you?'

Gerald stared across at Sir Nicholas, the loud hailer forgotten in his hand. For a moment Cosima thought he might leap at his adversary's throat; but then he slung the megaphone to the ground and turned upon his heel.

'Oh, do whatever the bloody hell you like,' he said. 'Come on, boys. Let's go back to the house.'

He strode off across the yard, Stefan and Marcus following sheepishly behind him. Marcus was still trailing the *Fascists out!* placard as though he did not know what else to do with it. When they had gone William gave a great noisy shiver and at once ran off into the trees.

'If you ask me,' muttered Roddy, 'you've let them off damn lightly.'

'We'll see,' said Sir Nicholas. He turned towards Brian Edwards, who was glowering beside the flint wall of the stable block, and gave him a brilliant smile. 'Well, Brian. Shall we go back in and try again?'

'Bugger that,' said Brian. He took a white handkerchief from his pocket and wiped his large damp face with it. 'I'm not being funny, but if I'd wanted to see people waggling shotguns around I'd have stayed in the East End. Believe me, I would.'

Alastair, Tom's boss, stepped forward, dark and dashing in his navy suit.

'What Brian means,' he said suavely, 'is that he doesn't entirely trust the security of his investment in a venture where there obviously isn't full agreement between all the parties involved.'

'You bet I bloody don't. I can find better ways of chucking away my money, most of them a damn sight more enjoyable than this. Sorry and all that, but it's the plain truth.'

'Brian,' said Sir Nicholas, 'I realize you've found this

incident disturbing but if I can just reassure you by explaining the next step . . .'

He drew Brian to one side, out of Cosima's hearing. She gripped Tom's arm, overcome by a hot desire to weep.

'I'm really sorry if I hurt you,' Tom said, putting one hand to her torn waist. 'It's just I heard you scream, and then that damn gun went off – well, it was a reflex, you know?'

Cosima took a slow painful breath. 'It's OK. I should have guessed what Gerald was up to. I should have realized he'd ruin everything. It was so stupid of me not to realize.'

'Well,' said Roddy, 'that was a fiasco and no mistake.' There was a robust note of self-righteousness in his voice. 'Are you all right, little cousin? You ought to get Morag to put a dressing on your arm.'

'I'm fine,' said Cosima, grudgingly.

'An act of heroism, I must say, Tom,' Roddy went on cheerfully, adjusting his hold on Gerald's shotgun. 'Not many men would have the balls to knock a girl over like that.'

'Oh, lay off, will you?' Tom said. As he spoke he removed his hand from Cosima's waist. 'I just said, it was a reflex action.'

'A pretty bloody dangerous reflex if you ask me.'

'Please, Roddy . . .' Cosima managed to say. She was conscious that Tom and her cousin were squaring up to each other in the courtyard like boxers ready for the next bout. It was as though the arrested violence of Gerald's demonstration had remained in the air, waiting for another shape to occupy.

'If you ask me those art students are a menace,' said Roddy. 'Typical bloody parasites on the state.'

'Garbage. They're kids, that's all,' Tom said. 'Kids are always subversive. It goes with the territory.'

'That makes it all right, does it? Well, I'll remember that next time someone calls me a fascist and threatens

my cousin with a shotgun. Kids are subversive, I'll say
to myself.'

'Oh, don't be such a jerk,' said Tom, with scorn, and
he turned to Cosima. 'You ought to clean that graze
up, though.'

'Look,' said Roddy, 'why don't I drive you back to
Courtney Park and get you patched up? You're in
shock. You could do with some time out of this place.'
He stretched out and took Cosima proprietorially by
the wrist.

'Don't pull her around like that,' Tom said fiercely.
'She's not your property.'

'Stop it,' said Cosima. She tried to shake off her
cousin's grasp, although it seemed to her that the more
she struggled the faster he held her. 'Stop it. Both of
you.'

'Just let her go, will you?' Tom said, and he plunged
forward to seize Roddy's arm. The force of the blow
sent Roddy staggering inelegantly backwards, pulling
Cosima with him. The shotgun in his right hand
clattered to the ground.

'Tom, what the hell do you think you're playing at?'
thundered Alastair, who had been huddled in conversation with Brian and Sir Nicholas. 'Come here at
once.'

Tom let his hands fall to his side, abashed.

'OK,' he said, and, throwing one sheepish glance in
Cosima's direction, he sloped across to where Alastair
was standing. As he did so Cosima realized that Kate
was watching him, an expression of peculiar anguish
on her face. An emotion which she thought must be
guilt wrenched at Cosima's heart. Abruptly she pulled
her arm out of Roddy's grasp.

'Leave me alone,' she said, in a furious voice, and
turning on her heel she marched away from the
stables, breaking into a run as she passed the house.
Only when she had reached the shelter of the willow
trees did she stop and look back, across the pond, to
the courtyard. Roddy had picked up the shotgun and

was carrying it towards his Land Rover; Tom, his head bowed, seemed to be standing in silence beside Sir Nicholas, like a schoolboy in disgrace. There was no sign of Kate in her red suit. Cosima let out a deep breath, and slid down the slippery trunk of the willow until she was sitting on the damp grass, next to the statue-menhirs. It occurred to her to cry, now that she was alone, but she felt too exhausted and confused even to begin. Then in the middle distance she heard the crunch of footsteps. For a moment she was afraid that it might be her father, come to enact his revenge; but it was Derek Connor, picking his way gracefully along the path in his neat black polished shoes. He said nothing until he had reached the willows, and then, companionably, he sat down cross-legged beside her. He was smiling.

'Well, Cosima,' he said, 'so this is what you call a sheltered life, is it?'

Chapter Twenty-Three

'You realize, don't you?' said Alastair, leaning back in his chrome chair, 'that I could fire you on the spot. Not only for screwing up a major promotional event, but for jeopardizing our relationship with a very important sponsor. You do realize that, don't you, Tom?'

'Yeah,' said Tom, miserably. 'I realize that.'

It was the day after the fiasco at Mallingford, and both Tom and Alastair were back in London. Alastair had taken charge of everything after Tom's brawl with Roddy. He had deftly removed Roderick from the scene by suggesting that he was the most suitable person to deliver Gerald's shotgun to the police, and he had made lavish apologies to Sir Nicholas for Tom's behaviour; apologies which Sir Nicholas had waved away as being more or less irrelevant given the catastrophe of the day. Alastair had not been able to mollify Brian Edwards as far as the Mallingford project was concerned, but he had persuaded him to meet for lunch the following week to discuss other ventures.

Tom himself Alastair had sent back to London immediately, even before the last visitors had left the stable block, deaf to his insistence that he must stay to help with the clearing up. This meant that Tom had not had the opportunity to talk either to Cosima or to Kate. Cosima had vanished into the Mallingford gardens, and although he lingered by his car as long as he dared before driving away, there was still no sign of her. As for Kate, when he offered to take her back to London, she had coolly announced that she would prefer to go with Alastair. Since Tom had keys to her flat in Fulham, he could have gone to find her later that evening, but he did not, for the simple reason that he did not really know what he wanted to say to her. The vision he had had, under the chestnuts at Mallingford, of declaring his love to Cosima now seemed far-fetched and impossibly romantic; you couldn't build your life on visions like that. At the same time, though, he could not imagine carrying on with Kate as if nothing whatsoever had happened. He gave an inward groan and swallowed the burnt coffee which Shabnam had brought him.

'There's also the fact that once the local papers come out it'll be open season on the Courtneys,' Alastair went on. 'They'll make a meal of it, I guarantee you, and I wouldn't be surprised if the nationals didn't pick up the story. We're just lucky that Derek Connor won't blow the gaff. From the conversation I had with him afterwards he's more interested in writing Stella's biography and he doesn't want to bite the hand that feeds him. Otherwise we would have been in seriously deep shit. The fact is, Tom, you've screwed up, and you've screwed up big. You know that, don't you?'

'Yes,' said Tom, 'I sure do.'

'Good,' said Alastair, running his hand through his dense bluish hair, 'I'm glad you know it. Because I'll tell you something else. I'm going to give you a second chance. Do you want to know why? It's because I think basically you're a sound man. Most of the time you've got your head screwed on. You just got carried away with this Mallingford project, and forgot the first rule of business: we're in this to make money. I don't want to go into the personal side. That's your affair. All I'm saying is that what went wrong here is that you had divided loyalties. Roddy Courtney was our client, and you should have been thinking about what he wanted, not worrying about whether that loony old man would have his fair share of the loot or whether those paintings would get to a bigger audience. Sure, there are times when you have to play a double game, make people think that you're on their side. You weren't wrong to try schmoozing Cosima Deighton and her father. The trouble is, my son, they ended up schmoozing you. Big mistake.'

'It's not as simple as that—' Tom began. He got up from his seat and strode restlessly towards the window. The sky outside was iron grey, thick with cloud. It made the room seem cramped and oppressive.

'Yes, it is,' said Alastair. 'That's the point, Tom. It is as simple as that. Every time it's as simple as that. And I don't ever want you to forget it again. *Comprende?*' Idly he reached out and refilled his coffee cup. 'Now, let's see where we are, and what we've managed to pull from the wreckage. I'm doing lunch with Brian next Tuesday, and as long as I take him somewhere ridiculously expensive and give him the works I dare say I can bring him round to this champagne scam. It'll appeal to him, that one; he'll enjoy bragging that he's got his own brand of fizz. I think you'd better steer clear for the time being, though, Tom, and let me handle him on my own.'

Tom, at the window, gave an acquiescent shrug. He did not care if he never set eyes on Brian Edwards again.

'No, I think you'd better lead on this Belmont campaign,' Alastair continued. 'There's a fair bit of background work to be done if we're going to clinch it, making sure we've checked out the market research, find out the billboard sites that might be available, that kind of thing. You could manage that, couldn't you, Tom?'

'Manage what?' said Tom, who was still thinking about Brian Edwards. One of the things he found most painful was that, by his public quarrel with Roddy, he had somehow lost his natural superiority over Brian. The idea gnawed at him that he could now legitimately be ranked alongside a lout who was unable to sit through the first scene of an opera.

'The Belm   campaign,' Alastair said patiently. 'You know, t   fag we're launching.'

'But what a..ut Mallingford?' said Tom. 'We're not just calling it a day, are we? After all the work I put in?'

'Jesus, Tom. Haven't you been listening to me for the past half-hour? Watch my lips. Yes. We are calling it a day. *Finito*.' Alastair made the abrupt brutal gesture of a hangman. 'If you ask me we're lucky to get out this side of bankruptcy. I'm not even sure we're justified in whacking an invoice to the Courtneys, although Sir Nicholas is such a gent I dare say he'll cough up.'

Eagerly Tom crossed the room once more and sat down, leaning towards Alastair with his elbows on the desk.

'Yeah, but I know I can make it work,' he said. 'I can make it work without Brian. I can probably make it work without the Courtneys. You saw how wild all those people were about the place? Derek Connor was raving about it. At least half of them would hand over some cash to get things started. And in a lot of ways it would be easier to work with Gerald Deighton directly rather than having to manoeuvre around him the whole time. That's what went wrong. He was acting out some kind of vendetta against the Courtneys. If we'd had his real co-operation in the first place it would all have been just fine.'

Alastair sat quite still, his blue eyes fixed on Tom's zealous face. 'For Christ's sake, Tom,' he said.

'What?'

'You're obsessed, aren't you? Completely bloody obsessed. Shit. I should never have let you go ahead with this.'

'But I can make it work,' said Tom. 'Believe me. I can make it work.'

'You won't give up, will you?'

'No, I won't. Why should I?'

Alastair said nothing. He rose to his feet and crossed

261

the room to the sleek chrome drinks cabinet. Still in silence, he took a bottle of Polish vodka from the fridge, poured a shot into a heavy glass tumbler, put back his head and swallowed it. Then he turned once more to Tom.

'All right,' he said. 'All right. I've got a meeting in half an hour. Before I go I'll do the paperwork and write a cheque for whatever I decide your payoff's going to be. It won't be astronomical but it will be generous, and I suggest that if you know what's good for you, you don't quibble over it.'

'What?' said Tom. 'What are you talking about?'

'I'm letting you go. That's what I'm talking about.'

'You're crazy. You can't do that.'

'Oh, Tom,' said Alastair, 'watch me. Just watch me. Look, you're a great guy, and it's been terrific working with you. But I can't carry passengers. I certainly can't carry passengers who've got private obsessions with hopeless projects.'

'It's not hopeless. I've just explained to you—'

'Yeah, yeah. I know. No hard feelings, Tom. If you can find someone else to back you on this one, great. Good luck to them. But it ain't going to be me.' Alastair leaned down and put the vodka back into the fridge. 'Now, if you don't mind, I'd like to get everything sewn up before this meeting. I'll leave the cheque with Shabnam, OK? You can pick it up when you hand over your car keys.'

Tom stared for a moment, his brain fizzing with shock. Then, slowly, he got to his feet. 'Fine,' he said, stiffly. 'Fine. If that's how you want it. In that case I guess I'll go and clear my desk.'

'Good,' said Alastair, in a crisp voice, taking a chequebook from his drawer. 'To be honest, that sounds like the best idea you've had in weeks.'

It took Tom forty minutes to pack what he wanted from his cubby hole of an office. He did it with a sense of unreality, as though he were tidying up to go on holiday, not leaving for good. As he pulled open the drawers he realized that his fingers were trembling, but he was not conscious of any distress; he was conscious only of the need to maintain a front of absolute dignity in front of Shabnam. She passed him a slim white envelope from beneath the curved desk with her eyes averted, as though it might be bad luck even to look at him now that he had fallen on hard times; but as he turned to go she looked up and said: 'Goodbye, Tom. Good luck.'

'Oh, OK,' said Tom. 'Thanks, Shabnam. Same to you.'

His first instinct, when he left the office, was to look at his cheque, which he had been much too proud to do in front of Shabnam. Instead, though, he stood by the traffic lights, gazing at the ornate terracotta façade of the Cambridge Theatre, at the huddles of tourists and foreign students consulting their multicoloured street maps. The air was heady with car fumes. I need a decent cup of coffee, Tom thought, and he crossed the road to the Italian café in Moor Street, where he often had doses of caffeine to revive him on hangover mornings. It was only when he was sitting down, a black inch of espresso in front of him, that he pulled the envelope from his jacket pocket. He opened it very carefully, as though he might need to reuse it, and drew out the cheque. It was for fifty thousand pounds: a year's salary. There was no note from Alastair, only a couple of official-looking forms which Tom did not bother to read. He stared at the cheque as though the figures upon it might change shape, or dissolve before his eyes. His first thought was, this is freedom. I can spend as much time as I want down at Mallingford, I can really make that place work. Then another fantasy struck him: flying home to the States, swanning around New York or Boston with his British credentials and his tidy bank account. He would have enough cash to play the field for a while; maybe enough to set up his own business. The image flickered and beckoned. I could just take off, he thought, tomorrow if I want.

There's nothing to stop me, and nobody would be any the wiser. It was then that he remembered Kate. I'd better tell her what's happened, he thought, I owe her that, at least. He slipped the cheque back into his pocket, and set off, on foot, for Kate's office.

Kate worked in a large modern block near Berwick Street market, which housed several other magazines besides her own. Tom had been there often enough for the security guard to recognize him and nod him through to the lift. He made his way into a large open-plan office, criss-crossed with tall blue screens. There was a hum of voices, one or two louder and more strident than the rest. Tom padded along the makeshift aisles to where he knew Kate sat, at a little brown desk piled high with press releases and free samples. She was on the telephone.

'Yes,' she was saying, in her brittle jolly work voice, 'I'm disappointed too. I thought she'd be a great find, someone to take the pressure off the regular team. But when I asked her to do me a piece on the new generation of lipsticks last week, all she could say was, they're red. And that's not what I pay freelancers for.'

Tom strolled forwards and stood in front of her. Kate lifted her head. She was wearing an emerald blouse with a high Russian collar, and even more make-up than usual. The expression on her face did not change.

'Listen, must go,' she said, into the telephone. 'See you later. *Ciao.*'

'D'you get that from Alastair?' said Tom. 'Saying *ciao* like that?'

'Lots of people say it. It's considered stylish,' said Kate, sticking out her chin. Despite her efforts her voice was not quite level. 'What are you doing here?'

'I've been fired,' said Tom. 'I thought you might want to know.'

'Oh,' said Kate. 'He told me he was planning to give you a second chance.'

'He was. But he changed his mind. Listen, Katie, can we go somewhere private? I really need to talk to you.'

264

'Well . . .' said Kate, doubtfully, 'I've got a lot on this morning. On account of wasting a day down in Sussex.'

'Oh, come on. Please.'

'I suppose we could use the meeting room,' said Kate, pushing back her chair, 'as long as it doesn't take too long.'

The meeting room was an airless, windowless cubicle with a round modern table in the middle of it, lurid with fluorescent light. Tom sat down, propping his face on his fists.

'Thanks, Kate,' he said. 'I really do appreciate this.'

'So,' said Kate, coolly, 'what are your plans?'

'Well, he gave me a pay-off. Alastair, I mean. Fifty grand.'

Kate whistled. 'What will you do with it?'

'I don't know. That's why I need to talk to you.'

'Why me?' said Kate. 'When have you ever listened to me?'

'Look, Kate,' said Tom, rubbing his forehead with the heel of his hand, 'I just don't know what I want any more. Alastair let me go because I said I wouldn't give up on the Mallingford project, and – well, sure, I really think I could make it work, but then – I don't know, I was looking at Alastair's cheque and I thought, maybe I should just cut my losses and go back to the States. Maybe that would be best for everyone.'

'Run away, you mean?' said Kate.

'It wouldn't be running away. It's an alternative, is what I'm saying.'

Kate gave a deep sigh and tilted her head to the white panelled ceiling. Her green enamel earrings gave a soft rattle.

'Tom,' she said, 'I think you're infatuated by Cosima Deighton. I think that's what the problem is.'

'Kate . . .' Tom said. She lowered her head and their eyes met across the table.

'You are, aren't you?'

'Yes,' said Tom. 'I guess I am. Not that anything's happened, believe me—'

'Oh, I do believe you. Funnily enough. If you'd actually slept with her you wouldn't be so bloody obsessed with the woman. But the fact is, until you get it out of your system you'll be no good to anyone. So if you want my advice I should go down there and sort yourself out.'

Tom said nothing. He was struck by a sudden admiration for Kate in her frankness, and with that admiration came a sly resurgence of his passion for her. He remembered the one holiday they had spent together, a beach holiday on a Greek island, and how Kate had lost her urban self-consciousness and frolicked in the sea like an eight-year-old. He remembered her face, damp with tears and mascara in the Glyndebourne gardens, saying, I need to know if you're serious. He remembered, in rapid but detailed succession, all the nights they had spent together.

'Kate,' he said, in a tentative voice, 'the thing is, I'm not sure I want to lose you—'

'Tough,' said Kate. 'What do you think I am? Some kind of masochist? I don't want you while you're busy fantasizing about a little eighteen-year-old you think is all pure and unattainable. Grow up, Tom. You've got this whole big romantic thing about that wretched place. Stella and her sodding paintings, that crazy old man. And if you don't do something you'll spend the rest of your life mooning over it. So just get on with it, will you? And don't waste my time.'

Tom spread his hands out on the table, examining the glossy teak surface between his fingers. 'I don't deserve you,' he said.

'Damn right you don't deserve me. Now push off, will you? I meant it when I said I was busy.'

'One thing, Kate. What made you realize about Cosima? Was it because I had that fight with Roddy?'

Kate shook her head. 'No. It was when the boy let

266

off the shotgun and you took that flying leap at her. You'd never have done that for me.'

'Oh, I don't know,' said Tom, as he got to his feet.

'No, you wouldn't. Not in a million years. Come on, Tom. I said push off.'

'OK,' said Tom, making his way to the door.

'Mind you,' Kate said, in a more friendly voice, following him out of the meeting room, 'I'm a fool to myself. That fifty grand Alastair gave you would have made a nice deposit on a bijou little maisonette. I saw a place the other day that would have been perfect for us.' She gave him a wry smile. 'I thought you were a completely different sort of person, you know. I thought you were the sort of person who made the best of what you'd got. Well, as I say. More fool me.'

'Kate,' said Tom, 'you're a good kid, do you know that?'

'And you're the kiss of death. No, don't touch me. If you touch me I'll cry, and I'm damned if I'm going to cry about you. Besides, if I cry I'll end up looking like a football, and they're taking staff photos for the mag this afternoon. Just go, Tom, will you?'

'All right,' said Tom. 'All right. I'll see you around, Kate. Take care, hey?'

Kate nodded, wordlessly, lifting one hand in an ambiguous farewell. Then she turned her back and sat down at her desk once more. Tom marched away between the blue screens of the office. As he went he was conscious of a sharp dragging fear, as though he had made a terrible mistake. This fear was so powerful that for a moment he had to stop and make himself breathe deeply and rhythmically before the spasm of it lifted, and he could move again. Then, out in the street, he looked at his watch. It was still only half past eleven. I could hire a car, he thought, drive down to Sussex. If I'm lucky I could be in Mallingford by three; four at the latest. Picking up his briefcase he almost ran in the direction of the tube station.

Chapter Twenty-Four

Sir George Courtney was buried in the village churchyard on a scorching cloudless day in July. At the
funeral his daughter-in-law Alicia wore an expensive
black wool suit and a toque with a veil, in which she
was much too hot. Violet, who came with her timber
merchant husband, wore a cotton print frock and cried
all through the ceremony; further proof to Alicia that
she was now déclassée. Alicia was not exactly glad
that Sir George was dead – she had in her way been
fond of the old man, and was conscious that he had
always treated her extremely well – but she could
not help feeling a sense of satisfaction that life was
proceeding as it was meant to proceed, according to
hereditary patterns, and that her son was now the
master of the Courtney estates. Charles had grown
plumper, his physique expanding to match his status,
and his cheeks had taken on a peculiarly English
ruddiness, most visible when he was irritated or when
he had enjoyed an excellent dinner. He had married
the timid sister of one of his fellow oarsmen at
Cambridge, who discharged her wifely duties by pro-
ducing an heir, christened Nicholas George, precisely
ten months after the wedding.

The village church was crammed with local people,
pink-faced in their best clothes. There was a distinct
smell of mothballs and of human sweat; not a smell
Sir George would have relished, but one he would
have tolerated on the grounds that it did him honour.
Knowing this, Alicia did her best to ignore it, burying
her nose from time to time in a lace handkerchief
sprinkled with eau de Cologne. She also did her best

to ignore the Deightons, mother and son, who sat in a pew at the back of the church. As usual they looked handsome and, for all their physical solidity, somehow other-worldly. Since the death of Sir George Alicia had been quite unable to stop her avid brain from making plans for the redistribution of what was now her son's property. Charles and his wife, whose name was Penelope, would almost certainly wish to leave their London house and live permanently in Courtney Park; what better for her to do than move to Mallingford, where she could keep a weather eye on Penelope's housekeeping without being seen to interfere? And so when Alicia angled her head away from Stella as they passed in the churchyard, it was not so much from dislike as from a consciousness that she was about to make the woman homeless.

Stella and Gerald, meanwhile, had called a ceasefire in their battle for supremacy. They had not discussed this any more than they had discussed their private grief at Sir George's death, but in silence they put on tidy sober clothes and in silence they walked side by side along the lane to the village, Stella shielding her face with a dark blue silk parasol which Cloris Bohun had left behind. Neither of them wept. They managed however to nudge themselves forward through the flock of villagers to the graveside, so that they could stand alongside the family and see Sir George's smooth honey-coloured coffin being lowered into the ground. When the burial service had been read Gerald dropped into the grave a spray of white roses from the Malling-ford gardens, their stems tied with ribbon. The roses fell noiselessly upon the ornate wreath Charles Courtney had laid on his grandfather's casket.

There was a large funeral tea served in the church hall after the burial, where the boiling of the tea urn added to the atmosphere of heat and humidity, and Charles in his stiff white collar made a rather pompous speech about how public-spirited Sir George had been. Afterwards the Courtneys and the rest of the local gentry retired to Courtney Park for dry sherry and the reading of the will. The Deightons, naturally, were not included in this select group and as a result they had no idea of what the will contained until two days later, when the useful Mrs Maybrick brought them the village gossip.

'No doubt you'll get a letter from the solicitors,' she said, sitting demurely in the Mallingford kitchen, 'but everyone's talking about it, so it must be true.'

'And he's left the house to both of us?' said Gerald, eagerly, leaning across the table.

'Oh, yes. To Mrs Deighton for her lifetime, and then to you. Rent-free,' she added, with a note of triumph in her voice. She had always favoured the Deightons over Sir George's blood relations. 'I expect the family will challenge it, but from what I understand Sir George has made the terms of it watertight. Lady Courtney – the elder Lady Courtney, that is – is furious. I think she was planning to decamp here herself.'

Stella sat upright, unusual tears pricking her eyes. She could not bring herself to speak at this marvellous and unlooked-for generosity.

'He was a good soul,' said Mrs Maybrick, herself prompted to weep by the sight of Stella's unshed tears. She blew her nose energetically instead. 'And when are you expecting Mrs Bohun? I thought she might come home for the funeral. She was always so fond of Sir George.'

Stella and Gerald looked at each other.

'Oh,' said Gerald, 'no. She still has family business in London. We don't know when she'll be back.'

'No,' said Stella, 'we don't know.'

Mrs Maybrick was right: the Courtney family did challenge Sir George's will, arguing that he had no right to divide his grandson's patrimony in so cavalier a fashion. Sir George, though, had obviously taken legal advice before making the bequest, and his wishes were clear. Moreover, as the Deightons' solicitor artfully observed, the gift was not irrevocable: Mallingford would revert to the Courtneys in due course, even if it would be too late for Charles and Alicia to benefit. It was pointed out to them that technically they still had the right to use the out-buildings, but they regarded this as more of an insult than a concession. What use could some stables and a semi-derelict dovecote be to them when they were deprived of the house itself?

During the months of the dispute Stella and Gerald lived together at Mallingford in a continued state of truce. Gerald did not harass his mother by his constant presence; indeed, for much of the time he left her to her own devices while he tramped around the country, visiting many of the places where he and Sir George had been together, in a sort of posthumous pilgrimage to his benefactor. Stella herself lived from day to day. Most of the time she spent in her studio, staring at her own ageing face in the mirror, painting endless self-portraits. In many of the pictures she wore a straw hat, trimmed with artificial cherries, which Cloris had given her, as though it were a symbol of her lost lover, indicating Cloris's continued and all-absorbing presence in her mind.

When Gerald did come into the stable block he made no attempt to disturb his mother. Instead he occupied himself by painting the wooden screens which divided the L-shaped studio, doling on the paint in bright whorls of red and green and yellow. Stella, observing, noted that the pattern he had chosen closely resembled something she had done, as an experiment, on the walls of the dovecote, but she said nothing to her son, not wanting to breach the uneasy peace between them. Now that Gerald had stopped tormenting her she felt such relief that it seemed not to matter that he was still at Mallingford. At times it was almost restful to hear his footsteps creak through the house at night, to smell the pungent scent of his tobacco floating up from the kitchen, to listen to him shuffle around the studio while she continued her work. In a part of her mind Stella assumed that once the question of the lease was settled Gerald would, whatever happened, move on and leave Mallingford; in another part there seemed to be no reason why they should not continue indefinitely in this strange symbiotic way, treading carefully around each other.

The letter from Cloris came just before Sir George's will was settled in favour of the Deightons. The moment Stella saw her lover's handwriting she realized that she had been thinking of Cloris as if she were dead: her departure had seemed so final, putting her beyond the human sphere, never to be retrieved. For the first time, as Stella tore open the envelope, she wondered why she had not thought to pursue Cloris to London, where she had almost certainly gone (and indeed, the letter had a London postmark), in an attempt to fetch her home. She wondered too, for a moment, why Gerald had not followed Cloris either, but her mind at once shimmied away from that thought as too painful to dwell upon.

Inside the envelope was a page of very cheap notepaper, with no address at the top. It was a letter begging for money. *I know I have no right to ask you,* Cloris wrote, *and I would not ask except that I am desperate.* She named a day and a time when she would be at Victoria Station, waiting at the platform where the Lewes train arrived. *I will understand it if you do not come but the fact is I have no-one else to help me. And I mean it when I say I am in despair.*

Stella told her son nothing about the letter. She merely said that she had some business in London, and was not sure for how long she would be away: possibly a day, possibly more. She drew a hundred pounds from her bank account; then she caught the train to Victoria, to arrive at the time Cloris had appointed. She did all this like an automaton, the emotions within her so vast it seemed impossible for them to be translated into anything she might actually

272

recognize as feeling. Only as she alighted upon the platform and smelt the familiar sooty smell of London did her throat catch in anticipation. She could not really imagine what a desperate Cloris must be like: her abiding memory of her lover was as an infinitely resourceful woman. Striding towards the barrier Stella felt a rush of the purest joy, that at any moment she would see Cloris again.

It was the clothes she recognized, the dark velvet cloak, the little squashed hat, both of which Cloris had worn on the evening they met. Stella's first thought was that Cloris looked well, her body as plump as ever. Then she looked at her face. Her skin was the colour of dirty linen, grey and crumpled, and her brown eyes seemed unnaturally large.

'You're ill,' said Stella. Cloris gave a whisper of a smile. She was half leaning against the wall, supported by one sparrow hand.

'Thank you for coming,' she said.

'You should have told me your address,' said Stella. 'I would have come to find you there.'

'I don't have an address,' said Cloris. 'Did you bring the money?'

'Yes, I did,' said Stella. 'Let's go to the restaurant. You need food.'

Cloris shook her head. 'I don't eat very well,' she said. 'I'm out of practice. When I have solid food I throw up. You'd better just let me have some tea.'

'You should be in bed,' said Stella, putting out her arm so that Cloris could lean upon it. As Cloris did so the worn folds of the velvet cloak shifted, and Stella realised why her lover had seemed plump. It was because she was pregnant. Both women gazed at Cloris's protuberant stomach as though it were a third, faintly unwelcome person who had just joined them. As she stared Stella remembered the revulsion with which she had seen her own stomach swell when she was carrying Gerald. Then, with a shock, it occurred to her whose child it was growing in Cloris's ruined body. Instinctively she withdrew her arm with a jerk.

'I'm afraid so,' said Cloris, in the same wry objective voice she had used when she said, I don't eat very well. Stella did not speak, unable to take her eyes from her lover's distended stomach. There was a moment in which her very soul screamed at her to take flight, to leave behind her the chaos of human connections, as she had all her life endeavoured to do. It was a moment so powerful that she thought she might be physically sick. Then, overcoming her nausea, she slowly stretched out her hand once more to take Cloris firmly by the elbow.

'Come on,' she said. 'We'd better find you somewhere decent to stay.'

For the next week Stella looked after Cloris in a couple of rooms which she found in a back street in Pimlico. They belonged to a pallid widow of indeterminate age who lived on the ground floor of the house and who appeared resolutely incurious about Cloris's state of health. There was a bedroom with ancient rose-printed curtains where Cloris slept interminably, as if rehearsing for death, and a sitting room with a day bed and a gas ring where Stella could heat soup and brew tea and, occasionally, doze. Even at the height of her obsession with Cloris Stella had never dedicated herself so entirely to the needs of another. She found the days passing with a peculiar speed, at once intense and monotonous. Sometimes she would sit looking out of the window upon the foggy November street and watch her neighbours come and go as if they belonged to an alien species. She had no real awareness of day or night: she told the time only by whether Cloris was sleeping or not.

During her rare waking hours Cloris told Stella a little of what had happened to her since she left Mallingford. At first she had managed well enough, living in a cheap bed-sitting room near Tottenham Court Road, finding herself odd bits of modelling work. But her pregnancy made her tired and sick, too ill to carry out the jobs she had, let alone look for something better. Gradually her savings dwindled: she could not afford to eat properly, but lived as she had done before during lean times on weak tea and bits of bread, and the lack of food made her weaker than ever. She had written to Stella when she realized that she could no longer pay the rent, driven not so much by fear for herself but by the deep-rooted desire at all costs to preserve her child. What she would have done if her letter had not been answered she did not say, and Stella for her part could not bear to ask, any more than she could bear to ask questions about the baby. She did not allow herself to savour the irony that if Cloris had not been with child she would never have begged for help; instead she treated Cloris's pregnancy as an illness from which, with luck, she might recover as completely as if it had never happened. Neither of the women mentioned Gerald's name.

Cloris went into premature labour ten days after Stella had rescued her, at four o'clock on a bitterly cold morning. Stella at once roused their landlady, who went for the doctor. He was a youngish freckled man with a straggly ginger moustache, smelling of tobacco. He examined Cloris with a weary thoroughness, while Stella boiled a huge enamel pot of water on the gas ring. She did this not because she thought it would necessarily be of use, but because she had to have something to do, and watching the bubbles gather and the steam rise seemed as sensible a task as any.

'Her first child, is it?' the doctor said, when he came out of the bedroom. Stella nodded. He crossed to the sink and washed his hands rapidly so that the soap foamed between his fingers. 'How far gone is she? Six months?'

'I think so,' said Stella.

'Well, we'll be lucky if the baby survives. I'd like to get her into hospital but I don't think there's time.' He

275

dried his hands on the towel which Stella gave him, and looked across at her. 'She seems undernourished for a woman of her class. Anaemic too, probably. It doesn't bode well, you know.'

'Can I go in to her?' said Stella, her face flushed from the steam.

'Yes,' said the doctor, 'of course. I'll need you to help me later, in any case.'

Cloris was lying flat, her hair untidy on the pillow. Stella took her hand and squeezed it in reassurance, but it was like holding a damp rag.

'I have to see Gerald,' said Cloris. She said it in a voice from which all colour was absent, a voice without charm, without anger, without irony. It was not a voice with which Stella could argue.

'All right,' she said. 'I'll send a telegram.'

And that was how Gerald arrived in London in time to see his first child and his first lover die, just as the doctor had predicted. Although she had asked for him by name Cloris never seemed to be aware of Gerald's presence. It was as though the moment the baby was born her body surrendered to the black exhaustion which she had for so long held at bay. She began to haemorrhage, and when Gerald reached Pimlico she had lost so much blood that she seemed only to skim the surface of consciousness. Certainly, according to the doctor, she would never have known that her baby lived for less than an hour. It was Gerald who took the child, a scrawny little girl with a face like a walnut, wrapping her in Stella's cashmere shawl. He had never seen a new-born baby before and he sought furiously for some resemblance to himself or to Cloris; but his daughter seemed to him less a human creature than a rare amphibian, disturbed before her metamorphosis was complete. Something about this very monstrousness, this failure to be like anyone else, moved Gerald to the point of heartbreak. Three or four times the child gulped blindly at the air, her red starfish hands fluttering; then, together, the gulping and the fluttering

276

stopped. The ginger-haired doctor at once put out his arms.

'I'll take her now, shall I?'

Gerald shook his head. 'It's all right. I know what's happened.' He looked once more at the shut wrinkled face of his dead child, his own monster. 'I'd like to keep her a while.'

The doctor lifted his eyebrows, but he did not argue. With one freckled hand he pulled the cashmere shawl a little more closely around the baby's neck; then he stepped back through the door to the bedroom.

Stella showed no interest whatsoever in the baby. She sat beside Cloris, dry-eyed, watching her grey features sharpen irrevocably until, just before morning, she too slid away into death. If Stella had expected some final declaration from her lover she was disappointed. Cloris died in silence, without admitting regret; or love, for that matter.

'We ought to give her a name,' said Gerald to his mother. They were alone, standing on either side of the bed in which Cloris lay. Gerald was still holding his daughter in her Paisley shawl. The doctor had left, and the landlady had gone to fetch an undertaker.

'Give who a name?'

'The baby. My baby. We should give her a name.'

'Oh . . .' Stella raised her hand in a small exhausted gesture as though she could not be expected to consider such things. She was gazing at Cloris, still and straight in her rented bed.

'The will was upheld, you know. Sir George's will,' Gerald said. 'I heard the news just before I got your telegram. Mallingford's yours, if you want it. And then mine.'

At this Stella lifted her head and looked at her son. There was no expression in her eyes but to Gerald it seemed that this was how the last people left in hell would look at each other.

'I want never to see you again,' said Stella. Her voice was quiet, almost conversational. Gerald gave a grimace that might have been a smile, and gently he adjusted his grasp upon the baby in his arms. Then he let out a long slow breath.

'Oh,' he said, 'I think I'm ready now to grant that wish.'

Chapter Twenty-Five

'You're mad,' said Cosima, with conviction. 'Gerald, you're mad.'

Gerald smiled and struck a match to relight his cigar, which in the drama of the moment he had allowed to go out. He was sitting in the studio beneath the charcoal sketch of Stella which Cosima had, with such care and optimism, hung two days before. The milky afternoon light flooded through the stable windows.

'I don't think so, Cosima,' said Gerald, serenely. He turned towards the art students. 'You don't believe I'm mad, do you?'

The art students, who were standing around Gerald in his canvas throne, shook their heads. They looked like pale-faced avenging angels, especially Kirsty, with her purple lipstick and her lank dark hair.

'I think it's poetic justice,' said Stefan, doggedly. 'Well, artistic justice. Liberating Stella's art, you know. Giving it back to the cosmos.'

Gerald gave a brief snort, as though this were too whimsical a notion even for him; but aloud he said: 'Quite. Stella was very fussy, for instance, about who she would allow into the dovecote. Personally I think she'd rather have seen the place go up in flames than have the hoi polloi trample through it. As Stefan says, it's a form of justice.'

'It's arson,' said Cosima, 'that's what it is.'

'Oh, my dear. You are a Courtney after all, aren't you? Such respect for property. Even your mother wasn't so conventional.' Gerald sucked once or twice at his cigar. 'Really, Cosima, can't you see the funny side? The Courtneys turn up mob-handed to reclaim the outbuildings – which they're bound to do any day now, I guarantee – and they find them burned to the ground. Imagine young Roddy's expression. I couldn't sleep last night for laughing.'

Cosima stared hopelessly at the ecstatic row of faces before her. 'I don't expect you'll be laughing when you end up in court,' she said. 'Arson's a criminal offence, remember. They send you to prison for it.'

'Oh,' said Gerald, airily, 'don't be so bourgeois. And who's to know, after all, that it wasn't an accident? A semi-derelict place like this, full of old junk? It's ripe for a fire, I'd say.'

'There's a lot of chemicals here too,' volunteered Marcus. 'Meths and stuff. That's inflammable, isn't it?'

'Exactly. To be honest, I'm amazed nothing like it has happened before. I don't see how anyone will be able to prove that we lent a helping hand. That is, Cosima, unless you decide to welsh on us again.'

Cosima gave a half-articulated groan, and turned towards Morag the housekeeper, who was standing at the back of the white room, her hands stolidly on her hips. 'Morag,' she said entreatingly, 'you agree with me, don't you? Tell Gerald he's mad.'

But Morag only gave a half-hearted shrug, and adjusted the blue butcher's apron which she was wearing. The front of the apron was covered in flour: she had been making bread when Gerald had summoned her to the studio.

'I don't know,' she said, thoughtfully. 'It's one way of making sure the Courtneys don't clean up at our expense. They can't make capital from Stella's name if there's nothing of hers left, can they?'

Gerald gleamed approvingly at the housekeeper. 'Quite,' he said. 'Thank you, Morag. Well, Cosima, it seems to me that you're significantly outnumbered. I vote that we get on with it. There's no point wasting time, after all. We may not get the chance again. As I say, I'm sure it's only a matter of hours before the Courtneys invade.'

280

'Right,' said Stefan. 'I'll go and get some petrol, shall I?'

Cosima rubbed her hand against her forehead so roughly that it hurt. 'Gerald,' she said, in despair, 'listen to me. I want no part of this. If you ask me this is nothing but vandalism.'

'That's all right, Cosima,' said Gerald, in a magnanimous voice. 'I'd hate you to go against your conscience. You don't mind if I ask Morag to keep an eye on you, though, do you? Just to be on the safe side.'

'Oh, for God's sake,' said Cosima. She turned and flung her way out of the studio, scarcely able to see where she was going. Her heart thumped painfully in her chest.

'Cosima,' said Morag's voice, behind her.

'Just leave me alone, will you? You're as crazy as he is.'

'Listen—'

'I told you. Leave me alone,' said Cosima, and she began to run across the courtyard towards the back door. Morag caught up with her as she lifted the latch.

'Have some sense,' she said, putting one squat red hand firmly on Cosima's arm. 'Cosima, listen. There's no point arguing with him; not when he's in a state like this. It's obvious he's made up his mind. If I hadn't agreed with him he'd probably have tried to lock us both up or something. This way we've got a chance of stopping him from torching the whole place.'

Cosima stared at the housekeeper through a fog of confusion. 'How?' she said.

'I'll take the van and drive to Courtney Park. Tell your cousin Roddy what's going on.'

'But we can't do that. Gerald will never forgive us.'

'Well, what's the alternative?' said Morag, in a matter-of-fact voice. She led the way along the dank passageway into the kitchen. 'Do you want to call the police?'

'Of course not. Don't be silly.'

'Silly yourself. If we're not careful, you know, we could end up being charged as accessories before the fact. And I for one don't fancy getting a criminal record at my time of life.' Morag pushed open the kitchen door. 'No, I'm afraid we'll have to bite the bullet and ask your cousin for help. There's no other way that I can see. And it shouldn't take me long to get to Courtney Park: we should be in time to stop Gerald doing any serious damage.'

Cosima let herself fall into one of the yellow kitchen chairs. 'But surely he'll be suspicious if you take the van and drive off?' she said. 'I mean, when he thinks you're watching me? He's bound to smell a rat.'

Morag bit her lip. Clearly this had not occurred to her. Even in so crowded a moment the thought gave Cosima a spark of satisfaction.

'Yes, you're right,' said the housekeeper sourly. 'He will be suspicious. There, you see. If you hadn't been so busy playing the prima donna and telling your father he was crazy—'

'What about Will?' said Cosima. 'He can run really fast when he wants to.'

Morag looked doubtful. 'Do you think he'll go? He hates Courtney Park.'

'Oh, he'll go. All we have to do is tell him why. Do you know where he is?'

'I saw him going to the vegetable garden ten minutes ago, when what's her name – Kirsty – came to fetch me.' They looked at each other for an instant; then Morag said: 'I tell you what. You stay here while I fetch William. Slump on the table or something and look as if you're crying. That should put them off the scent if your father or one of those students comes in. If they ask where I am say I've gone to the lav.'

'All right,' said Cosima. 'Be quick, though.'

'Of course I'll be quick,' said Morag, scornfully, and she was gone. Cosima stared at the kitchen table, strewn with flour from Morag's interrupted bread-making. She did not, for the moment, slump, as the housekeeper had suggested, but leaned back in her chair, lifting her face to the stained ochre ceiling. Unbidden the thought came to her mind: if only Tom were here. At once she censored so pointless a desire. During the long miserable night that she had just spent, it had dawned upon Cosima that she would probably never see Tom again. Now that the Mallingford project had so clearly foundered, there was no reason on earth why he should come back to Sussex, especially after the humiliation of his departure. She had not known Tom for long, but she knew him well enough to guess that such loss of face would rankle horribly: he would wish only to put the whole experience behind him. Instinctively Cosima put her hand under her shirt collar and touched the strawberry mark on her neck, fading but still tender, where his mouth had been. She felt a shadowy fear, which she did not want to admit, that he had simply been flirting with her, that it was Kate, his clever sophisticated Kate, whom he really wanted. It was not that she thought he had been insincere, exactly, but she could not rid herself of the idea that he had kissed her only because he was bewitched, caught up in the excitement of their plans and the magic of Mallingford itself. She remembered how, standing by the statue-menhirs in the uncanny moonlit night, he had said, I'm in love with this place, you know. It seemed there had never been any question of his being in love with her. Cosima's head drooped forwards. She felt the tears slowly inching down her nose and watched them fall one by one on the table, dark against the white flour, as though all this were happening to someone else.

'Where's Morag?' said Gerald, shoving open the door. Cosima lifted her arm and wiped her face on her sleeve. Whatever Morag had advised she did not really want her father to see her crying like this.

'Gone to the bathroom,' she managed to say. Gerald crossed towards the sink and turned on the tap, noisily. His face and hands were covered in black smuts. He looked extraordinarily cheerful, as though he had just shed an enormous moral burden.

'All right,' he said, reaching for the block of cheap pink soap. Then he looked more closely at his daughter. 'You've been blubbing, haven't you?'

'Yes,' said Cosima, angrily. She dug her hand in the pocket of her jodhpurs, vainly seeking a handkerchief.

'I don't know why. This will make our lives much simpler. I wish I'd thought of it before, instead of going through that pantomime yesterday.'

'Oh, shut up,' said Cosima. The fact that she could not find a handkerchief seemed, paradoxically, to make her cry even more. Gerald put down the soap and came to sit beside her. His chair scraped against the stone floor.

'Cosima,' he said, in a surprisingly gentle voice, 'shall I tell you what you ought to do, once the dust has died down? Do what Nicholas says, and go and live at Courtney Park. Take William with you. Your uncle will make sure you're both all right.'

'What?' said Cosima. The prism of her tears blurred her father's face, but she could see his eyes clearly, those grey eyes so like her own.

'I mean it. It would be much better in the long run, especially for William. The Courtneys value boys, you know. They'd send him to a good school, get him to make proper use of that infernal mechanical brain of his.'

'Don't you want us to stay here with you?' Cosima said blindly. All the anger and frustration she felt towards her father was abruptly transfigured to simple pain. Gerald, who so rarely offered any sort of physical contact, let alone a caress, let his slim papery fingers lie for a moment against her clenched fist.

'That's not the point. I'm thinking of the future.' He paused, withdrew his hand. 'You should go to art school, Cosima. Start developing your talents. That's what you really need. You shouldn't be wasting your time on all these wretched schemes to resurrect Stella.'

'There won't be much left to resurrect at the rate you're going,' said Cosima sourly. Gerald smiled.

'Don't abuse your intelligence, Cosima,' he said. 'You know perfectly well what I mean. I may be a selfish father but I'm not an entirely unobservant one. You have gifts of your own; you don't need to trade on your grandmother's reputation.' He got to his feet and strode back to the sink. 'And, by the way, whatever's been happening between you and the American boy, I wouldn't tie yourself in knots over it. There are plenty more fish in the sea: always remember that.'

Cosima was, for a moment, too startled to speak. Gerald had never said anything so personal to her before. She stared at him as he soaped his hands.

'Well, all right, I will,' she said at last, in rather a gauche voice. 'I don't expect I'll see him again in any case.'

'That's what you think, is it?' Gerald grimaced for a moment, thoughtfully. 'I suppose it's possible. Either way, though, I wouldn't take it too seriously.'

'No,' said Cosima, obscurely disappointed. She had half hoped that Gerald might have some secret, almost psychic, knowledge about Tom's intentions. He might not be right, but she wished nevertheless that he would say, oh, don't be silly, of course he'll come back. He's in love, don't you know?

'It's very dangerous to have obsessions,' Gerald said instead, rinsing his hands beneath the tap. 'Particularly if you're obsessed with someone who's absent. That's probably the most dangerous obsession of all. It's the kind of obsession that can eat you up.'

'Oh,' said Cosima. It occurred to her that Gerald was talking, not about herself and Tom, but about something quite different. She hesitated, wary of trespassing; then she asked: 'Do you mean you were obsessed with Stella? All those years when you never saw her?'

'What?' said Gerald.

'Is that why you want to burn the studio down? Is it?'

This frankness was too much for Gerald: Cosima saw it at once. His head swerved sideways and he shook his wet hands in her direction as though she were a fly he might shoo away.

'Oh,' he said, in a cagey dismissive voice, 'I don't know why I'm telling you this. Nobody ever learns from the foolishness of others. It's one of life's tragedies; or comedies, depending on how you look at it. I'd see it as comedy if I were you, Cosima. It'll make things much easier.' He grabbed a linen tea towel and began to scrub his forearms dry. 'Where the hell has Morag got to?'

'Here she is,' said Cosima, as the housekeeper came through the door. Her face was faintly mottled with the effort of running, although she was doing her best not to wheeze and gasp.

'Sorry, Gerald,' she said. Gerald dropped the towel on the floury table, and gave a grunt; then, without speaking again, he hitched up his trousers and marched from the room. Cosima turned at once to Morag.

'Has William gone?' she asked, in a whisper, just in case her father was hovering beyond the door.

'Yes, he's gone. He went straight away.' The house-keeper looked at her watch. 'If he keeps his speed up he should get there in – what? Twenty minutes?'

'Let's just hope they take him seriously,' said Cosima. 'Otherwise we really will be in trouble.' She picked up the tea towel Gerald had cast aside and dabbed at her eyes and nose.

'Yes,' said Morag, 'personally I wouldn't trust those students to do anything properly, even light a fire. It wouldn't surprise me if they didn't end up setting light to the whole house.' She eyed Cosima more closely. 'Well, you look as if you've been crying pretty convincingly. Well done. You've got flour on your left cheek; did you know?'

Cosima rubbed her face impatiently. 'So,' she said, 'what do we do now?'

Morag pulled back one of the kitchen chairs and plonked herself down in it. She looked like a squat ancient sibyl, half enjoying the portentousness of the situation.

'We wait,' she said, in a lugubrious voice, 'that's all. We wait.'

Chapter Twenty-Six

Gerald kept his word to Stella. The next time he saw her was in a hospital mortuary in Lewes. She did not, in death, look so very different from the woman he remembered from thirty years ago. Her hair was white, of course, and the lines between her nose and mouth were more deeply etched, but her face had retained that serenity which Gerald all his life had found both enviable and provoking. In her latter years she had taken to wearing spectacles, and the nurses reverentially handed him the pair she had brought with her to the hospital, in a dull brown snap-shut box.

Her death was not unexpected. Although they did not meet, Stella and Gerald exchanged occasional letters, cool amiable letters which were mainly to do with money. After the war Stella became richer than ever, despite the fact that she never appeared in public, and she started giving her son a hefty annual allowance, as though trying to pay off a deep and irredeemable debt. Every year Gerald cursed this money, which seemed a nagging affront for his failure to match his mother's fame, and every year he swore that he would not accept it; but when the next year came it passed as usual into his bank account, and he said nothing. He lived very much from hand to mouth. He painted a good deal, although he hardly ever managed to sell his pictures; instead he found other ways to make ends meet, designing posters for friends with fashion shops or theatre groups, sometimes teaching or modelling for life classes. In a part of his mind he regarded this life as somehow provisional, a way of killing time until his circumstances changed, although he could not have said what he thought that change would be.

In the last of her letters, which Gerald got in the spring of 1967, Stella wrote, quite dispassionately, that she was suffering from emphysema, and that if he wanted to assert his right to Mallingford under the terms of Sir George Courtney's will he should be prepared to move quickly. She seemed neither eager nor reluctant for him to claim the house, any more than she seemed eager or reluctant at the prospect of her own death.

'Maybe I should go down to Sussex,' said Gerald idly, scratching his thigh as he read the letter. He was lying in bed in his small rented flat in Soho, with a black-haired young model called Irina who took cocaine and claimed to be a Russian aristocrat.

'I thought you didn't want to see your mother?' said Irina, pulling the grubby white sheet over her breasts, which were fashionably small and hard. She reached for a packet of cigarettes from the bedside table and lit one of them.

'No, but I don't want to miss getting the house,' said Gerald. Without asking he took the cigarette from Irina. 'It's my inheritance, you know. The only inheritance I'm likely to get.'

Irina shrugged, philosophically tipping another cigarette from the packet. 'Isn't it tedious, down there in the country? I don't think I'd like it. I don't think I'd find it very amusing.'

Gerald swung his legs out of the bed. He noticed as he did so that his feet were beginning to show his age, with blue broken veins around the ankles and calluses, yellow as cheese rind, on his big toes. He was for the most part proud of how he had kept his looks. The years had given him a sort of raddled glamour, in practice far more seductive than the golden beauty he had had as a boy: Irina was only the latest in a string of much younger women who had graced his bed. None of them lasted more than two or three months, but that was his doing, not theirs. He had lost count of the tears and tantrums his slovenly rooms in Old Compton Street had witnessed every time he announced that it was over, that he was bored, that he had found someone else.

'Darling,' he said now, flicking ash out of the small fly-blown window, 'you're being presumptuous. I haven't asked you to come with me, have I?'

Irina stuck out her lower lip sulkily. Then she said: 'Well, all right. While you're in Sussex I shall work very hard and earn pots of money and when you come back to London we'll spend it all on champagne and lobsters and dope. Would you like that?'

'Oh, I expect so,' said Gerald. 'I expect I'd like it very much. Now, come on, Irina. Out of bed: chop chop. If I'm going I'd better get a move on.'

It was not difficult for Gerald to find news of Stella once he arrived in Sussex. Although since Cloris died she had lived in a state of perpetual and more or less reclusive mourning, she was too famous to go unnoticed; famous not only because of her status as a painter, but because of her feud with the Courtneys. All the villagers in the pub where Gerald was staying, just up the road from Mallingford, had their own tale of the feud, some of them as far-fetched as the stories which had circulated long ago about Dora and Molly and the ill-fated Julius Murdoch. Gerald sat at the bar with his inch of whisky, sweetly smiling as he listened to how Sir George Courtney had been besotted by his mother, how Alicia – now dead – had cajoled and begged him not to give Mallingford to Stella, how Sir Charles still lived in fear of some impostor appearing, claiming to be his grandfather's love child by this improbable liaison. The only useful piece of knowledge that Gerald gleaned from the villagers was that his mother had been admitted to hospital in Lewes, and that she was not expected to return to Mallingford.

This opinion was confirmed by the doctor, to whom Gerald revealed his identity.

'Three, four days at most,' he said, doing his best not to eye Gerald with unprofessional curiosity. 'She seems very calm. Are you sure you don't want to visit her?'

Gerald shook his head. 'We made a pact,' he said, simply, as if this explained everything, and he scribbled down the number of the village pub. 'You'd better telephone me when it's all over.'

The call came through two days later, while Gerald was eating a vast fried breakfast in the smoke-stained room behind the bar. Stella had died at four in the morning; quietly, the nurse said, in her sleep. Gerald stood in the draughty passageway, the black receiver pressed to his ear, the taste of bacon still salty in his mouth. He felt as though he had been holding his breath for an inordinately long time, and now at last could let that breath go.

'All right,' he heard himself say. 'I'll be over in about an hour.'

The staff at the hospital treated him with a sort of distant sympathy, giving him Stella's belongings, asking if he wanted to go and look at her. It was obvious that all the nurses had been in awe of his mother. Gerald's first instinct was to say, no, I won't see her, as though even now he ought not to be in the same room as Stella; then he realized the absurdity of the thought, and he followed the doctor along a dismal antiseptic corridor, clutching the paper bag which the nurse had given him containing Stella's things.

'There,' the doctor said. 'Very peaceful, isn't she?'

Gerald did not answer. Looking at his mother he felt strangely, shabbily disappointed. He did not know what he had expected: remorse, perhaps, or anger, or simply a vast sense of freedom; a large grand emotion in any case. But the question instead which sprang to his mind was, is this all? Is this what all the pain and passion had come to, that he should stand silent, a brown paper bag in his hands, gazing at the shut

291

parchment face which both was and was not Stella's? He cleared his throat, feeling obscurely cheated.

'I'll leave you for a moment, if you want,' the doctor said tactfully.

'No,' said Gerald, 'no. It's all right. I've seen enough. And anyway I ought to get on.'

The doctor looked mildly surprised, but he angled his head gracefully in Gerald's direction, and opened the door.

'Thank you,' said Gerald, clearing his throat again. 'You've been most helpful.'

Outside the hospital Gerald found a wooden bench where he sat down and shook out the contents of the paper bag. As he had expected, a large bunch of keys came tumbling out, half sliding through the slats of the bench. He retrieved them, and shoved the other things – the nightdress, the spectacles, the small gilt-framed photograph of Cloris – unceremoniously back into the bag. Then he got to his feet, to go to Mallingford. That, after all, was why he had come down to Sussex in the first place: not to have any dealings with Stella, alive or dead, but to take possession of the domain he had inherited.

He hired a minicab in Lewes, intending to arrive in style; but as the car drew nearer he decided instead to let it go, and to walk the last couple of miles along the mudtrack, as he had done so often in his boyhood. The may was in blossom, smelling sweet and heady. It was a scent Gerald had always found faintly sickening, and it heightened his sense of unreality. He felt he must have dreamed up Mallingford, in one of those long prosaic dreams which seem to regurgitate real life; and now the clump of chestnut trees, the piglets on the weather vane, the row of gabled windows, all brought back to him, not memories, but faint echoes of that dream. It was only when he saw the curve of the dovecote that his stomach gave a real lurch of recognition. He had, in the intervening years, forgotten all about the dovecote, as if in self-defence. It had never once figured in his remembered images of his home; if he had been asked to describe Mallingford he would have omitted it entirely.

For a moment Gerald dangled the keys from his fingers. He ought to go inside and start the business of sorting through his mother's papers, but he wanted first to reclaim this place from which he had so long been absent, to blot out Stella's presence and stamp his own there instead. He dropped the brown paper bag beside the back door, and he crossed the courtyard towards the outbuildings. His mother's career as a painter had only really begun when she came to Mallingford; maybe that would be true for him, too. Maybe the reason he had never quite succeeded, had never quite managed to lose himself in his work, was because he had been expelled from the creative paradise of his childhood home. Well, he thought, it's mine now. This is where my real life begins.

The gardens had been well cared for: according to the village gossips his mother had found another couple to look after the place once Mrs Maybrick died; a very *discreet* couple, his informant had told Gerald, rather regretfully. He smiled, remembering that regret, and put his hand out to turn the huge iron key in the door of the dovecote. As he did so he realized that it was unlocked. He gave the door a gentle push. It swung open, into the shadowy space beyond. There, staring at the painted walls, was a girl of about twenty, with long fair hair hanging loose on her shoulders. She was wearing a purple shift dress of fine cotton which came halfway down her thighs.

'Hello,' said Gerald, startled. The girl turned her head.

'This is private property, you know,' she said, with an unmistakably upper class twang. She did not seem to be in the least alarmed.

'I know,' said Gerald. 'It's my property, actually. I have it on loan for my lifetime.'

'Oh . . .' the girl breathed out. She looked at Gerald again, this time with interest. 'You're the son, are you? Goodness. Daddy will be awfully cross. He thought you'd been blotted off the face of the earth.'

She gave a ripe gurgle of laughter, as though her father's crossness was a source of great amusement. Gerald, himself much given to laughter at the misfortunes of others, was charmed.

'No,' he said, 'I'm sorry to say that I'm very much alive. As you can see.'

'Oh, don't be sorry. It doesn't bother me.' The girl spun back towards the dovecote walls, her pale hair flying behind her. 'These pictures are terribly *strange*, aren't they? I thought that if we got the house back I'd paint over them and buy some doves to keep here. Those pretty white ones with the fantails. I thought it would be rather fun. But I don't suppose I'll be able to do that now.' She paused for a moment, gazing at the portrait of Cloris with bloodstained talons; then she said: 'Oh, well. I expect I'd have got bored with them in any case. It's always nicer planning things than doing them, isn't it?'

'That's a very decadent thought, you know,' said Gerald, stepping closer to the girl. Her face lit up in delight.

'*Is* it?' she said.

'Terribly decadent.'

'Oh,' said the girl, in a different voice, 'you're teasing me.'

'No, I'm not. There's nothing more decadent than knowing that whatever you do it won't live up to your imagination. Whole civilizations have foundered on that idea. It's driven sane men to suicide; women too, probably.'

The girl smiled at him. Her skin, like her hair, was golden, and above the dankness of the stone Gerald could smell the expensive French perfume she was wearing. He wondered exactly who she was, which branch of the Courtney family she belonged to. He had no idea what had become of Sir George's descendants; it was not the sort of thing his mother had ever mentioned in her sparse businesslike letters.

'Are you an artist too?' she asked.

'Yes, I'm an artist. I live in London; that is, until now I've been living in London. I've got a nasty room in Soho which stinks of turpentine and cigarettes.' He paused. 'And where do you live?'

'Oh, at Courtney Park, of course,' said the girl. 'It's very boring. I'd like to get a flat in Kensington and do cordon bleu or something, but Daddy won't let me.' She gave another gurgle of laughter. 'I had a bit of a disaster while I was a debutante, and now he says he won't let me out of his sight.'

'You're out of his sight now,' Gerald observed.

'Oh, yes, but you know what I mean. He doesn't think I can do much damage stuck down here in Sussex.' The girl looked around her once more at the damp plaster walls. 'Let's go outside, shall we? This place is a bit creepy. I've never been inside before; have you?'

'Once,' said Gerald.

'I wanted to come and look over the house, just in case, you know, but it's locked up,' the girl said. She led the way out of the dovecote. 'Is it true your mother's dying?'

'She's dead. She died during the night. I've just been to see her.'

'Oh,' said the girl. There was a moment's silence, in which Gerald waited for her to add, I'm sorry. When she did not he felt a sudden relief, that he did not have to explain his emotions or mimic bereavement, followed by an odd sense of respect. This might be a frivolous girl, but she was not one to waste her breath on platitudes. She was also, now that he saw her in daylight, exceptionally beautiful. Her face had the strong features that make for lifelong handsomeness rather than a pretty girlhood, and her eyes were a striking, uncannily pale blue. Her legs, revealed by her short dress, were very slim and a delicious biscuit colour.

'What's your name?' asked Gerald.

'What? Oh, I'm Annabel. Annabel Courtney. Sorry, I should have told you. It's just that everyone round here knows who I am, I don't expect to have to tell people. So will you come and live in the house?'

'Probably,' said Gerald. 'I grew up here, as a matter of fact. I've always loved the place.' He paused for a moment; then he said, rather archly: 'I hope that doesn't interfere too much with your plans.'

Annabel gave a shrug, and began to amble across the courtyard, flicking back her hair. 'I told you. It doesn't bother me.'

Gerald followed her, matching his pace to hers. 'I've got the keys to the house, you know, if you want to look at it,' he said. 'I'll show you round if you like. I don't suppose it's changed much since I was here last.'

Annabel glanced at the gold watch on her wrist. It was so tiny Gerald wondered how she could even see the hands, let alone tell the hour.

'I should be getting home,' she said, rather gloomily. 'It's twenty to one. Nearly lunchtime.' She did not move, however, but dallied in front of the house like a child, scuffing up stones with her cream sandals.

'Tell me about your disaster,' Gerald said, in a friendly voice, to keep her there. 'The disaster you had when you were a debutante.'

Annabel glanced up, wrinkling her face against the sunlight. 'Oh, that,' she said. 'It was the usual, you know.'

'No, I don't know. What is the usual?'

'Oh, I had far too much to drink at a party and I went off and slept with an undesirable. Well, Daddy called him an undesirable; I thought he was rather nice. He was a waiter. Italian or Spanish or something.' She stole a look at Gerald, and went on, sounding defensive: 'Lots of girls do it. A few, anyway. It was just my bad luck to get caught.'

Gerald laughed. He was both shocked and delighted by this story. Without thinking about it he had assumed not only that Annabel, the gilded Courtney heiress, must be a virgin, but that her virginity would be impossibly hedged about with moral scruples. The notion that she might be available – and so casually, so gloriously available – gave him a thrill which was almost disturbing.

'There you are,' he said, playfully, to conceal this sudden prod of lust, 'I told you that you were decadent.' Annabel said nothing. There was a moment's silence; then, more softly, Gerald asked: 'Have you really got to go home for lunch?'

'Yes,' said Annabel, reluctantly. 'You know, if you're careful about the small things, you can get away with murder.'

'Murder, eh?' said Gerald. 'I'll look forward to that.'

Annabel raised her extraordinary blue eyes. Then, unexpectedly, she leaned forward and brushed her mouth against Gerald's. He felt for an instant the dampness of her lower lip, like a promise.

'So will I,' she said, and with a wave of her arm she disappeared along the dusty lane.

Chapter Twenty-Seven

The first Tom knew of the fire was the smell. In the beginning he thought it was woodsmoke, lacing the evening air as he drove along the mudtrack, just as it had done when Cosima brought him back from Chanctonbury; then he realized that the stench was too powerful for that, and much too acrid. His hired car, a white Ford Escort, juddered on the unmade road. It had taken him far longer to reach Sussex than he had expected. Once he had collected the car, he had decided to go to his flat and pick up some clothes; then the traffic leaving London had been murderous, clogging the motorway as far as Gatwick. By the time he took the turn to Mallingford it was eight o'clock, and starting to get dark.

'Jeez,' he muttered, accelerating towards the gateway. Now that he was closer he could hear the distant crackling of the fire. A dense cloud of smoke hung on the low horizon, although no flames were visible. The back of Tom's neck prickled with fear. What in God's name was going on? Then, as he drew into the little valley, he realized what was happening. It was the stable block that was burning. The windows had not yet shattered, and through them he could see a seething inferno of red. The roof was beginning to smoulder, the smoke billowing thickly around the tarnished weather vane. In the courtyard about a dozen people were huddled together, watching the fire as though in thrall to it. At the sound of his engine one of them turned. Through the haze Tom saw Cosima's face, pale and horror-struck. He braked at once, and leaped from the car.

'Tom,' said Cosima, 'oh, Tom,' and she came hurtling towards him. The next thing he knew he was holding her in his arms, her head burrowed against his shoulder. Her hair smelt brackishly of smoke.

'Cosima,' he said, 'thank Christ you're all right. What in hell's been going on?'

But before Cosima could speak they were interrupted by the blare of sirens behind them. A fire engine was powering along the mud track, its lights flashing in the dusk. Tom pulled Cosima to one side, out of its path. As he did so he noticed that there were two other vehicles parked on the gravel: a Land Rover, which he assumed was Roderick Courtney's, and a police car.

'What's been going on?' he asked again. 'What are the police doing here?'

Cosima did not answer. 'Come on,' she said, urgently, taking Tom's hand and running towards the burning stables. Half a dozen men in yellow helmets had sprung from the fire engine and were, with speedy precision, uncoiling a hose.

'About time, too,' said a nasal voice which Tom at once recognized as Roddy's. He was standing with his hands in his pockets, next to an anxious-looking policeman. The three art students were hunched together under the eye of a second officer. Despite the heat of the fire they were shivering. Tom looked around him. He could see Morag and William, who was holding his cat tightly in both arms, but there was no sign of Gerald.

'Well, sir, we do our best,' said one of the firemen, serenely. 'Is everyone who might be in the building accounted for?'

'No,' said Cosima, at once. 'We don't know where my father is.'

'And you think it's possible he's still in there?'

'It's possible—' began Cosima; but Roddy broke in.

'He did a bunk when the police arrived,' he said, in a brusque voice, 'probably because he's the person responsible for this act of vandalism. I should bear that in mind before you risk your lives going after him.'

'All right,' said the fireman, unperturbed. 'All right. So we have one person not accounted for. Now, if you can all stand well back—'

There was a sudden brutal crack as the windows burst. The flames, which until now had been contained in the thick flinty walls of the stable block, leapt into the air like freed spirits. Kirsty let out a great wail of fright.

'I said, stand back,' hollered the fireman, stretching out his arms as if to shield them from the blaze. The group of watchers swayed and in ragged formation took a pace backwards. A great blast of heat struck Tom's face.

'Oh, God,' whispered Cosima, gripping his arm. He could feel her fingers grind against the bones of his wrist.

'Where did Gerald go?' he asked.

'I don't know. I just don't know. Roddy's right: he disappeared when the police came. Ran off towards the dovecote. He might be quite safe, he might be hiding in the trees or something, but I don't know. Oh, Tom . . .'

'It'll be fine,' said Tom. He could hear his own voice, sounding far more confident than he felt. 'Honestly. Gerald's got more sense than to get stuck in there. Besides, these guys know what they're doing: look at them.'

The hose was in position now. A great stream of water arched through the air and hit the burning stables, with a hiss. In the distance Tom could hear another siren, as a second fire engine swept along the track towards Mallingford.

'Good news,' said the fireman who seemed to be in charge of the operation. He was a burly man of indeterminate age, with brown eyes and a pock-marked face. 'At this rate we should get it all under control in no time. The roof might go, but with any luck we'll be able to save the rest of it.'

'I'm glad to hear it,' said Roddy. He was wearing a blue-striped business shirt, flecked with bits of soot, and he seemed to be gaining a morose satisfaction from the catastrophe. 'I don't know what my father's going to say about all this. Thank Christ we took all our paintings back to Courtney Park last night. Ah, hello, Tom. I see you've arrived much too late to be of any use to anyone. So what's new, eh?'

'Shut up, Roddy,' said Cosima fiercely. 'Gerald might be trapped in there for all you know.'

'Well, if he is, it serves him damn well right. The man's a maniac. Thank God Morag had the sense to raise the alarm. The whole place could have burned down, and you with it. I hope you realize that.' Roddy blinked as a scrap of charred paper blew past his face. Then he turned to Tom. 'I think we ought to get everyone into the house, don't you? It could be dangerous out here.'

'I'm not going anywhere until I know where Gerald is,' Cosima said, in a stubborn voice. 'And I don't know why you're acting so smug, Roddy. It's all your fault. None of this would have happened if it hadn't been for you.'

'Oh, yes, of course,' said Roddy. 'I'm the bloody vandal who sets fire to valuable buildings just because I can't get my own way. Of course it's my fault.'

'You know what I mean,' Cosima said impatiently. 'You and your clever plans for opening up the studio. That's what did it. That's what made Gerald go over the edge.'

Roddy stared at his cousin for a moment, his blue eyes paler then ever; then a faint provocative smile crossed his long face.

'Ah, but you agreed to it, little cousin,' he said. 'You agreed. You even conspired with me against your father. Just you remember that. Whatever happens, Cosima, it may be my fault, but it's your fault too.'

Tom heard Cosima take a sharp breath, as though she had been hit. He knew that Roddy could not have said anything more calculated to wound if he had lain awake night after night, dreaming of revenge on his cousin.

'You bastard,' he said, and he put his arm round Cosima. Roddy gave an elaborate shrug, guying innocence.

'Well, I'm sorry,' he said, 'but it happens to be true. Doesn't it, little cousin?'

Cosima opened her mouth to answer; but the next sound was William's voice, not hers. It rang shrill and clear against the clatter of hosepipes and the crackling of the flames.

'The dovecote's on fire!'

Tom spun round to look. Sure enough, a plume of flame was flickering from the lantern on top of the dovecote, livid as sherbet against the night sky.

'Bloody hell,' said the fireman. 'That's all we need. OK, lads. Hose number two over this way.'

'But how can it have spread—' Tom began. Then he realized what had happened. It was Gerald. Gerald must be hiding in the dovecote; Gerald must have set it alight. Tom guessed this at exactly the same moment as Cosima. Their eyes met for an instant, sharp with their knowledge; then Cosima pulled away, and before Tom could stop her she had plunged past Roddy, past the firemen, towards the dovecote. Through the steam and smoke he saw the green of her shirt as she tussled with the key; then the door opened, with a great flash, and she disappeared into the foaming red heart of the building.

'Cosima!' yelled Tom, in a frenzy.

'What the hell is she playing at?' the fireman shouted. His face was black and wet and contorted with effort. 'She'll get herself killed.'

'It's her father,' Tom managed to say. 'Her father's in there.'

'Oh, Christ,' said the fireman. Then, without

speaking again, he shoved his helmet more firmly upon his head and started running towards the dovecote in his heavy fire boots. Tom watched, in an agony of helplessness. His face felt stiff with heat and fear.

'Has he gone to fetch Cosima?' asked William, in a sharp panicky voice. He still had both arms locked around Salvador, who was uttering little squeaks of distress. Tom nodded, unable to utter a word. He put his hands on William's shoulders. The boy was tense and quaking, like a frightened bird. Through the open door of the dovecote Tom could see the flames still leaping. There was no sign now of Cosima or of the fireman.

'He will find her, won't he?' said William. Tom squeezed the boy's shoulder.

'Yeah, sure,' he said, in a frozen voice. A single thought rebounded through his head: if she doesn't come out alive I'm going to kill Roderick. I don't care how I do it, or what happens to me afterwards: I'm going to kill the bastard. Then he felt William wriggle beneath his grasp, and he realized that the boy was pointing towards the dovecote.

'Look!' he said.

At first, with a leap of his heart, Tom thought it must be Cosima emerging from the flames. Then he saw what William meant. On the roof of the dovecote, beneath the burning lantern, was Gerald. He wore a smeared white shirt, and he was clinging to the roof slates with both hands. Through the smoke it was hard to see the expression on his face, but he did not seem to be troubled or afraid.

'How the hell did he get there?' breathed Tom.

'You can climb up by the creepers and things on the walls,' said William, his eyes fixed upon his father. 'I didn't think Gerald would be able to manage it, though. Don't shout: if you scare him he might lose his balance.'

'It's OK,' said Tom. 'He's seen us.'

He raised his arm and waved at Gerald. The firemen

303

had spotted him now: they were manoeuvring one of the engines into position, to climb up the ladder and bring him down. Gerald loosened his grip on the slates to return Tom's salute, his hand sardonically lifted like a prophet's. Something about the gesture seemed familiar to Tom, and he realized with a shock what it was. The whole scene resembled Gerald's lurid successful painting from the 1970s: *Zenox confronts His enemies*. My best-known work, the old man had said to Tom, that night in the drawing room at Mallingford, his voice salty with irony; and Tom had seen, as he saw now, the burning buildings, the huddled crowds, the white-haired messiah with his piercing candid eyes. Then Gerald faltered, and at once snatched back his hand to grip the slates. The flames were beginning to spread now, licking hotly around the sides of the roof. A flurry of burning debris fell from above Gerald's head, just missing him, and landed smouldering on the grass beneath.

'He's going to fall,' hissed William.

'No, he's not, Will,' said Tom. 'The ladder's nearly reached him. See.'

The ladder touched the roof of the dovecote just as a huge dark figure appeared in the doorway below. It was the fireman, carrying Cosima in his arms. He seemed to be struggling with the weight of her. Her head was tipped backwards, her blackened hands trailing inertly.

'Cos!' screamed William, trying to break free and run towards her. Tom dug his thumbs into the boy's shoulders, as though his very life depended on keeping him there, keeping him safe. The cat let out an unearthly shriek.

'Don't, Will,' gabbled Tom. 'Don't. She'll be all right. Believe me. She'll be all right. She's got to be all right.'

The fireman staggered forwards, away from the dovecote, and bending down he laid Cosima face upwards on the grass. Her eyes were shut. It was impossible to tell whether or not she was breathing.

'Oh, Christ,' whispered Tom, still gripping William's shoulders. It was then that he looked up and realized that Gerald, from his precarious position on the roof, had seen Cosima, carried out from the fire as if she were dead. Through the smoke he saw the old man's face change. Tom in that moment knew that he had never seen a face change like that before, and that he would never, as long as he lived, forget it. It was like seeing a soul damned beyond redemption, as Gerald stared down at his daughter spreadeagled in the grass.

Then the fireman on the ladder stretched out his arms to the old man. 'Easy does it,' he called. 'Easy does it. You're nearly there. One little step, that's all.'

Gerald, confused, reared up as a horse might. From the lantern above another shower of sparks fell, this time striking his head and his arms. With a muffled cry of pain, he raised both hands to put them out, but not before his hair had caught light, flaring abruptly and dramatically like a struck match. His foothold on the slates wavered. The fireman made a grab for him, lunging forward just too late to stop him from plummeting, his hair still burning, to the ground.

After that everything happened so quickly that Tom could not remember it in any sort of order. The firemen abruptly closed ranks around Gerald, shutting out Morag and the three art students, who were shrilling like banshees. At some point Tom caught a glimpse of Roddy's face, ashen with horror amidst the chaos, and to his astonishment he felt a twinge of pity for him. An ambulance arrived, its blue light eerily flashing, and more uniformed figures spilled out from its doors. But the next thing Tom recalled properly was crouching next to William on the grass as together they raised Cosima's head, and hearing the wonderful choking noise that meant she was alive.

Chapter Twenty-Eight

Annabel announced that she was going to marry
Gerald one Sunday over lunch at Courtney Park. She
picked a day when as many people as possible were
present to hear this announcement: not only her
parents, a couple of aunts and the local vicar, but also
her brother Nicholas and his wife, who had come
down from London especially to show off their latest
infant, a plump little girl called Henrietta who bore
an unfortunate resemblance to a pug dog. The family's
reaction was satisfyingly volcanic. Her mother,
Penelope, burst into hysterical tears, and her father –
that same florid Sir Charles who had delivered the
oration at his grandfather's funeral – turned a violent
purple, and they had to call the doctor to come and
sedate him.

'Oh, Annabel,' said Nicholas, wearily, retrieving
from the carpet a blue rubber hippopotamus that the
howling baby had just flung down, 'how could you?'

'Yes,' her mother chimed in, 'you're so irrespon-
sible. You know, you'll kill Daddy one day if you're
not careful.'

Annabel gave one of her characteristically lofty
shrugs, as if to say, it's nothing to do with me; and
taking advantage of the chaos she had caused she
wandered out of the house, hopped into her brother's
maroon Jaguar (he had providentially left the keys on
the hall table), and drove to Mallingford.

She found Gerald at work in the studio, retouching
the Art Deco screens he had painted years ago, which
had grown blistered and faded with time. Since his
arrival at Mallingford he had not yet progressed to

starting any pictures, although he had bought and prepared some canvases, one of which was standing on an easel ready for him to begin.

'Hello, my darling,' said Annabel. She unbuttoned her ivory silk blouse and slid it over her head as she unhurriedly crossed the room. 'I've escaped.'

'So I see,' said Gerald, drily, unfastening his leather belt. Neither of them spoke again. In silence they took off their clothes, lay down on the studio floor and made rapid and enthusiastic love. They had done this, more or less without preamble, almost every day for the two months since their first meeting. Gerald had known, after that meeting, that Annabel would come back, although he had not expected her so soon. In fact she rang the doorbell the next afternoon, at about half past three, while he was in the sea-green drawing room ransacking Stella's desk. He offered her tea, which mockingly she refused, sprawling on his mother's horsehair sofa in a white voile dress which showed both her knickers and her nipples. Gerald's mouth was dry with wanting her, and with the fear that this might after all be only a game.

'Would you like to go to the bedroom?' he asked, in the careful, serious voice which had paid dividends with so many of his conquests. Annabel pulled a face.

'What's wrong with the sofa?' she said.

After this they had had sex – although Annabel's preferred term, which Gerald found faintly offensive, was fucking – in every room and on practically every surface in Mallingford. Once or twice it crossed Gerald's mind that he could have discovered no more thorough way of profaning his mother's memory, but for the most part he was too besotted by Annabel ever to think of Stella. When she was not physically present he was tormented by endless elaborate fantasies about her, like a pornographic movie which it was impossible to switch off. He spent whole hours wandering around the house and gardens, looking for new places where he could make love to Annabel,

307

beside the pond, beneath the chestnut trees, in the stable block among Stella's discarded drawings, as though Mallingford had become no more and no less than the arena in which he performed these acts of passion. Oddly, the only place where Annabel refused to have sex was in the dovecote. It was too creepy, she said, in a flat decisive voice; she would feel the eyes of the paintings, watching them.

'So how did you get away so early?' Gerald asked, when they were getting dressed again. Although Annabel was cavalier about taking off her clothes she was very careful about what she did with them once they were off: her ivory blouse and her black and white check skirt and her hand-made broderie anglaise bra and pants were neatly folded on a chair, unlike Gerald's things which were strewn across the dusty floor.

'Oh,' said Annabel, and she told him how she had left Courtney Park in a state of uproar. She was a gifted and heartless storyteller, who did gleeful justice to her tale, conjuring up with relish her father's blustering turkeycock face. Gerald laughed.

'I must say, I wouldn't shed a tear if your father did drop dead of apoplexy. I've never liked him. I always remember the patronizing bloody speech he made at your great-grandfather's funeral: I wanted to punch him on the nose.' He buttoned his paint-streaked moleskin trousers. 'But why on earth did you say you were going to marry me?'

'I thought it might be a good idea. You're not married already, are you?'

'No, I'm not, but that isn't the point—'

'The thing is,' said Annabel, 'I'm probably pregnant. Well, actually, I *am* pregnant. I think it was that first time, on the sofa upstairs, before we started doing, you know, precautions.' She paused for a moment, and then went on, in the same casual voice, as if she were talking of a dinner party or a holiday destination: 'Of course, if you really don't want to marry me I could

308

get rid of it. That's what my brother Nicholas thinks I should do. His wife does some sort of charity work with underprivileged girls so she knows lots of people. She could probably fix me up. And I expect Daddy would pay.'

Gerald stared at her. Since his first disastrous coupling he had had a morbid fear of impregnating his lovers, although he never took time to consider how that fear had originated. If ever he thought about it he assumed that it was a symptom of his profound reluctance to be tied down, not uncommon in one of his sex or his profession. Now, from the subterranean depths of his memory, came the image of his daughter by Cloris, that beloved monstrous creature with her wrinkled face and her fluttering red hands. He had buried the image for so long that he was not quite sure what it was that he was remembering: a picture from a natural history book, perhaps, or something glimpsed in a film. Yet still the shape quivered in his mind, refusing to be obliterated.

'No,' he said to Annabel, in a curiously offhand voice, 'don't do that. I can marry you if you really want.'

'Oh. All right.' Annabel paused in the act of zipping up her check skirt and blinked at him beneath her silken eyelashes. Gerald waited for her to ask, are you sure? just as he had waited for her to say, when he told her Stella was dead, I'm sorry. But she did not speak. Instead she tossed her car keys in the air with one hand and caught them again, with a deft snatching movement.

'Well,' she said, at last, 'I ought to be getting back.'

'Stay, why don't you? You'll only get in a ruck if you go home.'

'Yes, I know, but I swiped my brother's Jag to get here, and I suppose I'd better take it back, or he won't be able to drive his wretched family to London. Besides, if I'm going to move in I'll need to bring some clothes.' She leaned across and gave Gerald's mouth a perfunctory kiss. 'I'll see you later, my darling.'

The campaign to prevent Gerald from marrying Annabel started the next day. In the beginning it was comparatively civilized. Annabel's brother Nicholas, who despite the timely return of his Jaguar had stayed overnight at Courtney Park, paid Gerald a visit and allowed himself to be shown courteously round his own property. Gerald had expected to loathe Nicholas, and he was disconcerted, not only by the young man's friendliness, but by his resemblance to his great-grandfather Sir George. Nicholas had the same long benign face, the same disarming combination of modesty and natural authority, which were quite absent from the florid and swaggering Sir Charles. Gerald caught himself being drawn into a sort of upper class male camaraderie, where he and the young man could join in mockery – affectionately meant, of course – of Annabel's flightiness. As they were having tea in the kitchen from those same lustreware cups that Sir George had once used, now rather chipped around the gilt rims, Nicholas explained in a confiding tone that Annabel had always been a headstrong young woman, prone to sudden passions. She had been spoilt, he admitted, partly because she was a girl, partly because she had been conceived so late, when her parents had given up hope of further children, and it meant that she had not been taught the self-restraint a young woman with her good looks and (let's face it) her wealth should have learned. The upshot was that her family were obliged, really, to protect her from the consequences of her own behaviour. Of course if she married without her father's consent she would be disinherited, but that wasn't the point, was it? The point was that she was hardly ready to be a decent mother, and it would be much better for all concerned if she got rid of the child and started again with a clean slate. Nicholas angled his head closer to Gerald's, and in that same man-to-man voice offered him a hefty sum of money if he would promise to leave Annabel alone.

Gerald in response gave a great bark of laughter, noisily pushed back his chair and proceeded to show his guest the door.

Things got nastier after that. First there were solicitors' letters; then there were visits from the police, who had been informed from an unidentified source that Gerald was a drug-dealer, and turned the house upside down at regular intervals. There were also endless screeds on perfumed writing paper from Lady Courtney, begging Gerald not to blight her only daughter's life. When none of this worked Sir Charles paid a private detective to dig up whatever he could find on Gerald's amours in London, a project in which many of his ex-lovers, including Irina, co-operated with zeal. A copy of the detective's report was delivered by messenger to Annabel as she dangled plumply in a hammock in the Mallingford gardens. She had arrived at Gerald's door minutes after he kicked out her brother Nicholas, in a taxi crammed full of exquisite Italian pigskin cases, and had stayed there ever since. The report gave her hours of delight. For weeks afterwards whenever Gerald heard her shrieking with mirth he could guess that she was reading it.

'And this one – what's her name? oh, the coward, he's just called her Miss B – she says that after she met you at a party and agreed to go to bed with you, you *made* her have sex five times in a row. Five times. Oh, Gerald. You're brutal.'

'I know,' said Gerald, cheerfully taking the opportunity to demonstrate his brutality, 'I know.'

Nevertheless he was in private appalled by the Courtneys' systematic efforts to obliterate the creature growing in Annabel's body, to deny it life simply because it was his. Gently he laid his hand on the bulge of Annabel's stomach. He could feel a stirring of sorts, as though the baby recognized his touch.

'They're savages, your family,' he said. 'Sodding bloody savages.'

311

'Oh, no.' Annabel yawned. Sex these days always made her feel deliciously sleepy. 'They're not savages. They're just rather boring and conventional. They think they've got a God-given right to have things their way. Can we get married in London? I'd like to have a party at the Savoy. I know my family won't come but I've got an awful lot of chums up in town. People I did the season with, you know. They'll think it's a hoot that I'm getting married.'

'Well, all right,' said Gerald. 'But remember, we don't have much cash for parties. We don't have much cash for anything, to be honest, now your father's cut you off without a penny. And soon there'll be three mouths to feed.'

Not normally preoccupied by money, Gerald had been dismayed to find, from his examination of his mother's affairs, that her estate was worth surprisingly little. Most of what she had she had already given him, in the shape of his much-resented annual allowance, and although there were plenty of sketches and half-finished canvases in the studio there were only a few saleable pictures. Besides, in the year or so before Stella's death fashions had shifted, and her paintings no longer sold for the astronomical figures they had attained during the 1950s: anyone with any sense would hang on to what was left and hope for the market to change once more. The question of how he would provide, not only for himself, but for an extravagant wife and a child, was beginning to gnaw at the edges of Gerald's mind.

'Oh, don't be boring,' said Annabel, thumping the pillow with her fist. 'We'll manage. Sooner or later I'll get round Daddy and he'll start coughing up again. He always does. He's so soft.'

She nestled her cheek against the thumped pillows and promptly fell asleep. Gerald sat beside her, watching that golden conscienceless face in repose. Not for the first time he felt afraid. It was as though, just as his life was opening up, just as he was ready to

312

celebrate his freedom from Stella, he had somehow been sidetracked, caught in the web of this beautiful witch; and now he feared that he was doomed to waste his remaining years in her service. To reassure himself he slid his arms round her, cradling her swollen stomach with his cupped fingers. Once again he seemed to feel the baby stir and leap in acknowledgement. Consoled, Gerald pressed his face to Annabel's smooth honey-coloured back, and he too dozed off.

They were married in London on a damp January day, when Annabel was eight months pregnant. She wore a short A-line dress of cream lace which, as she observed with an uncharacteristic lack of narcissism, made her look like a beach umbrella. Several of Gerald's old flames turned up, by coincidence all dressed in black with their lips painted a very pale pink. If they had been sitting together they would have been a terrifying sight, but because none of them were on speaking terms they were dotted around the register office, and as a consequence looked rather silly. Annabel at any rate thought the whole thing a scream. Throughout the ceremony she kept whispering in Gerald's ear: which is the one who snorts cocaine? which is the one who thought oral sex was illegal?

Gerald found his wedding an unsettling experience. For one thing, apart from the registrar, he was the oldest person in the room by a good fifteen years. He also realized, when they got to the Savoy for the reception, that nearly all the guests were friends of Annabel's, plump-cheeked young creatures in their twenties, with loud hooting voices, who talked all the time about horses and skiing. The only face he recognized was Irina's, her eyes lined with black as she made scornful inroads into his champagne.

'I suppose I owe you that,' he said, joining her by the window, which overlooked the Thames. It was raining, the drops shirring the grey surface of the water.

'Damn right you do,' said Irina. She emptied her glass with Russian aplomb. 'I just hope you're marrying her for her loot. Will she support you while you get on with your work? Is that it?'

'Not exactly,' said Gerald, in a rueful voice. It was weighing upon him that he had just agreed to do some paintings for a popular series of science fiction posters. The young man who commissioned him – a very young man, not much older than Annabel – had been refreshingly cynical about the enterprise. I know they're crap, you know they're crap, he had said, but the public loves them. And who are we to argue? Who indeed? Gerald had politely said, pocketing his cheque.

Irina took another flute of champagne from the silver tray. They both watched Annabel for a moment, her grandiose silhouette swaying as she shrieked with laughter at some unknown joke. It was like the laughter of strangers overheard in a crowd, remote and somehow alienating. Irina downed her fizz and began to gather up her things, her shiny black handbag, her rabbit-fur stole. Then she kissed Gerald on the cheek. It was the most asexual kiss she had ever given him, as though she had suddenly realized that he belonged to a different generation.

'Well,' she said, in a voice which against all odds he thought must be sincere, 'I wish you joy.'

Annabel gave birth three weeks later, in a small nursing home near Lewes. At the last minute her father had relented and paid for her to have private obstetric treatment, although none of her family actually came to see her. From the moment she went into labour she started screaming at the top of her voice, despite the fact that, according to the midwife, it was a quick and uncomplicated birth. Gerald did not stay in the delivery room to watch: instead he sat outside, in the bare February garden, feeling the wind buffet his face. When the nurse came to fetch him his ears were ringing with cold.

'You've got a little girl,' the nurse said. 'A lovely little girl. Mother's all right, too, no stitches or anything.'

Gerald nodded, unable properly to take in what she was saying. Through the doorway he could see Annabel. She was lying on the bed in a white smock, her face hectic and sullen with tears.

'I tell you something,' she burst out, when she caught sight of Gerald, 'I tell you, you're not coming near me again unless your *whole body* is covered in rubber.'

Gerald saw the nurses exchange sly smiles. Then one of them took up a bundle wrapped in white honeycombed wool and passed it to him. Automatically he stretched out his arms. After the frozen garden the sudden frowsty warmth of the room was making his head spin.

'There we are,' she said. 'There's your daughter.'

It seemed to Gerald that Annabel's sobbing receded into the distance. He gazed at the baby's face, purple and wrinkled as that other baby's face had been, thirty years before. But in her face he had seen no resemblance to anyone, not himself, certainly not Cloris, who had been dying silently in the room beyond. This child looked oddly like Stella. Her eyes were still bluish and cloudy, not storm-grey like Stella's, but there was something indefinable in the line of her cheek and the height of her brow that reminded him hauntingly of his mother. To his own surprise he did not find the similarity displeasing.

'What are you going to call her?' asked the nurse, poking at the white shawl with a tender and officious forefinger.

'I don't care,' wailed Annabel. 'Can't someone fetch me some more pain killers? I'm still in pain, do you realize that? I don't give a damn what it's called. You can call it Pocahontas for all I care.'

'We had thought—' Gerald cleared his throat. 'We had thought, Cosima. She is going to be all right, isn't she?'

'Oh, yes.' The nurse lowered her voice. 'Between you and me, she's making a fuss about nothing. She'll be fine when she's had a cup of tea and a nap.'

'Actually, I meant the baby.'

'What? Oh, yes. Nothing wrong with baby. A very healthy little girl.'

Gerald looked once more into the face of his daughter, sliding up his hand so that his palm cradled her small downy head. For the second time in his life he felt a wave of unqualified love, as though all the old rivalries and resentments and misunderstandings had been swept away, leaving in their wake a new beginning, clean as the empty canvas on his easel at Mallingford. My life will be different from now on, he thought, with a thrill of certainty, and he watched Cosima's eyes reel and waver, as they tried in vain to fix upon something solid.

Chapter Twenty-Nine

'It's no good,' said William. 'We can't stay cooped up here, Cosima: you know that. We've got to get on. Uncle Nicholas says I should be starting school as soon as possible. I've already missed the beginning of term.'

It was nearly two weeks since the fire, and Cosima had got out of bed for the first time. She was wrapped in an enormous square of royal blue cashmere, having tea with her brother in their sitting room at Courtney Park. They had been brought back to the house by their uncle Sir Nicholas, who had arrived at Mallingford just after Gerald's fall from the dovecote roof. He had managed everything not only with efficiency but also with consummate tact. It was Sir Nicholas who had persuaded the police to let the three art students go free with no more than a caution, arguing that it was Gerald, after all, who had been the prime mover in starting the fire; a piece of generosity which Stefan, Marcus and Kirsty were for the present far too stunned to appreciate. He had sent Roddy up to his bachelor flat in London for an indefinite period, so that his cousins, especially Cosima, need not fear encountering him; then, despite Lady Courtney's view that what the children needed was fresh air and company, he had ensured that they were given a small private suite of rooms at one end of the house, to which the servants discreetly delivered their meals. Other than this Sir Nicholas had left them alone together, to recover from the shock of their father's death.

'Do you want to go to school?' Cosima asked William now. Her voice was huskier than usual, and her chest ached from the quantity of smoke she had inhaled. Her blistered hands were still swathed in bandages, although the doctor said that there should be no lasting damage from her plunge into the flames. From time to time as she sat on the squashy toile de Jouy sofa she mopped at her face with a white handkerchief. Ever since the fire Cosima had been crying more or less constantly, not with particular distress, but as if her eyes were taps which could be turned on and off at will.

'Well, yes, of course. I always did, you know, it's just that I could never really say so. Not without being disloyal to Gerald.' William lowered his head and sniffed at his teacup. 'This is Earl Grey. I said we wanted Darjeeling.'

'Oh, Will. Does it matter? When did you see Uncle Nicholas, anyway? He said he wouldn't bother us till we were ready.'

'I bumped into him in the garden yesterday. I went out to stop Salvador from chasing those stupid mangy peacocks, and he was putting some things away in the summer house.' William reached for a toasted teacake from the plate, ate it in three bites and put out his hand for another. He had suddenly developed an appetite of monstrous proportions: Cosima was sure he had grown at least an inch in the past fortnight. For all his fierce resistance to the idea of moving to Courtney Park, now that he was actually here William had settled in cheerfully. It had helped, of course, that Sir Nicholas had had both the cat and William's hens transported with him, rather to the dismay of Lady Courtney. Salvador spent his days gorging in the kitchen and provoking the dogs, while the hens were already roosting in the once immaculate privet hedges.

'So where will Uncle Nicholas send you?' asked Cosima, in a bleak voice. She was disconcerted by the way her brother had so readily adapted to their new life, growing plump and sleek and confident on regular meals from the Courtneys' kitchen. It felt like a betrayal, although quite what was left to betray she could not have defined. She stretched out her hands upon the lacquered coffee table, staring at her fingers in their gauze bandages. Cosima had found in the pain of her physical injuries a peculiar relief. It had been somehow far easier to concentrate on her burned hands, her hacking cough, than to begin to think about what she was feeling: grief at her father's death, the grinding sense of responsibility for that death. She had shut herself up in these quiet rooms, keeping the curtains closed, seeing no-one except her brother and the doctor, ever since she had been discharged from the hospital. During this time she had grown increasingly dependent on William, who talked to the servants and ordered their meals and answered the door with a high-spirited competence she would not have thought possible during his reclusive years at Mallingford.

'He says there's quite a good private school round here,' William said, his mouth half full of teacake, 'so I could stay at Courtney Park if I wanted. Or I could go to boarding school. Uncle Nicholas says it's up to me. He's going to pay for it, obviously. Oh, please don't cry, Cos. You know we can't stay like this for ever.'

'Sorry,' Cosima mumbled, burying her face in her handkerchief. It was made of soft, well-washed cotton and bore her uncle's initials in blue satin stitch.

'It isn't your *fault*, Cosima,' said William.

'It is. Some of it really is my fault,' said Cosima. 'Oh, look, Will, it's much too complicated to explain.'

'Well, then, don't explain it. I mean, don't try to explain it. If you ask me that was what sent Gerald barmy. He was always going over things in his head. And telling those stories about Stella all the time, as if by telling them he could make something different happen. That's what was wrong with him.' William bit into a large wedge of fruit cake. 'Come on, Cos. It's not as if you can change anything.'

'I know, but if I could just understand—'

319

'Well, you can't,' said William robustly, chomping at his cake. Cosima looked at him. His down-to-earth wisdom annoyed her – surely it *was* more complicated than that? surely it was? – but at the same time she could not help feeling respect for her brother's new air of certainty. She wondered, rather helplessly, quite where it had come from.

'Uncle Nicholas wants to talk to you about your plans, too,' William was saying. 'He says he's got a lot of ideas, but it depends what you'd like to do next.'

Cosima felt her eyes blurring, the tears hot on her face. 'Gerald thought I should go to art school,' she managed to say. 'It was practically the last thing he ever said to me. In the kitchen, while Morag had gone to find you to raise the alarm. He said I should stop trying to resurrect Stella and use my own talents.'

'Oh, Cosima,' said William. In silence he poured another cup of tea for his sister, and crossed to hand it to her. 'Drink this. It'll make you feel better.'

'All right,' said Cosima, surprised by her own obedience, and she swallowed the thin scented tea.

William watched her for a moment; then, in a tentative voice, he went on: 'The other thing Uncle Nicholas asked was – well, I know this sounds nosy but I'm sure he didn't mean it that way. He's just concerned for your future.'

'What did he ask?'

'Well, he wondered if there was anything serious going on between you and Tom.'

'Oh, God,' said Cosima. 'Oh, God, Will, I don't know. I don't know anything any more.'

She pressed her face into the upholstered back of the sofa and began wholeheartedly to sob. Of all the visions which had haunted her since the night of the fire the memory of Tom's face had been the most confusing. She had felt such pure relief when she saw him drive along the track into Mallingford, as though everything would be all right now; and indeed he had told her, in his deep reassuring voice, it'll be fine, Cosima, these guys know what they're doing. But then Roddy had smiled and said, ah, but you agreed, little cousin, and there had been that nightmare instant when she realized that Gerald was in the burning dovecote, and then the sudden horror of the flames, knowing the moment she dived into them that it was quite impossible she would find her father there, that she had been mad ever to think that she could rescue him from something so furious, so uncompromising; and then there had been nothing, not even the sense of her own failure, only pain, and, worse than pain, the terrible fear that she would never get out alive. And in all this Tom was somehow implicated, like a collaborator in a shameful crime. His face had been the first thing she saw when she came to, choking, on the grass, too afraid to ask what had happened to Gerald; and she saw his face still, when she woke now at dawn to find the whole tormenting drama spinning once more through her head. The doctor had given her sedatives to help her through the night, but they did not stop this early morning delirium.

'The thing is,' said William, carefully, 'he's been here a few times. Tom, I mean. He came every day in the beginning. But Uncle Nicholas and I thought you weren't well enough for visitors.'

Cosima straightened up. There was a damp patch on the back of the sofa where her face had been, darkly staining a sepia shepherdess and her crook.

'Have you seen him, Will?' she asked.

William squirmed for a moment, looking cagey. 'Well, yes, I have. I've seen him a few times. He drove me over to Mallingford, one afternoon when the doctor had given you an injection to make you sleep. We had to fetch one of the hens that Uncle Nicholas had accidentally left behind.'

Cosima did not speak for a moment. Then she asked: 'Did he say anything?'

'What do you mean? He said lots of things. He said

321

– well, I don't know if I ought to tell you this, but he said that Uncle Nicholas has offered him a job. He thinks he might open Mallingford to the public after all, now it's his again, and he asked Tom if he wanted to help.'

'And what did Tom say?' asked Cosima. She was conscious of her heart thumping.

'He hasn't decided. He told Uncle Nicholas he needed time to think about it. He said he might go back to America instead.' William stretched out for another slice of cake. 'Cos, please don't start crying again.'

'I can't help it,' said Cosima. 'I'm sorry, Will. I just can't help it. Didn't he say anything at all about me?'

William thought for a moment, eating his cake. 'Well, he asked how you were. Every time I saw him he asked that. And he said he hoped you didn't blame him for everything, and that you would want to see him when you felt better. Except that he said it in the sort of voice you use when you think something isn't going to happen.'

'Oh, God,' said Cosima, and she smothered her face in the handkerchief once more. As she did so the tears and phlegm caught in the back of her throat. She began to cough, ticklishly at first, then in sharp uncontrollable bursts that seemed to rip at her chest. It was through the noise of this coughing fit that she heard someone knocking, gently but firmly, on the sitting room door.

'Cos?' said William doubtfully. He was standing up, hovering between the sofa and the door, uncertain what to do. There was another, more strident knock. Cosima leapt to her feet.

'Bedroom,' she said, between spasms of coughing, and she pushed her way out of the sitting room, through the small lobby and into the room which had been hers since she came to Courtney Park. It was a small room, decorated in chintz, which would have been pretty if it had not been rendered both airless and untidy by Cosima's illness. The counterpane was

322

bunched up where she had shoved it back, and the cherrywood table was strewn with medicine bottles and old magazines. Cosima sat down on her rumpled bed, her cough beginning to abate. She could just hear the deep murmur of a man's voice from the sitting room, her uncle Nicholas, perhaps, or the cook from the Courtney Park kitchens; then William, sounding shrill and firm; then the click of a door; then silence. She sat quite still on the edge of her bed, counting the seconds. When she had reached sixty, and still heard no sound, she got up and walked slowly back to the sitting room. William was standing behind the sofa, looking towards her with an air of expectancy; and beside him, his face taut with nervousness, was Tom.

'Oh,' said Cosima, startled. She made to close the door once more.

'Cosima, please,' said Tom. 'I just have to talk to you. Please don't run off.'

Cosima looked at him. The expression in his eyes was at once hopeful and wretched. She took a step forward.

'All right,' she said, in a rather defeated voice. William grinned.

'Tom, do you want some tea? I'm afraid it's Earl Grey, although I asked them for Darjeeling. And the fruit cake's rather good. There were some toasted teacakes but I've eaten them.'

A whisper of a smile crossed Tom's face. 'Yeah, I'll take some tea. Even if it is Earl Grey.' He tweaked at the knees of his trousers and sat down on the sofa.

'Elsa's settled in very well,' said William, as he poured tea. 'My hen, you know. The one you brought back here. I think she might even have started laying.'

'Is that right?' said Tom. He lifted his china teacup, examined it, put it down again. Then he said: 'Was it really Morag I saw just now, when I was coming out of Sir Nicholas's study? Jeez, what a transformation. Just shows what expensive clothes and a good haircut can do for you.'

'Yes,' said William, rather smugly, offering cake. 'She does look smart, doesn't she? Did I tell you, Cos? Uncle Nicholas has given her a job too, helping him with his charity work. She didn't want to take it at first, because of Dad always being against Uncle Nicholas, but in the end he persuaded her.'

Cosima let herself drop into one of the armchairs. 'So,' she said, in a caustic voice, 'all's well that ends well.'

Tom shot her a look of pain. 'You think she shouldn't have done it?'

'Don't ask me. After all, I was the first person to knuckle under and take the Courtneys' money, remember? I've got no right to criticize anyone else.'

As she said this Cosima was aware of a stillness in the room, and of both William and Tom watching her closely. Then she heard Tom say, softly: 'Will, be a good fellow and scram, would you?'

'All right,' said William, sounding good-humoured. 'I'll go and make sure that Salvador's been fed.'

When he had gone there was a long silence. Cosima found herself staring at her swathed hands, quite unable to lift her head and meet Tom's eyes. Her throat burned from her coughing fit. At last Tom said, in that same low voice: 'Cosima, do you really hate me?'

She glanced up for a moment, caught a glimpse of his anguished face and at once looked away. 'No. Why should I hate you?'

'Because I screwed up,' said Tom. 'I screwed up all the way down the line. I should have realized that your father would never let this thing happen, that it was too much for him to handle. Christ, you even warned me that he might crack, that day up on Chanctonbury. And then I didn't even have the sense to stick around after the open day, when I might have been some use to you. When I might have stopped – well, you know. I don't need to tell you.' Abruptly he crossed the room and, crouching at the arm of her chair, put one fingertip on her swaddled hand. 'I couldn't even stop you trying to kill yourself.'

'I wasn't trying to kill myself. I was—'

'Yeah, yeah. I know.' Tom straightened up, without looking at her, and walked over to the window. 'I saw his face, you know, Gerald's face, when the fireman brought you out. He thought you were dead. I'll never forget that, not till the day I die. I'll never forget his face.'

Cosima watched him standing at the window, his hand plucking at the bobbles on the curtain's hem.

'Will says you're thinking of going back to America,' she said, trying to make her voice sound normal, unemotional, as though she did not care how he would answer. Tom shrugged.

'Yeah, I might do. Alastair paid me off. Paid me off quite well, as a matter of fact. I could set up something in the States if I wanted.' He glanced at Cosima across his shoulder. 'And you know Sir Nicholas has offered me a job, don't you? He thinks we could patch up what's left of the studio and turn it into a going concern. Especially now we'll have access to the main house.'

'Will you do it?' asked Cosima. Tom gave another shrug, and let fall the curtain hem.

'I haven't decided. It depends,' he said. Cosima waited for him to expand on this, to tell her on what exactly his decision depended, but he did not. Instead he gazed across the room, his eyes fixing on her hands. 'Do they hurt still?' he asked.

'A bit. The doctor says they shouldn't be badly scarred, though. I suppose I was lucky.'

Tom let out a breath which sounded almost like laughter, except that it was too sardonic. 'Damn right you were lucky,' he said. 'That's the understatement of the year.' He hovered by the sofa for a moment, as though about to sit once more; then he said: 'Look, Cosima, I'd better let you get some rest. I wanted to

325

see you, that's all; see that you were OK. I won't disturb you any more.'

He put his hand to the door, slowly. If he goes now, thought Cosima, he might go for good. He might go to America without another word, and I shall never see him again. For an instant the pain of this idea seemed appropriate, all of a piece with the general shipwreck of her life; then she heard herself say: 'Tom, will you take me to Mallingford?'

'What?'

'William said you drove him to Mallingford the other day. Will you take me?'

Tom stared at her. 'You're not up to it, are you?'

'I'll be all right,' said Cosima. She stood up, pulling her blue cashmere wrap around her. 'I suppose what I mean is that I won't be all right until I've been there. I've got to get it over with. Please, Tom.'

'OK,' said Tom, in a rather grudging voice, 'you're the boss.'

They drove along in the white hire car without speaking, past the bridge where they had watched the stream together, along the mudtrack, more deeply rutted than ever from the toing and froing of the fire engines. Cosima noticed that it had been raining, and that the leaves in the hedgerow, dotted brightly with hawthorn berries, were still wet, and that the late afternoon sunlight had a pellucid quality, like beauty in old age, richer and warmer than the thin grey dawns which woke her at Courtney Park. After so many days of crying, so many days of turning everything over in her mind, Cosima was surprised by her own calmness now she was actually here at Mallingford. Tom pulled up on the patch of gravel beyond the gate. The house itself had been undamaged, although the side of the building closest to the fire was grimy with smoke; but Stella's old studio was a ruin, the roof gone, the walls charred and crumbling. The weather vane had melted in the heat, and the gilt sow was now as shapeless as her three piglets. The air of the little valley still smelt acrid, its sourness punctuating the scent of ripening apples.

'You all right?' asked Tom, in a gruff voice, as Cosima slowly got out of the car. She noticed that he seemed reluctant to touch her, even to help her from the low passenger seat.

'Yes, I'm fine,' she said, flicking her blue shawl around her neck. She felt shivery in spite of the mild September day. For a moment she looked around her, at the landscape she had known all her life, so abruptly disfigured. Then she walked purposefully towards the outbuildings. The dovecote was intact apart from the stone lantern on top, which looked as though it had been torn off the building by a brutal giant hand, leaving only a couple of blackened stumps. The door was standing half open.

'I guess it could have been a lot worse,' Tom said. 'Sir Nicholas has had some estimates done and they think they'll be able to rebuild the studio practically as it was.'

Cosima nodded, but she did not answer. She could not believe how little she felt, looking at the place where her father had fallen to his death, where she herself had so nearly died. It was still too familiar: she could not adjust to its changed significance. She stepped across the scorched grass, littered with broken tiles and fragments of burnt stone. As she walked she was conscious of Tom following her, two or three paces behind, a watchful guardian spirit. Their feet made no sound on the turf.

The inside of the dovecote was damp and black, the walls bearing the marks not only of fire but of the jets of water which had blasted against them. Stella's glorious cave paintings had been more or less obliterated, although here and there were glimpses of colour, like bits of a buried mosaic. Cosima put out her hand and touched the moist plaster. The part which had been best preserved was the fresco showing Cloris as a winged bird-woman: her brown eyes still gazed

327

across the small space between the dovecote walls with an expression of gentle amusement.

'Derek Connor will be sad,' said Cosima, in a thoughtful voice, as though the journalist's emotions somehow had precedence over her own. 'He thought this place was marvellous.'

'Derek? Oh, yeah, the newspaper guy. He's still keen on writing a biography of Stella, though. Sir Nicholas wrote to him about it the other day. He doesn't seem to think it will matter that – well—'

'That Gerald's dead, you mean?' said Cosima, glancing at Tom with a faint smile at his confusion. 'No. He said to me at the open day that he thought most of Gerald's stories were made up. He was probably right, too, when you think about it. After all, Gerald went for years and years without speaking to Stella. He can't have known as much as he claimed. All that stuff about Virginia Woolf and the war and Charleston. I bet he made it up.'

'I guess so,' said Tom. He stepped forward and stood at Cosima's shoulder. She was staring once more at the bird-woman. 'That's supposed to be Cloris Bohun, isn't it? I wonder why Stella painted her with those claws.'

Cosima stared at the winged figure with its grasping talons. 'Well, I think I sort of know,' she said, 'but I'm not sure I could explain. I think it's to do with the claims people have on you when you love them. Whether they mean to or not.' She felt tears welling up and in a brisker voice she said: 'I always wondered what happened to Cloris. Derek Connor says he read somewhere that she died in childbirth, but I'm not sure he can be right. It seems a bit unlikely.'

Tom did not seem to be listening. 'Yeah,' he said abstractedly. Then, in a hurried tone, as though he could not bear any longer to wait for an answer, he asked: 'Cosima, what will you do now? Will you stay at Courtney Park?'

'I don't know,' said Cosima, startled by the

suddenness of the question. 'I might go to art school. In London, I suppose. In fact, I think that's probably what I will end up doing, once I'm really well again.'

'Ah,' said Tom. From his expression she could not decipher whether he was disappointed or not by this reply.

'It's the logical thing, after all, if I want to paint,' she went on. Tom gave her a lop-sided smile.

'Following in Stella's footsteps, then?'

'Well, not quite,' said Cosima, in a sober voice. 'I'd like to think that if it comes to it I'll be a more considerate parent.'

Tom's smile widened for a moment. 'Right,' he said. Then he drifted away again, towards the open doorway, as if he felt that he should put distance between them. 'Do you want me to leave you alone for a few minutes? Give you some space?'

Cosima gathered the comforting folds of her shawl around her. 'No, not specially,' she said. 'I thought it would be really dramatic coming here, really – you know – cathartic, but it isn't. It's just a bit strange and sad. As though the spirit's gone out of something.'

'I know,' said Tom. 'That's how I feel too.'

'I mean, somehow it doesn't matter that Uncle Nicholas is going to take the whole place over. There isn't really anything left to take. It'll just be a sort of replica.' She paused for a moment, looking once more into the bird-woman's deep-set eyes. 'We can go now, if you want.'

Tom did not move. His brown fingers were tightly gripping the edge of the door. 'Cosima,' he said, at last, 'I shouldn't ask you this. It isn't fair, when your father's only been dead two weeks, and we haven't even had the inquest yet. I know I shouldn't do this, but I can't help it. The fact is, I can't make any sort of decision until I've asked you.'

'Until you've asked me what?'

Tom rubbed his free hand miserably across his forehead and through his crisp hair. 'You know your

329

uncle's offered me a job. Carrying out my original proposal to turn Mallingford into a study centre. It's not incredibly well paid, compared to what I was getting from Alastair, but it's interesting, and I'd like to give it a shot.' He took a breath. 'The thing is, I don't feel I can stay here and be around you if you really do hate me still for everything I've done.'

'But I don't hate you,' said Cosima. 'I've already told you that. I don't honestly think any of this is your fault.'

Tom pulled a face, half wry, half embarrassed. He let go of the door, shoved his hands into his pockets and at once took them out again. Then he said: 'I guess I'm still not being frank with you. What I'm really saying is that it would drive me crazy working here if – well, if I knew for sure you didn't want me. I couldn't stand it. I'd rather go back to America and start from scratch.'

Cosima looked at him. The space between them seemed at once vast and infinitesimal. 'What about Kate?' she asked, her voice small.

'We broke up. Right after the open day. It was kind of mutual, I guess.' He flapped his arms like a huge bird in a single helpless gesture. 'Oh, for God's sake, Cosima, who am I kidding? I'm in love with you. I've been in love with you for weeks, although I guess I didn't realize it. I know it's not fair to land you with this when your father's just died and you're still sick, but I don't know what else to do. I love you: that's all.'

He gazed across at Cosima, waiting for her to answer. His face, which had been contorted with anxiety, seemed now that he had declared himself to be smooth and curiously empty. She allowed herself to picture, for a moment, how that face would be transfigured if she said, yes, I love you too; of course I love you. The temptation to give joy was so boundless that it made her feel dizzy. But when at last she spoke it was to say, in a wary voice: 'I'm not really sure what I feel right now.'

330

'Oh,' said Tom, 'OK.'

'The thing is, I don't feel that I can make any promises to anyone. I don't feel I'm ready to do that. If you understand me.'

'Yeah, I understand.' Tom swung away through the open door. 'Thanks for being so tactful.'

'I don't mean—'

'It's all right, Cosima. I needed to know, before I could reach a decision. Well, now I do know. Shall we go back to Courtney Park? Then when I've dropped you off I can go see your uncle Nicholas and tell him thanks but no thanks.'

'Tom,' said Cosima, without moving, 'wait.'

'Look, you've told me what the score is. Don't let's spin this one out, eh? In case you hadn't noticed I'm finding it rather painful.'

'You're being unfair,' said Cosima. She could hear her voice tremble as she spoke. 'First of all you say you don't want to put pressure on me, and then when I tell you I don't know what I feel you jump to conclusions and assume I don't care. Well, it isn't as simple as that. I don't want to be responsible for whatever you decide to do. I made myself responsible for Gerald, and look what happened, look where that got me. More to the point, look where that got him. But it doesn't mean that I don't care if you catch a plane to America and I never see you again. It doesn't mean that at all. You're being so arrogant.'

On the word 'arrogant' she realized that her mouth tasted of salt and that the tears, those familiar companions of the past fortnight, were once again streaming down her cheeks. She stood in the middle of the floor, her shoulders quaking, not moving to wipe her face, listening to her own sobs as they echoed around the scorched circle of the dovecote. Engulfed as she was she did not see Tom approach her; the first thing she knew was that he had put his arms gently around her, and with his tongue was slowly, delicately scooping up the tears from her cheeks. His tongue felt

331

slightly, pleasurably rough against her skin, like a cat's. She could smell the expensive leathery scent of his aftershave.

'Don't—' she began.

'Hush,' said Tom, in a quite different voice, 'hush. It's OK. Really, sweetheart, it's OK.' He waited until eventually she had stopped crying; then he said: 'I'm sorry. I guess I've always been a stumblejohn. When I want something I blunder right ahead. I don't suppose I'll ever learn what you might call finesse.'

Cosima allowed herself to smile. Enveloped in Tom's great arms she seemed to feel the warmth going to her head as a shot of brandy might. It made her feel at once sleepy and euphoric.

'You won't go back to America, will you?' she said.

'Not for a while, I guess. You're right. We need a bit of time to sort things out.' He wound his arms more tightly around her. 'I don't know what I'm going to say to your uncle, though.'

Cosima was silent for a moment, feeling the thud of Tom's heart against her cheek. Their bodies seemed to fit so well together, it gave her a sudden overwhelming sense of rightness. She remembered how William had said, with that boyish confidence, don't try to explain if it's all too complicated.

'Tell him you'll take the job, Tom,' she said. 'Just take it. One way or another it'll work out.'

'Oh, sweetheart,' said Tom, and tipping her face upwards he kissed her. Cosima had re-enacted his past kisses so often in her mind, as if they were mysterious manuscripts to be pored over and endlessly scrutinized, that she was startled by the physical reality of feeling his mouth on hers: there was nothing abstract about it, nothing to be imagined or idealized. It seemed to her that in the distance, just beyond the feeling of security that she was once more in his embrace, there fluttered some other, stranger sensation, unknown and, so far, unlooked for. She wished that her hands were not bandaged so that she could have reached up, touched his face, pulled him more closely towards her.

'Cosima,' said Tom, at last, drawing back, 'you know, I meant it when I said I loved you. You're the most surprising woman I've ever met.' He slid one hand along her face, pushing her hair back from her forehead. 'And now I guess I'd better drive you home to Courtney Park, before you collapse with exhaustion and I get it in the neck from your uncle and the doctor.'

'OK,' said Cosima, reluctantly, although she knew that he was right. She was already beginning to feel great waves of physical tiredness, like a tide ready to drag her under water. 'We can come back here, though, can't we?'

'Oh, sure,' said Tom, with a grin. 'We can do whatever you want. Wherever you want.' He took her by the elbow, half supporting her. 'Let's wait till you're well again though, hey?'

Cosima turned and looked for the last time at Cloris Bohun's face, gleaming from the blackened wall with her flamingo-pink feathers and her crimson claws. The eyes still seemed to be watching her in tender irony.

'I hope we make a better fist of it than they did, that's all,' she said, quite suddenly. 'You know. Stella and Cloris. And Gerald. Especially Gerald.'

Tom kissed the top of her head. 'We will, sweetheart,' he said. 'I promise you, we will. Come on, Cosima. It's beginning to get dark. Let's go.'

And they crossed the overgrown courtyard just as the moon, a thin silver crescent, swung up into the dusky sky above the quiet house and the ancient chestnut trees.

THE END

A MISLAID MAGIC
Joyce Windsor

'I LOVED IT. I THOUGHT IT FRESH AND SHARP AND FUNNY,
WITH A MOST WONDERFULLY ECCENTRIC CHARM'
Joanna Trollope

All the beguiling charm of Dodie Smith's *I Capture the Castle*
combined with the witty view of Britain's upper classes portrayed
in Nancy Mitford's *Love in a Cold Climate*. A totally compelling
first novel which is funny, sad, and utterly delightful.

Lady Amity Savernake, neglected, rather plain, and youngest
daughter of the Earl of Osmington, was seven years old when her
stepmother (disparagingly referred to within the family as Soapy
Sonia) took her to London, bought her a fitted vicuna coat with a
velvet collar, and introduced her (at the Ritz) to Rudi Longmire,
the genie who was to change their lives.

It was Rudi's idea that there should be a midsummer Festival of
Arts at Gunville Place. The ugly Dorset pile, seat of the Savernakes,
would be transformed into a pastoral paradise; singers, actors,
musicians and exotic visitors – as well as the family – would
bring enchantment into their world. As Rudi, Master of Revels
and Lord of Misrule, drew each and every one of them into his
exotic plans, so excitement spilled out into the countryside. A
dead may tree threw out leaves and blossomed. The local white
witch absentmindedly gave her pig a love potion, and two village
maidens were accosted in the woods by a genuine Dorset Ooser.

And within the family it seemed the enchantment would solve
their various discontents. Soapy Sonia, Grandmother Mottesfont,
even Claudia, Amy's corrosive and rebellious sister, bloomed in
the midsummer revels. And young Amy watched and listened and
for a brief childhood span was given the magic of complete
happiness – a happiness she never forgot – not even in the
disruptive aftermath of that heady summer, or in the years
that followed.

'IT HAS ALL THE INGREDIENTS OF A FAIRY TALE . . .
WHIMSICAL . . . SHARPLY FUNNY IN PARTS'
The Times

0 552 99591 6

BLACK SWAN

THE VILLA MARINI
Gloria Montero

The house, built in the style of a classic Mediterranean
villa, lies abandoned behind tangled ferns and rusted gates.
Its history is one of obsession, of tragedy, of a chain of
events evolving from the day Mariano Grau and his daughter,
Marini, arrive in the town of Junction on the North
Queensland coast. They had been driven out of Cuba and
nothing has prepared them for the life that awaits them
in the swaying cane fields of a primitive new country.
Behind them is the loss of a huge sugar plantation and
the memory of Mariano's young wife.

Now his whole life is spent in a passionate encounter with
the land. He builds a simple house on stilts for himself and
the child but promises that soon they will build a house like
the old home in Spain, the one he remembers from his youth.

Marini, the child, grows up isolated, withdrawn. Driven by
her father's vision it is left to her to fulfil the dream. She
uses not only her own life and will to feed her ambition, but
also that of the weak, tormented man she marries until,
finally, she discovers that at the heart of self-willed creation
lie the seeds of destruction.

In a narrative of exotic imagery, Gloria Montero has drawn
an unforgettable picture of a period and place of
overpowering richness and beauty.

'WITH BEAUTIFUL IMAGERY AND A STEADY PACE,
MONTERO CREATES A SLIGHTLY MAGICAL WORLD,
POPULATED BY HAUNTED AND HAUNTING
CHARACTERS'
Publishers Weekly

0 552 99711 0

BLACK SWAN

A SELECTED LIST OF FINE WRITING
AVAILABLE FROM BLACK SWAN